Night + mare: A spirit that in northern mythology was reputed to torment or suffocate sleepers. A morbid oppression in the night, resembling the pressure of weight upon the breast.

—Samuel Johnson (1709–1784)
A Dictionary of the English Language, 1755

I am not born to tread in the beaten track; the peculiar bent of my nature pushes me on.

—Mary Wollstonecraft (1759–1797)

The Nightmare

A MYSTERY WITH
MARY WOLLSTONECRAFT

Nancy Means Wright

2011
McKinleyville / Palo Alto
John Daniel & Company / Perseverance Press

A Perseverance Press Book
Published by John Daniel & Company
A division of Daniel & Daniel, Publishers, Inc.
Post Office Box 2790
McKinleyville, California 95519
www.danielpublishing.com/perseverance

Distributed by SCB Distributors (800) 729-6423

Book design by Eric Larson, Studio E Books, Santa Barbara, www.studio-e-books.com

Cover image:
The Nightmare, 1781 (oil on canvas) by Henry Fuseli (Fussli, Johann Heinrich) (1741–1825)
Detroit Institute of Arts, USA/ Founders Society purchase with Mr and Mrs Bert L. Smokler/ and Mr and Mrs Lawrence A. Fleischman funds/ The Bridgeman Art Library

10 9 8 7 6 5 4 3 2 1

LIBRARY OF CONGRESS CATALOGING-IN-PUBLICATION DATA
Wright, Nancy Means.
  The nightmare : a mystery with Mary Wollstonecraft / by Nancy Means Wright.
    p. cm.
  ISBN 978-1-56474-509-5 (pbk. : alk. paper)
  1. Wollstonecraft, Mary, 1759-1797—Fiction. 2. Murder—Investigation--Fiction. 3. Art thefts—Fiction. I. Title.
  PS3573.R5373N54 2010
  813'.54--dc22
                2010040566

The Nightmare

*For the Reverend Johanna Nichols
whose caring ministry; promotion of justice, equity,
compassion in human relations; and enthusiasm for
Unitarian history and its religious Dissenters
has been a continued inspiration for me*

Acknowledgments

Grateful thanks to my sine qua non editor, Meredith Phillips, whose overall expertise, insight, and knowledge of British history and etymology brought this novel to full fruition. And to Susan Daniel, publicist extraordinaire; my dedicated publisher John Daniel; and to talented book designer Eric Larson.

Praise be to my helpmate, engineer Llyn Rice, who walked with me down the winding streets of Wollstonecraft's eighteenth-century London, photographed at my command, and offered helpful feedback on the manuscript. Gratitude for the support of my beloved extended family; for the wisdom of the Reverend Johanna Nichols, to whom I've dedicated this book; and for the continued interest of members of the Champlain Valley Unitarian Universalist Society in Wollstonecraft and her circle of Dissenters.

Thanks again to Kathy Lynn Emerson, whose *How To Write Killer Historical Mysteries* I read and reread, and to the late Kim Malo, KG Whitehurst, and other members of the online CrimeThruTime group who answered numerous picky questions on eighteenth-century dress, habits, money, etc. Appreciation for other readers of early drafts of the novel: Chris Roerden, Alison Picard, my daughters Catharine and Lesley, members of two writers' groups; and for the many knowledgeable fans of my Facebook page, "Becoming Mary Wollstonecraft."

Once again, I am indebted to the imagination and scholarship of the following books:
Bruce Alexander: *Blind Justice* (fiction)
Philip Baruth: *The Brothers Boswell* (fiction)
M. Dorothy George: *London Life in the Eighteenth Century*
Lyndall Gordon: *Vindication: The Life of Mary Wollstonecraft*

Diane Jacobs: *Her Own Woman: The Life of Mary Wollstone-craft*

Kirsten Olsen: *Daily Life in 18th-Century England*

Frances Sherwood: *Vindication* (fiction)

Janet Todd: *Mary Wollstonecraft: A Revolutionary Life; The Collected Letters of Mary Wollstonecraft*

Claire Tomalin: *The Life and Death of Mary Wollstonecraft*

Peter Tomory: *The Life and Art of Henry Fuseli*

Amanda Vickery: *The Gentleman's Daughter: Women's Lives in Georgian England*

Janet Warner: *Other Sorrows, Other Joys: The Marriage of Catherine Sophia Boucher and William Blake* (fiction)

Also nonfiction books and novels of the period:

Fanny Burney: *Evelina; Cecilia; Camilla*

Henry Fielding: *Joseph Andrews; Tom Jones*

William Godwin: *Memoirs of Mary Wollstonecraft; The Adventures of Caleb Williams*

Mary Hays: *Memoirs of Emma Courtney*

Elizabeth Inchbald: *A Simple Story*

Charlotte Smith: *Emmeline; Desmond*

Mary Wollstonecraft: *Mary, a Fiction; The Wrongs of Woman; Thoughts on the Education of Daughters; Original Stories from Real Life* (illustrated by William Blake); *A Vindication of the Rights of Men; A Vindication of the Rights of Woman*

Eighteenth-century plays by Fielding, Goldsmith, Sheridan, and Steele

Contents

The Nightmare

London: Spring, 1781

Prologue

❧

HENRY FUSELI had run through three models already, each unable to hold the pose he demanded. Now the fourth girl, Sophia, was complaining, "I have to move. I can't feel my arm. The blood is running to my head. I may faint."

"No," Henry said. "Not yet." The girl was lying on her back; head, neck, and left arm hanging off the bed, fingers twitching. He waved away her plaint. The pose was nothing for a girl of sixteen years. Why, he himself had lain on his forty-year-old back for weeks in the Sistine Chapel, musing on Michelangelo's ceiling!

The girl's cheeks were tinged with pink, her hair a lemony pool on the Turkey rug. Turning back to his canvas, he painted an incubus squatting on her breast, its head toward the viewer, an impish smile on its thin lips for what it was about to do.

The arrangement was perfect: folds and pleats of reddish drapery; the arm white as milk; the soft curves of flesh—he touched the nipple with his brush, let it linger there. He stood back to contemplate the painting. It was coming to fruition; still, it lacked something. He wiped his hand on an oily rag and breathed in the turpentine, the linseed oil. He squeezed his eyes shut, straining for the vision that had come to him the week before, when he had woken from a bad dream. The raw pork he had eaten for dinner did that to him: bad dreams. But then the images came flooding, like this one—idea and image, fused. The sleeping woman, the incubus, the light from the south window illuming her body, and in the upper left corner—*ja!* He would paint a horse, that ancient sexual symbol. Just the horse's head, the pointy ears, the bulging eyes of the voyeur, the open mouth—saliva on the tongue.

He was painting furiously now, deaf to the model's whimpering;

he applied a dab of burnt ochre with a fine brush. When the candle burned to the nub he lit another. He was inside the painting, inside the dream. He was horse and incubus, voyeur and participant. Horse and devil, unseen by the sleeper but instilling in her its terror. He was the female sleeper as well: dreaming, unaware of horse and devil, yet filled with its dread. Wanting and not wanting to be taken, ravished.

But how to show the literal—the reality?

A looking glass, *ja!* There would be a looking glass, showing only the sleeper—not the incubus, not the horse—only the sleeping woman in her nightmare. Nightmare... The title of the work came to him. *The Nightmare!* Night-mare. He laughed out loud at the pun; with his trembling right hand he picked up his mug, tipped the strong ale down his throat, and let it spill into his collar. He glanced at the young model and saw she had fallen asleep. The fingers were quiet. It was better that way. Later he would take her to bed and she would have her reward.

He took up the brush again in his left hand, and leaning forward, propelled his vision onto canvas.

Midwinter & Spring, 1792

CHAPTER I.

An Insulting Proposal and an Impious Painting

&

WHEN THE knock came, Dulcie was in the sitting room of the Store Street house in London, curled up on the shabby green sofa, and sipping a dish of freshly brewed China tea. She did not bother to get up. It was probably a tradesman, come for payment of last night's mutton chop or the bottle of claret the mistress had ordered for her publisher's supper. Miss Mary disliked having to deal with tradesmen—usually she owed them money. She had nightmares enough without *that*, she said. She had instructed Dulcie not to open the door.

But when the knock sounded louder and a voice with it: "Open up for the love of God, I've an offer of marriage for the lady of the house, I ain't got all day!" Dulcie slapped her teacup into its saucer and tiptoed to the front window. A bent stick of a man in a grease-stained coat was standing on the doorstep with a withered rose and a paper in his grubby hands. Surely it wasn't himself making the offer? Miss Mary would fell him like a fly with a crack of the swatter.

"Open up!" he shouted. "The master awaits 'is reply. 'E's a colleague of 'er bookseller's printer. I were told by Mister Johnson, the lady'd be in. The gentleman's a-waiting, I said."

"One moment, if you please," Dulcie called, then sat back to finish her tea. Did he think she had nothing to do all day but wait on his rude words? Dulcie did not consider herself a menial, but an "unservant," a "helper-about-the-house." She had made that clear when she took the position, and Miss Mary understood. She was swallowing a last bit of raspberry jam when voices erupted outside on the step. Good Lord—it was Miss Mary herself, home from her walk—and already accosting the fellow. Grabbing a broom, Dulcie began a vigorous sweeping by the window.

For a moment there was quiet. She peeked through the curtain. Ah yes, her mistress was by the street door, reading the note, the offer of marriage. Dulcie giggled. She knew what was coming next. For one thing, the mistress did not believe in marriage. "Marriage is merely a legal prostitution," Miss Mary had read aloud at the writing table one day—and Dulcie had sharp ears, something a non-servant–lady's maid–cook like Dulcie had learned to cultivate.

"A marriage proposal for me?" The authoress sounded amused. "From whom, may I ask?"

A moment later she was in shock—or so it seemed. "Edgar Ashcroft is it? That arch-conservative who belittles women in his editorials? Why, he'd have me lisp and play at cards and spend five hours a day at dressing and never read a book. I could not do it. No!"

"Dear madam," came the whining voice of the scraggy go-between. "'E just 'eard you was wanting for money. 'E owns a newspaper, 'e does. 'E can 'elp with your writing."

"What help do I need with my writing? I have all the help I need in here." She jabbed a finger at her forehead. "I do not want Mr Ashcroft's money. I do not need his advice."

A yellow carriage with ornamental red wheels and the image of a sunflower with a woman's smiling face halted in front of the house. A man in a red satin coat and tight black breeches leapt out, arms extended as though he would embrace the mistress. Seeing her step back, he flung himself on his knees. The mistress looked down, and laughed.

"*Mister* Ashcroft," she cried. "Here is your answer." She ripped the paper from the envoy's fingers, and flung the pieces in the air. A fragment landed in the man's high-crowned hat; another caught in his collar. "So much, Mr Ashcroft, for your scribbling-women-should-be-banished attitude. For your adulation of King Louis and his gaudy queen. Oh, I read your anti-Revolution piece: Hang the mob? Save the monarchy? I say, down with kingcraft and priestcraft. Up with the people. Up with women writers!"

"But madam," Mr Ashcroft stammered, stumbling to his feet. "It was your own publisher, Mr Johnson, who told me of your, er, impecunious state. I own my newspaper. I own two dress shops. You shall have your pick of gowns, you shall be—"

"A fool," she said, "that's what I'd be. Now, pray, go." She took a giant step forward, risking a pile of dog droppings on the cobble-stones. "And do not come to me again as if I were a—a hapless female needing charity. I may be poor, sir. But I belong to myself. No other. And certainly not to you, sir!"

"But past the marrying age, if I might say so, 'scuse me, mad-am," said the sly envoy.

And got a whack on the cheek as she stepped forward to pluck a fragment of the torn offer out of the underling's bobwig. Faces peered out from a passing carriage; a man and a woman snickered. The suitor's face darkened.

Behind the window glass, Dulcie gave envoy and suitor a fist. Past the marrying age indeed! True, Madam was two years past thirty—but made no secret of it. And if she was not ready to marry, she was surely ready for love—and this rude fellow offered money, not love. It was the notorious artist, Mr Henry Fuseli, who might offer love—or so Miss Mary hoped. Dulcie had seen the flames that lit up her face and neck whenever the Swiss artist came to call. She opened the door wide and the mistress swept into the entryway, her beaver hat askew, the hem of her black greatcoat and dress splashed with a putrid brown. The man was angry. Dulcie saw it on his face as he stalked back to his gaudy carriage.

"For God's sake, pour me a glass of claret," Miss Mary said, and flung herself, exhausted, onto the sofa. One arm hung down to the dusty floor and Dulcie was chagrined that she hadn't finished the sweeping. But the mistress didn't seem to notice.

"I did for him, did I not, Dulcie?"

"Aye, you did, ma'am—for the both of them. 'Twas a wonder to witness." She watched the pleasure of the victory creep slowly over the mistress's full lips.

Dulcie thought of the black look Mr Ashcroft had given as he left. Folk did not like to be humiliated—especially in front of oth-ers. They did not like to be laughed at. Were the mistress a man, he might throw down his glove and demand a duel. What, she won-dered, might he do to a woman?

MARY was not in the best of moods when she arrived at No.72, St Paul's Churchyard, where the bookseller, also her patron and publisher (along with many other such) had his home, shop, and salon in the shadow of the great cathedral. She set down the first six sheets of Part Two of *A Vindication of the Rights of Woman* for typesetting. Part One was already in circulation, and despite the shock and outrage from certain conservatives, it was applauded (to her delight) by the cognoscenti, and Joseph Johnson wanted a sequel.

She was still smarting from yesterday's encounter with Edgar Ashcroft. And she was unhappy that no opportunity was given to revise her work. Pages were rushed into print as soon as they were written, by the surly printer, Hunt, and set in stone, as it were. Hereafter she would give Mr Johnson the entire manuscript at once—she would not do it his way. She told him so.

"And so be it, my dear," said her publisher, with a stiff little bow of his slight body—then, accommodating as always, a wry smile, a shy wink.

He had a way of saying nay with the same indulgent smile, as though Mary were his daughter and he was refusing her request for chocolate because they both knew it marred her complexion. She could not help but smile back at him. Such a funny little asthmatic man he was in his rumpled blue waistcoat, his grey-black hair tied back with a stained blue ribbon.

"Sit down now and I'll tell you what I've arranged for this afternoon. Something you've been wanting to see." He thrust a glass of cider and a chocolate biscuit into her hands. A forthright, earnest man in his fifties, with large, dark blue eyes that probed her every mood and foible, Joseph Johnson had taken her in when she was penniless and exhausted from a somewhat humiliating year as governess in Ireland, and set her up in a small house, rent free. Now he touched her cheek with his ink-stained hand. "Why, you're all in a heat, my dear."

"Why should I not be, after that dreadful man came to my house. You set him on, Mr Johnson, admit it! He claimed to be a colleague of Cyrus Hunt."

And there was the printer in the shadows, crouched over a manuscript the publisher had handed him to take back to the Fleet Street print shop. She knew the toady was listening; she saw the muscles work in his sallow cheeks.

"Consider now," Joseph said, getting up to reset the mahogany grandfather's clock that had just donged the wrong hour. "A little money would see you through your sequel to *Vindication*. Not that I encouraged Ashcroft, no," he said when she held up a hand. "He came to tea with a friend—and will not come again, I assure you. He is *not* one of us."

Mary took a gulp of the cider and squared her shoulders. She did not want to alienate her benefactor—she owed her very life to him. But the proposed marriage implied nothing less than a prostitution of her person for a maintenance. Her cheeks ripened. "I'm proud of my poverty," she cried. "I will not be insulted by a superficial fop!"

"There, there," he said, patting her hand, "no one is asking you to. You've given your answer, you must stand by it. Oh, absolutely. We'll see how much money the new book makes for us. In a month or two we'll take our trip to Paris, shall we? See what's going on with the Revolution? Watch the world change before our eyes, hey?"

"Shall we?" she said, clapping her hands, her mood altered with thoughts of France, the uprising of the people. Oh, but she did long to see history in the making. And she wanted to meet the liberal Marquis de Condorcet who shared her advocacy of equal education for girls and boys, and who was writing a plan, she heard, for the schooling of French females. Why they might write one together! She wanted to change not only her own, but all women's lives. She wouldn't allow a man to keep his unhappy wife's baby as her brother-in-law had. Or an inheritance, the way her brother Ned had kept their grandfather's legacy for himself alone—ignoring his needy siblings.

Joseph was refilling her glass, pressing another chocolate biscuit into her hand. It was worth a blemish or two, yes. She could cover those with powder.

He leaned closer and she tilted her head. He had said something about an arrangement for this afternoon—an outing, perhaps. He was a good man, a kind man, the father she didn't have. Her own father was a drunkard, a man who had killed her mother with his womanising ways. A man who sent letters twice a week, demanding his "rightful" share of her money. What money?

But here was the publisher grinning at her, full of his plans. She squeezed his hand. He returned it and wheezed a laugh. "So what is it, sir," she asked, "this arrangement, this wintry afternoon's outing?"

"I have arranged with our mutual friend Henry Fuseli—"

Ah, Henry, as she'd hoped! She felt the blush coming on. She had been full of Henry Fuseli ever since they had met at one of Johnson's literary suppers. The artist was romantic, dangerous, diabolical. He was the grand passion she had been longing for. Years of male betrayal had brought her low. Now Henry Fuseli's love—well, he did greatly admire her, did he not?—was bringing her to life again.

It would not be physical, no, nothing like that. She was still a virgin. A virgin at thirty-two! Ah well. She glanced over Johnson's shoulder to see *The Kiss*, a painting that Henry Fuseli had loaned, a painting that carried the effect of the kiss from the lips down to the thighs, and even the quivery toes. Ah...

"To see the original of *The Nightmare*," he said. "The painting is back from Russia, home now in his private gallery. It is a bit shocking, my dear, prepare yourself. But I think you should see it."

Joseph was narrowing his eyes at her: he knew her all too well. He had seen her conversing with Henry Fuseli. It was the way the artist probed her psyche with those black orbs that melted her bones; the way he cocked his head slightly to listen to her, smiling, as though he agreed, as though he thought her a genius, like himself. Had he not said so one time? But with him she had met her match. Along with Joseph, he was her teacher.

"Shall we go then, my dear?"

She looked down at her old wool dress, the black worsted stockings still mud-stained from yesterday's encounter. Her hair was at its lankest under the old beaver hat. "But you might have warned me. I can't go like this!"

"Oh, dear me, he's seen you in that gown," Joseph teased, and she smiled.

So she had worn the black wool every day the past week. What did she care about fashion? To dress fashionably suited neither her inclination nor her purse. "All right then. But let me scrub the mud off the hem. Brush my hair."

She ran down a flight into the kitchen to find a basin of water; then two flights up, her wet hems dragging, to the looking glass on the wall of the spare bedchamber. A scissors was lying on a nearby table. She trimmed her hair until it curled about her face. She looked like a fringed curtain, but no matter.

"Ah, Henry, my dear..." she whispered into the mirror, and pinched her cheeks to summon up the blood. She was ready, yes, for an afternoon's adventure.

MARY was unprepared for what she saw on the wall at the Fuseli gallery. A sleeping woman in an attitude of utter abandon, looking naked as a summer day under the translucent white shift. She lay against a crimson-draped background, her fair hair and plump shoulders dropped back over the edge of her couch. A grinning goblin crouched on her chest. Mary gasped. In the left corner of the painting, the ghostly head of a horse loomed, its flaring nostrils and staring eyes inflamed at the sight of the reclining virgin.

The Nightmare.

It was horrible. It was wonderful. It was fascinating. She could not stop looking. She put a hand to her cheek and it burned. Earlier she had walked past scenes painted from Shakespeare and Milton depicting hunts, battles, deaths, despair, horror, exalted emotion. She saw faces with staring eyes, slumped bodies, heaving breasts, tensed and muscled thighs. Incubi and succubi, witches, magic steeds, dreams, fire. A Lady Macbeth like a maenad with daggers. A naked Richard III, visited by ghosts.

But *The Nightmare*...

People called the artist vain, sardonic, lecherous—they were wrong. Mary's friend William Blake, who had illustrated her *Original Stories*, called him a genius. And so he was. Why, Henry Fuseli was kind, humane, and thoughtful! Mary formed her judgements quickly and stuck to them. Her first instincts were often right. Though when wrong, she conceded, very wrong. In future she would try to correct such failings.

A man loomed behind her: a tall, lean, pallid fellow in his thirties. "*Mon Dieu*, a painting of genius!" He spoke in a thick French accent; he had a brown mole on his chin that he kept stroking. "This entire room: a mélange of terror! Blood and murder! Fuseli was eating raw pork, that is what brought on *The Nightmare*. Imagine! See the way he uses light, the way the shadows fall on the drapery. The muscularity of his figures—one thinks of Michelangelo. *C'est merveilleux!*"

Mary was not looking at the light. Or the texture. She was looking at the goblin that was squatting on the sleeping woman's breast. It leered, as though it would bide its time, then plunge to ravish her. The woman was asleep, yet one could sense her terror the way her head fell back, exposing her bare throat. Mary thought of her own recurring nightmares, and shuddered.

"A priceless work! But surely not one for ladies." The Frenchman gave a short laugh. "Allow me to introduce myself: I am Alfred de Charpentier. *Le Comte de Charpentier,*" he hastened to add. He had recently fled the flames of Paris; he was now living in a shared enclave of émigrés. "You see, I value my head highly," he said, with another laugh. "But perhaps you do not know all that is happening in *ma belle France.*"

Mary knew quite well, she informed him. She had followed the news with great interest—even joy. She pitied this count, truly she did, but he must see how important for the world this revolution was, how corrupt the monarchy, her own English king and queen as well. "Indulging themselves," she said, "pampering, eating pastries and cream while the people starve."

Monsieur was not prepared for her eloquence. He was not a monarchist himself. "*Mais non!* I am aristocracy on my mother's side only, but targeted by those starving people."

When Mary told him her name, his eyes lit up. He had heard of her earlier work, *A Vindication of the Rights of Men,* a work she had written to rebut the conservative Edmund Burke. "It is indeed revolutionary. I congratulate you on its publication. But I am afraid I cannot read it and smile. I have lost my home and title as a result of that revolution." He moved on, bowing gracefully.

Henry Fuseli came up behind and clapped a hand on her shoulder. "He's not a bad fellow. You turned him away, did you?" He laughed. "One more impecunious émigré, living off the fat of the English land. Drifting with the tides of public opinion. Trying to save his ugly head. London is full of them."

He saw her glance again at the painting. "Shocked, eh?" He seemed pleased with her reaction. "They all are. But they'd like to get their hands on it. In Russia they shot a fellow for trying to steal it." He laughed, and she gave a tremulous smile, but could not look at him. All that voluptuous flesh lay between them. He was married now, but no matter. She wanted only to share his mind.

He was half an inch shorter than she (though she was tall for a woman), small-boned, but such an aura of mystery about him.

Those penetrating eyes that drilled right through her gown. The hair unruly, unpowdered like her own—she liked that; it was white from some long-ago, mysterious illness that had afflicted his hands as well as his hair. Even now she felt a hand tremble on her shoulder. So much trauma in those fifty years that had known the love of woman *and* man—oh yes, there were rumours about Henry Fuseli.

Whatever the artist had done was his prerogative. A genius need not abide by the rules of the majority.

The genius pulled her about to face him, his movements quick and catlike. She squinted into the dark eyes, mesmerized. Then he turned her toward *The Nightmare*, and she looked back into the eyes of the voyeur horse.

She felt torn in half, as though the beast in the painting were stalking her, taming her, propelling her towards a bedchamber. She grew lightheaded, she had to sit down. She pushed past him, out of breath, out of words. Mary Wollstonecraft, out of words?

"I told you it's powerful, that *Nightmare*." It was Joseph Johnson, bending solicitously over her where she had collapsed onto a scarlet settee. "But you wanted to see it. I couldn't refuse you. Every painting in here, brilliant. But *The Nightmare* is Fuseli's favorite, like the child he's never had—or acknowledged. A masterpiece, indeed. It hung for a time in my own house, did I tell you? He made me lock all my doors."

"Oh," she said, imagining tea and crumpets in front of all that eroticism.

"But my housekeeper kept covering it up. So I gave it back. And then all the museums in Europe wanted it. He's thrilled to have it home now in London."

The artist was standing at the gallery entrance, and at the moment he didn't seem thrilled at anything; rather his eyes were hot with anger. It seemed directed at a young man and woman standing before him. Behind them, the blond Sophia Fuseli stood smiling, triumphant, as though she had brought her husband a pair of sweet cakes.

The man, Mary saw, was Roger Peale, a dark-haired young radical who had lately taken part in the weekly gatherings at the publisher's house. He was poor, a struggling artist—talented they said, though she had not seen his work. Joseph had given him, in good faith, an assignment to critique Fuseli's Shakespeare paintings at a local gallery. And what did the impetuous Peale do, Joseph whispered to Mary, but belittle the work: "'Not his cup of tea,' he wrote. Well, all right, but then he went on to call it 'crude, indulgent, filled with gratuitous violence.' The knave disparaged it in no less than three newspapers. And now he presumes to enter the private gallery?"

Mary struggled to her feet. And was pulled back down. "Wait," Joseph said. "Let's see what happens."

Henry was ordering the pair out of the house, his cheeks swollen with resentment. The young woman, too, looked upset; she was trying to pull her companion out with her. Mary recognized Lillian Guilfoy, who had once accompanied Roger Peale to the publisher's. Mrs Guilfoy painted teacups with roses and lilies; she was pretty with her dark curly hair and wide cornflower eyes, the smooth white bosom peeking above the snug bodice.

Mary had once seen Henry Fuseli peering down that bodice. She curled her hands into fists.

Mr Peale was here to review *The Nightmare* for *The Times*. He would be open, he was shouting; he would be objective. "You must take the bad with the good, sir. You have dozens of disciples. Why are you so worried?"

He was not worried, Fuseli growled. "Not from an *objective* reporter. You, sir, are hardly *objective*. Now leave the premises or I shall have my man escort you out!" His Swiss accent thickened, Mary observed, when he was upset. He signaled to a footman; the blond, hulking fellow took a menacing step in the young artist's direction. Peale was a slight but handsome man—*poetical* was how Mary would describe his features.

She hoped there would be no violence. She tried to stand again, this time in favour of young Peale, but Joseph had her arm.

"It's hard for Peale to be objective," he whispered. "I didn't realize when I first assigned him a piece."

"And why not?"

"Think," he said. "He's in love with the Guilfoy woman. She had a child, you know. They say it was Fuseli's."

Mary did not know. She looked at Henry Fuseli. She was feeling lightheaded again.

"Perhaps it was his, my dear. Though he denies it. And Henry

wanted nothing to do with any child. What *could* he do? He was
involved with that cousin of his at the time. 'Twould have been
damned embarrassing. He gave Mrs Guilfoy a painting. But she
destroyed it. Over his head, I believe."

The intruders were backing away. The blond footman resumed
his stance by the wall. Sophia Fuseli was in tears. She had made a
mistake by letting them in: "It won't happen again," she said, wiping her eyes. Her husband did not comfort her.

"It was naive of Mrs Guilfoy to destroy it," Joseph said. "A
Fuseli painting would take care of the child's education had she
sold it. I can't understand such carelessness."

Mary understood. One day she would call upon Mrs Guilfoy;
they would talk, woman to woman.

The artist's face was a wreath of smiles. He had rid the gallery of
his biased critic. He moved swiftly toward Mary, reaching for her
hands.

"You look be-eau-ti-ful today," he told her. "What have you
done with your hair?" His eyes gazed deeply into hers, and her
earth reeled about the sun.

Though when he turned away to speak to Joseph, she could see
only the brown goblin, leering.

CHAPTER II.

Stolen!

~

SATURDAY AFTERNOON Dulcie was a pool of perspiration. Charles Maurice de Talleyrand, Bishop of Autun, was coming for tea. But there was little tea in the jar. "And no muffins," she told the mistress. Why then, she must send to the market, said the mistress. But who was the person to *send* except herself?

"Then go, go," said Miss Mary. "We must not keep him waiting. You know who he is, do you not?"

"Who else is the Bishop of Autun but a bishop?" said Dulcie, shoving her arms into the tight sleeves of her old winter greatcoat. The lining was full of holes, and outside, a late February gale was blowing. A day to stay indoors, and here she was, running errands for some bishop who would ask her: "Where do you worship, my child?" And she would have to say, "Well, um—in my head, Father."

Oh, she did hope he wouldn't ask if she was baptized, for of course she was not. She was the love child of Mr Johnson's fourth cousin Penny, who'd died in childbirth. With the disappearance of the father, Dulcie was left to the parish of St Giles to be nursed, and then bred to Labour, Industry, and Religion. She cast off that yoke when her charity school sent her to work in the cotton mills of the north; Mr Johnson discovered her there, and brought her to Mary Wollstonecraft.

When she looked up from her reverie the mistress was still talking. Dulcie caught the phrases "progressive bishop... horses for the French army... aristocratic revolutionary."

Dulcie distrusted the word "revolutionary." The way the mob was said to be taking over Paris frightened her. *She* would not want to storm St James's Palace or even Newgate Prison the way the French people had broken into the Bastille back in '89, letting loose a bunch of ruffians. *She* would not demand the heads of

French lords and ladies, though thank God it was still nothing but talk. Louis and his queen were as good as prisoners in their own Tuileries, rumour said, but they were still breathing.

"Be off with you!" Miss Mary ordered, though her tone was soft. She was a good mistress on the whole: impulsive, opinionated, but kind at heart. Besides, when she was governess in Ireland, she'd known what it was to be a servant. Dulcie had heard about the selfish Lady Kingsborough and her rabble of dogs that all but suckled her breasts and supplanted her dozen children. She had heard about that lascivious Lord Kingsborough who broke into the governess's room one night and was rebuffed.

Dulcie couldn't imagine anyone taking advantage of spirited Miss Mary! Though Dulcie was suspicious of that Henry Fuseli who was rumoured to have a temper as violent as his paintings, and in spite of that, turned the mistress into a panting puppy whenever he came to visit. Why, one time she, Dulcie, took his coat to hang up, and three letters from the mistress fell out of the shallow pocket—unopened! Was that love? Was that devotion?

Now Dulcie couldn't find her winter gloves and the mistress was frowning. So she buttoned up her coat and straightened a parlour chair—one of two new parlour chairs, though there was precious little furniture in this place since Miss Mary had sold a highboy in order to send her sister Everina to Ireland—and went out gloveless. Behind her the mistress called, "And besides the tea and cream, fetch a bottle of French wine. Red. Be sure it's real and not watered down. Red, mind you."

"Wine at tea time?" Dulcie argued.

"He's French, French, I said! Now go. They'll be here at any moment. And Mr Johnson with them."

"And how do I pay for all this?" Dulcie called back. She reached into her pocket but found only a twopence.

"Charge it. What else?"

DULCIE dragged home through the frosty streets of London with a bottle of the cheapest French wine, cream, a sack of Chinese tea leaves, and six elderberry muffins—two for each of the two guests and one for Miss Mary. All of which she'd charged and been told she must pay up next time or no wine, no tea. Dulcie herself ate the sixth muffin.

A carriage was waiting outside at the kerb, and inside she found not two but three visitors. Mr Johnson introduced the uninvited person as Jacques St Pierre, a wiry red-haired fellow who looked like he'd been through a revolution and hadn't eaten since. The two were in England, the bishop told the mistress, to seek an alliance and to get money and horses from King George for the moderate Girondins in revolutionary Paris, who were struggling for power against the bloodthirsty Jacobins. The situation was becoming *désespérée*, the bishop said, sounding hoarse, like he'd been arguing all day but no one listened. His eyes followed Dulcie as she laid out the five muffins on a flowered tray. She avoided looking at Miss Mary, but felt the burn at her back. How was she to know there were to be three guests? She was told two, and she bought for two, and she was not about to accept a scolding, no ma'am.

The tea was steaming in the china pot and the muffins cut in halves to make do. She served the wine in flowered teacups—the mistress took the one with the chip—and Dulcie's task was done for the moment. She had only to stand at attention in a corner and observe. Maidservants (or unservants) were expected to be invisible and that was all right with Dulcie. Anyhow, Miss Mary would soon take over the conversation—the mistress bloomed like a rose in fine company—already Dulcie could see her putting out petals.

Though today it was Bishop Talleyrand who did most of the talking—largely about himself: "Regimes may fall and fail," she heard him say, "but I do not." Modest fellow, she thought. But he seemed a well-fed, middle-aged man with a rather sad-dog expression, except when he began his second teacup of wine, and then spots of fire reddened his cheeks. What interested Dulcie most was his left foot, on which he wore a large rounded shoe with a metal frame up the leg to the knee and attached with a leather strap. A gold-headed cane leaned against his chair, and when he got up to refill Miss Mary's cup, and then the Jacques Saint Somebody's, he had a heavy-footed limp.

The Saint Somebody simpered into the bishop's face as he took the wine. He was prettily, if shabbily dressed in a black coat, crimson waistcoat, yellow stockings, and black jackboots. He had watery blue eyes, and rust-coloured eyebrows that arched as he glanced about the room like he'd find something he'd been looking for. Money? If so, he wouldn't find it here.

The bishop had lately attended a reception at the English court, he said with a pout. "But King George was a block of ice and the queen turned her back. *Sacrebleu!*"

Mr Johnson and Miss Mary expressed indignation, but Dulcie understood. Why should the English king support a cause that hated kings? Dulcie could have told the bishop he would be scorned. But no one asked her opinion.

"And your sainted Prime Minister Pitt was not swayed from his most unsympathetic neutrality by anything I had to say. Hmph. Afraid to take a stand." An allied Britain and France, Talleyrand insisted, could together hold off invading troops from Prussia, Russia, and Austria—"All of them salivating on our doorstep!"

"But the English hate the French!" Dulcie cried, unable to hold back. "We always been at war with France. Ask anybody in the street. Only an hour ago the baker said—"

"Dulcie."

Dulcie shrank back into the wall, pinned there by the mistress's lifted eyebrow. There was a silence. Then the bishop began to laugh. Slowly at first, then louder and louder until his cheeks blew up like apples and his big left shoe pounded the floor. He was joined by Jacques Saint Somebody, and then by the bookseller-publisher.

"War!" the bishop roared. "True, my girl, for hundreds of years and unfortunately so. And that is what I am here to avoid. *Je suis un homme de paix!*" His big shoe tapped out the last six words while Dulcie watched, fascinated. The company was in agreement about No War; Miss Mary clapped her hands. Then Talleyrand called for more wine, and there wasn't any.

Without wine, the party fell into small talk. The conversation was mainly held up by Miss Mary complaining about King George III and Prime Minister Pitt, wishing she could that very moment sail over to aid the French.

"I do so long to visit and see for myself what glorious things have been happening," she cried, and went on about a trip to Paris she hoped to take in the spring. There was no mention of a helper coming along, and that was fine with Dulcie. She had no wish to go to that barbaric city.

Finally the talk turned to Miss Mary's new book—and Talleyrand bowed, seemingly amused by a book about the rights of woman. He gave a second bow when she handed him a signed copy and said she had dedicated it to him because of his work in educating young Frenchwomen. He must continue to do so, she warned, shaking a finger. Of course he said he would, with a wink at Jacques Saint Somebody. The latter patted Miss Mary's arm, and the mistress forced a smile.

Something going on there, Dulcie thought.

Publisher and Mistress were waxing on about the mistress's new book when someone banged on the door. Miss Mary shook her head at Dulcie to say, Don't answer it, but the door thrust open and there stood Cyrus Hunt, the publisher's printer. He was all in a stew, his waistcoat buttoned awry and his forehead a fountain of perspiration.

"She's busy," said Dulcie, running into the hall to hold him off. "She's entertaining."

"I came to find Mr Johnson," said Hunt in his Yorkshire accent, holding his sides to catch his breath. He had tracked in mud on Dulcie's freshly scrubbed floor. "I've got news for him."

"Mr Johnson is entertaining as well," she retorted. "The mistress won't want to have her party interrupted."

The printer brushed past Dulcie like she wasn't there at all. She protested, and then shrugged her thin shoulders. She'd done her best. The mistress would have to cope.

Mr Johnson looked up indulgently. But Miss Mary was nettled by the interruption: she didn't offer to introduce the printer to the two Frenchmen.

"A word with you, sir," the fellow said, sounding breathless. "In private. 'Tis vital. I was instructed to inform you at once."

Sighing, Mr Johnson excused himself from the company. Dulcie ushered him into the hallway, and lingered to polish the door handle. "A message from Mr Fuseli," said the printer. "'Tis *The Nightmare*. The irreplaceable original. Gone from his gallery. Stolen! You are to come at once. The painter is in a fury. He knows the thief, he says—he has evidence, something the fellow left behind in his hurry. Now Bow Street has sent a constable to arrest Roger Peale."

THE young artist was in the notorious Newgate Prison, Mary overheard when she arrived at Isobel Frothingham's Friday evening rout. Guests were whispering Peale's name—they loved a scandal.

Mary suspected that the authorities had found the painting on his person—why else would he be sent to await trial in that London bastille?

She had received an invitation to the soirée the week before, just after the brouhaha about the stolen painting, and in view of the recent publication of her book, she determined to attend. In six brain-racking weeks, she had poured a lifetime's complaint against the ill treatment of females into three hundred pages. Never mind the worm, Edgar Ashcroft, who in his biased *Chronicle,* called it "disorganized...in need of editing." His editing of course. She would keep an eye on the rogue. She did not trust him. So with the possibility of seeing Henry Fuseli as well, she had decorated her black muslin with a lacy fichu, poked a pink silk rose into her freshly washed hair, and sallied forth.

Besides, she was curious to see that grand brick house on Grosvenor Square, five storeys high and with an indoor water closet: a tangle of leaking lead pipes that the bluestocking's first, now deceased, lover had constructed before he willed the place to her. And Isobel's drawing room was elegant, yes, but filled with paintings too cluttered with plants and beasts for Mary's taste. The furnishings were a hodge-podge of French and Chinese, classical and modern. The mix of pea-green, ultramarine, and verdigris was enough to give one vertigo. The grand piano was piled high with books.

Mrs Frothingham, a poet and writer, draped in white like a Grecian matron, with a revolutionary red cockade over her right ear, was engaged in an animated debate about love versus money. The self-styled bluestocking, who had been known to nurture several lovers, even simultaneously, was on the side of love. "'Nothing is less in our power than the heart,'" she quoted the philosopher Rousseau, "'and far from commanding, we are forced to obey it.'" When everyone applauded, she cried out, "What is marriage, but men rising from their silken knees and women sinking down on *theirs!*"

The quip evoked high-pitched laughter, along with protestations from the men. "Which is exactly where Edgar Ashcroft would have me," Isobel shouted above the din, "had I accepted his proposal."

Oh? But Mary did not speak of Mr Ashcroft's proposal to *her,* in case it had come after the bluestocking's refusal. That, of course, would be humiliating, given that she was obviously the younger of the two.

When Mary came near her hostess, the woman pounced on her. "Why, here is the authoress of that book everyone is talking about! Tell us, Miss Wollstonecraft: should one marry—if one marries— for love? Or money?"

The question could not be easily answered. "In my book on the rights of woman," Mary began. But no one here, it turned out, had yet read beyond the first page of *Vindication*. She was beginning to describe the purpose of the book when Mrs Lillian Guilfoy entered the drawing room with red-haired Jacques St Pierre in tow. The two were talking animatedly. There were sympathetic glances at the bereft lady, along with raised eyebrows.

Mary planted herself in their path. "I am sorry to hear about—" she began, and the lady interrupted: "No proof! Mr Peale did nothing! So he wrote an adverse review of Mr Fuseli's last exhibition, what was that?" She blinked into Mary's face. "Mr Peale had nothing against the artist. Would you have him lie if he dislikes a work of art?" Her cheeks pinkened with her indignation.

"Of course not, *absolument non*," St Pierre said before Mary could open her mouth. He squeezed his companion's arm. She gave him a warm look that suggested he was not at all a new acquaintance.

"Well, no," agreed Mary, who in truth had published some... well...plain-spoken reviews of written works, including a sentimental epistolary novel by Mrs Frothingham herself. Though privately she wondered about Mr Peale's judgement—when the whole world considered Henry Fuseli a genius, including Joseph Johnson, whose views Mary trusted implicitly.

"Miss Wollstonecraft, you must help us." Mrs Guilfoy held out her hands imploringly. "We know you're a friend of Mr Fuseli. You must speak, madam, to my fiancé's character. They have searched his quarters and found nothing. Nothing but the mate of a black leather glove—a monogrammed glove he must have dropped the day before when we were so rudely ushered out—he didn't dare go back after it! But my Roger would never steal. No!" She wrung Mary's hands until the fingers went numb. "You're a woman of feeling, madam. I've read your novel—*Mary, a Fiction*. It was written out of the heart, I could tell."

"Ah." So it was, out of the heart. And drawn from nature. Mary smiled at this desperate young woman who had read her novel. She massaged the small white hands in her own. "I will speak to him. I can't promise anything, but I will try."

"Monsieur St Pierre is helping, too," Mrs Guilfoy said, squeezing Mary's hands again. "He'll enlist the aid of Bishop Talleyrand."

"Indeed I will help." St Pierre placed a hand on the young woman's shoulder. "I will do everything possible to find the true culprit." He lowered his voice: "Look, *par exemple*, to Monsieur de Charpentier. He spoke of the painting only yesterday, at the coffee-house—*passionnément!* Talleyrand was there; he will tell you how the count looked. Fire in the eye! There is the bishop now," he pointed, "having a *tête-à-tête* with Madame Frothingham. We will ask him."

Mrs Guilfoy put a finger to her lips, and St Pierre turned to see the French count enter the room and head for the hostess and Talleyrand.

"But what did he say, monsieur?" Mary would speak to Fuseli, but she did not care to question Talleyrand, who had left behind the copy of *Vindication* she gave him at her tea party, as though he valued it little.

St Pierre leaned close to whisper in Mary's ear; his voice was hoarse: "You will not believe, madame. But he said—'I would kill—to own a painting like that.'"

Mary laughed out loud. "And so perhaps would *you*, sir, and a few others whom I know. As for myself, I wouldn't have it in the house—I've nightmares enough as it is."

She excused herself to take some refreshment, and was about to pour a glass of foaming pink punch when St Pierre came hustling over to refill his glass. "I did not want to speak in front of Mrs Guilfoy," he confided, "but you should know there is more to the theft than she has told you, poor lady. Peale, it was discovered, had been arrested once already for stealing a painting—or was it a gold frame? One or the other, yes. So it was not difficult for Fuseli to persuade Bow Street to hold him in Newgate for trial—and without bail."

THE Bow Street Magistrates' Court was just ending its Friday afternoon session, and ignoring his wife's protests—for they were on their way to Mrs Frothingham's rout—Henry Fuseli jumped out of the carriage and ran inside. Six days since the theft and Peale still hadn't confessed; there was no other suspect, and he wanted his painting back. "Six days," he called out to the magistrate. "And you have done nothing to find my painting."

The man stood up at once—Henry was an important man, he had clout. "But Mr Fuseli, sir, we have done all—"

"All you can, *ja*. But you have the evidence, sir: Peale's glove in my gallery. You are familiar with the man's suspect background. And you know that my footman saw Peale in my gallery the night of the theft. *Saw* him, I say!" Henry wasn't wholly certain of that fact, but Benjamin had started to speak of someone he saw—a man running out of the unlit gallery. And then the coach arrived to take him and Sophia off to the bluestocking's foolish rout. Henry disliked clever women, they were only trouble.

"It was Peale, I know it," he cried at the bewigged magistrate. "An inveterate thief! Make him tell what he did with my painting!"

The man stared back at him, his face a flaccid pudding, his eyes a pair of squashed grapes. "But the perpetrator, Mr Fuseli, sir, is already awaiting trial. He will not admit to taking the painting. What more can we do? The law takes its due course."

"To hell with due course! I want my painting, I said. Six days and it could be in China. Or the bowels of a shipwrecked schooner." Henry sighed. The man was a dunce. The Bow Street Runners had deteriorated since the blind magistrate, Sir John Fielding, died. "And you, sir," he said, "more concerned with a lout who stole a lady's purse than a masterpiece worth thousands? Find the painting. Find it, I say! You will have your reward." Wheeling about, he made his way through the crowded chamber.

"Hurry, Mr Fuseli, we'll be late." Sophia poked her curly blond head out the carriage door, and then squealed. "It's raining! My hair will be ruined! Get in, quick! And don't bring the rain with you. Ooh, I've lost a feather—shut the door, will you?"

"Damn the feather," he bawled, climbing in. "Damn the constabulary. Hang that upstart Peale. Hang him, I say! Make him tell where my *Nightmare* is." He was breaking down, though he tried not to show it.

"But my dear," she murmured, stroking his quivering cheek, "if you hang him, he won't be *able* to tell."

"I don't care how," he cried, spilling his outrage into his wife's damp ear as the carriage bumped on into Oxford Street. "I want the blackguard *made* to confess!"

SOMEONE was warbling in a high soprano, and Mary turned to see Isobel Frothingham at the pianoforte, which held a song book of French tunes. The singing was off-key, though that did not seem to bother Alfred de Charpentier, who stood beside her in a frayed red satin coat, blue stockings (at Isobel's request), and shoes with red heels and shiny gold buckles in the shape of hearts. Every now and then he lifted a leg as if to admire the footwear.

Isobel swayed as she sang, glancing off and on into his shuttered lids. The Frenchman bent toward her, but just as his powdered face had almost reached her breast, she jumped up, her song ended. She gave a tap with her fan as if to say, "Go away, I can't bother with you now." Smirking, he pulled the red cockade out of her hair— and she snatched it back and swung away from him.

"Idiot," Isobel said, coming to stand close to Mary's ear. "That one will never have me. Besides, he smells bad." She held her nose.

Mary wrinkled her own nose, though she smelled only a rancid perfume. "I wonder... Would the count have coveted that painting, do you think? *The Nightmare*? He admired it. I heard him say so myself in Henry's gallery."

"Did he really?" said Isobel, dropping a low curtsy to a passing Talleyrand, who had caught her eye and winked. Mary, too, curtsied—though not so low. But the fickle bishop was not looking at *her*.

Isobel reattached the cockade over her ear. "But then Mr Peale is equally suspect in this nightmarish theft, is he not? Apart, that is, from whatever he might have done in the past. And he did write scathingly of the painting in *The Arts Forum*."

"He did. But I understood that Charpentier was the one who assured Henry—right or wrong—that Peale was the thief. It might have been he who went searching for Peale's past? Or made it up, do you think?"

"It was Fuseli's solicitor discovered it—it's true." Isobel fanned the air so vigorously that a bit of her lightly powdered hair blew into Mary's eyes. "Besides, if I were to give in to Monsieur Charpentier as he has been insisting with his daily offerings of chocolates, would I get half ownership of the painting? I would hang it there—beside that new painting by Angelica Kauffmann—*Sappho Inspired by Love*. An intriguing contrast?"

"Would you really want it?" Mary would not want the painting in *her* house. Now, though, there was no painting to hang. The magnitude of the theft left her breathless.

A maidservant brought in a fat little pug dog, and it leapt into its mistress's arms. "By the way," Mrs Frothingham said, cradling her dog and leaning in towards Mary, "I would like to borrow your housemaid Friday next to bake that iced plum cake she made one time for tea at your house. I'm expecting Bishop Talleyrand for dinner, and Cook will be off.... *Arrgh*," she groaned, to see a fellow in pink spit crumbs from his lips as he chattered to a giggling female.

"I'll see that she comes," Mary said, not admitting that iced plum was the only kind of cake Dulcie had ever been known to bake—she'd learned it from Johnson's cook, and only baked it for the one tea party with the bluestocking—the ingredients were too costly.

A footman announced Mr and Mrs Henry Fuseli, and Mary sucked in a breath. Overdressed in pink satin, Sophia Fuseli moved like a marionette, with Henry's guiding finger on her scapula. The pair was heading towards Talleyrand—until Lillian Guilfoy rushed forward, cutting them off from the bishop. Mary pulled on Mrs Guilfoy's arm, but too late. The distraught woman was hanging on to Henry. "Mr Peale—he would never! Pray, release him! You have no proof. He dropped that glove, I tell you, when he and I came there. He went home with only one—"

"Then why, my girl, was the glove not found sooner?" Henry said, looking quite smug. "Our servants are exceedingly meticulous."

"I don't know! I can't tell you that. Perhaps your dog..."

"But we have no dog, my dear. Only my wife's cat. Who has never been known to wear a glove."

"Oh, I don't know, I said!" Lillian Guilfoy cried, waving her hands.

"Of course not." Mary put a hand on her shoulder.

"But pray, Mr Fuseli," said the beleaguered woman, calmer now, "let the law release him. He'll find the thief for you. He can't go to trial for some minor mistake in his youth. Get him released, Mr Fuseli, for the sake of our child!"

"Mis-take, yes," Henry said reflectively, as though he were speaking to a child himself. And then, "What child? I have only *The Nightmare*—that was my child." Lillian's cheeks reddened as the artist's voice grew choked with his loss. "Now leave me. Has your thieving man not done me enough harm? Hey? Trying to destroy my reputation?" He looked closely into her face. "Where is my painting, eh? Tell me where."

She stared at him. He turned his back; she pummeled it. He moved implacably on.

"Patience." St Pierre took the young woman's arm. "There are other ways," he said loudly, and glared at Henry's retreating back.

"I know that man." Mrs Guilfoy pursed her lips. "He's made of iron. But he's not an impregnable fortress. He'll listen to reason. There were mitigating circumstances in Roger's past. He'll have my fiancé released. You wait."

She ran up to Henry again and spoke pleadingly in his ear. This time he gave a throaty laugh and grabbed her hands. "Come now, my lady, come. If your man is innocent he will be set free. I will see that he has a fair trial. Now leave me. And you," he went on to St Pierre, "I would advise you to stay out of this affair. Unless it was you—" he pointed a shaky finger "—who stole my painting."

St Pierre protested; Mary could see the anger in his face. He excused himself, squeezing Lillian Guilfoy's hand when Henry moved on.

"You see I am quite alone," the young woman told Mary.

"But you have your French friend."

Lillian gave a half smile. "We were seeing one another, Jacques St Pierre and I, in Paris—it was before I met Mr Fuseli. And Monsieur St Pierre has remained a friend. He despises the man. Oh, I know how you feel about Fuseli—it's inscribed on your face. I felt that way—once. But he was unkind to me, denying my child. I'm telling you this as, well, as one woman to another."

Mary nodded, she understood: she had already been the pawn of four men. Though with Henry, she vowed, it would be different. She must give Lillian Guilfoy a copy of her *Vindication*—it might offer sustenance.

"And I want you to meet my Tommy," Lillian said, wiping a damp eye with her handkerchief. "He'll be six years of age next Wednesday. We'll have a tea party and I can explain a little—about

my Roger's past. At four?" Mary agreed; she might like to see
Henry's child—if indeed it was his. "And you will speak with Mr
Fuseli?" Lillian added.

"All in good time." Mary looked coolly at the artist, who had
just put a hand on Isobel Frothingham's white silk bottom. And
the bluestocking offered no resistance.

"HENRY," Sophia cried on their way home from the Frothingham rout. "Look!"

"Bloody fool," Henry muttered as a blue coach-and-four bore
down on the Fuseli carriage, raced past on the wet cobbles, veered
left again, and rammed against an elderly hackney cab in its path.
The hackney horses reared, and the cab slammed over on its side.
The coach-and-four galloped on by, spraying mud and dung on the
cab, like a final blow to the fallen. A crowd quickly gathered about
the stricken hackney, blocking the entire lane.

Damnation, Henry thought: he was tired, he had drunk too
much at the rout—he watched impatiently as the hackney driver
picked himself up where he'd fallen into the street, and with the
help of a bystander, yanked open the righthand door of the hackney and pulled out the injured body of a man in the black-and-gold
livery of a footman.

"It's Benjamin," Sophia cried. "It is! We must help him! Is he
dead?"

It was a damned inconvenience, but no, Henry did not want him
dead. He jumped down out of the carriage and pushed through the
crowd of pedestrians and backed-up traffic. "Give him room. No,
here. You two fellows, over there. Carry him into that shop. That
one—the haberdasher's. Careful, careful now!"

The man opened his eyes, and Henry wiped the bloody forehead with the fellow's pocket handkerchief; he ordered the stunned
haberdasher to send an apprentice for his personal physician. He
liked Benjamin: the footman was dumb but devoted, the kind that
would give his life to save his master's. Henry reached deep into his
coat pocket and let the man sip from his flask.

"Thankee, sir," the man whispered as if in apology. "I wanted—" The voice failed; the blue eyes shut. And then opened again,
though the lids hung low.

"Wanted to tell me something, yes," Henry said. He could smell
the blood, and through it, the man's fragrance. On his way to an

assignation, perhaps? Male, most likely—dangerous—the English frowned on such things. "Then say it, man. Is it about the painting? Say it."

Benjamin was heaving up breath. Struggling with the words. Finally he said, "I saw someone...dark hair..." He groaned, and the lids slid over the dilating blues.

"Saw who? Was it Peale you saw? Dark hair, *ja*. Say it, man. Was it Peale?" But the footman was out of words. Though he nodded, did he not? Henry was certain he saw him nod. But he was in shock, no doubt—or worse. A weak pulse: the poor fellow seemed barely alive. Henry could hear Sophia's quavering voice calling for him; heard horses snorting outside the shop, the traffic moving forward again.

"Where's that physician I sent for?" he shouted at the haberdasher. "Get him here! No. Never mind," he said as he dashed out of the shop. "I'll fetch him myself."

"Do you think it was deliberate?" Sophia asked as they drove on. The rain was coming harder now; mud and pebbles splashed up on the glass. The carriage hit a pothole and lurched to the right; Sophia cried out.

"Of course not, why should it be? Just bad luck, that's all. Those hackneys are always off-balance. They pitch over at the slightest breath of wind."

"But that coach-and-four rode directly at the hackney. I was looking out, Henry, I saw it. The coachman pulled on the reins and made the coach turn into the hackney."

"You saw that, did you?"

"I just told you I did. The coachman pulled on the reins and—"

"*Ja*. I heard you. It was Peale then. To keep Benjamin from testifying."

"Not Peale, Henry. Mr Peale is in prison. You saw to that yourself, did you not?"

"Then he hired someone to do it. The man will stop at nothing. There, Hanover Square. My physician's house, stop there," he called to the coachman. "Stop, I said!"

WHEN Mary agreed to do something she did it. It was one of her principles. She was determined to bring Henry to heel. He would probably be having breakfast as usual with Joseph Johnson, so she took a sedan chair to 72, St Paul's Churchyard late Tuesday morning, where she found a small group of writers and Dissenters at their publisher's table. She had become a regular member of the celebrated Johnson circle since her recent publications—a matter of deep satisfaction to her as a woman.

There was Little Johnson, as she sometimes teasingly called him, to differentiate from the great, late Samuel. He was still in his blue slippers, a glass of coffee in his hand. There were Joseph Priestley, the chemist and clergyman; William Blake, the visionary artist; the lovelorn writer Mary Hays; and at the far end of the table, the radical American author Joel Barlow, who was to take Mary's brother Charles to America with him. The educator Anna Laetitia Barbauld sat across from her, grinning at the long-nosed William Godwin, who had criticized the structure of Mary's *Vindication*—Mary could understand Fuseli's hurt at young Peale's satiric reviews.

Even with eight people, the room seemed empty.

Joseph acknowledged her presence with a wave of his hand. Seeing her glance about, he said, "Henry is upstairs, my dear. And I must warn you he is feeling prickly. He has just heard that his young footman died."

"Ah, I'm truly sorry to hear that," Mary said, and took her seat. The talk was not only of the footman's death—a hackney accident that Henry Fuseli was evidently calling murder—but of a friend of Joseph Priestley's, who had been burned out of his house. She couldn't find an opening in the dialogue, so she sat down to listen—although listening didn't come easily to her. But she pressed her lips together and tried.

"And only yesterday one of ours, a Unitarian, was attacked in the street," Barlow was saying. "It was those bloody, king-kissing conservatives."

"Another Birmingham riot on the horizon?" said Godwin, referring to last July's mob violence against Priestley and dozens of other religious Dissenters.

"God help us if that happens," cried Priestley. "My papers stolen and handed over to that devil, Pitt. A blasphemy! And worse, as you know—" His lips quivered.

"Worse?" said Joseph Johnson, who seldom took the floor, but asked a pertinent question now and again to stimulate conversation.

"My laboratory, you know that!" the chemist sputtered. "The work of years—destroyed, irrevocably lost! Without your help, I'd

have been destroyed myself. And still may have to flee the country.
But for you, the worst is coming—"

"Worse again?" It was Godwin and Hays in concert.

"All our dissenting academies proscribed. The government calling them nurseries for revolutionaries," Priestley hissed.

"And so they are—for revolutionaries. Hurrah!" cried Mary,
though the others looked solemn at the news of such oppression.
"I mean," she amended, "that they must persevere—in spite of the
injunction." The academies, she knew, taught history, science, and
economics, along with a questioning approach to the Bible. Mary
had not been able to attend such a school. But she had suffered:
hers was an empirical education.

"They stimulate the imagination," said Will Blake. "They teach
men to see angels in the wheat fields."

"They teach men to think for themselves," murmured a more
rational Barlow.

"And women," said Mary, echoed by Hays and Barbauld. "What
of the women?"

"Aye, the women," the men murmured, and turned to smile at
the three women, as though surprised to see that they were indeed
women, and not just shorter members of the circle. A matter of
respect? Mary thought. Or simply familiarity... Yet she herself felt
respected here, though Mary Hays claimed to feel a certain conde-
scension.

Mary drew in a breath, for Henry Fuseli had entered, like a ge-
nie rising from its bottle and spilling all over the room. Five steps
took him across the room and into the chair opposite hers. When
he lifted an eyebrow at her, the other faces blurred. She leaned
across the table. "Sir. I understand your personal loss, but—"

"Another blow at the Dissenters, that theft," interrupted Godwin. "I'm certain of it. Look to Burke, look to Ashcroft. Look to
any of a hundred bigots out to destroy us."

"Look to Peale," growled Fuseli. "He likely hired someone.
Now my footman is dead—because of Peale—it was murder! If
Peale has destroyed that painting—" he clutched at his throat "—
it's like taking a life. It *has* taken a life. My life," he said hoarsely.
"And Peale will hang for it—if I don't strangle the knave first!"

"Calm yourself, Mr Fuseli," said Mary, who loved a lively discussion, but not a biased one: "I can't imagine him hiring someone to
kill your poor footman. Such accidents happen every day, sad to say."

"It was Peale, I said!" Henry cried. Tears stood out in his eyes, and Mary was quiet. Henry was good to his servants. He would miss that loyal footman. Mary tried to imagine how it would feel to have a manuscript stolen that you had worked on for months, even years, and her lungs filled with indignation. She stretched out a foot to tap his shoe.

"But Peale is one of us," said Barlow. "He was here just a fortnight ago."

"Yes, he's young and hotheaded, that's all." Mary was grateful for Barlow's defense. "There was evidently some mistake in his early youth. Haven't we all made mistakes? Surely I—" She quieted, certain events of her own crowding into her mind. Joseph smiled back at her—he read her like one of his books. Mary could see Henry more clearly now. He was dressed in the usual black: it offset his crown of white hair. His hand trembled as he lifted a glass to his lips. She thought of the long-suffering Hamlet.

"I had a witness, madam, and now he is dead. But Peale will not thwart me. I have still more confirmation." Henry pulled his foot away from hers and glared. She frowned back. This was not her fun-loving Henry who loved to pull apart her theories so he could fence with them and poke holes.

"What confirmation?" she asked coolly.

"Then hear this, and I quote," Henry cried. "'Could I get my hands on that painting, I would tear it to pieces and feed it to my horse!'" He glanced about to gauge the others' reactions. "This, in Peale's own handwriting, *ja*! A colleague has confirmed it."

"What colleague," she asked. "Who?"

Henry's eyes probed hers. His hand squeezed her wrist, hard. "My girl, I have promised not to tell. Let us just say it was in writing. I will produce it at his trial. Do you doubt me?" He smiled—that devilish smile that always left Mary breathless.

Breathless, but not subdued. "That, sir, is no proof he took the painting."

"Perhaps not, but it reveals a motive. And there is the matter of the found glove as well. So let that be an end, *meine Liebe*, to this inquisition." He held up his hands, palms out. They were an artist's hands: strong and sensitive, with a criss-cross of delicate blue veins on their backs. Painterly fingers. One could not help but admire them.

His eyes left Mary; he turned toward the men. "So what were you saying about our academies? Proscribed, you said?"

"It was Pitt proscribed them," Anna Barbauld said, and the talk moved on to a condemnation of the prime minister. He was a Burke man, Anna said, and they all assented; they wanted Pitt out of office. Joel Barlow mentioned Mary's "powerful" response to Burke's anti-revolutionary diatribe, and the men nodded at her; Priestley and Blake applauded. She felt a warm swelling in her chest. "It is a farce," she had written, "to pretend that a man fights for his country, his hearth, or his altars, when he has neither liberty nor property."

Her cheeks, too, were flushed with the recognition she'd received—for that response, and for her work in the *Analytical Review*—copies were scattered about on a table. Recognition by all, that is, but Henry Fuseli, who was thinking only of his painting.

She got up to leave, and Joseph rose to walk her to the door. "Will you help Mrs Guilfoy?" she urged, clutching his arm. "Poor distraught woman, with her lover in Newgate. What reason would Peale have to steal Fuseli's painting? Would I steal one of your books because I didn't care for it? Never! Mr Peale was your guest—he's one of us. Do help."

"Give her this," Joseph said, pulling a guinea out of his pocket in atonement. Or was it a bribe to get her to quit his ear? "Tell her to buy her beau some nourishing food. Money talks in Newgate. I'll speak to Henry. When his reason returns, that is." He unclamped her hand from his arm, coughed, and shuffled back to the meeting room in his slippers.

Mary glanced back at Fuseli, who was talking closely into Barlow's ear; he didn't seem to notice she had gone. She snatched up the blue hat she had worn for this failed mission, and headed for the door. A woman had to do for herself in this world. She could not depend on a man.

Nor should she, she thought as she hailed a sedan chair outside the bookseller's shop, and directed the chairmen to Fleet Street. She would stop in the Cheshire Cheese for a hot chocolate. For once, she would indulge herself. If she didn't, who would?

CHAPTER III

No Such Prospect as Escape

～

THE FLEET Street printer glared at the sheaf of paper Isobel Frothingham had handed him, and then at her. "What's this?" he grunted.

She was here to arrange a private printing of her poems with Cyrus Hunt. Joseph Johnson had published her romance, *Scarlette*, but these were too personal to be sold to the public. Anyway, Hunt needed her patronage. He was a sour-faced little man, slightly hunchbacked, but with strong, nimble hands from rolling and un-rolling galleys of type. He would have to do.

"Twenty-two poems, Mr Hunt. I want you to make a booklet of them. Perhaps forty copies. You needn't read them yourself, I might add." Though there was no need to warn him. He would set the type, she knew, the way a servant might straighten and rehang a valuable painting, seeing nothing in it beyond a jumble of colours and figures.

"You can pay my fee?" he asked. He meant, of course, that just because he was known to her, he would not do the work for nothing.

"You know I can pay. When can you have them ready?"

"Can't say." He frowned. "I got other work ahead of yours. I'll get to 'em when I can."

"Next week. I have friends waiting to read them."

She wanted them soon—before she changed her mind. They were poems about her childhood; poems about her feelings, her loneliness, her fear of losing her looks. For this was her deepest fear: of growing old, losing her power. She didn't think she could bear that. Her sympathetic female friends would understand.

As for Cyrus Hunt, she thought as she left the smelly print shop and the footman handed her into her carriage—he would not prate about her poetry in public. He was too literal a fellow, too proper. A bit backward, she thought privately—but he knew his trade. She had the coachman take her to a bakeshop for a sackful of chocolate biscuits, and then to the Foundling Hospital in Coram's Fields. She came every three or four months. There was someone there she had to see.

Inside the ornate building she found several dozen girls in brown serge dresses with stiffened bodices—but no whalebone stays, thanks to a freethinking physician who had the good sense to declare that stays deformed women's bones. A moment later a scrawny, carroty-haired girl in white cap and apron came running at her. "Missus Frothingham! What'd you bring me?"

The girl was a smallpox survivor: her face looked as if someone had taken a fork and made light dents in her cheeks and forehead.

"Chocolate biscuits. In anticipation of your, um, birthday (*Isobel had just realized*). Why, you'll be thirteen years of age this Friday. Did you know that? And we'll have a frosted cake, shall we?"

"'Course I know, I ain't stupid," the girl cried, sticking her hands on her non-hips.

Such dreadful grammar. Isobel felt more aggrieved at abandoning the child to bad grammar than at leaving her at the hospital. A dare from a friend, along with multiple glasses of claret, had led Isobel to seduce a prominent guest one careless night after one of her routs. It left her with child and in shock. In vain she visited the local "wise woman," but the child was stubborn; it clung to the womb.

The last person she would have told, of course, was the child's father.

An aide motioned Isobel to a small table outside the kitchen. The girl, named Ann after the wife of one of the hospital governors, plunked herself down in the straight-backed chair and began to stuff a biscuit into her mouth, and swallow it, half-chewed.

When the girl reached out for a second, Isobel said, "Not now. I don't want you ill. You'll enjoy it more on Friday. Or should we share these with a friend?" She glanced at a group of children who were sweeping and mopping.

"I got no friends here," said Annie, as she preferred to call herself, pulling the sack closer.

Isobel thought of her own childhood: the absent, abstracted father; the rigid mother to whom appearance was everything, who allowed Isobel few friends for fear of smallpox or ague. She thought of her child's birth: how she had brought her to the orphanage posing as "an aunt of the mother." The governor had seen right through her, of course. She did not have to explain what a scandal it would be for a woman of her class to have a child out of wedlock. She pretended to go to Switzerland "on holiday."

She had simply been required to affix on the child a distinguishing token so she "might be known hereafter if necessary." So Isobel offered a locket containing a handwritten poem that began: *I grieve to give away my lovely child but...* The child wore it on a ribbon around her neck and told anyone who asked that her mother would one day come to claim her. She would go, she'd once declared, with no other.

Though no other wanted her, Isobel knew, not with that pocked face, or that arch I-can-do-it-myself-I-don't-need-you attitude.

"Ah, child, I think you've grown since I saw you last. Stand up and let me see."

The girl inched back in her chair. "Aye, I've done, and not because of the food here." She glared accusingly into Isobel's face. "They feed us coarse brown bread and butter with no jam (*her voice slowly rising*) and only a glass of sour milk for breakfast. Uck!"

"But pure milk, I know," Isobel said defensively, "and the hospital makes its own fresh bread. And look at you. In the pink of health." Seeing the girl frown, she drew in a breath and went on. "And how, pray, do you spend your days? Productively, I hope?"

"How else should I, when they make us scrub the pots and sweep the floors and turn the spits and churn butter and I don't know what else—why, everything!" Annie stamped her foot. "We get hardly a minute's rest. We're slaves, that's what."

"But in that moment of rest, what do you do then?" Isobel would not be defeated. Besides, the child looked almost pretty with her flushed face. Were it not for the pox, she might have at least found an apprenticeship with an artisan. Now, in her unruly adolescence, she seemed destined to become a domestic servant.

The girl glared at her, her mouth set in a tight little bow, as though she knew it was Mrs Frothingham who had abandoned her. But Isobel was not going to feel guilty, no. In truth, she had all but come to believe that the child was not hers, but a poor foundling, dropped on a doorstep somewhere and brought here.

"I read," Annie said. She folded her arms across her thin chest and looked at Isobel through the mother's own sea-green eyes.

"Ah, I recall that you started to read more. And what are you reading now?" The school had a policy of teaching the teachable to read, to exercise, to keep set hours of play—a far cry from the wretched workhouses where children slaved a seven-day week with no play time. The girl should be thankful that Isobel had brought her here.

"*Gulliver's Travels*," declared Annie. "I like those horses—those Houyhnhnms. I'd like one of them for a parent." She narrowed her eyes at her visitor. "And I just begun *Clarissa*. Miss Nasty over there—" she pointed at the aide "—takes it away from me, so I keep it under my pillow."

"But that's a naughty book!" was all Isobel could think to say—though she had read Samuel Richardson's work herself, cover to cover.

The girl smiled. Not a mean smile, but a warm, triumphant, glowing kind of smile.

Isobel felt her heart breaking out of her chest and spilling over. The girl was so much like herself—she had begun to realize this during her last few visits; had tried to suppress the thought. She had even considered bringing the child to live with her. She could not admit to the world that it was her own daughter, no. She would keep the girl on as a—charity child, yes. Other fashionable women took on a foundling for a time as a Christian thing to do, and so might she. She would direct the girl's reading: Rousseau, Shakespeare, Anna Barbauld...her own novel, of course.

For Isobel was lonely, in spite of her company, her routs, her assemblies, her series of tedious lovers. The life of an intellectual woman was not the carefree world it seemed—especially with some like the narcissistic Fuseli, who mocked her soirées.

She knelt to the child's level—and then got up again when she saw that the girl was as tall as she, but for an inch or so. "Would you like to come home with me, Annie? Live with me and read my books? Go to the opera and attend my book discussions and walk with me in Vauxhall Gardens and visit the bishops in Westminster Abbey?"

The child's green eyes penetrated Isobel's. For a moment she resembled her father when he had struggled to resist Isobel's love-making but finally gave in. Isobel looked back at her, and smiled.

The girl said nothing.

Then she gave a shriek and flung herself at Isobel. Isobel grabbed hold of a nearby chair—it slipped, and the pair went head-over-teakettle onto the floor. A servant came running to help them up. "But no dead bishops," cried Annie, gasping for breath. "And I don't know about any opera. But I'll go pack. You wait here."

"Oh no, no, child, not yet, we can't just walk out today." Isobel laughed at the notion—she felt a moment's panic. "Tomorrow perhaps. Or Friday, on your birthday. Or the day after. There will be papers to sign, you see. I'll have to speak to the hospital governor."

"No more coarse bread," Annie shouted at her peers. "No more sour milk and stinking drink-water. I'm leaving tomorrow, hurrah!"

"Not tomorrow, I said, no—it takes time," Isobel called after the girl. "The authorities have to confer." Already she was beginning to regret her quick promise. She would think it all through tonight. It might be wise to take the child on consignment, as it were, the way one pawned a watch or ring. To see how things worked out.

It might be time, too, she thought, to inform the child's father of his paternity. It took money to bring up a child. And Isobel was having trouble paying her creditors lately.

She bypassed the director's chamber for now, and left the hospital. She had to go home. Company was coming the next day. Important visitors: one had to keep up, save face. Her carriage was waiting; the coachman handed her in.

It was only after she was settled in the soft cushions that she thought of Mary Wollstonecraft who had passed her without a word outside the print shop. She had her chin up in the air, oblivious, as if she were counting clouds. But that embarrassing new book of hers! Isobel, too, was an independent woman, but there was no point shouting it out to the whole world. The authoress advocated schools for girls and boys alike, Isobel had heard, and oh, breast feeding? Thank God she had avoided all that.

Besides, Isobel had seen the way Miss Wollstonecraft looked at Henry Fuseli at her rout: like a puling adolescent. Independent, was she?

∾

MARY loved to hear about other people's lives: it gave an opportunity to tell her own story. And indeed, her life had parallels to Lillian Guilfoy's. The two women were seated together on the sofa Wednesday afternoon, after Lillian's other guests had left.

They had both grown up as the genteel poor, with tyrannical fathers—Mary recalled sleeping on the landing near the door of her parents' bedchamber to keep the drunken father away from her ailing mother after his night's carousing. Lillian's father brought his mistress to live with him *in* the house where her mother lay dying. "Look!" She lifted a lock of hair to reveal a shiny scar. "Boiling water—thrown because I refused something that woman wanted me to eat."

Stunned at the coincidence, Mary told the story of her father's taking a younger mistress while her mother was on her deathbed. "Yet even then my mother would scold if I uttered a word against him. Or especially against my brother Ned who could do no wrong in her eyes. He was always her pet."

Mary felt better for all the talk. She was quite at home in Lillian's little box of a house on George Street, not far from St Paul's Churchyard where Joseph Johnson lived and worked. And why not, for this was today's greatest coincidence: the house had been Mary's residence when she had arrived, exhausted from a year of near slavery in Ireland.

"How can you afford this place?" Mary asked. "In my case," she offered, to soften the question, "Mr Johnson rented it to me for a pittance."

"For me as well. That is, he does it for Henry Fuseli, who helps with the rent, of course. It's only right he should do so!" The muscles tightened in the young woman's face. "Tommy is his child, you see, though he denies it in public."

"Ah," Mary murmured, pretending surprise—though she already knew.

"And I want nothing more to do with the man—after we free my Roger, that is." Her face was flushed with the effort of admitting her dependence on Henry Fuseli.

Mary waited. It would all come out, though she burned with questions.

"Mr Fuseli was working in Paris with another artist, and I was spending two weeks with an aunt after my husband's death. He was much older than I." She lowered her voice, as if her late husband might hear. "A marriage of convenience, you know; I was eighteen, I didn't know any better. It was a relief when—well, you can understand."

Mary nodded, though in truth, she preferred the company of older men. They usually had more to *say*.

"So I went to see the other artist with the thought of taking lessons. The man liked my work. He liked—me. But I held him off, I did! And there I met Mr Fuseli."

Mary gripped her hands together. She was not sure she wanted to hear this.

"I think you know what he's like at first meeting. He makes you feel you're the only woman on earth, that you're beautiful. Somehow he becomes his paintings. He's there with his winged horses; you want to mount behind him and ride off into the sun."

"Yes." Mary half closed her eyes. Though she was at war with the thought.

"Erotic." The young woman offered the word that Mary was afraid to say. "The paintings are so erotic. And when I met him, I was, well, shocked at first. Then captivated. You can gather what those two weeks might have been."

"I can," Mary said, and squeezed her eyes shut.

"Tommy was conceived. Then Mr Fuseli went on to Rome and I stayed in Paris. When I discovered I was pregnant, I wrote to him. I hoped we might marry. But he insisted it was his colleague's child. I was devastated!"

Mary held up a hand; she could hear no more. "Your fiancé—does Roger know that Mr Fuseli helps with the rent? Would that not bother him? Would it—" She took a breath. Would it make him angrier, she wanted to say, give more reason to steal a painting....

Her hostess crunched hard into a biscuit. "I've told Mr Peale I have reserves, a little inheritance from that aunt. Though not much to speak of, really."

"Ah." Mary sipped her tea. She was feeling a bit dizzy with all this talk about the passion Henry had offered other women.

"I understand you don't believe in marriage," Mrs Guilfoy said. "You wouldn't know how I feel. When Mr Peale and I marry—that is—if..." Her voice broke.

Thwarted love. One day Mary would decry dependent relationships in a novel. She would get back at Fuseli for marrying that ninny, Sophia.

"I must tell you about Mr Peale's past. I know you're wondering." When Mary shook her head, Lillian cried, "Of course you are, who wouldn't be! It was years ago—five to be exact; he was eighteen and his apprenticeship was almost over—"

"Ah, I didn't know he was—"

"Apprenticed, yes, to a frame maker. He was the fifth son of a middle-class family that had suffered losses—and so his father sent him to a friend who made frames. He was clever at it."

"I've no doubt of that."

"But he'd painted his mother's portrait for her birthday, and at his work, made a beautiful gold frame; but the master said it was not for Roger to keep. So he—he—"

"Appropriated it," Mary whispered.

"Yes," Lillian whispered back. "And the master had him arrested. It was six months before the master, who knew the family, relented, and Roger was released. Now Fuseli's solicitor has dug all this up, and misconstrued! And my darling is back in prison."

"Monstrous," Mary said. It was the only word she could think to say. The pair sat in abject silence for a time and then Lillian jumped up to point to an oil painting. "It's Mr Peale's. Actually a copy of George Stubbs's *Haymaking*. Copying, you see, is how a young artist learns. Look at that sweet old workhorse! Nothing like the cruel horse in *The Nightmare*. But over there above the breakfront—that's his own. It's a portrait of me, with cherries in my hair."

Mary squinted. She was a bit short-sighted, but she would never wear those foolish round spectacles in public. The painting was a good likeness of Mrs Guilfoy. The young artist had talent. She noted the way he used tiny dots of colour to paint Lillian's cheeks and hair. It was innovative, romantic. He was not, like Fuseli, diabolically inspired. Still, she might suggest to Lillian that he eat raw pork before he painted.

Two raps sounded at the street door and the nursemaid, a pasty-faced woman with a slight limp, shuffled into the room to answer, the boy at her heels. When the door opened wide and St Pierre strode in, rosy-faced from the cool wind, bowing deep over Lillian's hands, his eyes bright with adoration, Mary was stirred. Like herself, St Pierre was obviously a victim of unrequited love. And here was his beloved: using him only to gain back his rival.

St Pierre had come, he said, to take Lillian to Newgate Prison where Peale was awaiting trial. He had arranged a visit, he told her: "For today—we'll hope. Tomorrow at the latest. And that footman who was run down? He saw someone, I hear—with the painting. But he died before he could speak further."

"You mean that *someone* would have actually carried out the painting in front of people?" The woman's cheeks were on fire. "But it's huge!"

"*Non, non, ma chère*, the painting would have been taken later that night." (*When the glove was found*, Mary told herself, and then banished the thought.) "The thief just wanted to negotiate, no doubt, with a pawnbroker, perhaps, for a painting he hoped to sell. Monsieur Fuseli, I hear, has been visiting the pawnbrokers. He thinks the man was—"

"I know who he thinks. Let's hurry then," Lillian cried, running for her cloak. "I want to see my Roger! I pray they've treated him humanely."

Was the Frenchman unhappy? He would like to have the young woman for himself, would he not? And yet he wanted Lillian's favour—would perhaps risk his life to gain it. Mary considered herself a student of emotions and motivations. The reactions of others, she hoped, would help to understand her own conflicted ones.

"If all else fails, I have a plan," Mary heard him tell Lillian as he helped her on with her cloak; and then heard the latter's breathless "Oh! And what plan is that, pray?"

Excusing herself, she picked up her skirts and rustled out the door. Mary ran after her with her publisher's guinea and the abstracted female pocketed it with barely a nod.

"You'll have to pardon Madam," the nursemaid said. "She would set her man free by any means. There is no stopping her." She lowered her voice so the boy wouldn't hear. "She's obsessed with that young painter. She calls out to him in her sleep."

"Obsessed, poor girl," Mary murmured. "She'll have to get over that, will she not?"

She turned away to hide the flush that was colouring her own face and neck.

ᕁ

NEWGATE was a massive stone building, rebuilt over the ancient
prison after the place was randomly destroyed in the anti-Catholic
riots of 1780. It was as cold on the inside, Lillian Guilfoy discovered
Thursday morning—they had been denied entrance the day before—as it looked on the outside. It was a pit of lost souls who were
allowed but a penny loaf a day, and that, as Jacques St Pierre reminded her, was merely a bit of bread boiled in water. "Poor Monsieur Peale," he said, "gave all the money he had to tip the warder
so his chest might be branded with a warm iron rather than a hot."

The warder stopped them to examine the sack. He dropped the
bread on the greasy floor—would have trampled it but Jacques's
quick hand rescued it. At the last the man gave back the bread and
cheese but kept the ale. For the entrance fee, he said.

Inside, Lillian saw two- to three-score men and women in a
room no more than thirty-by-twelve feet and low enough for only
a middle-sized man's head to brush the ceiling—too low for her
Roger. The air was ripe with the sweat and stench of the prisoners.
Above all, she could smell fear. Or was it her own fear? She held
tightly to Jacques's arm.

"Mr Peale!" she cried out, and was rewarded with a dozen
hands thrusting through the grating, begging for money, food, and
mercy—for a way out.

"In the next cell." Jacques drew her to a second room, just as
crowded, just as foul. There in a corner on the straw-covered dirt
floor, head sunk in his hands, shirt torn and dirty—was Roger. He
struggled up to see her; he thrust his fettered hands through the
grating. She held his fingers tightly to keep herself afloat. Already a
ragged old man was reaching out for the sack of bread and cheese
she had brought.

The sack would not fit through the grating, so she tore off
hunks and thrust them through, one by one. Roger stuffed them in
his mouth and apologized for eating in front of her. "They fed us
an elegant meal," he said, "but I didn't care for the Champagne."

Lillian could not manage a smile at his humour.

"There's a tap room somewhere down the corridor," Roger
went on, "and you can buy a dram of ale or gin. I haven't the
money. I can pay you back." He appealed to Jacques.

"Get it for him, for God's sake," she told Jacques, handing him half a crown. She was glad of the latter's absence for a moment alone with Roger. She pressed her lips to the cold grating; her lover's fingertips warmed after a moment's pressure. She told him what Jacques had said about the footman seeing another suspect, and Roger laughed.

"It's me Fuseli wants. It has nothing to do with a dropped glove. The man can't bear a word against his art. Oh, he's brilliant in his own way, I'll give him that. He knows how to mix his colours—but he throws his tints onto the canvas with abandon. Is all that distortion and violence—art?"

"He claims to be inspired by the devil—he once told me that."

"Ha! I wouldn't doubt it. The fellow has the confidence of a Satan. You saw the way he critiqued *my* work, tore it to bits, and all because I'm doing something new. Why the fellow's fifty-five if he's a day! He's out of the mainstream."

"Fifty-one." Lillian pushed back her hair where it had fallen across her eyes. "My friend Miss Wollstonecraft is in love with him, I think. She says she'll try to help us, but she has conflicting interests—though she means well."

"Over here, wench! Gimme a kiss, me pretty?" A bald fellow with an earring in his left ear, his right ear cut away altogether, waggled his eyebrows at Lillian, and she cried out.

Roger gave the man a shove. "You shouldn't have come here. It's no place for a lady." Her fiancé's cheekbones stuck out under the bruised skin; his eyes were dark holes in the starved face. It was more than unfair what Henry Fuseli had done to him—monstrous!

Still, Roger was beautiful, even with the ankle irons: shoulders lowered as though bearing the world, and bowed down by it. She held his gaze with hers. Though there were iron bars between their bodies, their eyes kept them connected.

Then Jacques returned, and Roger's eyes focused on him and what he held in his hand. "You'll have to find a turnkey to bring that in to me," he said.

When Jacques bribed the burly gaoler to open the cell and thrust in the tankard of ale, a dozen hands groped for it. The turnkey knocked them roughly aside, spilling the drink on Roger's shirt. Lillian wept to see her lover lick the ale from his lips and the back of his hand, then hurl himself at the grating. "The place is killing me, love. I can't paint, I can't think! A man died here last week, I heard—he'd been almost a year awaiting trial! Speak to Mr

Johnson, will you? He has friends with influence. I must get out of here—discover who really did steal that painting."

"Monsieur St Pierre has an offer of help, love. You must listen to him."

"Not now." Jacques laid a hand on her shoulder but she shrugged away from him. The turnkey was watching, reading lips perhaps. "Distract him," Jacques whispered, and reluctantly Lillian approached the man. He was repellent. Yet here she was, diverting a gaoler so her lover could have a private word with his failed rival. It was madness!

She heard her hoarse voice; she cleared her throat. "I've a guinea in my purse, sir, and if you could kindly fetch my friend a dram that he can *drink*, and tonight bring him a decent supper, you can have it." She held out the bookseller's coin.

When the turnkey sauntered off with the guinea, Roger and Jacques pushed their heads as close together as the grating would permit. She saw the concentration on Roger's face as they spoke; his expression changed from surprise to doubt and then to something like hope. When the turnkey returned, Jacques moved away, while Roger stared after him, open-mouthed, as though he still had something to say, or ask.

The turnkey opened the lock to hand in the dram, and Roger's thirst overcame his pride; he gulped it down. The turnkey snatched away the mug and proclaimed the visit over. Lillian could only press her lips to the grating and murmur, "*Je t'aime.*" And offer a smile, for she must be brave.

"Lady, lady, come kiss me, lady," cried the man with the earring. "Bed me, lady!" A roar and a thump from Roger brought a howl from the bald offender. She felt faint, and let Jacques lead her away.

An escape, the Frenchman whispered as they passed through the outer gate of the prison, was planned for some time in the following week. He would go back to Newgate to work out the details. "To bribe a turnkey. It's easier now while your man is awaiting trial. Once convicted—they never get out of that bastille, I hear, until—" He closed his fingers around his throat, jerked upward, and she cried out.

"A thousand pardons, *ma chère*," he said, "that was thoughtless of me to say. But we will find a way. Though I might need help with…" Flushing, he rubbed his fingers together.

Money? Where was she to find money? There was her small inheritance, of course. Though it was all she had for herself and the boy. "But monsieur, an escape? What if they capture him? Is there no other way?"

She panicked at the thought of the risk, as if he were indeed guilty: men hunting him down like a beast. She pictured Roger hanging outside Newgate, like a youth she'd seen the year before: feet dangling, a purple bruise spreading over the neck; a crowd of voyeurs below. The victim was only a boy, not much older than her Tommy, the weeping mother yanking on his feet to hasten the death. He had stolen a lamb....

Oh, God. She did not want an escape. But was there an alternative?

Henry Fuseli, she thought. Once again she would have to lower her pride and plead with him.

THE three golden balls of the pawnbroker J. Grippe hung out over the street from an iron rod with an arrowlike point. Henry would like to run the point straight through Roger Peale's heart. From the outset he had been convinced of the young artist's guilt and nothing had happened to change his mind—Bow Street had come up with no other solution. The footman had died before he could speak further of what he saw, but Henry remembered that nod when he mentioned Peale. It was a nod, yes, he was sure of it. It was Peale he saw in his mind with the painting.

Grippe himself was behind the counter, an obese, red-faced man who looked as if he might die of an apoplexy if you crossed him. There was something confident yet ingratiating in his voice as he handed over a guinea for a cookpot and eight silver spoons a woman with liver-spotted hands was handing him. "But they're worth far more," she cried, tears running down her withered cheeks. "Feel them, they're genuine silver, my grandmother's heavy silver. I wouldn't sell them—but we've had reversals...."

"One guinea," the pawnbroker grunted. "It'll be less for you to pay when you come to retrieve them."

Retrieve them, ha, Henry thought. It was common knowledge that one of every two pawned items was never redeemed, for want of money. The woman knew it, too, for she pocketed the coin, and hunching her shoulders, trudged out of the shop. That the spoons were her grandmother's silver, Henry had no doubt, although this

J. Grippe had a reputation for being a counterfeit broker, a receiver of stolen goods. It was for this reason Henry had come.

He whistled in a breath to think of that rogue Peale stealing his masterpiece. The blood rushed to his head, but he took another breath to calm himself. He was already fifty (or was it fifty-one?) but he was not ready for an apoplexy. He had work to do. Nothing was more important than his work. He had the acclamation of the whole art world, had he not?

Yet there had been others like Peale in his past who dared disclaim it—jealous, petty men, who might have stolen his work had they had the opportunity. *Ach!* The rogues, past and present, were trying to poison his reputation. He could not have that, *nein*.

He announced himself to the pawnbroker and requested the painting. For Peale was poor, he knew that. And in love, God help him, engaged to be married—he needed the money. Yesterday Henry had gone with a constable to look for the painting in the fourth-floor garret in Chelsea that he shared with another artist, and the paucity of furnishings was astonishing: a table, a chair, an easel, a dozen miserable paintings left to gather dust—three of them copies of George Stubbs. Copies!

Was that why he took the painting, to copy it? Sell it as an original? The arrogance of the man. The insolence! He would never get away with it.

Henry had not really expected to find his *Nightmare* in those dingy quarters. Grippe's pawnshop was only a few blocks from the thief's residence, and a thief—or a pawnbroker—would want to be rid of his purloined art as quickly as he could, would he not?

But one never knew. There was a long-ago time in Rome when Henry himself had taken a master's painting. But only to study it, learn from it—nothing more! He had sat up with it all night, returned it the next morning. He would never keep it to copy, or to resell. The thought made him want to hurry back to his studio, to see if Peale had returned it.

But Peale was in prison. There was no returning it. *Nein*, he must have the man whipped. That would make him tell where the painting was!

Unless, out of sheer malice, Peale had destroyed it? *Mein Gott!* What a thought! A masterpiece, destroyed? Better he had killed someone....

But no, Peale needed the money. The pawnbroker would know.

The theft was in all the newspapers, the man knew that. Pawnbrokers connived, one with the other. The painting would make its way from one broker to the next until it arrived in America. And who was to get it back from those outlaws?

He lifted his head and stared at the man. The scoundrel was smirking, he had no respect. He was too ignorant to know a master artist when he saw one—and the author of eight books, *ja*! Though his art was superior to the books, and he'd stopped writing them. "And you think the thief would have brought it here, do you?" Grippe said, leaning over the counter, his raisin eyes squinting into Henry's. "And they would throw me in Newgate and I'd never again see the light of day? Am I that stupid I would accept a famous painting like that? As if I would take in the *Mona Lisa* and have the whole world wanting my head?"

Henry was somewhat appeased to have his painting compared to *Mona Lisa*, even though he privately felt that *The Nightmare* stood on equal legs. Surely his sleeping beauty was more sensuous, more erotic than that simper.

He would not be defeated by this arrogant pawnbroker.

"Of course you took it in. You gave Peale the money he asked. Then you passed it on." He took hold of the man's cravat and twisted it in his hands. "Where is it? Who did you sell it to? I must know. There is a reward out, you understand. You hear that? A reward! Yours. Speak up, man!"

The pawnbroker's perspiring nose shone under the greasy whale oil lamp. His nostrils appeared to inflate as though he knew he had the upper hand. "Let me go and I'll ask around," he said. "I'll try to find out for you. But I don't have it, you understand. I do... not...have...it. Peale never brought it in. Not to me! You must try other pawnshops—try the publicans—The Blue Cat takes in stolen goods. It was not me." Grippe peered closely into Henry's eyes. His breath came hoarse and sour through the thick lips. "Peale did not bring it here," he repeated. "Not to me. Never."

Henry was sinking into his shoes; he could hardly stand. He released the fellow and held on to a stool to keep from falling. Tears blocked his vision. He was ready to break down. But he had his pride. His dignity. He was a master painter.

He gripped his hands together until the knuckles whitened. There was only one recourse. To go to Newgate. To see that Peale was made to talk. How, it didn't matter. Peale would talk, *ja*. Talk or be hanged.

NEEDING solitude after the anguish of Newgate, Lillian parted company from Jacques and walked on, alone, down the windy streets, looking absently in shop windows. It was almost March but winter was still in her breast. She had gone only two blocks when she saw Henry Fuseli approaching. He looked like a lion, the way his whiskers grew around the sides of his face—like a lion approaching a kill. He was moving rapidly, his arms swinging with purpose, eyes wide and staring ahead as though if he blinked, he might swerve and miss his goal.

She saw her chance for a last appeal: "Mr Fuseli." When he didn't stop she shouted, "Henry Fuseli! We must talk."

He halted, clicked his heels together, bowed, and smirked. "Madam, I am afraid I cannot stop. I am on business. Some other time we will talk. The boy is well, I presume?"

He was hurrying in the direction she had just come, and she turned to match her step to his. "It's not about the boy—*our* boy. It's about my fiancé, Roger Peale. Have you ever been in Newgate? Do you know the horrors inside—even for those awaiting trial? Men herded together like animals! I saw a young man with a rash covering his entire body, an old man who looked like a leper. Who knows what diseases run rampant with such proximity?"

He stopped for a moment and glared at her: "Madam, we can take care of that, the proximity you speak of. A cell to himself, *ja*. He deserves it, does he not?"

She stood a moment, uncertain of his meaning. He would have Roger moved to a better place? Henry Fuseli in a moment of humanity? The old Henry she had once loved? Though what was human about any kind of imprisonment? "Henry, wait," she said hotly—for he was moving forward again: "He did not steal your painting. I would have known if he had! He is an honest man, learning his craft. He is—"

"An arrogant puppy. A parasite. Sucking up the master's juices, consuming his mind. Do you think I have had a moment's sleep since the theft of my master work? Do you, hey? *Nein! Nein!* Now go. Do not pester me about this. I do what I must do. I seek justice and only justice. It will be done."

He strode on up the hill. A passing cart splashed her with mud and she raced at his heels: "I hate you, Henry Fuseli. You're a barbarian, a monster! You're making your son grow up a bastard. Your own son! How could you?"

He turned his head and grimaced. "Watch your language, woman. They will haul you off as a woman of pleasure." He moved on and she stopped running. Spent, she held on to a hitching post in the road. She imagined Henry on his way to have Roger put into solitary confinement. In her inner ear she heard the cell door clang shut.

"Madam?" A hand stretched out to pull her up. She had fallen to her knees. It was a middle-aged man, nicely dressed, a boy at his side. "I'll find a sedan chair for you."

Dazed, she let him hand her into the chair. "Take this lady to her home and see that she gets in safely." He gave one of the chairmen a gold coin.

"Forty-five, George Street," she whispered, and sank back into the chair. "Thank you, sir," she called out. But the man was already far up the street with his boy.

At least, she thought, there is some kindness left in the world. Then thinking of kindness, she changed her destination. "Wait!" she called out to one of the chairmen: "Take me to Store Street—near Bedford Square."

LILLIAN Guilfoy's unexpected visit was beginning to wear. She had planted herself beside Mary on the new second-hand sofa, and was raving on about Henry Fuseli's cruelty. Mary sipped her tea and closed her mind to such thoughts—had Henry not given a gift of ten pounds last week for her brother Charles to study agriculture in view of his sojourn in America, and then sent over a vaseful of holly and ivy for *her*? Henry was not cruel. He was simply, well, wholly preoccupied with his art. Lillian must try to understand that. It was one reason, perhaps, that Henry had left her. Though Mary would never intimate that, heavens, no.

"And now there is to be an escape," Lillian said, turning to look at Mary. "I was not to speak of it, but I had to tell someone. I knew you would keep it to yourself."

"What?" Mary was incredulous. "An escape? From Newgate?"

"Newgate, yes." The tea trembled in the young woman's hand.

"Impossible," Mary said. She thought of the French royals' escape from the Tuileries where the revolutionaries had imprisoned them. How they had reached Varennes near the Austrian border in a coach overloaded with family and memorabilia; how they were caught and returned to Paris. The *sans-culottes* kept their hats on when the coach passed through the streets; they shouted and cursed and hissed their disapproval.

She thought of Thomas Paine, his life in danger after the publication of his inflammatory *Rights of Man*. The Dissenters were urging him to escape. But where to?

There is no such thing as escape, Mary thought, recalling the flight with her sister, who had abandoned her abusive husband, lost her child, and now could never remarry. It took an act of Parliament to divorce: proof of incest, sodomy, bigamy—none applicable to poor Eliza who had simply begun to go mad from living with the man. The baby, abandoned, now dead, never ceased to wail in Mary's nightmares.

"Impossible," she said again, "the whole situation is impossible."

Lillian agreed. She would speak to Jacques, she said, and urge them not to try to escape the prison.

A moment later she disagreed. "But Mr Peale cannot stay in that black hole! You can't lock up an artist. He must be free to work. And free, he says, he can hunt down the real thief."

"Perhaps," Mary said. "But even free of the prison, he would be in hiding. How could he hunt a thief?"

She thought of her year in Ireland with the autocratic Kingsboroughs. To the latter she was just a servant. She wore no shackles, but she was never free. What was "free" anyway? Who was ever free in a society where everyone knew everyone else's business? Oh, dear God, she couldn't think straight. Her temples were pounding. Being in love was not freedom either. It was thralldom. She knew Henry's faults, but could not help herself. "Then you must help to find the thief," the young woman cried. She flung herself at Mary and tea spilled in both their laps.

"Poor dear," Mary said, "don't worry," and mopped up after them both. People alter with misfortune, she thought. Most people, that is. Herself, she had learned to endure. When Lady Kingsborough had poked her rouged face towards Mary's and said, "You will pack your things and go," she'd had a moment of panic. But then went straight to London to see her publisher, to thrust her novel *Mary, a Fiction* at him—and there it was now, on her bookshelf.

"You are not the only one with troubles," she said, thinking of that autobiographical novel. "Yet good things can come from adversity. You will come to see that, yes."

Her young friend did not see at all; she was holding a handkerchief to her face. What more could Mary do to comfort her? She had been up half the night working on the *Vindication* sequel (Joseph Johnson had advanced her ten pounds—already spent on her brother James); then, in despair, for she'd written little of worth, she'd torn up the pages.

"You will help find the thief," Lillian implored once more, standing to take her leave; she leaned over Mary and squeezed her hands so tightly they felt like empty gloves. "You're a celebrity now, you can do that."

"I'm a celebrity?" Mary said.

"Your *Vindication* has been translated into French—Mr Johnson didn't tell you? A Parisian publisher. And they have it in America as well, Miss Hays told me that. It's in the Boston bookshops."

"Boston? And translated into French?"

"Yes! And do you want to know something?" She leaned closer as if to divulge a secret. "Fuseli is jealous of you."

"Of me?" Mary was incredulous. How could that be?

"Yes! Miss Hays says so. Because your fame from the new book is greater than his, and he's a man who can't stand to be surpassed by a woman. No woman, I've heard him say, can create a lasting work."

"Oh, the scoundrel!" Mary cried. But jealous? She almost laughed. But Lillian was still talking.

"That's why I'm asking, Miss Wollstonecraft—nay, begging you to help free Mr Peale. You know the right people. Get them to help before someone—dies."

"Dies?" But someone already has, Mary thought, remembering the hapless footman.

She rose from the sofa as if the thought alone had lifted her up to take action. "I'll try then, I shall." (Though first she needed a nap. She could neither pursue a thief nor write without rest. She must spend more time on her protest against the biased laws of inheritance, her greedy brother Ned an example.) "Tomorrow," she said, "I am to go to St Paul's Churchyard to discuss the new work with Mr Johnson, and I've naught to show but bits of ripped paper."

"It's Fuseli, is it not?" said Lillian, narrowing her hyacinth eyes at Mary. "The man is wronging us both. You must look closely, my dear, and see who he really is inside. You must understand he cares only for himself—and that miserable painting. Can you see that? Can you?"

Mary sighed and clutched her empty cup. Her reason could see. But oh, her heart could not. She was not free at all. One could not escape oneself.

CHAPTER IV.

A Breaking Window

◡

DULCIE GAVE a deep curtsy on Friday morning as Mrs
Frothingham had instructed—then lost her balance and
pitched into the bluestocking's bosom. The lady pushed her off.
"Who taught you to curtsy like that? You must put a leg back to
balance yourself, then lean slightly forward. Like this." She per-
formed the curtsy with a sweeping curve of her arm. "Now do it."

Dulcie tried, and failed again. For one thing, she was hampered
by the costume Mrs Frothingham had made her wear: a striped
poplin gown, a pair of dimity pockets, a black silk bib, a gauze cap
with a lace border. "I'm not a real maid," she declared. "Miss Mary
does the greeting. I just clean up a little."

"Really?" Mrs Frothingham said, lifting an eyebrow. "But you
make an iced plum cake. That's what I borrowed you for. And to
polish the silver and the plate. I've royalty coming for tea. Cook is
off to bury an aunt."

"Yes, ma'am." Dulcie did an awkward half curtsy, and the mistress groaned.

A barrage of instructions followed: how to polish this, how to
shine that, how to scour the pans, how to mend the fire. Then,
thankfully, the lady left to tend to "business in town. I must leave
you alone." She warned, however, that she would return within
two hours. "Foundling Hospital," Dulcie heard her tell a chair-
man.

"Alone" meant two footmen who sat down at once to play at
cards, and maids of various shapes and sizes who were at work
washing, ironing, scrubbing, and gossiping. One of them deigned
to help Dulcie make a fire. Another slapped down a pair of bowls to
mix batter in. While the cake baked over the kitchen hearth, Dulcie

moved with a feather duster about the house. "I was told to dust," she fibbed to a suspicious parlourmaid.

Mine, all mine, she imagined as she floated and dusted past Chippendale tables and cabinets, pink-and-green satin settees; past the open door to the wine cellar—a red-faced footman was coming up with a bottle in his hand. "None of your business," he said, though she hadn't spoken. (Miss Mary would be amused to hear about that.) Her duster tinkled the glass droplets of the candelabrum that overhung the zebra-wood dining table. Polished stairs led her up to the bluestocking's bedchamber, her recipe still in hand—*oohhh*. For Dulcie, bedchambers were the heartbeat of a house, the secret soul. It was in the bedchamber that Miss Mary did her writing, those not-so-secret revolutionary words about the rights of woman. Though of late she did more tearing up than writing down, and Dulcie knew why. The only one who did not know was the mistress herself.

This bedchamber did not disappoint: a dressing table with a hundred coloured vials and bottles, brushes, combs, and looking glasses. A basket with stuffed animals: monkey, rabbit, mouse. A child's hobby horse that looked worn and bent from riding. A birdcage with a dozen red-and-yellow stuffed birds on gold perches. The four-poster bed with pink silk curtains and a pink embroidered counterpane, where Mrs Frothingham would bring her lovers. She flung herself full length upon it, breathed in its rosewater fragrance, imagined a dark-haired man leaning over her, whispering, *You're beautiful.*

Would anyone ever say that about her round, freckled apple face? She was beginning to doubt. None of the tradesmen she dealt with were interested in her *face*.

She heard a scraping sound and jumped off the bed. Ha! it was only an ugly little pug dog, skittering across the hardwood floor; a long-haired silvery-grey cat, pushing its head against a wooden stool.

Papers littered the mahogany writing desk—mostly letters, written on scented paper. Dulcie examined them, careful not to get them out of order. One was from Talleyrand: *I will see you Tomorrow. Be ready with the Object of my Heart.* What object might that be? One was an unfinished note: *Dear M. de Charpentier, I must beg you to withdraw your interest in me. I have been unable to discern a*

*single thought in common between us. Your incursions on my person
have become Most Disagreeable. Now I must ask you to*
The letter ended there. Dulcie could only imagine what the lady
must ask him to do. To disappear, most likely. She opened a stack of
letters from one Mr Elwell H: *Madam: I might Venture to Presume
to Grosvenor Square tomorrow morning. Or may I flatter myself with
the Hopes of seeing you in the Park or Gardens or at the Exhibition, or
at the Opera some Evening, or at Ranelagh?*
At the bottom of this letter the bluestocking had scrawled *Over
my dead body!*
Most intriguing of all was not a letter but a document in a lower drawer. It was from the Foundling Hospital, where Dulcie had
accompanied Miss Mary one autumn morning. Dulcie had been
moved by the squall of motherless babes, and the poor women
crowding the entrance with unwanted infants. "Seduced and re-
duced," Miss Mary had said, and Dulcie vowed right there and
then to avoid the advances of the smelly tallow chandler's apprentice who'd been staring at her bosom.
The document was brief. It read: *Brought in this day of March* 7
*in the year of our Lord seventeen hundred and seventy-nine a healthy
baby girl, aged ten days; green eyes, red hair.* It was signed by that
same Isobel Jane Amelia Frothingham. Dulcie subtracted on her
fingers. Ten days from March 7 would be today's date: February
25. Thirteen years ago. And today Mrs Frothingham had gone to
visit the Foundling Hospital.... Why, she was going to visit the
child on its thirteenth birthday! Which one of the lovers, Dulcie
wondered, had fathered that child?
The secret might lie in the drawer. She lifted out another packet
of letters, tied in pink ribbon. Then, hearing a male voice in the
hall, she crammed papers and letters back inside, and tidied up the
bed. The red-faced footman leered as she plumped up a fat pillow.
"I don't think you should be here," he said, and sticking up her
chin, she fussed a moment longer with the bed curtains. Then she
plunked down the pillow and walked slowly past the fellow, not
deigning to meet his lustful eye.
But, ha! if Mrs Frothingham had a secret, so now did Dulcie.
One never knew when it might prove useful.

IT was not royalty come for tea the next day, Dulcie discovered
as she brought out the silver tea service and the muffins and the

plum cake, but that lame-foot Bishop Talleyrand, along with the red-haired Monsieur Saint Something and the bishop's lady friend, Madame de Genlis. They were seated in the drawing room that Dulcie had swept and polished till her fingernails broke off.

Madame de Genlis grimaced as Dulcie gave her awkward curtsy, but a smile formed on her lips as she bit into the iced plum cake. "I should take you home with me," she said in her French accent. Now it was Dulcie's turn to grimace: why would Dulcie want to go to bloody France? Though she might like to see the French ladies' gowns. Madame was wearing a low-cut scarlet gown sewn with small diamonds, and around her neck, she announced, a stone from the Bastille. She'd had it polished and set in gold.

"Ah, to have such a memento," Mrs Frothingham breathed inside her Grecian gown, and said she was thrilled to think of Madame's bravery in procuring such a stone. Madame said, oh no, it was Monsieur Talleyrand had procured it for her, and the bishop winked and looked smug. Mrs Frothingham poured champagne in Venetian-red glasses and the bishop got up to toast his hostess's beauty. When she must be forty-five years of age or more, Dulcie thought, observing the crinkles beside her eyes, the pleated lines under her nose.

"If only we could start a rebellion here," said Mrs Frothingham, patting the red cockade in her hair, "and eliminate Mad George and his frumpy queen. What relevance have they to our lives? I say, Up with the People!" She lifted her glass high; the champagne bubbled over the top and between her upthrust breasts.

"Le peuple, la patrie!" Madame cried, hoisting her glass. Monsieur Somebody raised his glass, but slowly, Dulcie noted, like he wasn't wholly in agreement.

Dulcie was sent into the pantry for a second platter of cake, and on her return heard the group discussing the theft of *The Nightmare*. This was a subject beginning to weary Dulcie. She had seen a cartoon of the stolen painting in the papers, and she did so hope the party wouldn't mention that horrid little goblin that was squatting on the sleeping woman's bosom. Or she might throw up right here in the drawing room.

But too late. Here was Mrs Frothingham describing the painting in sick detail, and the Frenchwoman interrupting with *"Ooh! Ooh! La! Quel horreur!... I should like to paint my own version,"* she cried, "with a man lying back on the couch and a female goat gnawing on his breastbone. See how he likes that, eh! I'm thinking I might write a piece about it. To sympathize with the *thief* of the painting."

"*Touché!*" said the bluestocking, laughing out loud, choking on her bubbly, wiping her lips and neck with her serviette.

"Who do you think stole it?" asked Bishop Talleyrand, leaning back in his gilded chair, slurping his wine, his big, misshapen foot stuck out on a stool.

"Mr Fuseli has thrown young Peale in Newgate," said Mrs Frothingham. "But in my opinion, Mr Peale had nothing to do with it." She lowered her voice. "Personally, I think it was a woman who stole it."

"*Non, vraiment? Quelle bravoure!*" cried Madame, clapping her hands.

"Hmm," said the bishop, grinning, "a woman getting back at the fellow for getting her with child?" He sucked on the knuckles of his left hand, then coughed. He knew a thing or two himself about child-getting, Dulcie had heard.

"Exactly," said the hostess. "And we all know whose child he begot and then denied. Though I understand he pays the rent for her house."

"Ah," said Madame de Genlis, fanning herself vigorously. "A sure sign of guilt. And is this woman capable of theft? That is, alone, without male help of some kind?"

"No, she would not." It was Monsieur Somebody speaking, his face as dark red as his thatch of hair. His tone was sharp; they all turned to stare at him. Madame, like the bishop, was smirking; Mrs Frothingham, too.

These women eat men, Dulcie thought. They are chewing on the plum cake like it's a male heart.

There was a silence, and then Mrs Frothingham laughed her full-throated laugh. "We did not mention any names, did we? How then can you speak for her?" Madame laughed, too, and stroked her Bastille stone. "Oh," said the bluestocking, "we all know who it is Monsieur St Pierre loves, do we not? I heard he has vowed to protect her to the death—even to help her lover escape his prison. What do you say to that, monsieur?"

"I did not say that!" cried St Pierre (Dulcie had the name right now), turning a hot pink. Couldn't he see, Dulcie thought, that they were laughing at him? But true, she had happened to overhear a plan of escape when Mrs Guilfoy dropped by Store Street for tea.

"Help," he croaked, "but not help to *escape*. Why would I endanger myself?"

"Of course not," said Mrs Frothingham in a sugary voice, like she was speaking to a child. "You would never sacrifice your neck. Why else did you escape from France?"

"But I support, well, the *ideals* of the Revolution!" said St Pierre, colouring again, looking at the bishop for agreement. "Even though I am an émigré, I am only from the *petite aristocratie*. I had an English grandparent, recently passed on. I support the people, *absolument*." He looked again at Talleyrand, and the bishop cried, *"Mais oui!"*

"A wise decision indeed," said Mrs Frothingham, patting her cockade again. "And the lovely Mrs Guilfoy was already here in England, was she not? With her pale young artist? He, too, is a close friend of yours?"

She was playing cat and mouse, Dulcie saw. She was trying to pull out secrets—though Dulcie wagered she would keep her *own* secret hidden to the death. Did even the child's father know about the girl in the Foundling Hospital? And what would happen if he found out? That could open up a Pandora's box! Dulcie would like to see that.

St Pierre was a shiny red, from his nose to his scarlet stockings. He was stammering something but could not get it out. Madame de Genlis said it for him. "Because he is a gentleman. A gentleman in love would give up everything for his lady. Even when what he must give up *is* his lady. Is it not so, monsieur?"

St Pierre's lips quivered; he nodded.

A footman announced the arrival of Monsieur le Comte Alfred de Charpentier, and the fun was over with St Pierre. Now the new arrival would be given the inquisition. Though Mrs Frothingham did not seem overly pleased to see him. Dulcie remembered that letter she'd read of rejection—had he received it yet? But the bluestocking was polite in front of company. This was an age of "make-believe," according to Miss Mary, who spoke her thoughts plainly, without all the crooking of little fingers, so to speak.

Now Dulcie had to bring in cake when there was no more to be had. She whispered this embarrassing fact into the hostess's ear.

"Then find something else and be quick about it," the bluestocking snapped.

Dulcie marched back down into the kitchen and had a shouting match with the parlourmaid, who was munching the last biscuit in the house, and marched up again, with empty hands. No wonder the lady took in lovers, she thought. For here was the French count, arguing that he would send Dulcie out to the market for a cake and fruit—he held out a handful of coins.

Dulcie was not pleased. She could see the sleet coming down beyond the window. She had come to bake a cake, not to run here and there at some foreign count's whim.

"Here," the man said, pushing the coins into her hand. He looked at her, like he expected a curtsy. She nodded briefly and ran down the steps. She would see that there was a cake for herself as well. She was *not* going to all this trouble for nothing.

ISOBEL loosened her stays and sank gratefully onto the sofa; kicked off the satin slippers and let her legs splay out. God, but it felt good! Visitors, servants gone—that impudent young housemaid departed after dropping one of her new blue Wedgwood plates—a hairline crack. No tears, just proud, like her mistress with that big, demanding book of hers that Isobel would never read. Isobel was not to be told what to think. She had worked too long, too hard for where she was now. For what she was.

Her own mother, sending her out her first four years to a wet nurse on a pig farm in York. Her father in debtor's prison when they brought her home, just in time to see the furniture carried out of the house: the Linnell dining table her mother mourned like a lost child, the flowered draperies purchased from the Spitalfields weavers. A tiny girl in petticoats too big for her small frame, she had stood, mute, and listened to her mother howl. Right then as she huddled, forgotten, like a child's toy not worth the bother to retrieve, Isobel had determined that no one would take anything more away from her.

A pretty face and body helped to achieve that goal. It was her aging lover Robert who set her up in this house, and when he died, willed it to her. After that it was a series of men, all wanting a part of her: body, brain, her creative self—for hadn't all her friends lauded her published romance? Mary Wollstonecraft's review in the the *Analytical Review* was not so favourable. Yet Isobel saved face, invited Mary to her routs. She would offer a copy of her poems. The authoress might be useful, who knew?

Isobel revenged herself on any adversaries by inviting them into her den. Once inside, she bent them to her will or confined them. She had learned that from watching the spider. A child at the wet nurse's, she had seen a spider weave a fly into her web, squeeze it in spun silver, watch it buzz then slowly wither.

This very evening she had been the spider. The bold Alfred de Charpentier stayed on after the others had taken their leave and triumphantly pulled a bottle of her favorite Bordeaux from a pocket of his greatcoat. "Pray, remain then," she said with her slyest smile, "we will make a toast to the Revolution." Of course she knew that the count was afraid of the Revolution. He had lost an estate and all its treasures in Normandy. But she wanted to see his hypocrisy at work.

"Ah, bien sûr, la Révolution!" the hypocrite cried, and touched his glass to hers. He leaned towards her on the sofa. His fleshy lips touched her neck. She wiped the moist spot with a handkerchief and passed a plate of the tasteless cakes the housemaid had brought back. He waved them away—it was not cakes he wanted. He swilled down two more glasses of wine, breathed deeply for a minute or two, his eyes bulging in his large head, then lunged sideways at her, knocking her back onto a cushion. "Aha!"

But she did not cry out, no, she was still the spider.

She let him wriggle his body onto hers, unlace her bodice, and bury his ugly head there. He drooled onto her skin. "Wait!" she cried, "not here. The bed—it is far more comfortable. We'll go up to my bedchamber. But first, Champagne! It's in the cellar. Here," she said when he eased up his big soft body and she gasped in a breath, "take a candle. Turn right at the bottom. The Champagne will be on your left."

He stood there, huge, clumsy, red-eyed like a fly, in the candlelight. The golden hearts gleamed on his red-heeled shoes. "You'll find it worth your trouble," she teased. He wheeled about and stumbled towards the stairwell under her guidance. He never felt the thread she had drawn about his body, a thread she was about to cut. He looked back once more and she blew him a kiss, then shut the door behind him. Bolted it. Ha!

But that door did not lead to the wine cellar. There was no wine on that level, only steps leading to a door that opened to the outside. The fly was out in the cold. A lucky escape, though he didn't realize it. She heard him buzz a while, and pound on the door.

Howl his muted howl. Until finally the noise stopped and she was free to go to bed.

Now, blessedly alone, her decision made to take the child—she would fetch Annie tomorrow—she went upstairs to the bedchamber, unlaced her stays, and naked, her body gratefully free, slipped between the pink satin sheets. Her Persian cat leaped up to nestle in beside her, his grey fur long and luxurious against her bare hip, his purr soothing, somnolent. She sipped the last of the Bordeaux, nibbled on a dried apricot, and read the first chapter of Charlotte Smith's *Desmond*—a new book, fresh from the publisher. It was an epistolary novel like hers: she loved the sequence of personal letters. Already the writer had captured the reader: ...*I have determined to relinquish the dangerous indulgence of contemplating the perfections of an object that can never be mine.* Ah, pray, what object? Why *dangerous?* Would the speaker return? The writer knew how to toss out the hook.

She took another gulp of the wine and read on to the end of the second page. By now she had read of Geraldine. *But is it possible she can love him?* Then the print began to blur; the cat's purring dulled her brain. She blew out her candle, snuggled deep into the covers, and felt sleep wash over her like a soft sea wave....

AT first the crackling and crashing noise was part of Isobel's dream. She moaned out loud; the cat knocked over her book and jumped off the bed. She opened her eyes wide and reached for the candle, but it had burned to a stub. It was not a dream. It was—*aahh!* her chamber window breaking! Horrified, she saw the frame lifted away with a crack. And as she screamed for her absent servants someone entered; a hand grabbed hers. She looked up at a fevered face: "What are *you* doing here? Go. Go!"

DULCIE had forgot not only her recipe for iced plum cake but the pan she'd baked it in, and Miss Mary ordered her back to Grosvenor Square to retrieve it. Grumpy from being waked up before six, Dulcie protested. "But the servants won't be there yet! There was no one but Mrs Frothingham when I left. How will I get in?"

"You'll find a way," said Miss Mary. So Dulcie was up at the crack of dawn with no expectations beyond a miserable walk through the rank, rainy town. She had no money for a chair, and the mistress, whose nose was deep into a book, offered none.

At least Dulcie was able to get in the house. The cook was hurrying down the street with a dozen keys hanging at her waist and a squirming sack over one fleshy shoulder. "Eels," she said, "I were lucky to come by 'em. Missus Frothingham is partial to 'em, y'know. I was buryin' me old aunt. The mistress borrowed ye again for the day, did she?"

Without waiting for an answer she thrust a large iron key in the door, turned the creaking lock, and lunged in. Her sack of eels made a mewling noise as they struck the side of the door.

"Missus Frothingham? I got eels. I got raspberry muffins, too," the cook cried and started upstairs towards the bedchamber. "Mercy, she's let the fires go out," she complained as she heaved her heavy body up the steps. "'Tis cold in here. Now we'll have to work in the damp till we get 'em going again. Housekeeper's late, I see."

Dulcie despised eels—the thought of the creatures slithering through her belly made her nauseous. She hurried down the back steps into the kitchen to find her baking pan and recipe. The scoured pan was on the table where she'd left it, but the recipe was nowhere to be found. Then she recalled she might have left it on the bluestocking's writing desk when she leafed through the letters. Though how was she to explain how it got there? If the footman had told....

"Oh lud," she moaned, "oh saints, help me now! Mrs Frothingham will tell the mistress I been minding someone else's business and she'll give me a talking to'll turn me deaf."

Upstairs there was a scream. A long on-and-on scream that only grew louder and longer as Dulcie hurried up to the drawing room and then up again to the bedchamber, where the scream had reached such a high pitch it would wake the dead.

But the dead was not to be waked: she saw that at once. It was a sight such as she'd never in her nineteen years come upon and hoped never to again. A woman, naked as the morning light, her hair hanging off the edge of the mattress with its pink satin sheets, one arm trailing on the floor; and squatting on her breasts a stuffed monkey with a grin on its raggedy brown face. At her feet a hobby horse with a wide-open, grimacing mouth.

Dulcie opened her own mouth to let out a scream, but it crept back into her throat and threatened to choke her.

CHAPTER V.

The Nightmare Revisited

ﾟ

IT WAS *The Nightmare*, just as Dulcie had heard it described. But crude, ugly, cruel—no pretty brushstrokes of yellow, red, and blue-green the way it would have been in the painting. And on Mrs Frothingham's face: no sleeping sigh but a mouth wreathed in agony, for the lady had been strangled. A blue silk stocking was twisted about her neck. Her face and throat were a dark red; purple bruises shone on the back of her neck where her head was turned towards the window. A silvery-grey cat crouched at the foot of the bed, alive and purring, like it was waiting for the mistress to wake up and feed it. The pug lay beside the bed. It growled when it saw Dulcie.

"It ain't right to leave the poor thing naked like this," Cook said, her voice a grating whisper after all the screeching. She snatched up a satin sheet and draped it over the body. The cat jumped off the bed. It was then Dulcie saw the note—the cat had been sleeping on it. In large, neat block letters it read: BLUESTOCKINGS BEWARE.

Dulcie clapped a hand over her mouth. Cook ran shrieking out of the chamber, crying, "Justice! Justice!" Dulcie couldn't seem to move her feet. She was still rooted there when Cook came back with a slightly tipsy justice of the peace, and a pink-cheeked constable, hardly more than a boy. The latter took one look at the corpse, turned pale, and crumpled into the carpet.

Dulcie got her feet moving again. "Give him smelling salts," she told Cook. "Go on. In the drawing room." While Cook ran downstairs for the salts, and the justice was preoccupied with the body, Dulcie scooped up a pile of papers from the desk and thrust them into the cotton pocket she wore at her waist. Though she'd deny it, she wagered that Miss Mary would read them with relish—after all, she was a writer. When the justice called, "Come back! I've got

78

questions," she pretended not to hear, and raced out the chamber
door and down into the street where a ballad singer was grinding
out a tune with a monkey on his shoulder. "Move off!" she cried.
"With that ugly monkey! There's a dead woman upstairs. You got
no feelings?"

And then she thought: how shall I break the news to Miss Mary?
For the mistress was a bookish person. And she owned a pair of
blue stockings. Worsted, to be sure, not silk—but blue. Oh God in
heaven—oh sweet Jesus on a cross—Miss Mary could be next!

MARY had scrawled two pages of script that read *Henry&Mary,
Henry&Mary* over and over until she fell back to sleep, head down
on the writing table. The purring cat and the pen rolling off onto
the wooden floor were the last sounds she heard before the old
nightmare took over: the carriage racing down the street with
her and Eliza—then a brown goblin leaping into the carriage and
jumping on her back....

The dream was shattered by a screeching in her ears. "Madam,
wake up. Wake up! Murder most foul!"

Mary opened her eyes. It was Dulcie, who seemed to be halluci-
nating, out of her mind. Had she taken opium? Mary occasionally
took a bit of laudanum to calm her nerves or stimulate her muse,
but she drew the line at opium: she was not a Fuseli, or a young
Sam Coleridge, arriving at the bookseller's supper with a notebook
full of fantasies from his opium dreams.

"Calm down," she told Dulcie. "Have a cup of hot chocolate.
I'll have one, too."

Dulcie would not calm down. She was ranting on and on about
a dead woman. A stuffed monkey. A broken window. "It's Mrs
Frothingham!" she cried, "she's dead. Dead from a blue stocking!"

This was altogether too much. How could someone be dead
from a blue stocking? Getting up, Mary took the maid firmly by the
elbow and marched her toward the kitchen. "Hot chocolate, I said.
An antidote to whatever you took."

"I took nothing, I swear it." Dulcie stood before the kitchen
steps, blocking Mary's way. The freckles stood out on her face; her
chest was heaving. "I went back to the Grosvenor Square house to
get the baking pan and the recipe. Cook let me in, and then she
went up to the bedchamber. I heard her scream."

"Oh?" Mary was beginning to listen now. The dream of goblins and racing carriages had faded. What was it about a blue stocking?

Dulcie described *The Nightmare* almost exactly as Mary had seen it hanging in Henry's gallery, except that it was not a stuffed monkey as Dulcie said, but an incubus on the sleeping woman's breast. No hobby horse either, but a bulgy-eyed mare. Henry was in love with horses, especially stallions. She tried to explain that to Dulcie. Mary would go down and make the chocolate herself. She needed the stimulus; her nerves were popping out all over. Dulcie, somehow in her confusion, had come upon the painting. My God, she thought. Had the cook stolen it?

"Not the painting, no, ma'am," Dulcie said. "Only *like* the painting. Mrs Frothingham is dead, I told you. It was murder, Miss Mary."

"Murder? No! You're certain of that? Then we must go at once!" Mary jumped up to find a fresh neckerchief. But none was to be found, so she smoothed out the wrinkled one.

"A justice of the peace is there. And the constable. He fainted. Oh, and madam, the murderer left a note. It said, Bluestockings Beware."

"What?" Mary's nerves were taking over her body; she was a walking nightmare.

"You must keep the house locked at all times, ma'am. Bar the windows."

"They are already bricked up, all but the front one, you know that, Dulcie. Mr Johnson wants to avoid the tax."

"Keep the doors locked then. Someone who hates bluestockings is on the loose!"

This time Dulcie broke down completely. Mary would give up on the chocolate and send the girl to bed. She took three deep breaths to quiet her skittery nerves and then pulled on her great-coat and set out for Grosvenor Square. I don't believe a word of it, she told herself: it is too outlandish a tale.

But what if it were true?

She stumbled on a slippery cobblestone and fell flat on her face. Her purse went flying against a shopper's overstuffed bosom. "Mind how you go," the woman growled, and left her lying in a puddle. Were the heavens falling down on her head—or was it hail? Hail, seeming as big as silver coins, battering her beleaguered brain.

At last she sacrificed a shilling for a sedan chair, and at Grosvenor Square was delivered to a scene of pandemonium: servants running in screeching circles, a dog howling, and a housekeeper with a face as grey as a pewter plate.

Upstairs, she gazed open-mouthed at the apparition on the bed; at the blue silk stocking around the poor woman's neck, the stuffed monkey on her breast, the hobby horse with its one shiny green eye. Someone had put a sheet over the nude body—Mary was thankful for that. Yet Isobel's open eyes looked flat, as opposed to the twisted mouth—and relatively calm, as if she had recognized the villain, had pleaded with him, did not believe he would kill her until the moment of tightening the stocking.

How long did it take to strangle a human being?

Long enough, Mary decided. Time would have already ceased to exist. What had passed through Isobel's mind in that last long, horrific moment?

Sadly, one would never know. It would have been quite a feat, she thought, to climb to the second storey, break a window, strangle a woman, and then arrange horse and monkey. This was no crime of sudden passion—it was a premeditated killing. Someone had planned out this horror to the last fold of sheet beneath the bluestocking's body, and then carried it out without remorse. She tried to close the staring eyes but they wouldn't shut, as though the eyes were the last to let go of life. "'There is murder in mine eye,'" she quoted aloud from Shakespeare, and then quieted when she heard footsteps.

"Step aside, madam, *if* you please," said one of the men—had he heard her speak of *murder*? He was a justice; "the investigating officer," he said, with a slight hiccough. An undertaker, sent for by the housekeeper, stood behind him, waiting to claim the body. The cook brought up a silver tray of biscuits and tea as though the mistress might suddenly sit up and take a sip. A whey-faced constable drank it instead, averting his eyes from the body.

The pug jumped up on the foot of the bed. It growled when the constable tried to remove it, then nipped the undertaker as he and a helper heaved the body onto a wooden pallet. A pale arm hung down; the helper tried to bend it back so it would fit on the plank but it had begun to go rigid.

Mary recalled her mother when they took her away for burial.

One arm was uplifted as if seeking help from God—but God was looking the other way that day. "A little patience and all will be over," her mother had said again and again; and finally it *was* over. And no help came.

Mrs Frothingham's long hair caught in the door latch on the way out and the sheet slipped off the naked body. The young constable made a gurgling sound in his throat; his arm knocked against a glass case full of stuffed birds. The housekeeper, tall, gaunt, and crisp-tongued, hustled across the room to wrap the satin sheet more securely about the body, and then, blinking rapidly, clipped a lock of hair to tie up in her handkerchief. Men and corpse lurched down the steps to ground level and out into a waiting hearse. The justice stuffed hobby horse and monkey into a cloth sack for "evidence," then squinted down at the note.

"You know what that means, do you not?" Mary said. "Bluestockings, beware? I, too, am one—well, more or less."

The justice turned to stare at her; he glanced down at the inch of black worsted stocking that showed beneath her petticoat and gown and ran a tongue over his thick reddish lips.

"It does not mean I always wear blue stockings," she said. "It means I am a literary person."

"Then you better watch out," said the tipsy J.P. "Or we be carryin' you out next." He grinned, and signaled for the constable to follow.

"You realize this has something to do with the stolen painting," she called after them, infuriated now with their insouciance. "You must look in that direction!" But already the door was banging shut. Fools, she thought: they would not have the brains to find murderer *or* thief.

Or perhaps murderer and thief were one?

But the murderer was not Roger Peale. She did not for a moment believe the young artist had caused the murder of Isobel Frothingham or the Fuseli footman. Mr Peale was in Newgate Prison. She hoped the unrestrainable Fuseli would consider that fact.

She glanced about the chamber. There had been a struggle toward the end: bed sheets dragged on the floor; bits of glass gleamed from the broken panes. The strangler would have escaped through the window he had entered. She looked down onto the busy square. Folk were lolling about, watching the body being shoved into the horse-drawn hearse. They were pointing up at the broken window. Across the square a sweep's blackened head poked up out of a chimney. A phaeton dashed down the street, its prancing horse's hooves hurling dust onto the corpse. The chairmen were squatting on the front steps, waiting for her as she had asked. One of them was peeling an orange—oblivious to the death.

There was blood on the window sill, where the killer had cut himself. The justice had tried to scrape it off, but what good did that do? He could not link it to any man. The authorities had less evidence than Mary, who at least knew the attendees at Isobel's soirée the week before. And at tea yesterday. Chatty Dulcie had described the tea party, down to the pauses in conversation. Mary counted the guests: Talleyrand and his confederate St Pierre—sometimes disagreeing. Madame de Genlis with the Bastille stone set in a medallion about her neck—Mary had heard about that stone: the word *Liberté* was inscribed on it in diamonds. Would Madame, who came from a noble but impoverished family, have envied her hostess's wealth? Alfred de Charpentier, who had arrived, uninvited, towards the end, undoubtedly an unwelcome guest—Mary recalled the frown on Isobel's face when he had sidled up to her at the piano.

And oh, she must not forget that arch-conservative, Edgar Ashcroft. He was not at the tea party, but like Mary, Isobel had refused his proposal of marriage. A vindictive fellow, she felt certain. Thinking of her own refusal, a frisson of fear came over her. Then vanished with a squaring of her shoulders.

Yes, Henry would have to look beyond poor Mr Peale. She would ap*peal* to him (she smiled slightly at the pun). He must see that her own life, as a more-or-less bluestocking, was in danger over his painting.

She leant an elbow on the window sill and propped up her chin with her hand. Danger? She rather relished the thought. If there were no money at present for a trip to revolutionary Paris, why then a London murder—two murders now—would have to do. A stolen masterpiece—and a young artist planning to escape from an impregnable fortress? What folly!

ROGER Peale was struggling to keep himself awake in spite of the loud snorings of his cellmates—when someone, or something, jostled his elbow. The escape was scheduled for some time in the middle of the night—one had no way of knowing what hour in this foul blackness, or even what day. He sat up and listened. It was not St Pierre; Roger smelled only the unmistakable stench of the night turnkey. He was to be put in a separate cell, the fellow said. The key turned in the lock; the grate opened. The turnkey had a prisoner with him—another drunk by the sound of the protests; he thrust the man in, and then grabbed Roger by the collar.

"Yer bedchamber's ready for ye," said the vile fellow. "Nice and cozy, oh my, silk sheets, eh? Say yer bye-byes to yer playmates here."

Roger stumbled behind: his heart, like his feet and hands, in loose chains. He tried to think of nothing; he wanted only to sink into oblivion, to let his mind go—for that, he knew, was what happened in a solitary confinement—if that's where he was headed, for some inexplicable reason. No use to retain the rational mind when, in madness, one could dwell in a dream world.

It seemed like hours they staggered, even crawled, through the underground labyrinth of rat-infested halls and tunnels, past iron cages only big enough for men to squat in. Now they stumbled down crumbling steps, the turnkey unlocked a great squeaking door—and to Roger's astonishment, a gust of fresh air blew into his face! He breathed in deeply; felt a vertigo, as though he might drown in the air. He heard a clinking of coins, and the rustle of paper; the turnkey gave him a shove through a low door and pushed him out into the night.

He gulped in the air, and overwhelmed—collapsed onto the ground.

Then astonishingly, St Pierre emerged to pull him up, and shove him half-senseless over a back wall and into a waiting coach. "Take the south road out of the city," he ordered the coachman.

"Prisoner escaped!" It was the turnkey shouting drunkenly behind them. "I'm 'alf-dead I am, 'elp! Who give him the knife? 'E stabbed me! 'Elp! 'Elp!"

"I'll repay you," Roger whispered to the Frenchman when the horses started to run, "if I get out of this alive. What can I lose? Better to hang in fresh air than die in that dungeon."

St Pierre laughed. "*Mais oui, mon ami*, I should think so. And you can repay your lady, not me. I have scarce a farthing to my name here in England."

"But where would Mrs Guilfoy have found the money to pay off that fellow?"

The Frenchman shrugged. "Somewhere, I don't know. A desperate lady, eh? Here, lift your hands so I can get at those manacles. We'll unchain the ankles when we arrive at our destination. Just thank your stars, *mon ami*, you are free. Ah, *voilà*, they are off. Wave your arms, eh? Put your head back and rest. Your host has a copper tub: we will have you smelling like a rose. You will wake up tomorrow with your lady love by your side."

"And you? What do you gain from this?" Roger tried to exercise his arms, but they resisted: they were weights hanging from his shoulders.

"Your lady's gratitude. I would move heaven and earth for her friendship. I have just now moved it, have I not? Lucky you are not in the *old* Newgate. In those days, they tell me, no one got out—innocent or guilty. Here. Drink this—for your strength." He handed Roger a flask.

The coach, which was particularly malodorous, jolted them through a dozen narrow streets where frequently they had to back up for a rival coach, and then restart. They rolled over a bridge—Roger could hear boat whistles below in the Thames, shouts and oaths of the rivermen—and beyond the night lamps of London. Then on into a deep silence, except for the *clip-clop* of hooves. A light snow fell through the dark trees; it lulled Roger into a state of semi-consciousness. He was too fatigued to anticipate the meeting with his beloved, to ask when and where they would meet. Placing his trust in St. Pierre, he let his body ride on with the horses of the night, then let go into sleep....

"Your money or your life!" The coach jolted to a stop; Roger tried to sit up but his head lolled on its aching stem. He heard the thud of fists on flesh, grunts and groans, a shot; then St Pierre's voice, outside: "Save yourself! Make for the woods!"

Roger wouldn't—couldn't move—not with the shackled ankles. He had no money: the turnkey had taken his watch. He had nothing to lose but his life. And Lillian. Yes, adorable Lilly—somewhere, awaiting him. No, he was in no condition to fight—St Pierre should realize that. Let the highwaymen do what they would. He sank back against the head-rest.

Another shot rang out. A scream: "My leg!" It was St Pierre.

Through the glass Roger saw his rescuer writhing on the ground. This time he lunged for the door but it was locked. He fell back against the leather seat; already the horses were racing on with the coach. He could do nothing. He believed in fate: things happened or they did not. There was no going back.

Hours later—days perhaps, for all his muddled brain knew—the coach stopped. A man and woman came running to propel him up two flights of rotting steps to a small chamber with a cot and a grated window; a bowl of cold gruel sat on a scarred table, an insect floating in its center. He was hungry enough to drink it down. "What place is this?" he asked between gulps. "Who are you? Where is my fiancée?"

But they left without a word and turned the lock in the door. His legs were still fettered. He dragged himself to the cot and fell face down on it. He wanted only oblivion. Sweet oblivion...

CHAPTER VI.

Easy Prey

∾

LILLIAN OPENED the door, and shrieked. There in the rain
stood Jacques St Pierre: blood caked on his face and clothing,
a handkerchief wrapped like a sling about the left arm that was
"badly sprained," he said, "if not broken. A bullet wound in my
leg—a narrow escape indeed."

"Oh! Poor man." She didn't know where to look, what to do.
"And where is Mr Peale? Is he hurt?"

"Not hurt—the last I knew. But out of prison. I thought I might
find him here. May I come in?"

"Yes, yes, forgive me. It's just that—" She couldn't think what
she had been going to say. Roger was unhurt and out of prison,
ah!—then the escape was successful. But why was he not here with
Jacques? No, he was to be in hiding somewhere. "Where then, tell
me where!" She helped her friend over to the sofa, sat him down,
and summoned the nursemaid for hot water and compresses.

The woman cried out to see him. "Been in a fight, has he? Oh,
poor fellow. Mercy."

"And fetch a physician," Lillian ordered.

"No physician. Just a basin to wash in. And clean bandages."
Jacques looked helpless, creased and shabby, altogether done in
as though he'd had an arduous journey to get here. She dropped
numbly beside him on the sofa.

"Do not trouble to heat the water," Jacques called after the
nursemaid. "Just soap to clean the wound. A little alcohol."

"A wound!" said Lillian, feeling giddy, pushing her hands flat
on the sofa cushion for balance. "And Mr Peale—was he wounded
as well?"

"Unhurt, I told you—to my knowledge." He was sounding

peevish. "I was shot in the leg. Had I not ducked behind a tree, *Mon Dieu*! I do not know what might have happened." He closed his eyes as if to frighten away whatever image harboured there.

"Yes, yes, and how? Tell me!"

"I am trying, *ma chère*. Give me time. I came straight to see you after I found my way to an inn. The innkeeper would have taken me to a doctor. But I said, '*Non, non*, I must see Madame Guilfoy.'" He reached for her hand and she inched it away. She was not in the mood for his poor hopes. "It is still bleeding," he said.

"Oh," she said, chagrined she had not realized the extent of his injury. He was a friend, after all. He was helping Roger. But where *was* Roger! The nursemaid brought a basin of soapy water and a jar of alcohol. "Put it down," Lillian said, "I'll tend to him."

"A mere flesh wound," Jacques said. "I was fortunate. But you can clean out the dirt—and the blood, *s'il te plaît*." He looked as if he might faint and Lillian offered her salts. He waved them away. "I will tell you what happened. You should know."

"Tell me, yes." She dismissed the nursemaid, bathed Jacques's leg and arm, and cleaned the dried blood off his face and neck while he told his story. How he had bribed the turnkey at the prison, having to use a friend's money as well as hers; how he had hired a coachman to take them to the country house where he had a relative who would harbour Roger. "For he is still in danger, you must understand, a fugitive." He turned to gaze into her eyes, to plead with her. "It had to be done. In that prison, he would not last long. Not, *eh bien*, a—painterly soul like his. He begged me to help free him. Though it put both our lives in peril—you must understand that." He peered closely into her face. She could see the yellow flecks in his brown eyes.

"I understand, I do, yes. That monstrous prison! So you went off in the coach. You went to this émigré friend of yours." She was rubbing him too hard; he put out a hand to make her pause. Oh dear. She was no nurse.

"Went toward the cousin's estate, *oui*. But *hélas*, we never got there. We were attacked. A highwayman. Two of them. Masked!"

"Ah!" It was her turn now to use the smelling salts. Highwaymen! She pictured foul-smelling fellows in black, a glittering sword. Or was it a pistol? A pistol, yes, Jacques was shot. "But Mr Peale? He was not shot? He was not hurt, you said?"

He flung up his arms. "I was lying on the ground, unconscious.

When I awoke the coach was gone. Your fiancé was nowhere to be seen."

"But it was dark. How would you know?"

"I went back again today, in the light. No one! I knocked at doors—a gamekeeper, an elderly couple living on the edge of the woods. They had seen no one. I can only assume he is somewhere in hiding. You must have hope." He looked up at her pleadingly. "I tried. I did my best. They know already he has escaped. They will have sent after him. It is better, my dear, he does not come here. I did my best," he repeated. He looked wan. She must not forget all he had done for herself and Roger.

"Of course you did." She patted his hand while she gazed at the window where she saw her son playing with a stick, an imaginary sword, stabbing and stabbing at an invisible foe—so young to be so martial. "And don't think I'm not grateful. You *will* do your very best then? You will find where he is? You will help him?"

"*Bien sûr*—have I not promised?" He seized her hand and kissed it. She let him hold it a moment, but not too long. He had not yet fulfilled his promise. To find her Roger. To prove his innocence to the world.

Where was he then? Where! Ah. She must send a note to Mary Wollstonecraft. The authoress, too, had promised to help, had she not? To find him innocent of all those accusations. Stealing a painting? Killing a footman? Preposterous!

HENRY was leaving his house as Mary Wollstonecraft turned the corner of Queen Anne Street. He did not want his wife to see her—already she complained of his attentions to Mary. Sophia was a good homemaker, she was good in bed, solicitous—Henry did not require talk. A woman should be a comfort to a man, not a companion. He had all the companionship he needed in men. He had his art.

But Mary was running, holding up the hem of her skirt, near collapsing at the foot of his steps, crying out his name. "Henry Fuseli! Sir, we must talk."

Nein, he did not need this. The authoress had a good understanding, a first-rate mind—for a woman, *ja*. He had made the mistake of telling her once that he and she were noble minds, that they did not have to play by the rules like ordinary folk. He had said that mainly to get her into bed. He had almost achieved that goal when she started talking. And talking. But the talk veered off on the subject of platonic love: what it was, was it a truer love than physical love and so on and so on—*arrgh*—all the time gazing soulfully into his eyes. What did he think they had in common? she asked. What did he see in her, what did she see in him? Why did she love him when she did not even *like* him? That was a surprise! All the while, in her bedchamber, he was trying to remove her petticoats, the innumerable garments that she kept reattaching as he pulled.

Mein Gott!

She was a virgin, she said. At the last he had buttoned up, and left the house. He was tired of playing with no prize at the end. A virgin! At thirty-two? His Sophia was only twenty-seven. Lost hers at sixteen—and willingly.

Yet for all that, it was flattering to be loved. And Mary did look appealing today in her scarlet stockings—a welcome change from the boring black.

"And what is it brings you to my doorstep?" he said, determined to be amused, not to let her get under his skin. "The gallery is not open to visitors today. Not since the theft of my work. Here," he swung her off the steps, onto the cobblestones. He heard her quick, excited breath. "We shall take a walk, shall we? Look at the river? There is a fleet of boats fresh in from Holland. Shall we flag one down? Take a ride? And *ach*, look up! Sun is coming out."

"Mr Fuseli," she said, "We must talk. You heard about the nightmare." She turned her liquid eyes on him. That slight squint—one might call it *louche*, in one eye—most appealing; it gave her a look of *volupté*. Eyes the colour of burnt almonds. No, they looked green today. The woman was a chameleon. He should not trust her.

"My painting?" he said. "Have I heard about my painting, you ask?"

"Not your actual painting, Mr Fuseli. The fleshly rendition of it. The murder. Isobel Frothingham, strangled, and then rearranged to look like your painting. It was like walking into a madhouse. Truly horrible."

"Ah." He had heard about it. The whole world had heard about it by now. They were shouting it in the streets, house to house. Everyone locking doors and bricking up windows. "It was ingenious, yes? Clever. You have to admire the one who did it. A creative mind, surely."

She seemed shocked at his blithe reaction. "A morbid mind. A horrid, sick, murderous mind. A woman in her prime?"

"If you can call forty-five a woman's prime."

"Mr Fuseli." She was angry now. It became her, that anger: it coloured her cheeks and moistened her lips. Her eyes burned apple-green. He would like to paint them. "I suppose at fifty-one, *you* have not yet reached *your* prime."

A cutting remark. Close to the quick, the sardonic creature. "I think not," he said—though secretly he worried about getting old, losing his touch. The right hand was shaking more than ever, damaging his work. He had to spend longer now, at a painting. He had never been completely at one with his left hand.

But he would not give in. Never! He would not grow old. Space, height, depth, breadth, health—and youth, *ja*, all that, he needed in order to paint.

She was taking deep breaths; her chest was heaving with what she had to say. She was gulping in the smoky London air. They would walk down to St James's Park, then onto Westminster Bridge; he would let her cool herself in the breeze off the river. His mood was turning gay. Clever indeed, that murder. Well, a waste, perhaps, an intelligent, attractive woman like that—he'd had a night or two with Isobel before he married—neither took it seriously. But a creative act. A compliment to his stolen masterpiece. One must view the strangling in that vein.

Though the thought of the stolen painting turned his mood sour again. He had painted variants of *The Nightmare*, for the greedy printmakers of course—one had to make a little money. But this was the original! And it was stolen! They might as well have purloined his soul. At least, he thought, I had signed it. So if it survives, some art lover, in some unknown future, will know it is mine and hang it in a museum.

She was walking close to him; he could feel the weight and slant of her body next to his. A nicely shaped body, a handsome face. His friend Roscoe had commissioned her portrait. Henry had offered to paint her himself but she declined—did not want to appear like a ringletted Medusa, she said, and he had to laugh. A fragrance now from her neck: rosewater. A hair taller than he, perhaps—but one had to measure his height in relation to the force of his personality.

She said, "It is likely, do you not think, that Mrs Frothingham's murderer was also the thief of your painting?"

"Possibly," he said, indulging her, smoothing his Delft-blue cravat. She had a point. The Bow Street magistrate would deduce that. The murderer had to be familiar with the painting. Though hundreds had seen it, to be sure. It had hung since '82 in the Royal Gallery—and then gone to St Petersburg. George III had borrowed it to hang in his own drawing room, until Queen Charlotte made him take it down. Scandalous, she said. *Mein Gott!* The queen was such a prude.

"Then it would not have been Roger Peale who took it—he could not have murdered Mrs Frothingham." Her arm was hooked under his. She pinched his elbow.

"*Oww.* Stop that, woman! Of course he took it. And killed my footman and then the bluestocking, and trussed her up to defy me. Everything points to him. But enough. I do not wish to discuss that question further."

"But that's the point. It remains a question. Because Mr Peale is in prison. He is in Newgate."

"Yes," he said, "I saw to it he was put there. It will make him confess.To everything. Theft, murder—all the greed and envy that made him criticize my work."

"But if Mr Peale is in prison, he could not possibly have killed Mrs Frothingham. *You* know that—you were at her rout. She died only Saturday night."

"Oh? Well, how was I to know when? I did not kill her." Too much was going on in his head these days. To hide his confusion he unfurled his newspaper. The wench had caught him in her trap. But there was the front page headline: BLUESTOCKING FOUND DEAD IN HER BEDCHAMBER, and underneath, an artist's depiction of Isobel Frothingham as the woman in *The Nightmare*. It was ludicrous. He was fascinated. Mary snatched it away.

"But it was not like that," she cried, grabbing his sleeve, pointing at the painting. "The illustrator never saw her! It was not a real horse, it was a hobby horse. And a monkey to represent your demon—not a doll dressed as a devil the way they picture it."

"All the same," he said, shaking his head, reading on. "*Ach!*" It was not the artwork that shocked him. It was what was on the bottom of the page, in small print. PRISONER ESCAPES NEWGATE. He stopped walking to read aloud: *Art thief Roger Peale escaped after brutally assaulting a prison guard. The prisoner is now at large.*

He heard Mary gasp. He ripped the paper in his anger. Then

tried to pull it together again. When he failed at that, he tore it into tiny pieces and flung them into an alley and watched the wind take them. Escaped, indeed!

They walked on for a time in silence. Finally he turned to Mary. "How could he escape?" he said. "How, I ask? From Newgate Prison? Who was helping the man? Did he have a weapon? Someone passed it to him, eh? Was it that Guilfoy woman? *Ach*, I would not put it past her."

"She is in love with him. She is his intended. *You* should know what she's like. She was *your* intended for a time, was she not?"

"Never mine! She was sleeping with my assistant—he confessed it. That is how she got pregnant." When she looked sceptical, he pinched *her* arm. She cried out; it served her right. Her words were knives. Which made him think: "Peale had a knife, you think? To take on that guard? Then crept in through the woman's window and stabbed her?"

"She was strangled," Mary said, "not stabbed."

"Never mind. She was killed. That is the point! She was *killed*. The killer did not want blood. He wanted it to look like my painting. There is no blood in my painting. Ha!" He pointed a finger at Mary; he was feeling better now. "So Peale was free that night, eh? The man who stole the painting *was* the killer as well. He had already killed my footman Benjamin—why not one more? You were right. Aha!"

They were at Westminster Bridge. The stone towers of Westminster Abbey rose gloriously beyond it—they would bury him in that abbey, a famous artist, *ja*. He laughed hugely, and held Mary in a hard embrace. Now she was confused and he loved it. "You were right, clever girl, *meine Leibe*, you were right."

She did not return his embrace. She just stood there, her hat askew in the breeze off the bridge. He could see the frustration in her eyes, in the pout of the full lips. She had come to press a point, to ask for help for the young artist, and he had turned her theory on end. It was hilarious! "Come, come, my dear," he said. "We will cross the river. I know a little tea garden there. We will have tea and cakes—the almond ones you like? We will talk. *Ja*, by God, we will talk. Come along now. Come."

He tipped up her chin. She was in love with him: platonically she said, but he knew it was more than that. Much more. The virgin did not yet know her other self. If she could be awakened, ah, and he could do it for her if she would let him—together they would release a new woman to the world. Platonic, ha! There was no such thing as platonic. It was physical—or it was nothing. Look to the beasts! And what were human beings but animals at bottom? At *bottom*—he liked the pun. He had spent his life painting animals. Painting passions.

She was frowning. Her elbow slipped from under his. She was turning away, running back off the bridge, dodging the hawkers, skipping between the carriages and the snorting horses. "In a month or two," he called after her, "I will arrange with our friend, Joseph Johnson, an outing to Paris. He has been speaking of it. Paris, I said. Why not?"

That got her attention. She turned and blinked. He caught up with her. "You have been wanting to go to Paris, have you not? So we will go. You and I and Joseph, and Sophia."

"Oh," she said, dismissing Sophia.

"Well, she is my wife. And we need the bookseller to keep peace with her."

"Your wife, sir, will be afraid. The blood will flow in the streets and she'll feel faint and want to come back home. You would have to bring her back."

He laughed and took her arm again, squeezed it, planted a kiss on her right cheek; then fondled her right breast, and she let him. "There is no blood in the Parisian streets. Well, hardly any. Yet. Though it will come, I can feel it in my bones. I can smell it in my paintings. You have talked with Talleyrand, eh? He is a scoundrel in anyone's book. Untouchable, one would think. But he promises it will be safe to go in May or June. He will help with the arrangements."

"Will he come, too?" She was pouting; she obviously did not want a large party.

"No, no, he is still scrounging about for funding for his parliament. Hoping the king will come round, even though His Highness ignores him. He will stay here another month and keep trying. But come. That dish of tea. The cakes. They serve wine as well, eh? We will talk. You are always wanting to talk and I am always putting you off. Shame on me! Well, this time we will talk and talk! About our trip to Paris, eh? We will find time to sneak off together in one of the gardens and make love, shall we?"

She stood a moment, struggling to regain her dignity, her *reputation* as she called it. Her *Rights of Woman*. A muscle twitched in her cheek and she stilled it with a finger.

Then she smiled. She was a daring one at heart. That was why he liked her company. He caught her arm in his, and felt the return squeeze. He would not have to take her to Paris. She could lose her head right here in London. Lose more than her head, *ja*.

"No more talk now about that thieving artist," he said, and touched her pretty nose with a playful finger. "We're off to the tea garden!"

ROGER Peale woke to rain pelting his barred window. He was wearing a nightshirt so coarse it made his skin raw. When he tried to rise, one leg was too heavy to move. He saw that it was chained to a spike in the centre of the room so that if he were able to get up, he could walk only in a radius of four feet, between bed and window. What was this place?

He shouted as loud as he was able. He shouted and shouted—and no one came.

He was not back in Newgate. Not in that solitary cell the turnkey had threatened. This was no dungeon, for rain shone in the window and beyond was a dark green forest—trees and underbrush as far as the eye could see. He was not in London.

He remembered leaving the prison with St Pierre. The latter had bribed the turnkey—Roger would have to repay him—or was it Lillian who paid? He pushed his mind as far as it would go, but for the moment it yielded no more clues. He strained against the misery of his chained leg, his aching head, the vertigo when he tried to stand. They went off in a carriage, yes; he had fallen asleep from the exhaustion of the time spent in Newgate. Something happened then: shouted threats, a highwayman, yes. Possibly two. He had never before encountered a highwayman, only read of them in newpapers—desperate men, demanding your watch, your jewels, your cash. Riding off with the booty, seldom hurting one, no, for if caught, it would be the hangman for them.

Then why, why was he in this place?

There had been a gunshot, he remembered that, and St Pierre crying out. And when he tried to stumble out of the carriage in his leg irons: the door locked on the outside—and the horses starting up. I am being abducted, he had thought at the time—had he? But why? Who? Why had he thought *abducted*?

Memories were crowding back. They brought him here. A woman and man, stripping him of his clothing, of one manacle (he was grateful for that), throwing the coarse shirt on him, making him drink a bowl of ill-tasting gruel. Himself so starved he drank it down. And afterward, the bed, the deep, drunken sleep, nothing and nothing. Blessed nothing. Until he woke. And from the way the light struck the trees, he gauged it was noon.

He cried out, but again no one answered. Was he here alone? But then he heard a groaning in an adjoining chamber. "Hello, hello," he called, and the groan came louder. A voice shushed the groaner, and then feet padded to his door. He heard the scratch of a key in the lock; an old woman stood there with a tray: a bowl of porridge and a hunk of bread, a mug of something sickly yellow. Some drug potion perhaps.

He waved it away. "I don't want your poison. I've had sufficient sleep." He needed to be wide awake and stay that way. He needed to find a way to escape this place. For some reason he was prisoner here. When he had done no wrong; he had stolen no painting— why would he have coveted that piece of eroticism? But he had escaped prison. He was a felon; he was criminal in the eyes of the law. He dropped his head back on the pile of straw that served as pillow and turned to the barred window.

"No poison here, son," she said. "This be a licensed house. We don't serve poison. You better take the food. You look like you need it."

"What is this place then? Tell me that. Who brought me here?"

The woman shrugged her shoulders. She seemed a decent sort. A round, withered apple of a woman, with pitted cheeks and a tangle of white hair under a plain linen cap. A shapeless brown dress topped by a voluminous apron, with patches of dirt where she had wiped her hands a thousand times.

"I work here mornings. I don't know who brought you here. Your wife? Wanting to get rid of you? So she can have her honey to herself?" The woman cackled.

He balked at that. "I have no wife. But I have a fiancée who is crazed with worry this moment and I've no way to tell her I'm alive. Unless you—" He held out his hands. "Just paper, a pen, or a brush, a small brush will do. I'll send her an image. She'll know it's mine."

The woman laughed and plunked down the tray on a small wooden table by the bed. "I can't do that, son. This be a madhouse you see. A private madhouse. We had six here but one died and one got away. You make number five again."

"Escaped?" He sat up and clasped his hands together; felt a surge of hope.

"Oh no, son, nobody leaves here on his own. This one was took away by her husband. Seems he got religion, you know, *so* sorry he put her in, and now he come to take her out. Though she looked a fright, she did. Scared of him, aye. He had to put her in the waggon, still manacled so she wouldn't hit him. That's why they chain you—for your own good, is how they put it. So you won't hurt yourself."

The woman went out. He lay back again and stared at the scarred ceiling. It was full of holes as though someone had thrown darts. His leg ached from the iron. His head was an anvil, being hammered on; his mind, blank. He couldn't conjure up an image of Lillian or the garret where he painted, where he had been happy pulling images up out of his mind and his past.

Where was that world now? What had happened to it? What had he done to lose it? Why had his God forsaken him? For though he was a Dissenter, he still believed in a First Cause, a Presence. Some spirit that "rolled through all things," as that young poet Wordsworth described it one Tuesday at the bookseller's. The poet had been to see the ruin of some abbey, and the line just came to him, he said. He would use it one day in a poem. For Roger, a ruined abbey was an image for a painting.

He squeezed his eyes shut and prayed: "Blessed Spirit, hear me now...."

But when he opened his eyes again there was only this humble room, the sour smell of gruel, and the rain, slapping hard against the barred window. The chain on his leg, chafing, digging into his poor flesh.

The absence of hope.

CHAPTER VII.

Foundling with a Locket: Father Unknown

ᔐ

FROM THE doorway of the Essex Street Unitarian chapel Wednesday morning, Mary watched the men wrestle the closed coffin out of the hearse and enter the meeting house in which Isobel Frothingham, a declared agnostic, had prided herself on never setting foot. It was her single relative, a distant maternal cousin named Rose Wiggin, who had insisted on a church funeral, and so Mr Johnson arranged for it in his own place of worship. The expense, Mary assumed, would come out of the Frothingham estate, which would most likely fall into the purse of that lone relative. For Isobel had seemingly died intestate.

Six men in black, moving at a caterpillar's pace, carried the oak coffin down the aisle on their bent shoulders. Behind them came four honorary pallbearers: Joseph Johnson by the left front, gasping with the dust blown through the open door; to his right the American writer, Joel Barlow, looking pious; after him, Alfred de Charpentier, grieving like any widower; and on the left rear, the rejected suitor, Edgar Ashcroft. Both of the latter hoping, perhaps, for a share in the inheritance? Ashcroft's cheeks glistened—not from tears and grief, Mary felt, but from the effort of pacing the others as they trudged to the front of the chapel.

Behind the pallbearers came the cousin: a stout woman with black ostrich feathers bouncing on her black hat and raggedy ladders in her black worsted stockings. Her heels were worn down— she would profit nicely from any estate monies. Her husband followed: a bandy-legged fellow with the pinched snout of a weasel. Mary had not heard Isobel speak of this Rose Wiggin: the woman would have read the papers, and emerged like a mole out of the past from her northern birthplace. The cousin trod on Ashcroft's heels; he turned to give her a black look.

Someone shut the street door, and a good thing, Mary felt, for a crowd of onlookers had been hanging about the chapel; she had heard the whispered words *bewitched... the devil....* She stood in a pew across from a pair of theatre folk whom she had seen at the bluestocking's salon: she recognized the playwright Elizabeth Inchbald, and the actress Mrs Sarah Siddons, wrapped in something turquoise-blue and filmy. Her writer friends Mary Hays and Anna Laetitia Barbauld, more sensibly dressed, stood farther down in the same pew. There was a scattering of former suitors, as well as a male actor or two, for Isobel Frothingham loved the theatre.

A maroon velvet pall draped the coffin, silvered candlesticks sat on the pulpit, and white tapers illumined the sides of the sanctuary, interspersed with wax lights. Mary imagined *The Nightmare* superimposed on the coffin: the leering incubus, grinning horse, the sleeping woman's exposed breast. She saw William Blake in a far corner with his sketch book—she imagined the fantasy that would fill his sheet: this fey man who claimed he saw the face of God in a tree, and angels dancing on the head of a pin.

The pallbearers finally took their seats, and beside them, the feathered cousin and her obsequious mate. Next to them a space, where Mary imagined a thirteen-year-old girl—though Isobel had not yet adopted her, had she? There was only the receipt that Dulcie said she had found in the bluestocking's bedchamber. And what should Mary do about that? The kindest thing would be to leave the girl in the Foundling Hospital and let her graduate, so to speak, to domestic work with some decent family.

Did the Wiggin cousin know about her? Undoubtedly not. Could a natural child, not legally adopted, take precedence over a legitimate cousin?

The thought of the child nagged at Mary. In her view, the girl was the one true heir, illegitimate or no. Not that four-times-removed cousin who was even now dissolving into false tears and already contemplating, no doubt, a move into the sumptuous (if somewhat gaudy) rooms on Grosvenor Square. The girl made Mary think of Margaret King, her charge as governess in Ireland— a bright, independent-minded fourteen-year-old—now forced by her parents, at nineteen, into an arranged marriage.

Yes, Mary would go to see Isobel Frothingham's girl—orphaned, it would seem, for a second time.

But thoughts of the girl vanished when Lillian Guilfoy slid in beside Mary, her eyes moist under the black veil. It was not the memory of the deceased that reddened her eyes, though she gave lip service to the untimely death—but of her fiancé, Roger Peale. "Disappeared," she whispered. "A highwayman! Somewhere south of London. Monsieur St Pierre has been searching unceasingly. To no avail. We fear my dear boy has been abducted." Her eyes were whirlpools of bluish water.

Mary clucked her sympathy. How much ill news could one take in a short period of time? Poor Lillian. Poor Isobel. Poor foundling. Poor vulnerable females everywhere! "If for ransom, then you will soon hear something," said Mary, squeezing the woman's gloved hand.

"I've thought of that, but I've heard nothing. And how would anyone know where to find me? Poor Mr Peale escaped in his prison clothes! St Pierre brought a pair of breeches and a greatcoat for him, but the prison clothes were undoubtedly still in the coach. Suppose the robbers found and reported them to the prison governors? What if they're keeping him locked up somewhere till the constables can go after him?"

Not the constables only, Mary thought, but Henry Fuseli, who had vowed to find him. Though she wouldn't mention that to Lillian. "We must be patient and wait," Mary said aloud, thinking of her own role in Eliza's escape from an irate husband. And she and her sister listening to every footstep outside their rented room.

Heads turned. Someone in front said, "Shh," and Lillian dropped her veil. She sniffled into an embroidered handkerchief.

Mary sat back into her pew. "The service is beginning," she whispered to the weeping Lillian. "We'll talk afterward."

Though what was there to talk about? Roger Peale was missing. What could one say or do? She prayed it would not be Henry's men who found him.

The Reverend Theophilus Lindsey, the chapel's founder, was a pleasant-looking man with piercing blue eyes, a prominent nose, and a crop of unpowdered white hair. He had known Mrs Frothingham by reputation only, but he deplored her violent death, he told the mourners, and hoped she had now "found peace." His sermon was followed by testimonials from Dr Priestley and Joseph Johnson, and finally, by the husband of Mrs Wiggin who stood up, uninvited, to advise everyone in the room to fear the Lord, for His wrath had "thundered down upon the unhappy victim."

Mary drew the line at that. What had poor Isobel done to defy the Lord except to stay home from church and write novels and poems and offer the literary world a few bibulous routs and readings? And have a child out of wedlock, yes, but whose fault was that? At the very least the blame should have been shared by the unknown father. There were far greater crimes for the Lord to protest: he did not have time for a freethinking female.

Mary went up after the final prayer to place a crumpled rose on the coffin. What more could she do? She felt genuinely sorry for Isobel Frothingham—appalled at the manner of the death. And sorry for having criticized the woman's novel. Had she imagined that violent death, she would have critiqued more lightly. But who could foretell something like this happening? In fiction, readers would have said, Nay, unbelievable! But truth, Mary was beginning to discover, was far more eccentric than fiction.

As she turned to go back up the aisle—Lillian Guilfoy being detained by Mary Hays—Henry Fuseli emerged from a back pew. She gasped: he always took her by surprise. Put her in a state of shock, as it were. That wild white mane, those liquid eyes that spilled into her own. The furry black brows, the sensual lips that repulsed, and yet drew her. He moved up on her, smiling. He was always more affectionate without the restraining wife. He put a hand on her arm and rubbed.

"And did you feel the wrath of the Lord on your shoulders?" she asked, teasing, yet serious. Trying to (*deep breath*) relax.

"Moi?" he said, innocently. "And why, pray, should I feel the Lord's wrath?"

"Why, sir, if you had not painted *The Nightmare,* Mrs Frothingham would not have been strangled in such a deplorable way."

He drew back; he had no sense of humour these days. "Madam, I see no connection here. Had I not painted *The Nightmare,* she would have been arranged in some other way—perhaps hanged and de-tongued. For teasing but not always delivering—do you catch my meaning?" He gave a soft, sensuous laugh. Then grew rational again. "Someone had a grudge against her, that is all. This particular arrangement shows how much influence my work has on the world, eh? Another rave review just received from Zürich, where two of my works hang in the Kunsthaus."

Mary stiffened. She did not care for this arrogant, self-serving Henry.

No, she told herself. She loved and admired him—that is, his mind. No again: she both loathed and loved his mind, all at once. He was a destructive influence on her and she knew it. Turning, she breathed in the fragrance of the largely female mourners, already taking their leave. The wax lights flared, then dimmed in her vision. She thought she saw her publisher waving at her. Or was it the flickering light? "Pray, excuse me, sir."

Henry ran his fingers down her back, across her buttocks, stirring her juices. Oh merciful God! She was so vulnerable, so gullible. She hated that she was. She saw the Wiggin cousin watching, and tried to pull away from him.

"Did I tell you how charming you looked in those scarlet stockings?" Henry said, pushing a knee against hers. "Red becomes you. Absolutely. It freshens your cheeks."

She was not wearing the scarlet stockings today—she was wearing the black ones. "Charming" was one of his empty phrases. She looked coldly at him and squeezed through the crowd of mourners; she needed air. Joseph caught her hand and asked how she was "holding up." He told her that *Vindication* was about to go into yet another printing, that he was proud of her. She clung to his arm. This was love, the way she felt about this sweet man. This was what the words "platonic love" truly meant.

And yet there was no frisson, no lurch, no heat in the breast or groin, no sense of empowerment, or transport into some heaven, which Henry Fuseli gave. There was no rapture from Little Johnson in his stained coat, which smelled slightly of sardines.

Henry was by the outer door now, speaking with a tall woman in rose-and-grey silk with whom Mary was unacquainted. The woman's eyes were fixed on his face; she was holding the tip of her closed fan to her heart. In the language of fans, it meant, *You have my love.*

Mary would scream if he touched that woman.

SHE was told that the hospital governor was busy, but she barged through the study door anyway the following week and found the man at his desk, slurping chocolate, popping chunks of fresh-baked bread into his mouth. His triple chins chewed it back and forth, up and down.

"Do the children get hot chocolate?" she asked, and taken aback, he said, "Well, um, on special occasions. I do not believe we have met, madam. Are you here for—" He glanced at her flat belly; got suddenly busy, shifting papers about on his massive mahogany desk.

"I am Mary Wollstonecraft," she said, pulling back her shoulders. Her more-than-average height served her well. He was still seated; if he got up, the chocolate might spill. He did not offer her any. Her name obviously drew a blank. He was not a bookish man.

She did not offer to leave, although his nose was in his papers. "I have come about the child," she said, and halted, realizing she did not know the child's name. "Isobel Frothingham's child," she went on. "Surely you've heard that Mrs Frothingham is dead. Murdered in her bed, alas. There is a nice inheritance, I understand." Though she did not really know, did she? "Doubtless some part of it will go to this Foundling Hospital."

The word "inheritance" caught his attention; the hospital was always soliciting funds. Mary had once heard a magnificent performance of Handel's *Messiah* here. Deep in the inner sanctum was a hall hung with the paintings of English artists, William Hogarth's among them—he had helped to found the hospital and establish a gallery. None of Fuseli's erotic paintings, though—they might contaminate the minds of innocent orphans.

The governor knew about Mrs Frothingham's death, but not the manner of it. He lifted up a pile of papers to show that he was too busy to read newspapers or to heed gossip. She took a seat and described the death. "Oh my," he said, pressing his pudgy hands together. And again: "Oh my." He got up to rummage about in a tall wooden cabinet and emerged with a sheaf of papers labeled *F*. "I cannot guarantee that I will find the records—the mothers don't always tell their names."

The governor had a quivery, sensitive mouth. If he did not share his chocolate with the children, well, it was probably because there were so many of them.

On the other hand, Mary could have used a hot cup, but remained uninvited.

"She was brought here on March seventh, 1779," he announced. "A Mrs Frothingham, aye." He gazed up at Mary with eyes that matched the chocolate. "They all call themselves Mrs, of course."

Mary nodded. She thought of Fanny Blood's sister Caroline: seduced, abandoned—and destitute, forced into prostitution. Mary had sent what money she could, but the poor girl, it seemed, was lost. The thought galled her—she must write about this.

"But we do not divulge names, no, no," the governor said. "It is just because she is deceased, otherwise—" He cleared his throat, then spewed out facts and figures on the child: age, weight, height, moles, pockmarks, hair colour. "The mother left a poem as token— that is, inside a small locket. The girl wears it around her neck and we indulge her. She often recites the poem aloud." He cleared his throat again. "We give our charges a considerable amount of liberty," he said, pushing his fingers up into a steeple. "We offer lessons in morality; we instill a healthy fear of God."

"Ah," said Mary, "a *fear* of God."

"We have begun to vaccinate now against smallpox."

"Smallpox, yes," said Mary, impressed with the way he moved from God to smallpox. Though on second thought she did see a connection. Children sometimes died from the vaccination, she had heard. "But, sir, this child—her name? Did Mrs Frothingham..."

"*We* name them. This one is Ann. Though at first we called her Silence." He chortled at the memory, and explained that the child did not utter a word for her first three years. "But now, I understand, she has more than made up for that silence. That is, if she is in the mood. She does not always, um, respond when spoken to." The steeple collapsed in his hands.

Mary would not want a talkative child. There was noise enough in her house with Dulcie singing off-tune as she worked, interrupting one's writing with a hundred irrelevant questions. Now this man was humming as he explored the file.

Why, anyway, had she come here? She couldn't think. Ah. Not only to see the child, but to discover the true father, yes. It might have been he who strangled the bluestocking. Though for what reason, she could not at that moment fathom. Her brain had spun a tale: he was a nobleman; he had a wife but she died, and now he could claim the child, someone to nurture him in his old age. He was a Lear; he needed his Cordelia.

But why destroy the mother? Hate? Revenge of some kind?

"You have no record of a father?" she asked. "The man was not mentioned?"

"Oh no, no. They never say. Are you here to adopt the child? You might find her odd, but amusing. She always has her nose in a book. I understand, in fact, that Mrs Frothingham had planned to adopt her. At least the child has been spreading that tale. We usually discount such talk, however. An adult will come to look over the children, encourage one or the other, then not come back and the child is devastated. Unfair. Oh, so, so unfair." He lifted his eyes to the ceiling; blinked.

Adopt her? Mary had no such plan in mind. She had books to write! Although, well, adoption would be a charitable act. She closed her eyes and stood a moment in thought. Should she take the child for a short time, as an ostensible handmaid?

The man was looking at her. She coughed. "The girl would be thirteen now, I understand?"

He glanced back at the chart. "Aye, madam, as of February twenty-fifth. The reason, I expect, for the mother's visit. We had to explain to the child that the lady would not be coming back for her. Should she, as you suggested, have remembered us in her will—" He pursed his lips and glanced discreetly down, leaving Mary to supply the rest of the sentence.

"Mrs Frothingham, I understand, died intestate," she explained. "But a distant cousin has come to claim the inheritance. Is there no mention of beneficiaries in your papers?" She did not want the feathered cousin who had ignored and doubtless disapproved of the bluestocking during her lifetime, getting it *all*.

He brushed away a few crumbs and dropped his three chins back into the folder. He came up smiling. "There is indeed. Not a great deal, but something. 'In the event of my death,'" he read, "'two hundred pounds will go to the Foundling Hospital. You will find it in my will.'"

A will? Mary wondered. When she was told there was no will?

"We do ask this of the affluent ones," he said. "Most are too poor to give even a farthing."

"One is never too poor to give a farthing for a relation," said Mary, who made a point of succouring her siblings—something she had promised her mother on her deathbed. "Now, pray, take me to the child, if you will. I would like to introduce myself to her." A quick visit, yes; Mary was inclined to hasty decisions, and she must correct that fault. Eliza's infant, left behind to a husband who denied the child to a "runaway wife" (Mary must change this law) had died within a year—poor nurturing, Mary suspected. And now

her sister had no child. She was still married, though separated—
"separation from bed and board," they called it.

Was that why she wanted the Frothingham girl? To stop Eliza's
child from wailing in her dreams?

Mary rose and the governor rose with her. He rang a bell; an
aproned women told Mary to follow her. If she came again, she
would bring a copy of her *Original Stories*, the children's book her
friend William Blake had so beautifully illustrated.

In the kitchen, a tall, gangling girl was sweeping the floor. Her
carrot-coloured hair straggled under her cap into her face. She was
sweeping with one hand and reading with the other. The book was
Henry Fielding's *Tom Jones*. A grown-up novel for a girl of delicate
years, but Mary as a child had read books beyond her years, hiding
them under her mattress. It might be interesting to try to educate
the girl as she had Margaret King. An empty mind, needing filling. Mary might write a rebuttal to Rousseau's *Emile*, where he
described the education of a young boy, yet downgraded the education of females.

And there was Ann, the dust moving slowly under her broom—
the name recalled Mary's beloved Fanny; her heart staggered in her
chest. "I—I'll take her," Mary told the woman. "On trial for a few
weeks, to be sure we're compatible. No formal adoption, no. I'll come
for her, in a day or two. I will have to prepare a room and so forth.
So go. Tell the governor this moment and I'll approach the girl."

The woman hustled off and Mary sat down, bowled over by
her sudden decision. Already she wondered how she was going to
feed the child. She would have to appeal to her publisher, but how
much more could she ask of him?

"I am so sorry, Ann, about Mrs Frothingham," she said to the
girl, who had stopped sweeping and was staring at her visitor.

"Annie's my name," the girl said. "And Mrs Frothingham was
going to take me home. Why did she have to be killed?"

Why indeed, Mary thought. "It was a terrible thing, Annie,"
she said, "and I know how disappointed you must be. And I may
not be a good substitute, but I'll try. Would you like to come home
with me?"

The girl regarded her a moment longer and then burst into
tears. Whether from sorrow or joy, Mary couldn't tell. But suddenly the girl cried, "All right then," dropped her broom, and ran off.

In her place a woman she had not seen before stood on two pianoforte legs with the Fielding book in her hands. She was frowning at the bold frontispiece illustration. "She oughtn't be filling 'er 'ead wi' such nonsense," she said.

"I'll be the judge of that," Mary said. "So return the book to the child, please. I'll be taking her home—Tuesday next, I think—that will give me time to prepare. See that she is packed and ready, if you would."

Feeling light-headed, as though body and mind had parted, Mary went out—nay, floated, out of the building and into the noisy street. Her sedan chair had not waited; she would have to walk. It was growing dark, but she felt like walking. She would go down to the river; she moved briskly, filling her nostrils with the good smells of fish, baking bread, spices, roasted meats, and puddings. She swung her arms against the March chill and felt the breeze biting her face like a live thing. She walked and swung and sang until she glimpsed the water; then she turned right along Whitehall and Parliament Street towards Westminster Bridge.

She gazed down at the Thames rushing past with its flotilla of cutters, skiffs, scows, smacks, and cockleshells; a fleet of sailing ships in from a foreign clime. She was subject to melancholy—it was the Irish in her, her mother used to say, and she felt it keenly this afternoon. The wind blew through her body; it chilled her belly and heart. *Should* she have offered to take the child? What did she, a bookish spinster, know about mothering? Her siblings, yes, but how helpful was she really? Would this new undertaking end as one more nightmare?

Nightmare. That word again. The incubus, the grinning horse, the sleeping Isobel, superimposed on her sister Eliza's dead babe, lay behind her closed lids. She opened her eyes wide but the image remained, like a palimpsest on the grey surge of water some twenty feet below. She hung onto one of the piers. Each pier on the bridge ended in a small hooded alcove, like a night porter's chair. The alcoves were built as shelters for pedestrians, but footpads, it was said, adopted them as hiding places for stolen goods. On impulse she stuck her fingers into a nearby niche—but found nothing.

Had she hoped to find a painting?

How wonderful it would be to find that painting: to see Henry's face, his gratitude. She imagined him swinging her about, both of them laughing, joyfully embracing. She ran from pier to pier, thrusting her fingers into each of the alcoves.

Nothing.

Fool, she told herself. She was addicted to the pleasures of the imagination; she must return to reason. Stick to your essays, Mary. Stick to your facts. Alter the world with your words.

Yet she couldn't seem to write at all these days. Was it her own procrastination? Was it because of her obsession with Henry? Or had it something to do with *The Nightmare*, with that note at Isobel Frothingham's cold feet: BLUESTOCKINGS BEWARE.

She could hardly feel her fingers now; her face was numb. She turned back into the city, wanting now to go home, needing to warm herself by the fire, needing human company. Dulcie would have to do for today. Tuesday, she would go to the gathering at the bookseller's; she would tell them about the child—before she went to fetch her. It would help to share her concerns with like-minded company.

Her own nightmares might vanish, she thought, with the return of the painting and the resolution of the murder. *If* the bumbling constabulary could resolve it. *She* could not. How could she?

She hurried back past St James's and Green Park to Grosvenor Square where the Frothingham apartments sat vacant and drear. The street lamps barely illuminated the square; snowflakes flew into the glass globes, like winged ghosts. She imagined she saw the bluestocking rise up out of her bed to repulse her intruder—had she pummeled and scratched him? Had she cried out—though there was no one in the house to hear? Had her soul flown out through the broken window, free at last, leaving the tortured body behind?

Was there indeed a soul? Some ignorami said that women had no souls.

Mary's faith was breaking down. It was the killing and poverty and injustice that deflated her—those motherless children in the Foundling Hospital. She felt responsible for and yet helpless against the ills of the world. Who was she to save anybody: man, woman, or child?

Her foot crunched something hard, and when she leaned down to look she saw it was a small shard of glass—from Isobel Frothingham's window perhaps; she put it in her greatcoat pocket, along with a broken quill pen she found beside the shard. It might be the bluestocking's pen: something to remember the dead woman by, something the child Annie would treasure. And Isobel, she thought, might have used the pen as a weapon against the fellow. Should she look for a wound from a pen in the faces of all the men whom the bluestocking knew?

Alfred de Charpentier had been a pallbearer and she had not thought to communicate with him, nor Edgar Ashcroft. Nor St Pierre, nor Talleyrand. Had the latter two attended the funeral? Possibly, though she did not recall seeing them. She had seen only Henry Fuseli. The man had blinded her to all else.

She wound her way quickly through the labyrinth of shops and houses towards her own Store Street. Strong cooking smells assaulted her nose: cabbage, onions, pork—now she was ravenously hungry. The night-soil men were beginning to pull their waggons to pick up detritus from the garden privies and basement cesspits. Coal smoke hung heavy in the air. Figures loomed at every turn: drunken men emerging from taverns, young ruffians bumping their hips against her, prostitutes beginning their nightly solicitations.

She walked faster; she was sorry she had gone so far from home, dallied so long. Her nerves were weak; she should stay home nights with her books and her writing—although she used up candles, sometimes a week's supply in a night—writing letters to Henry Fuseli that he didn't answer. She should not go walking in the dark. The words *Bluestockings Beware* seemed more ominous now; she picked up her skirts and ran. She ran down Oxford Street and up Tottenham Court Road; she turned into Store Street, and hurried to the end where the small house sat dark as a tomb.

It was Dulcie's night off, she remembered. The girl had gone to visit a friend, she said, though Mary suspected it was that tallow chandler's apprentice. He had started calling on her—though Dulcie would deny any interest.

Almost home, she pulled out the key from her pocket and the shard of glass came with it. And fell. She stooped to pick it up and found herself flying through the air, shoved from behind into the street. A coach-and-four thundered towards her. Just in time she scrambled behind a plane tree. She looked wildly about for help, but saw no one. Had the shove been on purpose? Had the coach come to run her down as it had that poor footman? Was someone lying in wait—warning her of dire things to come? Or was this all in her imagination—had to be, yes. She had cut her face on the glass: that of itself seemed an omen. She was on fire with pain: she had turned an ankle, skinned a knee; her cheek was bleeding from the cut glass.

She dragged herself up the two steps to the front door and jammed the key in the lock. She shut the door behind her and fell back, trembling, against it. The fire was in ashes, the house cold as a—tomb.

Why did that word *tomb* haunt her brain? She pulled her body away from the door and lit a candle. Something crept toward her and she cried out. It was her black cat. The green eyes stared at her. Isobel's eyes.

Tomb, tomb, tomb, her mind wept.

CHAPTER VIII.

Beware: the World Has Gone Mad

✎

MARY WAS the center of attention at the publisher's Tuesday dinner. For once Blake, Priestley, Barlow, Coleridge, and Christie abandoned their boiled cod, beef, and rice pudding. They even abandoned talk of the Revolution—just to gawk at her battered self. Both men and women clucked and *tsk*'d—where had she got those scratches and bruises, that bump on the forehead? That cut on the cheek?

She had fallen, she told them. She did not say "pushed," but she did mention the bare miss of the rushing coach.

Had she seen a surgeon? Should she have a bleeding? Leeches on her arms and cheeks, someone asked? "Leeches are worse than the cut itself," Joel Barlow said, and some agreed.

"Mary, Mary, you must move in here with me!" Joseph cried. "Mrs Murphy will take care of you." (Mrs Murphy: the wrinkled, stoop-shouldered, scatter-brained non-servant who could scarcely lift a stool without help.)

"I have a child," Mary said. "How can I?"

That brought the clucking and *tsk*ing to a halt.

"But Mary," said Joseph, looking her up and down from her new black boots to her old blue hat, "there was no talk of a child last week. Where did this child come from?"

"You've been holding out on us," said Tom Christie with a wink. (Tom Christie, who had got a Frenchwoman with child, then left her to marry a wealthy English girl!)

Indignant, she explained that she was on her way this hour to fetch the child from the Foundling Hospital, and they leaned forward in their chairs. Barlow, who was childless, looked worried; children only "complicated one's creative life." Dr Priestley stroked her arm. Blake, ridiculous in a red wig to identify with the Revolution, stared at Mary as though he had seen a vision of Armageddon. Everyone knew he advocated free love, had even ogled Mary on occasion (she laughed him off).

For ten minutes they talked all at once, a regular cacophony; then went on with conversations that had begun before she arrived. "Those self-righteous Methodists—" Christie began, and they all joined in to malign the "Bible-toting moralists."

They had done for now with Mary and that was a relief; she rose to go.

"Bring the child here with you, Mary, it's all right," said Joseph, coming up behind, placing both hands on her shoulders. "Don't go. Stay, stay—at least for cheese and grapes." But she couldn't stay, she explained, she had only wanted to tell what happened. It was almost five o'clock: they were expecting her at the Foundling Hospital.

He was not listening. "Mrs Murphy will see to the child, so you can write. Is she a talkative child?"

"I understand she's a quiet child, and she reads. So I'll fill her up with books. If I write some juvenile fiction, will you publish it?"

The publisher massaged her shoulders. "Perhaps," he said. Her *Original Stories* about a governess and her young pupils had sold well, but mainly, she had to admit, because of Blake's inventive drawings. "Perhaps I shall," he repeated. He would do anything for Mary, and she knew it. She was his surrogate child. She leaned against him.

Dr Priestley came over to interrupt her ear: "Be careful now, Mary. I heard about that note—about the bluestockings. I know you've no salon—that frivolous sort of thing. But there are dangerous men out there in the world. It would have been a madman who killed Mrs Frothingham. We can't change the way we live to avoid them, but we must act with caution." He spoke with that sweet reason of his. He was a preacher, a liberal Unitarian. And a good father, like Joseph Johnson.

How lucky she was to have two surrogate fathers! Her biological one, had he known of the accident, would say: "Serves you right. Women should stay home, not go tramping about town, night and day, viewing corpses and wicked paintings." Then, done with paternal advice, he would turn away and belch. Oh yes, and a postscript: "Give us a guinea before you leave?"

"Move back in with me, why not?" said Johnson.

Why so? She was an independent woman. St Paul's Churchyard had served nicely for a time while she served her apprenticeship, and earned money on her own. For now she would remain in her home—one day she would repay her publisher. "But thank you," she said and kissed his creased cheek.

"Mind you, walk in company at night. It's a mad world out there." Johnson and Priestley were on either side of her now, seeing her out: the publisher laying her blue cloak about her shoulders; the preacher holding out her muff. Mrs Murphy thrust a sack of potatoes into her hand and straightened her neckerchief. It was half sleeting outdoors—spring was resisting. She had felt foolish wearing the muff her sister Everina had sent her, but today she was glad of it.

She promised not to go out alone, though knowing full well she would not be able to keep the promise. Why would anyone want to turn *her* into a nightmare? Many disapproved of her new book, she admitted, but wouldn't resort to violence—would they? The note about bluestockings, she conjectured, was simply to warn people off finding the killer. The note made her desire all the more to bring the rogue to justice.

Outside, the sedan chair was no longer there—chairmen made no money, waiting. Now she would have to break her promise and walk.

"Miss Wollstonecraft? *Allô, allô!*" She turned to see Alfred de Charpentier hailing her from the window of a "borrowed carriage," he told her. He would be pleased to take her wherever she was going; he did not want to see her get wet—"Such a pretty hat," he said, and she recalled she had stuck a spray of artificial roses on the brim, thinking Henry Fuseli might be at the publisher's. When the Frenchman stepped out, she saw that his hair was combed forward under his hat—to cover up a cut? The man who had entered through Isobel Frothingham's broken window would surely have facial wounds.

She declined his offer.

As he turned away, looking dejected—his habitual look, it would seem—she called him back. After all, the girl, Annie, was ready to leave—the hospital governor had sent a note. She was not familiar with this neighbourhood. It was indeed sleeting and she had come out without her pattens. The wind lifted his hair and she saw that his forehead was perfectly smooth. Ah. "Perhaps I shall after all. I'm going to the Foundling Hospital. No, no, wait. I must go home first, if you don't mind taking me there. I've an outgrown cloak to bring to the orphanage. I live on Store Street. Number twenty-nine."

Now she was worried. She had given the man her home address. The count would see where she lived, perhaps examine her windows, her basement door. Such a fool she was.

He gave a deep bow, left leg thrust back in his emerald green breeches, right hand sweeping his hat so that it touched the wet cobbles. She had to admire the French for their elegance, although his stockings looked threadbare, the red heels of his shoes worn down. Had the bluestocking been robbed? No one had said. Yet, judging from the manner of death, the motive was not money.

"It is not safe to walk alone in the streets—a lady alone, madame—that thief's escape—that 'orr-rible murder."

"I know," she murmured, "I went there. I saw."

"Oh, madame, you should not have—it was not a sight for a lady, *mais non! La belle Isobel...*" Monsieur handed her into the carriage and she immediately regretted it. But too late: the horses were surging forward. The count was telling the coachman to hurry on.

Then he turned his hot face to hers.

SHE would be leaving soon, the woman in the next room whispered to Roger through a jagged hole in the wall. Her voice was hoarse. They had been conversing now and then—whenever someone approached in the hallway the woman would shout nonsense as if talking to herself. She was forty-eight years old; she had been put in this madhouse by a cruel husband. It was his right by law, she said with a sigh, but after a while he would relent. There was no one home to cook for him, or warm his bed. It had happened twice before: each time he would come after a month or so to fetch her. This month was almost up—she had been marking the days on the wall with a spoon.

"Sometimes," she told Roger, "I think I'm just exchanging one madhouse for another." She burst into hoarse sobs. "One day he'll come and I'll refuse to leave."

He put his little finger through the hole and she touched it with her damp one. He told her his story, too—it helped to keep him sane. Without human touch he would truly go mad. Even now he wanted to cry out and punch the walls, flail his breast with a chain.

"I could help you," she said, and he held his breath. Waited. "When Rupert comes again," she continued, but still she gave no explanation. Again he waited. He had no voice at all now. His throat was parched: they hadn't brought water for hours. When they did bring it, it would be foul-tasting, as if it had come out of a trough. He coughed to show he was still listening.

"I can't leave my own house for long, but I could send something to your sweetheart. When I can get away, that is, I never know." Her voice broke; there was no sweetheart for her, she indicated thus; there were only the beatings and the bitter knowledge that her man would put her back here again. Roger's heart ached to hear her story.

"Can you write?" he said, summoning all his breath to speak the words. Home, she could write Lillian a note; tell her where he was. Lilly would find a way to rescue him.

"No," she said. "But Rupert can write. Though he would never—you know. 'Twould have to be something you sent. That your sweetheart would recognize. I would try to get it to her."

What could he send? They had taken everything from him, even the clothing St Pierre gave him at the hour of escape. If he only had a token his Lilly would recognize... Like the branch of cherries he picked when they first met and she bit into one and he kissed her— he didn't know which was cherry and which her sweet lips. Or the self-portrait he gave her when she wanted his likeness for her dressing table, and he portrayed them looking into one another's faces. She had held it to her bosom and wept. Wept! From the joy of it. And he, too, was momentarily blinded by tears.

But how could he find cherries—they gave him nothing so exotic here to eat. There was no ink or paper to make a sketch. There were only two links of rusted chain he had found under the bed, and the goosefeather quill an attendant had given him that he had no use for. He had hidden it anyway, inside the straw of his mattress. He could only scratch with it on the grated window. He could pretend he was drawing the chestnut tree outside: if he squinted he could see the bare outline of branches. There were still chestnuts hanging on, but he couldn't get at them. And what would a chestnut mean to Lillian?

He could think of nothing. And if this woman could actually break away and go to Lillian, and tell her who had sent her, and where he was, would his fiancée trust her? An unknown woman who herself had been locked into a madhouse? He pictured the woman's disheveled hair, the haunted eyes, the bruises on her flesh. His Lilly was shy with strangers, a little afraid of life after the betrayal she'd had from that villain, Fuseli.

Fuseli! If he got out of here alive he would go after the blackguard. He would stuff the man's gullet with his own foul brushes. He would knock him over the head with his satanic paintings! It was Fuseli keeping him here, he was certain of it. The highwayman who had halted them was Fuseli's man—had to be.

He dragged his chain to the window and beat his hands against the bars. Out, he wanted out! He beat and beat until his hands were cracked and numbed, and like a Lear, howled his grief. The matron's husband burst into his room and grabbed him from behind, threw him down on the bed, and strapped him to it.

Bound hand and foot, he was as helpless as his father had been the year before when a tree fell on him and it took three of them to heave it off his broken body. At least his father had his wife to comfort him as he lay dying. Roger had only the woman in the next room—fettered, no doubt, like himself.

He rolled toward the wall. He put his mouth to the hole. "I can't go on, I can't," he groaned.

"Count to a thousand with me," she whispered back. "That's how we'll keep sane. One two three…"

"Ten eleven twelve," he rasped, "…twenty-two twenty-three twenty-four…"

THEY had not ridden two streets filled with the count's false compliments, when the count lurched, giggling, at Mary, and grabbed at her neckerchief. He yanked her toward him, and began to kiss her throat and neck. "Leave me!" she cried. The devil was squatting on her breast; he was pulling back a layer of clothing, burning her skin.

"Get off—off!" she screeched. She swatted him with Mrs Murphy's sack of potatoes. He fell back into a corner of the seat; regained his equilibrium and scowled—and then grinned. With his big white teeth he reminded her of the leering horse in *The Nightmare.*

"Mademoiselle," he said. "Do not tell me you do not want this. I do not believe it, *mais non! Une belle femme comme toi!"* He lunged at her again, and pinned her into a corner. She balled her fist and hit him, hard, in the groin.

When he bellowed and clutched himself, she seized the opportunity. The carriage was slowing in the mêlée of horses and coaches; she yanked on the door handle and leapt out. She fell to her knees on the muddy street and banged her head on a stone. The vehicle halted; she heard him curse in French. "*Ces femmes anglaises*—they are all prudes!"

She stumbled up and ran. She raced around a corner and into an alley and out again: left, then right, then left into a square where smartly dressed shoppers were milling about, and into a fabric store. The shopkeeper glanced up, astonished at her disarray.

"I have been assaulted," Mary said, gasping out the words. And then held up a hand when the woman stared. "Barely escaped. Should never have accepted the ride. He was an acquaintance, you see, or I would not have..." She pulled up a breath and went on: "Tell me, pray, where I am. I live in Store Street. I must go there."

"Store Street," the shopkeeper cried. "Why, that's far, far, my dear, from here. This is Prince's Square. You'll never walk it in your condition. Let me get you a chair."

"I left my purse in his carriage. I've only a ring for barter. My friend Fanny gave it to me. She died, you see, in childbirth—my dearest friend. But here. Hold it, you have an honest face. I'll return the fee. I'll send my maidservant."

The woman shook her head. Her husband owned the shop. She would pay for the chair and Mary could return the money another time.

Mary would embrace her but her hands were grimy from the muck she had fallen in. "I promise you'll be repaid. I'll want a yard of that lace." She pointed to a heap of intricate Belgian lace—which she couldn't really afford, the kind she never wore but that Henry liked; she had seen his wife in a petticoat of such fine lace.

The woman was happy to be of help—and to sell the lace. "Take it now, take it," she said, letting the lace trail through her fingers, snipping it with her shears. "'Tis thirteen shillings the yard—a bargain. You can send it with the chair fee."

Mary thanked the woman and went out. The Frenchman was nowhere in sight—though who was that stout fellow in blue breeches lurking in a shop entrance across the street? Or the bald man peering out the window of an aged hackney? Everyone now was suspect. She ducked into the sedan chair the shopkeeper had hailed, and leaned back against the soft cushions. She just wanted to go home, but she had promised Annie. She would have to go to the orphanage without the cloak—surely the girl had something warm to wear.

"The Foundling Hospital," she called out. "And hurry!"

THE girl had been here two days, and already Dulcie was at her wits' end. What was she anyway? A ward, a guest, or a servant? A guest, it would seem, from the way she arose well after ten o'clock each morning and plunked herself down at the kitchen table, waiting to be fed. Then after she slurped a hot chocolate, heaping in the sugar, and buttered three hunks of the best white bread, she skipped upstairs and lay flat out on the sofa with a book.

A book! Dulcie had never read an entire book in all her nineteen years, nor had time for such indulgence. There were no books in her old charity school except the Bible, and she only pretended to read that. Though she had to admit that under Miss Mary's tutelage she was beginning to feel the pleasure of knowing her letters. For one thing, it made her privy to her mistress's thoughts. And someone needed to know what Miss Mary was up to, with all this *Nightmare* business. Dulcie still worried about Miss Mary coming in all bedraggled from an accident that Dulcie suspected was no accident.

BLUESTOCKINGS BEWARE the killer's note said, and Dulcie believed it, even as the mistress belittled it and went on with Part Two of her *Vindication* like it was all she had to think about in the world. Though the book seemed to shrink even as it grew. Just yesterday she had ripped up a dozen pages and flung them into the waste bucket.

Annie, the girl's name was. Annie, who hummed or sang loudly while she read, and then, while Dulcie was trying to revive a dying fire and concentrate on the next task—there was always work to do, always—the girl would ask a hundred annoying questions: "What did you put in that pie that made it taste so good (*or bad—the girl didn't hesitate to criticize*)? Who do you think killed Miss Isobel? Where did Miss Mary get that black eye? Do you think someone's trying to kill *her*? Will he try to murder us all?"

That was what came of children learning to read. This morning Dulcie had found the girl rummaging through Dulcie's hatbox, where Dulcie kept the papers she'd picked up at Mrs Frothingham's. It was luck she got there in time because there was information about Annie's birth and other documents the child shouldn't see. One of them was in a foreign language (Latin or Spanish, or Chinese). So when the girl left the room, looking sulky, Dulcie stuffed the papers under her straw mattress and locked her door. Let that teach the little snoop a lesson.

Now she faced the sofa. "Up, missy, help sweep the room. It's your duty."

"Who said?" the girl asked, peering over the top of her book. A grown-up book, too, from the cover—Dulcie was embarrassed to even look. *Tom Jones*? It looked naughty.

"Miss Mary said. You heard her. We all help around here."

"You're supposed to do it. You're the maid."

Dulcie put her hands on her hips and glared down at the girl. "I beg your pardon! I am the bookseller's relation. I'm just helping out. I can leave any time I wish. And what are you, missy? What do they teach you to be in that orphanage? A domestic servant, right? That's all an orphan can hope for. I know that for gospel. I once lived in a place like that."

"They teach us to find our own way in the world. And my way is not sweeping or scrubbing." The girl stuck up her snub nose. Come to think of it, Dulcie thought, she does look like her mother. Except for the pockmarks. Mrs Frothingham's complexion had been flawless. With help from a dozen vials and jars, of course.

"What's *your* way then?"

"To be a writer. Like my mother."

Mother? The word stopped Dulcie. Had the child been snooping very long before Dulcie found her?

"Miss Mary told me. This morning just. Before she went out. My real mother was a writer. She left me this poem." She patted her locket. "Miss Mary has my mother's novel, and I intend to read it."

"Oh." So the girl didn't yet know that Mrs Frothingham, in particular, was her mother. "Well then. You can try to be a writer

if that's what you want to be. But writers are poor. Look at Miss
Mary. You think she can afford to pay me? Uh-uh. It's Mr Johnson
what pays me. 'Cause writers don't make money and that's a fact.
Writers have to clean their own houses. Most of 'em anyway. Not
that Mrs Frothingham, though."

Now she'd said it! But the girl didn't change expression. "She's
dead. That Mrs Frothingham is dead. She was going to adopt me
and now she's dead."

"Don't I know that? Didn't I find her?" Though Dulcie hadn't
known that the bluestocking was actually going to adopt the girl.
That was sad. "Be careful," Dulcie warned. "Miss Mary's not planning to adopt you. She just took pity on you, that's all." Dulcie
wanted the girl to know this. It was for her benefit. Dulcie did not
want to have to speak like this; she was kind at heart. But this saucy
girl made her speak out. She was too forward a child. Pushy, one
might say.

Someone rapped on the door. "Don't answer," Annie said.

Dulcie had not been planning to. She had the fires to build up.
But the girl's response made her say, "Why not? It could be Mr
Johnson. It could be Miss Mary, forgetting her key. It could be a
neighbour, needing sugar for a cake."

"It could be that murderer," said the girl, "thinking Miss Mary
is here. Coming to kill us. He hates people who read books. And
write them."

"Ridiculous," said Dulcie, though her heart was banging inside
her chest.

The knock came again. Louder. The girl curled her thin body
into the sofa and held the book inches from her nose. Dulcie
worked furiously on the fire. She would hold on to the bellows—in
case.

"Open up!" a voice boomed. "Do you want me to leave this
manuscript on the doorstep? There's a nasty cold wind out here."

Dulcie recognized the Yorkshire accent. "Go and open the door.
It's just the printer," she told the girl. "Miss Mary will be angry.
It'll be something she wrote, and she'll want the proofs." But the
girl remained seated. Now it was a matter of Dulcie's pride: the girl
must obey. "Go, I said." She stood over the little minx and pumped
the bellows.

A spark fell in the girl's hair; Annie slapped at it and jumped up.
"You trying to burn me?"

"No, but Miss Mary will if she discovers you lounging about and won't do as you're told." The knock came again, insistent, and finally Annie got up and ambled to the door.

It was indeed Cyrus Hunt, the sour-faced printer. He was always polite, though, minding his own business. He never stayed and usually (not always) wiped his feet before he stepped over the threshold—Dulcie liked that. He took a side glance at the girl, wondering, Dulcie supposed, why there would be a child in this house. He held out a pile of scribbled pages. "Your mistress left these. She'll be wanting them to carry on from."

Dulcie took the pages from the girl, who didn't seem to know what to do with them. It was Miss Mary's handwriting all right, but worse than usual: the letters raced backward and forward, like her mind was travelling in two directions at once and couldn't find the right one. Seeing the printer look again at the girl, she said, "That's Annie from the Foundling Hospital. Miss Mary brought her here to help with chores."

"She did not!" Annie cried. "She brought me 'cause Miss Isobel was going to adopt me and then she got killed and Miss Mary felt sorry for me and brought me here. I'm not a servant. I'll never be a servant!" The girl's face was hot: there were moist beads dancing on her forehead; she was shaking with indignation. The printer's mouth hung open; he took a step back.

"All the same to me," he said. He backed out, slowly, in the direction of the door; bumped into a hat rack and pushed it aside; then, annoyed, he turned and said, "See that your mistress gets those. She'll be wanting them, I said."

The door slammed behind him. Dulcie threw a log on the fire and waved away the smoke. Now the girl was alienating the mistress's visitors; Dulcie was close to tears. Miss Mary would have to make a decision: the girl went or Dulcie did. She could not take these outbursts from a thirteen-year-old. Dulcie had nerves, too. She had feelings. The girl was back on the sofa, feet up on the shabby arm.

Pumping the bellows, Dulcie sent smoke in her direction, and she didn't even blink.

THE young girl attendant came to the madhouse once a week. Roger didn't know which day because, though they had unchained him and he tried to mark off the days by the weather outside his window, he had become confused, and lost track. But he had to try, to keep himself sane. He must never go wholly mad like some of the inmates he could hear down the hall, shouting, moaning, and scratching the walls. Just yesterday (or was it the day before?) he had heard one cry, "I be Jesus of Nazareth—sum'mun driving nails in me two hands—will no one he-elp me?"

That night Roger dreamed he, too, was on a cross: his body naked, the nails splitting his flesh. His own groans and outcries woke him; he was drenched with sweat. "It's all right, calm down, keep your head, sir." It was the woman next door, whispering through the wall. But the nightmare persisted, even as he heaved his body up off the stiff mattress.

On the whole, one bland day was like the next. Rain, partial sun, mud; the chestnut tree leaves coming into bud so it might be late March or even early April. One sunny afternoon he heard children's voices outside his window, and that was a blessing—but then the matron went out with a stick, and they ran.

His neighbour's husband was late coming. "He never took this long to be sorry," she hissed through the crack. "He'll be ill. Winters, his cough sends him to bed and he can't work the cows. We never had children—no sons to help. He blames me for that."

Roger had no children either, he told her. He was twenty-six. "But Lillian has a boy; we get on well. And when we're married—" He paused: *if* we marry, he thought.

"Twenty-six," the woman said: "you're just a babe. If she made one child, she'll make more. My Rupert wants a new wife but can't find one. His face so marked from the pox, front teeth gone—only me'd have him. I pitied him, you see. But it's the pox made him angry at life—I didn't count on that."

Footsteps came to the door and Roger gave two quick knocks, the signal to stop talking. It was the young aide; Roger was glad. He hadn't seen her for a while. She smiled at him. She knew he was not insane, she'd said, but what could she do? She brought porridge and "an apple. Ma don't know I stole it. Here."

It was withered, like an old woman's face, but he took it greedily. The juice was sweet and cold from storage. He even ate the core: it was soft from wintering over; it spilled down his throat. Afterward he asked, "Can you get me a cherry?"

She looked at him like he *was* crazed. "A cherry? Where on earth'd I get a cherry?"

He couldn't tell her. He only recalled he had painted cherries in Lillian's hair in the month of May. He gave a half laugh. "I can't say—someone somewhere must preserve them. I only know if you can find me one, I'll reward you when I get out of here."

With what could he reward her? A painting maybe. He would paint her holding a bough of cherries. "You're a pretty lass," he told her. "I'll do your portrait. You can sell the painting or you can keep it. I have a bit of a reputation, you know."

Well, he did have a reputation, but it was not for his art. It was for stealing a frame, when he was a desperate youth. And now a famous painting—or so Fuseli said. Though, true, he'd had two small exhibitions of his work: he had built up something of a following. And he would keep on. He had ambitions. Lillian believed in him; so did a handful of others. Even the renowned William Blake had looked thoughtfully at a watercolour Roger had given the bookseller and said, "Keep on." No praise, but no discouragement either. Just "keep on." And he intended to do that.

If he could get out of here before he lost his mind.

"If your mother kept apples, someone kept cherries. A farmer's wife, a squire's cook. Please can you find me a cherry?"

She was staring at him. She didn't ask him what he wanted it for and he was grateful.

She was a good girl, but they might make her talk. They probably pumped her for what he said, what he did when she was in the room. It wouldn't do to say too much. Though if she told them he wanted a cherry, they would think he *was* going mad, and probably that was what they wanted. Someone was keeping him here, for some malevolent reason.

Fuseli, he thought again: Henry Fuseli is keeping me here. Though once again that didn't make sense. If Fuseli had put him in Newgate, why would he take him to a madhouse? He would have gone mad enough, awaiting trial in that prison. He couldn't think why or why not, his mind was too disoriented. He could only think, *Fuseli, Fuseli, I hate Fuseli. I will avenge myself on him if I get out of here.*

"I'll try to find a cherry for you, but I can't promise," the girl said, and smiled. She liked the idea of having her portrait painted, he saw that. It was a small hope that she would find a cherry, but what had he now but small hopes? And even if she brought the cherry, how would he get it to Lillian? Could he pass a cherry through the rough whispering-hole without destroying it? No, he would have to ask the aide to give it to the woman. But the woman's husband had a cough, she said, he could be dying. Then no one would come to release her—she had no children. She would die in this madhouse.

As would he.

CHAPTER IX.

Rotting Cherries and a Cruel Reception

∽

MARY'S NERVES were frazzled: she drank a glass of ass's milk and lay back on the sofa with a copy of *Candide*. She sent Dulcie out to the cookhouse for a mutton chop and a York-shire pudding; she had Annie fan her. She had felt ill for over a week now; she had missed the latest gathering at the publisher's. Joseph had sent over a cake and a bottle of stout, along with a re-newed invitation to come stay with him. "Bring the girl with you," he'd insisted in a note. "Mrs Murphy will see to her."

But Mary couldn't move. The onslaught of accidents had quite undone her. It had flattened her out to a silhouette of her former self. She couldn't write a word on any of her projects. She could only lie back on the sofa, read, munch on grapes, and prepare for a slow death.

Annie said: "Why do I have to fan you when it's freezing cold in here?" The girl was sitting back on her heels, humming loudly (as usual), a new book—courtesy of Mr Johnson—in one hand, fan in the other. The book was Henry Fielding's *Joseph Andrews*—inap-propriate reading for a child, although Mary herself had found it to be delightful. But Mary had given up scolding. Let the child have her way: it was easier than trying to discipline her. At least she was reading.

"It is not freezing cold. *I* am burning up," Mary said.

The girl put her hand on Mary's forehead. "I don't feel a fever. You're cool as a wet sponge."

"It's all inside." Mary put a hand on her breast and closed her eyes. "I had another nightmare last night about my sister's dead baby. Someone killed Isobel Frothingham and now wants to kill me. But there is nothing left to kill. My heart is in ashes."

"Go on," said the girl, who despite her vivid imagination could be quite literal. "Nobody's heart is in ashes till the flesh burns. And your flesh is pink as roses. I can see you breathing big as life. You wouldn't be talking if you was dead, would you?"

"*Were* dead," Mary said. "And keep fanning." Hearing a knock, she added: "But first, answer the door. No, wait," she said when the girl groaned. "First, look out the window and see who's there. It might be a tradesman." It might be Mr Ashcroft, she thought—or worse, Alfred de Charpentier, who had sent her a profuse apology—she had "accepted the invitation to ride," and so he had "assumed..." et cetera, et cetera. She had torn it up.

"You're giving me too many firsts. Which first comes first?"

"The window, the window! See who's knocking."

The girl moved slowly to the window. "It's a man with white hair and bulgy eyes. He has a picture with him. A picture of a horse."

"Henry Fuseli!" Mary cried, and leapt up. She combed her fingers through her tangled hair, pinched her cheeks, and smoothed out her blue dress, which was wrinkled from lying so many hours on the sofa. Why had he not sent a note to warn of his coming? Henry was not thoughtful that way.

But he was already in. He flashed a painting of a stallion rearing up on its back legs, revealing its private parts—he loved to shock. He said the painting was to cheer her up; she found it depressing. Annie said, "Disgusting," and went back to her book. The cat purred beside her.

"I heard," Henry said, striding to Mary's side, snatching up her hand, pulling her back down on the sofa beside him. He put a gentle finger on the bruise that nine days later still coloured her cheek. "Who did this? Who marred this lovely complexion?"

She wanted to tell him, but she was afraid he would run right out and skewer the French count; accuse him of being in league with Peale to steal the painting. Henry was altogether too impulsive. "Act before you think" was his maxim. That it was often her maxim, too, she did not want to think—not today.

"A man, a perfect stranger," she lied. "He offered a ride and accosted me. I jumped out of the carriage and hit my head. That is all."

Henry was astonished. His right hand was a trembling leaf. "You accepted a ride with a perfect stranger? Have you gone mad, woman? Sometimes I wonder about you, mad-Mary. Ladies do not—"

"I know, I know. But it was raining. I was cold, I wanted to be home. I'd had that other accident as well."

Now she'd said it. He had to hear all the details, so she gave up and fed him. That first injury *was* from a stranger, it was true. Or was it?

He reached for her hand: his eyes were like lighted candles. She was afraid he might embrace her, right in front of the girl. Where was the girl? Ah, eyes on the book but ears wide open. Taking in everything: listening, watching—a little sentinel. Mary tried to pull away but Henry had her in steely fingers. "It all fits together," he said. "The stolen painting. Isobel Frothingham's murder, the note about bluestockings. But the woman in my painting was modeled on my wife, Sophia. She is not a bluestocking."

"But who knows that, if they haven't met her? Does she read at all?"

"Don't be naughty," he said. "Of course she reads. She reads *The Lady's Magazine* cover to cover, every issue."

"Ha. But I don't think the stranger's assault has anything to do with a murder. Or a theft. I'm convinced now that the earlier accident on my street was just that: an accident. As for the other—you were right: I should never have accepted a ride with a stranger."

"It was Peale," he said, sitting upright, his eyes widening as though he'd had a sudden revelation. "That's who your so-called stranger was—the man who assaulted you. Peale is a psychopath, my girl, did you not recognize him? Or was he in disguise... *Ja, ja,* of course, he was in disguise." Grabbing her hands, he forced her to look into his huge, shiny eyes. His brows resembled a pair of snowy hedgerows. "What did the fellow look like? What was he wearing? Where did he accost you the first time? Did he touch you here—or here?" He put a finger on her thigh, then her breast. "Where was his carriage? What colour was it? How many horses? Was it that faux-artist?"

Mary's hands flew up for peace. "It was not Peale, I can tell you that. I know Mr Peale, I'd know him even in disguise. *If* he were free, he'd have come to see Mrs Guilfoy, and I can tell you with certainty he has not been to see her." She took his hands in hers and looked pointedly at him. "The poor woman is in despair, not hearing from him. She is sure he's held captive somewhere."

Henry freed her hands and jumped up. "He is back in London—an escape artist. He is trying to sell my painting on the underground market. Soon he will leave for the Continent: he will try to sell it there. He will try in Switzerland, my native country. Just to flout me. He has a wicked mind. Wicked!" She could hear him grind his teeth.

Henry should be the novelist, she thought, with his flagrant imagination. "Think what you like," she told him coolly, "and pray sit down. It was not Mr Peale."

"I have men on the outlook." He pulled up a stool; then, adjusting the back flaps of his coat, sat with dramatic flair. "A justice in every village. We will find Peale, I assure you, we will spare no expense. He will hang, *ja*, he will hang. No punishment too lenient for that scoundrel. *Nein!*"

Mary gave up the argument. She was too unnerved. Now he was squeezing her hands again. She was only thirty-two—oh dear, thirty-three this spring, April 27—but she needed to see a physician to gain back her health. Annie was humming loudly again, trying for attention—though Mary was fond of the girl, in spite of all. Annie was taking the place of her pupil, Margaret King—married and already pregnant, she'd written—another fertile mind wasted.

"Don't ever marry," she'd told Annie, and the girl said, "Why would I?"

"I want him found, I want him drawn limb to limb," Henry was ranting on like an overwrought actor. "I want him—"

"Leave me, Mr Fuseli," she said. "I cannot hear any more of this hyperbolic talk. Come again when you're over this mad obsession with Roger Peale."

He was up again, a jack-in-the-box. Standing over her like a stern teacher. "First, madam, answer my questions. Tell me where and when and what about that man who accosted you. Tell every detail. Do not hold back. Quick! I am all ears." He cupped his ears. He had small, delicate ears—a surprise, where everything else about his face was outsized.

So she told the story again—embellishing a detail or two to placate him. This time Annie made no pretense of reading. She watched round-eyed, her mouth open like a noon flower.

"Details, I said. Speak."

She gave what details she could about "the abduction"—without mentioning the count. Then "Leave me be," she said. But smiled at his concern as she spoke. And changed the subject before he could rant on. He did worry about her, did he not? "You'll be at Joseph's breakfast tomorrow?" she asked.

"If you are there, my dear, how could I not be? I think I need to keep a closer eye on you—to keep you out of trouble." Bowing, smiling, he kissed her hands fervently, as though they were keys to the taking of Roger Peale.

Then he turned his gaze on Annie. "Resembles Isobel, does she not?" he said. Mary shushed him, but he kept on. "The curve of the brows, the bow-shaped lips. The pea-soup eyes." He was gazing tenderly at the girl. Yes, there was a gentle side to Henry, but it needed nurturing. If he and she could spend more time together, she thought—not as lovers, no. But as, well, friends, soulmates... A platonic relationship. A cerebral *ménage à trois*. She would immerse herself in books and Henry's mind; let the wife mend her stockings in a corner of the room.

Beyond the window she saw a grey tomcat mount a tabby. The female crouched, docile, accepting. Mary was fascinated.

The cats parted and ran off in different directions, and she turned back to watch the artist pull on his greatcoat and hat, smooth out his soft grey gloves, and with a quick wave, bang out the door. There was nothing quiet or reserved about Henry Fuseli: he wore his passions and prejudices on his sleeve. Was that a good thing or not?

"She was my mother, wasn't she, that Isobel," Annie said, jumping up, eyes flashing sea-green—her mother's eyes. "Don't deny it now. I know she was." Annie fingered the gold locket she still wore around her neck and refused to take off, even for bathing (when Mary forced her to bath).

Mary sighed. There was no use hiding the fact any longer. "I believe—she might have been." When the eyes flashed again: "Yes, she was your mother, she was."

"Then we must find out who killed her," said the girl, crossing her arms over her thin chest. "What are you laying about for?"

"*Lying*. Lying about," said Mary absently. "And I'll be up and off soon." She turned away to the window. But not to find any killer. No, she was going after Mr Fuseli. He had said he wanted to keep an eye on her. And if she didn't act at once on her dreams they would die, unrealized. It was time. She would make the long dreamed-of proposal to Henry and his wife: to move in with them. She would have greater influence with him, then, would she not? She would soften his heart on all accounts. On Roger Peale's account.

She patted Annie's head, and fluffed up her hair. Annie said, "*Oww.* Stop it." Mary laughed, and went up to her bedchamber to prepare. The Fuselis had a large house with maidservants, footmen, cooks. Annie could have her own spacious room instead of the cubicle she slept in now. Mary would bring Dulcie along as her personal maid.

She threw the three dresses she owned out on the bed: the black muslin, the black wool, the new jade-green muslin with a white fichu crossed at the breasts, slyly revealing—yes, she would wear the green, and the scarlet stockings Henry admired. She would wear them evenings while Sophia was doing needlework. Mary would be with Henry, talking books, art, philosophy, and Sophia would see that Mary was not a rival for his bed, but for his mind and spirit, something the childish blonde could never give him.

If Sophia was a model for his painting, Mary would be his muse.

Though she would not mind his painting her portrait—fully clothed, of course, in her scarlet stockings. She did have a reputation to uphold.

In the interim, she thought, as she dressed her hair with the fringe he had complimented, she would make him realize how futile, how cruel was all this hunting down of a poor young artist. How many goals would be gained by their mutual habitation, how many lives saved! And what safer place for *her* (she would tell him—though it wasn't his protection she wanted) than to live in his establishment? If he worried about her as he said, he would have to understand this.

On impulse, she stuck a sprig of hollyberries in her hair, just over the ear—she could still wear her hat. She might even put a touch of rouge on her cheeks, though they would heat up, no doubt, with what she had to say.

She squinted into the looking glass. Her hair was not at its best: she had a cowlick in the back that would not flatten out. She would have to keep her hat on. But her complexion was clear today: a little powder would remove the shine from her nose and cover the bruise on her cheek. She looked quite well; if she were to meet herself on the street she might turn her head and say, "Now there is a worthy woman."

When Dulcie returned with the mutton chop (divided in three, they would each have little more than a bite), Mary sent her running with a shilling to find a sedan chair—there was an unseasonable chill in the air. She put pattens over her shoes to save them from the dung, donned her new blue cloak, and let one of the men hand her into the chair. She stretched out her legs on the foot-warmer, lifted her chin, and repeated to herself that the course she was about to take was the right one, that it would fulfill a need for all three of them. Would not Sophia be ultimately abandoned without Mary to keep her husband intellectually satisfied?

"Take me to Queen Anne Street. And quickly," she told the chairmen. *Before I change my mind,* she thought. She pulled up a deep breath and felt altogether delirious. When a girl in a shabby gown ran up to the chair with her hand out, she tossed out a sixpence, and laughed out loud when the girl blew her a kiss.

LILLIAN Guilfoy opened the door to a girl of sixteen or seventeen, wrapped in a woolen shawl over a blue print gown patched at the hem. Her shoes were broken at the heels as though she had already walked to all the destinations of her short life.

"Is this the home of Missus Guilfoy, known to a painter called Peale?" the girl asked in a shrill voice.

Lillian cried out at the name Peale. Her stomach leapt to her throat. She clasped her hands to her breasts.

"Well, are you?" said the girl. "I can't stay. I'd a turrible time findin' you. He give me the address but he had no money. I had to pay for the coach to London and then beg for a biscuit to eat. He said you'd pay me."

"You've seen him? You've spoken to him!" But then Lillian hesitated. Who was this girl? Who had sent her? Someone who was holding her Roger hostage? Already three persons had come forward claiming to have seen him, and all had proved false, wanting only money. This one, too, held out a rough palm, her fingers twitching.

"It come to three shillings. Took half me wages I saved. Said he painted you with cherries. Like these." She pulled out a paper full of rotting cherries from under her grubby cape. "He said that's how you'd know I come from him. Couldn't come hisself, you know, locked up like he is."

Lillian's vision dimmed. She dropped into a chair. The girl might have been addressing her from miles away.

"Would I come all this way if I was goin' lie to you?" The girl was standing over her, her arms akimbo.

Lillian made a brave effort to sit up. It was no time to be swooning. She staggered out of the chair and motioned the girl toward the portrait of herself, holding cherries. She put a hand against the wall to support her weakened body. She had to hold herself together. The girl was pressing the cherries into her hand.

Locked up, the girl had said?

"You don't know how devilish hard 'twas to find these. Cherries don't come out this soon. I said that to him, but he kep' on. Cherries he said, find cherries. So I did. Granny Sopworth put 'em up last May. She made me work a full day to get 'em."

"I'll repay you. Don't you worry. Here's his painting. Look! He did it last spring, when we were first betrothed."

"Laws," the girl said. "'Tis a beauty aright, that painting. But he's in no condition to do one now. He's in a madhouse, he is, miss."

"A madhouse!" Lillian cried. The word struck her like a hurled rock. She felt as though her insides were bleeding. "What would he be doing in a madhouse? Why, he's as sane as I. Who put him there? He hasn't—" she felt the blood drain out of her head "—lost his mind?" But no, he'd remembered the cherries. Someone had abducted him, put him in that place against his will. "Where is he? Take me to him at once."

"No, miss, I can't do that. They'd know who told. I have to go back on me own. This is me one day off, Sunday. Me friend's meetin' me here—he had a delivery. We'll go back in his waggon. Anyway, miss, you can't get your man out. Not you alone. They got dogs. Big black ones. You got to make a plan."

"A plan," Lillian said. "What kind of a plan?" She was leaning against the wall. The floor was rising up to meet her eyes.

"That's up to you, miss. I got to go now." She held out a hand. "You said you'd pay the coach. Cherries, too, miss. Come to four shillings, sure. I need the money, I worked a whole day for them cherries. You ought to get him out, he's a young man. Nice lookin', too. Or was—when he first come."

Lillian stumbled to her desk to find the money. She took out four shillings. It meant no meat tomorrow for her and the boy. But if it would bring Roger to her...

"Tell me exactly where this place is. What town? Make me a map." She would hold back the money until the girl told her.

"Slinfold," the girl said, sounding impatient. "I don't know how to make no map. 'Tis just a village. Go to the public house and ask somebody for Madhouse Lane. Go to the end and turn left, down a cow path. The house be at the end. The dogs is mean when they gets loose. So's the folk what runs it."

The girl pocketed the coins, took one last look at the portrait with the cherries, and ran out. The door banged twice behind her. When Lillian went to the window the girl was already running up the street and around the corner.

Dogs, Lillian thought, a madhouse. She had once been to Bedlam, seen women in coarse white shifts, chained to the walls; men in strait-coats, urinating in their straw; folk shrieking and moaning, crying out, "Save me. Help me!"

A madhouse, she thought again. Unbelievable!

"*Allô* in there!" It was Jacques St Pierre banging through the door with a bottle of wine. She had not heard him knock. "Who was that girl? What did she want with you?" She watched him uncork the wine, and told him about the visit. He looked up, shocked, and then was quiet for a time. He said he couldn't believe what he'd heard about a madhouse. He pooh-poohed the integrity of the girl. "Someone else taking advantage, wanting money," he said, and poured the wine into two glasses.

She took a sip. For a time she believed Jacques's words. She had been duped by that girl. When he took her hand and looked hungrily into her face, she let him kiss her cheek.

But then she remembered the cherries. It had to be Roger. Only Roger knew about the significance of the cherries: where they had found them.

"No. I have to believe her." She pushed him away with her free hand. "He's in a madhouse—where? Yes, the village of Slinfold, the girl said. Slinfold. We must go there, seek it out—wherever it is. It was Henry Fuseli had him put there, I've no doubt of it. Can you find out where Slinfold is?"

Jacques sighed, and nodded. He drank his wine in a gulp, as though he needed the drink. He was a good man, Jacques; he loved her. He honoured her situation. He kept his distance.

"You will help me to find him. You will help to free him?" She put a hand on his arm, and let him place his hand over hers. "There are nasty dogs, the girl said."

Jacques was leery of dogs: he had been bitten once, he'd told her; he almost died. But he would do anything for her, would he not? His hand was trembling on her hand. "I will try," he said, "I will do my best. But if his poor mind is broken—"

"It is not broken," she said. "He remembered the cherries."

"Ah. But I cannot do it alone. I will need help. You must give me time."

She nodded. Time was all she could give him. And if he couldn't help, she would appeal to Mary Wollstonecraft—although the latter had seemed particularly abstracted of late. She withdrew her hand. Even if Roger were truly mad—and she was certain he was not—she would not be able to love Jacques, not in the way he wanted. Jacques was a friend. He could never be her lover.

HER scheme would work, Mary told herself as the chair bobbed and swung through the crowded streets. The truth was, Mary could no longer bear to live separately. She must see Henry every day. He had his faults, like this maniacal pursuit of young Roger Peale, but he had a superior mind; she could soften, bring about a change in him, couldn't she? And didn't her *Vindication* promote open friendship between men and women? Boys and girls in the same schools? And had not her hero Jean-Jacques Rousseau lived in a *ménage à trois* with his mistress Madame de Warens and another lover? Had he not written about a triangular relationship in his novel, *Julie*? In that novel, Mary recalled, Julie's friend Claire asks the tantalizing question: "Does the soul have a sex?"

No, Mary decided, it does not. The soul is androgynous. So her hopes were not unprecedented. And she was asking only for an intellectual intimacy.

Henry's carriage was in front of the house on Queen Anne Street—he was home. She stood on the steps, taking deep, ragged breaths. She ran her fingers through her wind-swept hair and pinched her cheeks. But her stomach was bloated; her feet stood frozen to the top step that was still damp from a rain shower. Overhead the sun came out for a moment and she was emboldened. She rapped the door knocker. No one appeared. She knocked louder and the door swung open; she nearly fell in. The maidservant caught her; she looked blankly at Mary, raised her eyebrows, and waited for Mary to speak.

"I am Mary Wollstonecraft, an authoress friend of Mr Fuseli," Mary said, and gained an inch with her foot. "I have come to see *both* Mr and Mrs Fuseli." The maid, a tall angular woman shaped like a bucket that someone had dented, did not move or seemingly care that an authoress was at the door. "Wait," she said, and put an outsized foot forward as if to say: the line is drawn here.

Mary waited; she rehearsed the speech she had prepared. The hallway was hung with Henry's paintings: a man in red contemplating a dead woman in white at his feet; portraits of Mrs Fuseli in curls and cap, her eyes discreetly down. Mrs Fuseli sleeping, in a black bonnet; an expressionless Mrs Fuseli warming her back at the fireplace; Mrs Fuseli with a switch, her breasts bare. In a corner, two paintings of nude madwomen: wild-eyed, wind and rain swirling about their heads—Mary felt herself to be one of them.

When Sophia Fuseli came out of a nearby door, Mary drew back.

"Yes?" The woman barely acknowledged her presence; Mary might have been a tradesperson, bearing smelly cheese or herring. She looked beyond for Henry, but he was nowhere to be seen. The words she had rehearsed went blank. She would have to improvise. "I have come," she stammered, "to make an offer. I—I wish to become an inmate of this house. I will be forthright. As I am above deceit, it is right to say that this proposal arises from the sincere affection which I have for your husband. For I find that I cannot live without—without the satisfaction of seeing and conversing with him daily."

When the wife made a guttural sound, Mary's voice rose: "I do not try to supplant your position as the legal wife of the flesh—not at all! I would be united to Henry by a mental affinity, a spiritual union. We—we have been friends. I am sure he would—yes!—he would approve this arrangement. If you would read Rousseau..." She stopped, feeling giddy—she put a hand on the wall to support herself.

Sophia Fuseli stood perfectly still, as though held hostage; her mouth hung open. Then she opened it wider to scream: a scream that penetrated Mary to the bone. She shouted towards the stairs: "Mr Fuseli! Who is this woman? What does she want?"

Mary widened her stance for balance. The woman was more obtuse than she had thought. "You know perfectly well who I am,

Mrs Fuseli. We have met on numerous occasions. And I have just explained what it is I want. I would help with the rent. We could travel together, to France—the three of us, to witness the Revolution. I have been invited by the Marquis de Condorcet to consult with him about female education. I would need your husband's help. I would need *your* help as hostess for the artists who would come to our soirées. I would—"

"My God!" cried Sophia Fuseli, holding on to the door handle. "*What* is this woman who would presume to enter my household? I am speechless." (She was decidedly *not* speechless, Mary noted.) "Leave. Get out of my house at once!" She pointed a tremulous finger at the front entrance. Her tight yellow curls shook with her indignation. Her breasts, Mary noted, drooped inside her pink dressing gown.

"Let me speak to your husband. He will understand. Henry Fuseli, where are you? I know you're here!" Mary cried. She ran towards the staircase. "Pray explain to your wife what I am asking, why—"

"You will *not* speak to my husband. You will *not* be part of my household. What? A spiritual union? Union?" the woman screeched, a lacy arm making dizzy circles in the air. "You will have no union. Now go. Annette?" she shouted at the maid, who was lurking by the entrance. "Show this arrogant woman out. And you, Miss Vindication," she bawled, pointing a finger at Mary. "Do not return. Never again! Never!"

The maidservant threw open the door and a gust of rain blew in. "Henry Fuseli," Mary cried, for there he was at the top of the stairs: "Pray explain to your wife, sir, why I'm here. Make her understand!"

But Henry turned away with a face the colour of a ripe raspberry; an upstairs door slammed. Slowly Mary's mind cleared and she understood that he was not going to help her. He was not going to interfere with his wife's decision. It was a betrayal of the most humiliating kind. When Mary had meant well, oh yes, she had meant well, had she not?

Outside the house, she stood on the top step, dazed. Behind her the door latched. Her legs and arms were logs. She could not move a foot or lift a finger. The wind blew off her blue hat and she watched it sail down the street as though it were herself being blown far, far from this house—out of London, out of England...

Henry had heard. He had heard everything and he had not come forward.

Her thoughts turned to the river. She felt herself divided, her heart at war with her reason. She was a compound of weakness and resolution. In her mind's eye, her feet moved down Regent Street, by Whitehall, past the Privy Gardens. She would go on and on, pushing against folk in her way—shops, carriages, horses, dogs, all a blur. She stumbled down Bridge Street, pausing only to put stones in her pocket. Poised on the edge, she stared a long time into the river depths.

Her life till now drifted through her head: her weaver grandfather, the six siblings, the pious mother, the abusing father. Her beloved Fanny, dead in Portugal; then the inhumane captain she'd forced to rescue the drowning French sailors. The frenzied flight from her sister's husband. The men who had betrayed her: Joshua Waterhouse, Neptune Blood, the poet George Ogle in Ireland. Henry Fuseli. Henry Fuseli. Henry Fuseli.

He would be glad to see her drown, would he not? "Out of my house!" his wife had said, and he allowed her to say it. He stood there like a pillar of salt and let her say it!

Should Mary give him the satisfaction of drowning herself?

Roger Peale's sensitive face glimmered in the shadows. Lillian Guilfoy's pleading eyes. Peale wronged, falsely accused, a victim like herself. With her gone, who would intercede for him? Who would help her sisters carry on with their lives and find posts as governesses? Take care of your siblings, her mother said on her deathbed, and Mary had done so.

No, she would not drown. She would not throw herself in front of a horse. She would not let Henry Fuseli persecute the young artist. She would not let him triumph over her. How many times had he mocked her work, her quest for the rights of woman? When a woman's life had as much value as a man's. Yes, by God!

Mocked. Ah. That was the word. And she had tolerated it.

She opened her eyes, wide. She would live. She would thwart Henry Fuseli. She would be dependent on no man. Why, she had almost lost herself, had she not? She would find Roger Peale. Precisely how, she did not know, but she would find him. She would enlist the help of her Dissenting friends. She would make Lillian Guilfoy pluck up her courage. She would pluck up her own courage. She would move forward until the end, be it bright or bitter.

She looked down at her feet where they stood, as if planted, still on the brick step of her betrayer's house. Slowly she moved one, then the other. She wiggled her fingers and thrust out her elbows. Then her whole body came alive and she ran down the steps, down the street to retrieve her blue hat where it was lodged in the crook of a tree limb. She slapped it back on her head and pinned it firmly on. When the hollyberry spray came free, she tossed it into a bush. She could feel the nerves coming alive in her neck, in her head.

She moved briskly towards home. She did not take a sedan chair. She did not care if her gown got muddy. She did not care if she stepped in dung.

She did not look back.

CHAPTER X.

I Am Going to a Madhouse

∾

ANNIE WAS at the tallow chandler's shop the next Tuesday morning, sent by the mistress for a pair of red candles. Red for Revolution, instructed Miss Mary, who had invited two men and a lady for tea. The lady's lover had been captured by a highwayman. Annie imagined the man coming to capture the lady as well, the lady falling in love with him and then having to choose between her old lover and the more handsome highwayman. Except that the lady would try to reform him so he wouldn't rob people anymore and that would be hard. And dull.

Some people, she thought, while the chandler waited on a large lady in a snug pink bonnet, you can't reform: like the head cook in the orphanage kitchen who didn't care if you were ill to the death but you still had to scrub the floor until you could see your sweaty face in it. Or a stuck-on-himself artist like Mr Fuseli, who let his wife shut the door on Miss Mary and did nothing to stop her. Though personally, Annie didn't think she should have gone there in the first place.

But the chandler had no red candles. "I can only dye one colour at a time," he grunted, "and today I did blue. So your mistress will have to take blue or white."

"I am her ward, not her servant, and she said they're meant to be red. Only red."

"Aye, young miss, you explained that, but then I explained I got no red, but only white and blue. So is it white or blue today? Or blue or white? Only two shillings, ten pence a pound. You won't find 'em cheaper anywhere in town."

"Neither," said Annie. "Miss Mary said to get red candles and that's what I'll do if I have to walk all over London to find them."

"That's what you'll have to do then, miss." The tallow chandler, a middle-aged man with wax in his thick black hair, winked at her, and turned back to his work. She saw his young apprentice laughing at her in the workroom beyond the counter. She thumbed her nose at him.

Anyway, she wanted to explore the town. The girls rarely got out of the Foundling Hospital except to walk in pairs under the big stick of one of the nurse-aides. Even then, if she dared to look around, a stick would smack her shoulder and make her stare straight ahead again.

She ran out into the warm spring air. The clatter of horses' hooves and the rumble of carts and carriages excited her. A group of ballad singers gathered on a corner, and though she didn't know the words, she joined in. Each new square was a symphony of bell-ringing collectors for the penny post, vendors of flowers and fish and quack medicines. She was thrilled with it all. London was a smelly romance of alleys, lanes, courts, and byways. She imagined her highwayman living in one of them, counting his stolen coins and timepieces, writing poems to his lady fair.

Annie had never seen London Bridge; she stopped a woman to ask the way. There had once been houses and shops on the bridge, torn down now she'd heard, but there might be vendors' stalls. Surely she'd find someone there selling red candles.

The woman didn't answer; she was going somewhere in a hurry. Next Annie came upon a young girl, hardly older than herself, sitting with her crippled legs stretched out, and between them, a basket for coins. "Point the way to the river, please," Annie said, and dropped a shiny pebble into the basket.

"You can smell it, can't you?" said the girl.

"No," said Annie. "Just tell me where it is," and the girl stuck out a thumb in a westerly direction.

Annie couldn't smell the river. There were too many other competing smells: onions, fish, horse dung, roasting chestnuts, rotting dogs—she took a wide berth around a terrier on its back with its four rigid legs straight up like it'd been trying to rise but couldn't. She took the direction of the thumb and moved on down the street, turned left, and when the next street ended in a cul-de-sac, she broke through a hedge and landed in someone's courtyard. She was still moving, she hoped, in the same direction.

"Out of my garden, young scamp!" a woman's voice cried out.

She started to run but a hand held her fast. "I'm looking for London Bridge," she said. "I been sent for red candles. If I come back without 'em Miss Mary'll be angry."

"And who, pray, is this angry Miss Mary?" the voice said. A pair of round raisin-coloured eyes set on top of a bulbous red nose stared her in the face.

"Why, the famous writer, Miss Mary Wollstonecraft. She's writing for *you*," Annie confided. "To give your rights back."

The woman gave a belly laugh. The fingers pinched her arm. "Well, I got my rights right here. And they don't include insolent girls tramping on me garden where young tulip shoots be coming up. Now get out afore I call a constable."

"How far to the bridge?" Annie yelled as she ran out of the yard and back to the street. But the woman only called after her with a curse.

After a time she found herself in Fleet Street. There, she knew from Miss Mary, was where the printers worked. One of them would have printed the romance her mother, Isobel, wrote. Her mother said she would give Annie a copy to read when she got bigger. But Annie had taught herself to read while she was still small, and when she got bigger her mother was killed. Her eyes filled with an overwhelming sense of loss. She pulled her locket to her lips and kissed it. She whispered the first lines of the hand-scrawled verse inside the locket. Swallowed the lump in her throat.

On impulse she turned into a print shop, and there was the man who had come to leave Miss Mary's manuscript. He was leaning over a table and laying paper on black type. "Whose book is that?" she asked. One day he might print her own book. She smiled at him, but he only grunted and went on with his work.

"I saw you at Miss Wollstonecraft's house. I'm looking for Mrs Frothingham's book." She tapped him on the shoulder. "It was called *Scarlette*. Did you print it or did you not?"

"If I did I've no copies of it here," he said without looking up. "Now leave and don't bother me again. If I was to tell Miss Wollstonecraft you were here, she'd give you a good hiding."

"She doesn't give hidings. She's kind, and patient. That is, she's patient when she has time and she's not writing or thinking."

This was true. If Annie interrupted her thoughts, Miss Mary would turn and look at her like she had no idea who this intruder was. She could be like that. Writers were an odd lot. Maybe Annie wouldn't be a writer after all.

On the way out of the shop she trailed her fingers along a shelf of books that had been published and sewn together. She saw a copy of *Vindication*, but not of *Scarlette*. It might have been another printer who did it. Or someone else in this place—for she spied a second man hunched over a table, and behind him a starved-looking apprentice. The older man looked like a teakettle, ready to spout boiling water, the way his bent neck was quivering as he set the type. She wouldn't want to be a printer either—too dirty. She passed a table strewn with papers. One of them caught her eye: *Life of a Bluestocking, A Portrait in Poems*. "By a Lady," it said. She peered at the first poem.

> *My mother was always nursing*
> *Her angers, my father away*
> *At his club, home late and cursing...*

Annie liked the way the lines looked on the page—not regular like a story but broken up in different lengths. Already this poem was telling a story. She flipped through the pages. A poem about a birdcage the poet kept in her chamber; a poem about her dog Jack.

> *'Tis with sad heart I leave you, child.*

She gave a shout. "It's *my* poem. Mine! The one my mother wrote for me!"

The teakettle printer swiveled his head. "Don't touch," he said.

"I just want to borrow it to read. I'll bring it back." She opened her locket, unfolded the poem, and took it to the first printer. "See? These are my mother's words. I can prove it. Look."

The printer's head swiveled towards her. He glanced at the tiny script, then stared her in the eye. It was as if he were swallowing her whole. "Mrs Frothingham had no child," he said. "Now put that down. It's not yet in print. It's not yours to take. She paid me to print it, were she dead or alive. And I do what I'm paid for." His face was turning crimson. He was angry. She would come here again with Miss Mary. The printer wouldn't dare glower at the authoress.

"I might be a poet myself one day," she said, stroking the poems.

The man came roaring down on her. A hairy hand picked her up by the collar like she was some mewling cat, carried her to the door, and dropped her in the street.

"And do not—do not, I repeat, let me see you in this shop again!" he croaked.

She had landed on her backside. She pounded the pavement with her fists. "You won't do that when I'm a famous poet! And don't think you'll be *my* printer. Oh no, not you! I'll see nobody takes their work to *you!*"

But the door of the print shop was shut tight. She was howling to the skies. A woman in a scarlet gown helped her up. "You be naughty, be you? Got no place to live? Well, I know a nice place you can live, oh 'deed I do. Come along, dearie, you can earn money for us, too; you got a pocky face, but a bit of powder—"

"I'm looking for London Bridge," Annie said. "Tell me where to find it, please. I need to buy red candles." What passed for sunlight in London was already on the wane. She had to get on or Miss Mary would have her revolutionary tea with no candles at all.

"Ah, we got candles in my establishment," the woman said, grasping her arm, pulling her along. "Come and see now. We do our work, dearie, by candlelight. You'll like that."

"No, I won't. I only read by candlelight, I don't work by it. I won't do your work!" She pulled loose and ran on; the cook at the orphanage had warned of such people. The woman called after her: "You'll not find London Bridge that way. That's Blackfriars Bridge."

She ran down the street anyway, and then left into another street, and right into another called Fish Street and suddenly there it was: the river. This time she could smell it. The Thames, teeming with boats and fish and people. And down in the fog: a bridge. She raced towards it, her heels kicking up like they weren't attached to her legs but had a life of their own. She was turning into a swift-moving cloud. She was free; she was near the river. One hot day the orphans had been taken to a pond, and an older girl taught her how to paddle her hands and churn her legs. She could jump in right now and she would stay afloat.

Or she could take a boat somewhere—she could go to China! She had read about China in a book at the hospital library. She would just visit though, she didn't want to be like those Chinese girls, their feet bound and shrunk. She sat a while on a grassy bank, and then lay back and closed her eyes to dream of China, and how she would go to free the Chinese females, and let them grow their feet so they could run.

In her dream she was fighting a Chinaman, telling him to unbind his woman's feet. He was trying to overpower her, grabbing her shoulders. "Open your eyes," he told her in her dream. "A female can't be telling men what to do. So don't interfere."

She yelled out her protest and a pair of rough hands *were* on her shoulder. "Quiet," a voice barked. "Come along quiet and you won't get hurt." The man yanked her up off her feet. Where was the dream now? Lost in the fog.

"I want to go home—let me go! I want—" And a hand clapped over her mouth.

WHEN her knock at the Store Street door was answered by the pouting maid, Lillian Guilfoy was greeted with a shout from the room above, and then the sound of running feet on the stairs. "Annie? Where've you been, Annie? I've guests coming for tea and only the nubs of white candles when I want red. You should be—"

The tall, robust figure of Mary Wollstonecraft came into view, the tousled, unpowdered hair. "Oh, it's you, Mrs Guilfoy. I'm so sorry. I thought—you see, the girl hasn't yet come home and it's almost four o'clock."

Lillian was sorry, too. She had come early before the other guests. She had important news for her new friend and wanted it savoured. "If you would rather I didn't stay…" She felt hurt. She was always close to tears these days, it seemed.

"No, no, I want you here. Pray sit down, I'm happy to see you. But forgive us, we've only a few candle stubs left."

Now Lillian had to sit down on one of the two uncomfortable parlour chairs—the cat was sprawled full-length on the sofa. Lillian had to listen to the story of how Mary had brought an orphan girl on loan, so to speak, from the Foundling Hospital. And how contrary the child was, yet bright and literate—though overly fond of sugar. "She's reading Samuel Johnson's dictionary now. She's already through *C*."

"How clever of her," Lillian said, "but—"

"I can't imagine where that girl is," an abstracted Mary went on. "She doesn't know London at all. They kept her so confined in that hospital. It's like having a dog on a chain and when it breaks loose it runs—but who knows what will happen to it? I'm such a worrier, I'm afraid. " She stared at the window as though that Annie person would suddenly climb through, red-faced and bleeding.

"I've news—about my fiancé," Lillian said—she had to speak out. "That's why I came early. I didn't want to say it in front of the others. To tell you we know where he is." Her voice shrank to a whisper. "He is in a madhouse."

"Oh!" Mary was sitting upright now. She had discovered her visitor. "A madhouse, you said? How dreadful!"

"A madhouse, yes. Where they put the insane. When my Roger is not mad at all, of course not! It's preposterous. Monstrous! It's Henry Fuseli put him there. Oh, I know you're friends, you and he. But you promised to help."

"And so I have been—at least trying. And Mr Fuseli is no longer my friend. But he wants your Roger in *prison*—not a madhouse! I'm told he has men out looking. Would he have men looking if he knew Mr Peale was in a madhouse?"

Lillian took a bite of the almond teacake Mary offered; she was confused. "Then why is he there?"

"That's what I'm asking," said Mary, with her mouth full of cake. "I want to help you find him, I truly do. Now tell me the story of this madhouse. What makes you think he's in one? What evidence have you?"

"Why, the cherries," cried Lillian, throwing up her hands, and she went on to tell the story, all in a breath. "And now Jacques St Pierre plans to go to this madhouse to find him. To try and free him. Slinfold—it's three or four hours south of here, they say." Lillian bunched her white kid gloves where they lay in her lap. She saw Mary watching her, then smoothed out the glove fingers, one by one.

"Madam?" Now it was the maidservant back in the room with two candle stubs. "Won't these green ones do?"

"No, Dulcie, no! Just go now, and gather up any red candle stubs you can find." She turned back to her guest. "Talleyrand will be here for tea, you see, and he prefers red. Red for revolution. He plans to leave England in two weeks—the king has quite ignored him. Your St Pierre will remain in England, I gather? To be of service to you?"

Lillian searched her friend's face for an opinion about Jacques, but finding none, went on. "Yes, who else can I count on? Monsieur St Pierre helped Roger escape Newgate, you know—this is our secret, remember—but then the pair met misfortune. The highwaymen are rife, they terrorize us."

"There you are then. It was the highwayman who put him in that madhouse. The proprietors would have paid him—I've heard of such horrors. Yet St Pierre managed to escape them, did he?"

What did that remark imply? Poor Jacques had had a terrible experience. But Mary was calmly munching her teacake—she was merely stating a fact. "Yes," Lillian said. "Fortunately. But he was hurt. We tried to call in a doctor, but he wouldn't have it."

"Ah," said Mary, "a stoic. But you don't want to go to that madhouse with him?" Mary was peering closely into her face as she spoke; it was disconcerting.

"With Jacques?"

"With your Jacques, yes. To find your fiancé? If it were my fiancé—though I've no use for one—surely I'd want to see him at once."

Now she was peering straight into Lillian's brain, it seemed, as though trying to sort out her guest's thoughts. Lillian supposed that Mary *would* go to the madhouse, and demand to see her lover, if she had one. Lillian had heard, well, things that Mary had said and done. That she had been dismissed as governess in Ireland for instilling revolutionary thoughts in her pupils' heads. That she had been intimate—only rumour no doubt—with her employer, Lord Kingsborough. And now, some said, with Henry Fuseli. A story was spreading about a demand to live with him and his wife. A *ménage à trois*? Lillian couldn't imagine such a thing!

Oh dear, how did one know what was true and what was false these days? She must not make assumptions. She was not wholly innocent herself, was she? She was shunned by certain ladies of society because of her natural child.

"We were speaking of St Pierre," Mary said.

"But he doesn't want me to come. It would be dangerous, he said. There are dogs, vicious ones, according to the girl who came with the cherries. Jacques was badly bitten one time, but he's going to brave them. Besides, he can't go at once. It might be as much as five days. Poor, dear Roger! Even then Jacques said he would need reinforcements to break down the madhouse walls, so to speak."

"If it were I," Mary began, and took a second cake; chewed it thoughtfully.

"Yes? You would go, see for yourself. But I want to go, you see. I do. I want my Roger freed. Though he won't be free, will he? With your Henry looking for his head?"

"He is not *my* Henry, I told you." Two spots of red appeared in Mary's cheeks.

"Oh. But at least out of that madhouse. Monsieur St Pierre has an acquaintance in the country who would hide him. But I can't go now, unprotected."

"Unprotected?" Mary said. "Oh dear. Then I'll go with you, yes. Surely the owners won't let the dogs loose on a pair of females. I've not been to Slinfold. It's in the Cotswolds, I believe? Shakespeare country?"

"South of here, I said. The Cotswolds are north."

"Ah. Right," said Mary. "But a madhouse! Where our own mad king might be headed, poor fellow. They say he recently mistook Queen Charlotte for a laundry maid." She smiled. She was looking quite handsome today in a new green muslin, with her brownish-auburn hair curling about her face.

Lillian bothered little with news of kings and queens. Now and then they rode about in carriages and people fell to their knees. To her, the monarchy was as remote as the stars. And might be doomed altogether, if the French had their way. Poor, dear Jacques.

One of her gloves dropped off her lap; she leaned down to pick it up, and wagged it bravely at the author. "When, then, shall we go?"

"Soon. This Thursday, or Friday. But first I must see to my Annie. I must know that she is home, safe. Though the girl might have gone to the Foundling Hospital to see an old friend—it's entirely possible. I'll walk out with you after we have our tea party. Though I've promised Joseph that I won't go out alone after dark—they say the watchmen are full of drink by then. But if we females sit at home all our lives out of fear, we might as well be dead. Don't you think?"

Lillian could not think at all at this point. "I am going to a madhouse" was the refrain running through her head. "I am going to the madhouse. I am going to find my true love and nothing can stop me." Her stomach heaved, she felt quite ill. And now she had pulled a hole in her glove. Her best pair of kid gloves.

It occurred to her that one did not need gloves to enter a madhouse. Who would care? Yet she had worn them on her one visit to Bedlam. And then was sorry when an inmate reached for her hand and almost pulled off her finger.

Lillian was waving away the offer of another cake when the door flew open and something in white burst past like a streak of lightning and raced through the sitting room. "Don't you never send me out after red candles again," the white streak squealed, "not ever, never!" and she dove onto the sofa. The sofa skidded across the wooden floor with her weight and rumpled the rug. The cat scampered upstairs, tripping the maidservant as she dashed into the room.

"What happened, Annie?" Mary cried, leaping up at once. "I only asked you to go to the tallow chandler's in Bedford Square. That was four hours ago," and the maidservant echoed, "You heard what Miss Mary said. Now stop that noise, Annie, and answer."

Lillian was too involved with her own thoughts to want to know what had happened to the girl. She was not feeling at all well. Black dogs growled in her head. She couldn't possibly stay to greet the other guests. "Pray excuse me, I am unwell," she shouted above the cacophony. "You can send me a note about you-know-what."

Mary wasn't listening; she was bent over the girl who was shouting about a "monster" who had "bruised" her shoulders, and feeding the girl cake to calm her. In fact, they were all shouting now: girl, maid, and mistress.

Lillian pulled open the door: the rasping noise struck a nerve. She had only wanted to ask Mary's advice; she had not expected Mary to offer to go to the madhouse with her. She did not have the courage that Mary had. She did not have the foolhardiness.

Yet she knew she must go. For her fiancé's sake.

"I am going to a madhouse," she repeated to herself as she moved out into the twilight. Her eyes were suddenly blinded, as if she were stepping over the edge of the world. "I am going to a madhouse. I am going to a madhouse. I am going to a mad—"

"Quite daft, poor thing," she heard one passerby say to another as she went to flag down a sedan chair.

Gracious heavens! Were they talking about *her*?

THURSDAY morning, and the girl was in the sugar again. It was infuriating; there was scarce enough for Dulcie's tea, and Dulcie was so looking forward to a leisurely dish of tea while the mistress was away. Miss Mary might be gone for a few hours or a few days, she'd said, when she went flying off at dawn that morning with Mrs Guilfoy, the pair play-acting like they were going to visit a friend in the country when Dulcie knew they were not. She had heard the discussion. They were going to a *mad*house to find Mrs Guilfoy's fiancé. If they weren't careful, they'd be locked up in it themselves.

She tiptoed up behind the girl and clapped a hand on her shoulder. Annie cried out and the sugar sprayed the kitchen table. At least the girl didn't try to lie. She was caught in the act. "So?" the girl said, and glared at Dulcie. "I'm entitled. I could've been killed by that man. Or worse."

"We can all be killed at any time in this lawless town. Today, tomorrow, next year," Dulcie said. "Now go fold those clothes. That's what you were told to do. You don't see the mistress sitting lazily around just because she was pounced upon, do you?"

Nevertheless, Dulcie did not like what was going on. Miss Mary twice attacked and now, maybe, the girl. Though she had heard two different stories from Annie, and each time things got blacker. First, the man who accosted her wore a grey coat and black breeches and silver-buckled shoes. In the next version he wore black boots and a black hooded cloak that went down to his knees. When Dulcie confronted her with the contradictions, Annie said, "I misremembered. It was a black cloak, aye—with a dragging hem. His black boots had yellow tassels on top. And he hurt me something fierce when he grabbed me. He looked like a killer, all right. I'll find him. I want him caught!"

Frankly, Dulcie didn't believe a word the girl said. All that part about how she threw grit in his eyes and then knocked him backwards and ran, screaming for help, and a passerby looked for the man but he'd vanished. It was all too much. How could a half-grown girl knock down a full-grown man? No, no, the girl just wanted an excuse for not getting the red candles. "And where is the money she gave you to buy them? Tell me that now," Dulcie said. But the girl just walked away with her pitted chin in the air.

Dulcie hoped Miss Mary would come home soon. The mistress had given instructions for the girl to stay indoors while she was gone, and that meant misery for Dulcie.

In any event, she planned to look through those papers she'd taken from Mrs Frothingham's desk. They might shed light on what was going on. Dulcie couldn't sleep with a murderer loose in town. Especially after reading that note about Bluestockings Beware. Dulcie wanted the man caught and hanged.

First, though, she would have to move the bowl of sugar, and sweep up before the ants came crawling. She would put it on the highest shelf where the girl couldn't see it, much less get into it. It was a terrible thing to steal costly sugar, never mind what the girl had or hadn't been through. Dulcie had been sent by Mr Johnson to care for Miss Mary, and that much she was going to do. Dulcie had a conscience.

"There now," the girl said, looking cross. "The clothes are folded." (*More or less*, Dulcie thought.) "I'm going upstairs to read. My mother wouldn't have made me do all this hard work. My mother wanted me to learn to be a lady."

"Is that why your mother put you in that Foundling Hospital? So you could learn to be a lady?" Dulcie said.

Then was sorry she'd said it when the girl exploded into tears.

"Here," Dulcie said, thumping up the stairs behind her, her own eyes blinking. A plague on the girl, for making her feel bad. "Here's a lump of sugar. But it's the last one. I'm hiding the bowl where you won't find it. Just stop feeling sorry for yourself. Or Miss Mary will hear about it when she gets back from her madhouse."

"WHEN will we get there?" young Tommy asked. They had been journeying no longer than twenty minutes and already, Mary saw, the boy was bored. Lillian had objected to the idea of her child coming along, but Mary persisted. A child would lessen suspicion, she had argued. There was nothing like a mother-father-son embrace to melt even the stubbornest of madhouse hearts.

"We'll get there when we get there," Mary told the boy. "Don't you want to see your mama's Mr Peale? He'll soon be your daddy, you know."

"Yes, but when?" the child asked. "He was going to take me boating on the river." Mary drew a deep breath. Did she ever want to be a mother? Lillian had dressed him in a royal blue waistcoat and breeches; he looked like a miniature adult. Children, Mary felt—and had indeed, written—ought to wear simple smocks and shifts so they could better exercise their limbs.

They were halfway to Slinfold, following the old Roman road, when Lillian began to complain. The coach seat was uncomfortable: "I'll not sit down again for days after this," she moaned. She was dressed all in yellow: ruffled, laced, and feathered, her hair tortured into a beehive—she had paid for a hairdresser. To go to a madhouse? Mary asked herself.

Then the young woman began to have doubts. "Are we doing the right thing? What about those dogs? Oh, I knew we shouldn't have brought Tommy." She pulled the boy close; he stared at Mary out of large, moist eyes, and then, let loose, ran the iron wheels of his toy carriage over her foot.

"How much longer?" he asked, and Mary sighed.

"Just a bit, not far now," Lillian said. She raised a questioning eyebrow at Mary.

"What will we do when we get there? Have you thought of what we'll say to the owners? Where we will take Roger afterward?"

"I told you, I have a plan. Just let me do the talking." Although Mary's plan, if anything, was no plan. She would simply meet the owners, and do and say what seemed appropriate. Mary had confidence in her ability to meet confusion head-on and still remain (more or less) rational. Had she not successfully rescued her sister Eliza? Well, no, not if you considered the baby left behind in the mêlée. The baby named after herself: Eliza *Mary* Frances. She would like to have known that child.

But she *had* fended off Alfred de Charpentier and arrived safely home by using her wits. She had sent Dulcie with the money for the lace she'd taken from the fabric shop; the purse she had left in the coach had mysteriously reappeared on her doorstep—at least the impecunious Frenchman was honest. She was pleased with the way she had handled the situation: fighting off the count, then bringing the shopwoman to trust her. The list of her shortcomings was a bit shorter, perhaps.

Though she had to admit: a small voice inside was always undermining her confidence. In truth, she was apprehensive about this madhouse.

They were riding through a wood about an hour and a half out of London, when Lillian shuddered and drew the window curtain. "I hope we won't meet a highwayman,"she whispered.

"Highwayman?" the boy said, looking thrilled and worried at the same time.

"Of course, we won't meet a highwayman," Mary said. "It's much too early in the day." Although she was relieved when another coach came rattling past, the coachmen cheerfully hailing one another. Be brave, she told herself, already sorry she had taken on the adventure, what with the impatient child and the madhouse ahead. She hoped this place would be "civilized," like Bedlam, where the attendants were ready to rescue visitors from the clutches of the insane.

The rest of the four-hour journey was long and cramped, chilly and uncomfortable. But when they reached their destination, life seemed quite ordinary. Slinfold was simply a quaint little place with a village green, a public house called Niblett's Red Lyon, and a small stone church from which a group of chattering women was departing. Lillian was cheered by the sight; Tommy was already standing up in the coach, pushing on the door.

They alighted, rearranging their dress, Mary fumbling in her purse for a coin to give the coachman for the public house. They would have a late breakfast and then take the carriage to the madhouse. If indeed there were big dogs there, why horses were bigger. And they had the coach to retreat to.

"Madhouse?" the waiting girl said when Mary made her enquiries. "Bludgeon's Madhouse?" she repeated, her pencilled eyebrows set in a frown.

"Is there more than one?" Mary asked, alarmed. Her plan now was to explain that there had been a mistake, that Roger was as sane as herself; then, after an impassioned embrace between man and fiancée, she would whisk him away.

"Depends, miss, on how you look at it," the waiting girl said, and flounced off to attend another customer.

Lillian was quite gay as the driver handed her back into the coach and they jolted off in the direction of Bludgeon's Madhouse. Tommy had filled his belly with pigeon pie and promptly fallen asleep. Mary alone was left to worry.

When the coach jolted to a stop in front of a grey three-storey house with three black dogs squatting on the front steps, she regretted the whole adventure. Lillian squealed with fright. "I want to go home," Tommy wailed. "Take me home."

"Wait here in the coach, both of you," Mary ordered, as she climbed out. An earsplitting scream issued from an upper-storey window and she stood still; then moved cautiously forward. She heard low growls from the porch steps, then a deep-throated barking. As she inched ahead she saw that the barks were coming from a single dog, crouching between two dogs made of black marble. The one live dog was chained.

Courage rose again in her throat. She mounted the steps, staying well to the right. The chained dog lunged at her; she almost slipped sideways off the steps to avoid it. The front door opened and a large woman stood there, filling it with her bulk. She was dressed in black, with a pair of black feathers in the ruin of her hair—Mary pictured a giant raven, ready to swoop down on its prey.

"State your purpose and if I don't like it, be off with ye. Stop that noise, Tiger." The dog gave two more woofs; then, cowed by the woman's eye, lay mute.

"I am Mary Wollstonecraft," Mary began, "an authoress, from London. You might be acquainted with my publisher, Joseph Johnson. I'm looking for—"

"Speak plain," the woman interrupted. "Or I unleash the dog."

Mary began again, telling the story of Roger Peale, but omitting the fact that he was a fugitive. When she had done, she waved to Lillian and Tommy to emerge from the coach. "Those are Mr Peale's loved ones—his fiancée's little boy who has no other father. You can see, can you not, that it has all been a terrible mistake? A painter, a young artist on the verge of public acclaim. Would you inhibit a young man's creativity?"

The woman held up her hands and grinned through her blackened front teeth. "Why, you're too late then, dears. Just yesterday they come and took Mr Peale away for a visit. We was sorry to see him go just then. We was going to have him repaint our house, we was. Make it look more respecable-like."

"What are you saying?" Lillian ran forward to confront the woman. "Who took him away? It was Henry Fuseli, I know it!" she cried, and covered her face with her hands.

Mary had come too far to be thwarted now. "Let us in, please. We would see for ourselves. Mr Peale has no one else who would come for him. He has only his fiancée. Now open up, I said."

"Come on in then, dearie, and see for yourself. No, not you," she said to Lillian and the boy. "You're too well dressed. There might be a speck of dirt on the floor. My charwoman don't see so good." The matron gave a nervous laugh.

"Mr Peale, can you hear me?" Lillian shouted. "Answer me, love!" But the door slammed in her face. Mary heard it latch.

The front room was furnished with a single hard chair, a small table, a wooden bench painted a dull green. On the table was a pottery vase with paper roses—so dusty their colour was not discernible. A square grated window hung in the wall above the table.

"Who brought Mr Peale here?" Mary asked.

"Why, his brother, that's who," the woman said. "Looked just like the patient, he did."

"Mr Peale has no brother."

"Ooh, you don't say? How was I to know? I can't go crawling inside folks' heads, can I now? He had papers with him. This way, dearie, you'll want to see for yourself he's gone." She pointed at a set of crooked stairs. Mary heard voices; a man and woman came tramping down, the man leading the woman, and she pulling back.

"I don't want to go with you, sir! Better this madhouse than living with you."

"But Joanie," the man said, "Joanie. I signed the papers, I did. You're free to come wi' me. Come on then, girl." He was a short, densely pockmarked man of middle age with a broad chest and arms. Grey hairs grew like withered weeds on his neck and jaw.

The woman held on to the banister. "And you'll just bring me back here again, you know that. Now go and leave me!" The man yanked on her arm and the woman came tumbling down the stairs. Just in time he righted her again.

Seeing Mary, he said, "Mad as hops, she be. Try to help her out and no thanks from her." He gave his wife another yank. This time she gave in. Mary thought of a rag doll she'd had as a child: you made it sing and dance, stand up and lift its arms—but then it fell slack, limp on the ground, just a rag after all.

"Leave her," Mary said. "She doesn't want to go with you. I'll find you a home," she told the woman, who was gazing up with huge liquid eyes.

"Who be you?" the woman whispered.

"Why, an authoress, she say," said the matron. "Curtsy, dear, to the authoress. She come to take away our dear Mr Peale. But too late, oh my, he's already gone. Took hisself off with relations, he did. Not to return, mayhap. Who knows?"

"Joanie's me wife," the man growled at Mary. "She belongs to me."

"Belongs to you!" Mary said hotly. "Why—"

"Sure she does, sure," the matron interrupted, and patted him on the back. "All nice and legal. We'll go in now and sign the papers. You," she told Mary, speaking harshly, "upstairs and first room to the left. Go see for yourself, your man's not there." She scurried to a door off to the right, ushered the husband into it and ordered the woman to "wait there." Mary saw a desk strewn with papers; a second black dog, chained to the leg of a table.

"You're Mr Peale's sweetheart," the wife whispered when her husband went through the door. She clutched Mary's arm. "He's gone all right, I don't know where. The matron was angry, she said it was him broke a hole between our rooms—when it was already there! I tried to tell her that but she wouldn't listen."

"Who? Who took Mr Peale?"

"I can't tell you that, miss. I only knew they took him from the room. I did hear the matron say he had to learn his lesson. Who knows the truth? They always lie to us. But maybe he's in a better place—he wanted out of here so bad. I was to help him but my husband didn't come. Not till today and now I don't care. I just don't care." She slumped down on the single chair and dropped her chin in her hands.

"Papers all signed and proper," the matron said, coming back into the room. Mary was reminded of a large sack on legs, filled with rubbish. "Go along now, missus. Your husband be good to ye, he promised, eh, sir?" She winked at Mary and Mary scowled.

The man took his wife's arm. "We'll have a good supper, Joanie. I got peas and rabbit pie. I shot the rabbit meself." He looked meaningfully at his wife. "Come on now, I got the waggon waiting back o' the house."

"Come with *me*, madam. You can," Mary called after the wife. Yet the woman only shook her head helplessly, and allowed herself to be hustled off. The matron gave Mary a nudge toward the door, but Mary eluded her and bounded up the stairs.

She would see for herself.

CHAPTER XI.

Curiosity Killed More than the Cat

༄

THE GIRL had been driving Dulcie to distraction, dancing about the house with a chair cushion, boxing with the cat, then flopping down on the sofa to read aloud some dribble about a foppish rogue who was ogling a young girl. She was doing it just to annoy Dulcie. So when she begged to go outside: "Just down the street a little," Dulcie gave in.

"Go then," Dulcie said. "But see you don't go more'n two streets in either direction. Or I'll tell Miss Mary and she'd be angry with both of us. Here's tuppence. There's a sweet shop in Russell Square. Buy yourself some almonds."

"Almonds get in my throat," the girl said. "They make me cough."

"Whatever you like then. Be it almonds or walnuts, I don't care. Just go. Go and be back by noon hour."

"You know I don't have a timepiece."

"Then look at the sky. The sun'll be overhead at noon."

"There's cloud. It's looking to rain."

"Go," Dulcie cried, "just go. Go!" Tossing her head, the girl went. The door slammed.

Now it was Dulcie's turn to dance about the house. She did a reel across the room, facing an imaginary partner. He wore a scarlet waistcoat with tiny pearl buttons that caressed her cheek as the pair whirled about. They danced up one side of the room and down the other, up and down, up and down. It didn't take long, the room was small. Finally exhausted—she hadn't slept well the night before because of a rat knocking about inside her wall—she fell back on the sofa and took a nap.

When she woke she looked at the mantel clock and saw it was

almost noon. The girl should be home soon. The fire was dying, the floor dusty. A mouse skittered across the raggedy blue-flowered rug Miss Mary treasured; it had been woven by her grandfather. Dulcie gave the impudent mouse a swish with her broom and it disappeared into a hole beside the fireplace.

Half-past-twelve donged and no Annie. Let a creature off the rope and it was gone. A disobedient child, aye. So then. Let her take her lumps. Dulcie trotted down to the kitchen to butter a hunk of bread and heat water for a dish of tea. Then trudged up two flights to her garret chamber.

She sat in the small rocking chair that Mr Johnson had lent her and sipped the tea. She chewed the white bread and butter slowly—it was sweet butter she'd bought at the marketplace. Dulcie wasn't up to making butter herself, all that churning! And Miss Mary just shrugged when Dulcie added butter to the list of victuals to buy—she liked a little butter on her bread. Dulcie was lucky to have such a distracted mistress, her friends said. Dulcie wasn't sure about that.

She dropped to her knees to pull the hatbox of papers out from under the bed. She had been born with a generous measure of curiosity. Too much, the parish nurse would say, making her go lie on her bed when she asked too many questions. When Mr Johnson rescued her from the cotton mills at age sixteen, he sent her first to work at William Blake's house over in Lambeth, where Mrs Blake did her housekeeping stark naked—Dulcie never knew where to look. When the latter dismissed her for getting blood on one of her prize pieces of Belgian lace (she'd pricked her finger on a pin attached to it), Mr Johnson sent her to live with Miss Mary, and it turned out to be a good match.

Curiosity was a good thing to have, the mistress said. Dulcie consoled herself with that thought when guilt washed over her now and again for taking the bluestocking's papers. She'd taken them on impulse, and now—well, what could she do but read them? And if she found anything that might relate to a killer, she'd give them to Miss Mary, who would know what to do. Miss Mary would praise her for this, wouldn't she?

But curiosity could get one in trouble, too, and that was Annie's problem. Lord knows how much *she'd* read in the papers Dulcie was spreading out now on the floor. She found a birth certificate that announced the birth of one Isobel Jane Amelia Frothingham on January 22, 1748: of Henry and Amelia Frothingham. Dulcie counted on her fingers. That would make the bluestocking four-and-forty years at her death. Four-and-forty! She had heard the lady tell another lady she was four-and-thirty. For good reason, all those jars of powder and milk of roses on her dressing table.

She pulled out a rough sketch of a young Isobel's family: Mother in a hooped gown and feathery bonnet, father in boots and cocked hat, and Isobel squatting between them with a sly smile—a spoiled child, to be sure. But then in the corner, a thin boy with his tongue hanging out, looking on. Who was he? A little brother? Cousin? Servant boy? If so, why was he in the picture? A neighbour boy maybe, or a ward. And why the tongue hanging out—was he hungry? Feeble-minded?

She slapped the picture face down with the birth certificate and pawed through sketches of waterfalls, houses, trees, flowers, birds, and geese. Then three more rough sketches of the same boy but each time with a frown or pout or some distortion of the face. He would've been a thorn in her side! She flipped through boring school reports and notes from teachers in Miss Harley's School: *Isobel Frothingham sang a lovely duet Friday last with Miss Jane Owen.... Isobel wrote a fine essay entitled Five Things a Proper Lady Should Not Do.* Dulcie never found out what the five things were because the essay itself was missing. And who cared, anyway?

Next Dulcie turned up a marriage certificate. Aha! it was in 1766, to one Mr Charles MacBride. Odd she hadn't taken his name. Too early for him to be the father of Annie. And sure enough, a death certificate in 1768: *Dead from a pistol shot,* it read. A duel? Dulcie wondered. If Miss Isobel was sorry, there was no sign. No trace of a tear on the document. But a copy of Charles MacBride's will said she was his full heir, there being no offspring. Five hundred pounds, two dozen books, six paintings, and a gold carriage-and-four went to Mrs Charles MacBride. So she *had* taken his name! But changed back to her maiden name—legally or illegally, and kept the Mrs. All part of being a freethinking bluestocking, Dulcie supposed. Nothing *she'd* ever want to be.

There were drafts of poems written to various lovers—including the man, now dead, who had set her up in the Grosvenor Square house, Miss Mary said, and left Mrs Frothingham his fortune. There were the packets of love letters Dulcie had earlier sampled. *Ma belle Isobel*, one began from Alfred de Charpentier, *You are driving me to distraction. Je t'adore! When I saw you last night I thought an angel had lighted on my chair.* Dulcie gagged.

She made her way through several documents relating to one Ann but with no father's name. *My child*, one began in the blue-stocking's hand, like it had been an immaculate conception. Aha! Was young Annie the French count's child? Mrs Frothingham had been in Paris, she'd said.

Mr Ashcroft's letters were mostly about money: how she would have clothing and apartments to rival the queen's, if he could but have a single night with her. In one letter he threatened to kill himself if she wouldn't have him.

Or kill *her*? Dulcie wondered. Miss Mary must see this.

Now she was growing weary of fumbling through papers. Dropping them back in the hatbox, she saw two pages clipped together. A legal-looking document—maybe a will? It began, in Miss Isobel's handwriting, with all the fancy words Dulcie had to sound out slowly, like they taught in parish school: *I, Isobel Jane Amelia Frothingham, of the city of London, Kingdom of Great Britain, and being of legal age and in full possession of my faculties, do ordain this my last will and testament. I bequeath to God a soul polluted with sins I have not always regretted.*

No doubt about that *polluted*, Dulcie thought. She glanced at the second page but saw no signature. Probably Miss Isobel meant to see a solicitor but got busy with her social affairs. Who would she want to leave her money and house to? Miss Mary had talked of some fat cousin who might want to claim everything.

Her knees were hurting: she needed to stand. Keeping out the will for further reading, she stowed the hatbox under the bed, and went downstairs. She would read the will whilst she finished her tea.

Hearing a knock, she dropped the will on a side table and opened the door to—speak of the devil—Mr Edgar Ashcroft, all in black and purple, like an aubergine. He looked right through Dulcie, like she was part of the wallpaper, and walked in. "Where is she?" he demanded of the ceiling.

"At a madhouse," Dulcie said, and then bit her lip. "I mean to say, she's gone off with a friend to visit the Bedlam, you know, to leave a gift of charity. Those poor folk in there need all the help they can get. And I don't think she wants to see *you*."

"She will when she hears what I have to offer," he said, "and it will not be a *ménage à trois*."

Touché, Dulcie thought. Everyone, it seemed, knew about the scandal. Dulcie could have told Miss Mary it wouldn't work to move in with Mr Fuseli's wife, but the mistress didn't ask Dulcie's opinion.

"Tell her I ask only for a hearing. If she then refuses, why, I shall fade out of her life." He took a step backward, though he could hardly fade away with that big belly and the two protruding teeth in the center of his grin. He smelled of perspiration and scent, and she stepped back herself.

"By the by," he went on, "I found this on your doorstep—someone must have left it." He tossed a wrapped packet at the sofa. It missed. When Dulcie made no effort to pick it up he stooped, grunting, fell heavily to one knee, and slapped it down.

"Thankee," said Dulcie, and waited for him to take his leave.

"I saw your orphan girl," he said, struggling up from his knee, "you might want to know that. She was in Eastcheap on Fish Street Hill, near London Bridge. Lot of young rogues about, ne'er-do-wells. I recognized her from the red hair. She looks like her mother." He frowned, like that was to be held against her. "Everyone knows now that she belonged to Mrs Frothingham," he told Dulcie. He coughed. "So. You might want to go and fetch her. Young girls oughtn't be in London alone. Someone could take advantage. Fact—I saw her talking with a fellow. Not so young, neither." He glared at Dulcie as though it was her fault the girl had gone there.

"I sent her for a packet of pins. There's a shop near there has good sharp ones."

Dulcie was lying, but she didn't want him blaming her. Nor Annie neither. She disliked this pompous man in his ratty chin whiskers and old-fashioned bobwig and coat with trimmed sleeves the colour of vomit. He took a dandy-like pose, one foot behind the other, and gazed at the ceiling with a curled lip, like he'd seen a worm crawling beneath him (herself) and didn't care to look at it.

"You'll find Miss Mary at the madhouse," said Dulcie, and made a monkey face.

He growled, and turning on his heel, slammed the door. "Good riddance!" she shouted after, though he was out of hearing.

A moment later a knock came at the door and she ignored it, until she heard Cyrus Hunt's voice, announcing he'd come from St Paul's Churchyard. "A book from Mr Johnson," he called out. "He says to tell your mistress he wants a write-up for the *Analytical Review*."

"Put it down," she said, letting him in, and pointing to a parlour chair.

She surveyed the packet Mr Ashcroft said he'd found. She wouldn't be surprised to learn he'd brought it himself, only pretended to find it on the doorstep. It was probably a chocolate sweet to try and woo the mistress with. She picked it up with her handkerchief and dropped it into the hall waste bucket, where it made a clunking sound.

As for that girl Annie, she, Dulcie, was not about to go looking. In Eastcheap with a not-so-young fellow indeed!

"Tell her he wants the review by next week," the printer said, and let himself out the door without a goodbye.

She thought she would take a walk, down to the tallow chandler's where she might run into Elbert, the apprentice, who would now and then sneak a candle stub into her pocket. Not that she particularly liked him. His nose was a beak, his ears stuck out like teacups. But it was nice to be noticed. A little teasing now and then never hurt a girl. It lent experience for when the real love entered one's life. If it ever did. The butcher's boy had come calling two or three times, but Dulcie had finally dispensed with him. Like Miss Mary, she seldom ate red meat.

The rain had all but stopped, she saw when she looked through the window; a hazy sun was pushing through. She left a key for Annie under a flat stone on the top step. If she hurried, she might see a rainbow.

And there it was: layers of red, orange, yellow, green… Like a painting the Lord hung in the sky. Dulcie wasn't much for religion, but *Someone,* she felt, made that rainbow. A stout woman carrying a squirming sack and a squalling baby bumped into her, not apologizing, and when she looked up again, the rainbow was already starting to fade.

It was like dying mothers, stolen paintings, runaway girls.

Here one moment, gone the next. Now there was only the empty smoky-blue sky overhead, the sun a bleeding circle so far above her stretched neck she couldn't begin to imagine the distance.

In spite of herself, she found her feet heading for London Bridge. She must find the girl before the mistress got home from her madhouse. Or else she'd have a tongue-hiding!

THE madhouse matron had lied. There *was* a man in the room on the left. Mary saw him through the slit in the door. He was sitting on the bed, dressed in rags; his right leg was chained to a spike in the centre of the room.

"Mr Peale!" she cried, and the man swiveled his head. His face was a waterfall of wrinkles, his chin whiskers grey and straggly. One arm had been cut off below the elbow. Had the artist been tortured, so radically altered?

The man pulled himself up off the bed; a fierce eye peered out at her. "I be Geoffrey Wineapple," he said. "Me daughter-in-law put me here—she be a sempstress. Said I took up too much room in her house. Help me, miss. Help me out o' here."

A chorus of voices set up along the hall. *Help me, help me. Set me free-ee... I'm Mary Magdalene. I saved our Lord. Tell 'im to save me. Save me-ee.*

"Don't listen to 'em, miss," the matron called up, sounding irritable. "Go home now. There's naught for you to do in this place. Your Mr Peale's not here, I said. Now go."

Mary was not ready to leave. Not yet. She required answers. "Do you always believe the people who bring in the poor devils?" she called down. "Like that woman who just left—who will be back in, she says, at her husband's whim? *Who* said Peale was mad when he was not? Do you have a conscience? Do you have a heart?"

The woman laughed. "Me husband and me be running a business, that's what. I be Mrs Bludgeon. I don't go looking for hearts. They pays their money, dearie, and we takes 'em in."

"Who put him in here? Who?"

"His brother, I told ye! Or claimed to be. Doctor's orders, he said."

"Would a doctor allow you to chain him up like that?"

"Policy, dearie, policy. We can't have 'em go running about, knocking the attendants down, can we now?"

Mary would write this into her sequel to *Vindication*: how a husband could lock up his wife at whim in a madhouse. How a daughter-in-law could incarcerate her father-in-law because she wanted his room for a sewing room. She would speak to Mr Johnson. She would engage a body of men and come back to rescue these forgotten folk.

Someone pinched her elbow; she was face to face with a toothless woman, dragging a long chain. "Too late," the woman squealed. "Too late, we all be doomed. We be going straight to hell." The mouth was a perfect circle, the flesh inside seemed grey and rotting.

Had Mary met up with one of the Three Fates? Alarmed, she ran down the stairs.

Mrs Bludgeon stood there grinning. "You see? You see why we're here, do you? You want to save that one, eh? Let 'er loose— trotting about, pinching folk?"

Mary didn't know, her head was spinning. She was suddenly afraid, as though the matron would see through her, detect a streak of madness and fetter her feet. She thrust through the front door and heard it, mercifully, lock behind her.

Lillian ran to grab Mary's hands. "Mr Peale? Was he there after all? Speak to me. Tell me, Mary, where is my fiancé?"

In hell somewhere, Mary wanted to say. But Lillian was so desperate, so needy, so desiring of his safety, she said only: "I think the matron was telling the truth. Someone took him away. I don't know whom. A relative perhaps. He may well be back home, she said."

"A relative, you think? He never spoke of such a person, but perhaps..."

"Or he escaped, and she didn't want to tell us."

"Escaped? Oh! And he might be home this very moment!" She ran toward the carriage. "Hurry, Mary. We must go home." She turned back. "Or perhaps he does have a cousin somewhere. I'll find out. It might be he or she who has him. Do you think so? Could it be?"

Mary was perspiring head to toe. Her skin was pinched under the whalebone stays. Why did folk think she had all the answers? When the truth was, she had none at all. She had only the questions. "I don't know," she said, "I just don't know."

She was struck with the magnitude of all she did not know about people. Selfishness, jealousy, envy, greed—noxious traits she had known in her own family, in her small circle of acquaintances;

traits she had read about in Shakespeare's tragedies of kings and queens. Traits she found even in herself at times, sad to say. But to find them everywhere, amongst all the classes... It was like a boulder dropping down on her head, briefly illuming her brain, her reason, then crushing her into bits. She thought of the Parisians, rising up against the nobility. Were the poor better at heart than the rich? Should she judge rich and poor equally?

She could not speak at all now. She could only wring her hands. She was like her mother in the power of her feckless father: he, bankrupt, contemplating yet another uprooting. Another failure in farming or whatever ill-suited occupation he turned his hand to. And for which he would covet the little money she earned from her books.

HER London house looked like the kingdom of heaven after that madhouse. It was already evening. Mary was spent, but oddly exhilarated. The daffodils were out in her small garden—she had come out of a madhouse, where it was forever winter, into spring. She had not found Roger Peale, but she had a new cause to write about—when, or if, that is, she would find the peace of mind to write. She fumbled for the key in her purse, barged into the house, and stumbled against the waste bucket that Dulcie insisted on keeping in the hallway; the bucket tipped, expelling its contents on the carpet. She called for Dulcie, but no reply. She called for Annie. "Answer me, both of you!"

Still no reply. She supposed they were out together. She had made Dulcie promise not to let the girl out by herself and she had to trust the maid. She had to have faith in the human heart—in Something, Someone higher. But with all that had been happening of late: the strangling of Isobel Frothingham, the Fuseli fiasco, the madhouse, she was beginning to have serious doubts. What just God would allow such perfidy?

She threw down her cloak and hat and flopped onto the sofa. Her whole body ached from that miserable coach. Her ears still rang from Tommy's piercing shouts and Lillian's outcries about Fuseli who, the young woman now feared, might have hired someone to return Roger to Newgate Prison. "Speak to Mr Fuseli, I beg you," she'd wept over and over, as though Mary were a magician and not the spurned female in a hopeless love triangle.

Mary could not speak of that triangle to Lillian: it was too mortifying. It was all over town now. Mary had shrunk in mind and spirit from the betrayal. Even her physical stature had diminished; returning from Lillian's house, she had seen herself reflected in a window—and yes, she was noticeably shorter. Let Lillian seek out Roger Peale's relatives who might have taken her man. Though, in retrospect, Mary felt that Roger might still be in that madhouse, hidden from her in some closed-off attic or cellar. Who knew? Mary didn't. For now she was done with madhouses.

But she couldn't just lie here. For one thing, her stomach was upset. Her body needed to eliminate. Our minds are prisoners of our bodies, she reminded herself; they are adjuncts to the flesh and bones. She pushed herself up off the sofa. She would use the necessary down in the cellar; for some reason she was shivering. She went back to the hall wardrobe for a shawl, and discovered the tipped-over bucket. Among the contents was a packet addressed to her, unopened. Something important perhaps, from the publisher, or the printer—how lax of Dulcie to let it fall into the waste! She dropped it on the sofa and went down to the cellar.

Squatting there, she contemplated the waste in her own life. The old guilts and humiliations pushed up again, even in daylight: Eliza accusing Mary of losing her child. Over and over Mary saw Sophia Fuseli, ordering her out the door—the loud, blond fury of her; Henry on the stairs, cold and silent. (Was he really jealous of Mary's new fame as Lillian Guilfoy had suggested?) She saw her sisters, unable to find and keep suitable employment as governesses. Her brother James, wanting to be a naval lieutenant, but with no funds to equip himself, awaiting a hand-out. The youngest, Charles, dreaming of America, but with no money or occupation. It was all laid on Mary's doorstep.

And here was Mary, needing a mother herself. And none to be had. She blew noisily into a handkerchief.

Then ordered herself to carry on: escape London—go to Paris and throw herself into the revolutionary maelstrom where women, with the help of Condorcet and outspoken females like Olympe de Gouges and Manon Roland, were beginning to be noticed as equals. "Persevere, Mary! Don't let wagging tongues fell you." Thrusting up her chin, she got off the pot.

Back upstairs, she slit open the sealed packet with a pocket knife—then sank back on the sofa in shock. Who had sent this? It was a poorly executed sketch of *The Nightmare*, stuck clumsily into a gilded frame. And on the bottom, scrawled in red ink: *Look in the wine cellar. You will be surprised what you find there.*

What wine cellar? Ridiculous, she thought. There was no wine cellar in *her* house.

Unless...

"Oh," she said aloud, and pulled on her spring cloak.

ANNIE thought it might be the same man who had earlier assailed her; she was standing near the place where it happened. He was not wearing a black hooded cloak, but he had dirty fingernails and a fat red nose, and a torn handkerchief around his meaty neck. Was it the handkerchief he'd strangled her mother with? No, that was a stocking. Even so, to be safe she ducked behind a pair of black-frocked parsons. The man might be her mother's killer, a man who hated bluestockings; aye, there were folk who did, Miss Mary said. He wanted to make an example of one, so he climbed in her window and *arrgh...* She had read a horror story like that in one of the books in the Foundling Hospital library. But then one of the parsons stepped forward to shake hands with the villain, and the red-nosed man grinned a toothy grin, and his voice was high-pitched and not the growl of the man who'd attacked her. So she moved on.

But she kept looking. She wanted to find that man. It was silly, but she had this hunch. Why else had he singled her out that time from among all the young girls idling about near the river? She walked up and down Fish Street a dozen times and then down by the riverfront, and saw a half dozen burly men in raggedy black but didn't see *him*.

She was squatting on a rock to watch the riverboats float by when she heard a woman's voice—and then a male voice answering. The voices were moving along the bank behind her and she scooted farther down to listen; then glanced up to see a pair of dirty black boots with ragged yellow tassels on the tops.

"Jib, honey," the woman's voice whined, "when'er you n'me goin' off on our own? 'Ow long that sister o' yours goin' run your life?"

"When the money comes in, Bett," the man's voice said. "Jus' a matter o' time. Me sister's fellow says so. Then she gets her share from 'im, 'n I get mine. And you get me."

He grabbed the woman and she giggled; she stuck a finger in

his big ugly belly. "Better not be too long or I might find me some other chap gimme what-for, eh?" She stuck out her tongue, and then ambled up the bank to the street. Jib laughed and jingled some coins in his pocket while Annie held her breath—he was close enough so she could smell him. And it was him, she was certain. And then he walked away.

He was the man, aye. He'd attacked her, she wagered, because he thought she knew something about him. Or saw something. Or because he discovered—she didn't know how—that she was her dead mother's daughter. She crept back up the bank and into Fish Street. Jib was standing there in front of The Flying Fish, peering into the pub's window. This was Annie's chance: to follow him, find where he lived, and then call a constable. If nothing else, to punish him for assaulting her before. Wouldn't Miss Mary be surprised?

As for bossy Dulcie, well, Annie couldn't wait to show *her* up. The man Jib was moving on now; she stayed ten paces behind as he swaggered along and turned the corner into Great Tower Street. They weren't far from the Tower of London—that was a monstrous place! Englishmen could be nasty mean, Miss Mary said; they shouldn't blame others who were just trying to free themselves from tyranny.

Tyranny. Annie repeated the word she had learned from Miss Mary; she let it roll on her tongue. Tyranny was what this man Jib might've done to her mother. She would see he was sent to the Tower and hanged and then disembowled (she'd read that in a book), and then thrown to the dogs. All for killing her lovely, poetical mother.

The thought of the mother she hardly knew brought on the sniffles. She wiped her nose on her sleeve and walked on. Jib stopped to talk to a woman standing by her gate, and Annie darted behind a tree.

It wouldn't do for the man to see her. She waited, breathless, not daring to look until she heard the voices cease. Then she peered cautiously out. But Jib was nowhere in sight. She'd lost him! She pummeled her thighs with her fists. She'd had her chance and lost it.

Blinking back the hot tears, she scurried on down the road, and turned right into Lower Thames Street. She walked into the shadow of an enormous church—St Magnus the Martyr. She wanted to go inside and light a candle for her martyred mother. But then she saw the man again! He led her past a dozen quays on the riverside and smack into the biggest, noisiest marketplace she'd ever seen in her life. Billingsgate, she heard a woman call it. Boats of all shapes and sizes were lined up on the river, full of stinking eels, codfish, carp, and who knew what other ugly fish, for Annie disliked fish of any kind. And the yelling, cursing, and shrieking...

She waited at a distance while Jib purchased a sackful of scallops, then haggled over the price, and finally tossed some coins at the fishwife and pinched her fishy cheek. Then he turned back a few yards and darted left into an alley—Dark House Lane, the crooked sign said. Annie moved cautiously into the lane, past a smithy, and then an ironmonger's—until a rumble of thunder made her pause and look up into the sky. If there was one thing she feared, it was thunder—and worse: lightning. As a child at the Foundling Hospital she would throw herself under a bed or table at the first bang.

A hand shot out from behind a tall bush and clapped around her wrist. She started to scream, but managed only an *arrgh* before the other hand stopped her mouth. She smelled beer, old sweat, urine. Her own fear.

"Followin' me, was you, young miss?" said Jib. "I was 'opin' we'd meet up again. I know some'un'd be real glad we 'ave. Well, then, welcome to me sister Peg's place. Come in and we'll have a hot dish o' tea, shall we?"

"I need your help," Mary told Joseph Johnson, whom she had found at home in his rocking chair, sitting with his feet in a pan of steaming water, his throat wrapped in flannel. He had caught a cold, he said, he ached up and down his body. He might be nearing his life's end; she should be advised.

She wanted to laugh at the theatrical way he said it, and now he was smiling, but the laugh caught in her throat. She loved Joseph—he mustn't die, no! She couldn't bear it.

"I must go to Grosvenor Square and hoped you would accompany me, but I see you're indisposed. So I'll go myself," she said. Though in truth, Mary would rather cross the Channel to the land of the revolutionaries than return to Isobel Frothingham's house-of-the-dead. It was Dulcie's tale of the footman stealing the wine that had made her think of Grosvenor Square. She laid a hand on

Joseph's forehead. It was not hot: he did not, thank goodness, have a fever. "Now don't say that again about dying," she teased, and ruffled his hair. "I won't allow it. But I do need your advice." She handed him the anonymous note about *The Nightmare*. When he started to speak, she interrupted. "Now I know what you're going to say. There are wine cellars all over England. But why send this note to me if there weren't one nearby? It may be fraudulent or it may not. But we must go and see."

"We?" He reread the note, muttering to himself, and mopped his brow with a handkerchief. He was loyal to his friend Fuseli, she knew that; he would want the painting found. Finally he lifted his feet out of the water and she knelt to rub them with a warm towel. "You and your curiosity—it kills more than the proverbial cat," he said. "So very well, I'll come. But not till after my tea. Barlow is back from Paris for the week, and will bring an old friend from Liverpool. They've revived our Society for Constitutional Information. This in the face of the mad king's proclamation against seditious meetings and political clubs! Publishers and writers are in dire danger. *You*, Mary, are in danger."

"Oh, I know that already." She handed back the towel, flung up her arms, and danced over to the door. "I'm in danger for any number of reasons. I crave danger—it makes me feel alive. Have I not lately braved wild dogs and a house full of mad folk? Well, more about that later. Shall I sit in my house all day, sipping tea? No! That note may be fraudulent and it may not. But I need to explore it. I need to put down Henry Fuseli. It's virtually all I think about now—making him pay. I must find the painting and prove the young artist did not take it. I must prove Fuseli wrong.

"Wrong, wrong!" she chanted, feeling her cheeks heat up as she went into the dining room where the men were singing *Ça Ira*, the revolutionary song. Joel Barlow was holding forth against the arch-conservative Edmund Burke, who cherished the monarchy, the holding of hereditary property, and class distinctions, and who now claimed the Dissenters were calling in foreign forces to help with their "plots."

"He would indict Priestley," Barlow shouted, "he calls him a dangerous man."

"Aye," Priestley cried, "well may they think so. We're all of us dangerous men—"

"And women," Mary cried out, her cheeks flushed.

"—if love of liberty," Priestley went on with a quick nod to Mary, "free speech, and conscience be dangerous."

"Hurrah," cried Blake, waving his red cap of liberty, "a toast to all dangerous liberty-loving men and women!" Barlow struck up another chorus: "*Ah! ça ira, ça ira, ça ira,*" they sang with him, "*Les aristocrates à la lanterne!*" Which meant hanging from a lantern post, Mary knew—oh dear. Blake emptied the remnants of his wineglass on his head, and everyone laughed to watch it running down the side of his face. Tom Paine raised his tankard to announce that he was soon to appear in court for encouraging revolutionary societies "in all of England. They accuse me of sedition. But will that stop me?"

"Nay!" cried the Dissenters, Mary among them. She was a staunch admirer of Paine.

"Aye and they will," corrected Blake. "From what I've heard, Paine, you'd be well advised to go to back to America at once. If you're not sought now, you soon will be."

"It may be," said Paine, "but first another round of wine!" He whistled at Mrs Murphy, who was leaning against the wall, to all appearances half-asleep. On the second whistle she thumped over to the cabinet for the wine. "*Vive* Tom Paine*! Vive la Révolution! Vive le vin rouge!*" the Dissenters cried, and raised their glasses.

Joseph entered the room in his blue bedslippers. He was looking quite pink-cheeked after his steamy footbath. He unrolled a handful of foolscap on the table: revolutionary pamphlets, with the watermark of a jester's hat on the covers—Blake's work on the fiery year of 1789, complete with illustrations of the fallen Bastille. Joel Barlow's pamphlet, urging the French convention "to establish a democratic republic on humane principles." The author read aloud, to cheers: "No standing army. No death penalty." To Mary he shouted: "Arrangements for your brother Charles to sail for America—alone, I'm afraid. Business calls me back to Paris."

Mary waved her hands. There was too much going on at once. For now she could think only of what she might find in Isobel Frothingham's cellar. It might be *The Nightmare*, and then what would she do with it? She prayed it would not be another corpse; she shook her head at the ghastly thought. She gulped the wine Paine was pressing upon her, and squeezed his wrist to show her support and sympathy. On her other side Joseph was now holding up a bit of sweet pork to her mouth and she swallowed it, though she ate little meat these days.

"One more nip of claret and then we'll go," Joseph said. "It'll be a waste of time, I fear. We'll undoubtedly find naught in the cellar but a pile of the bluestocking's poems. Hunt is printing them up. She paid him to do so, but they'll need censoring, says he: 'twould be an embarrassment to her heirs."

Her heirs? Mary thought of Annie. She had not seen the girl when she returned from the madhouse—where could she be this time? But Dulcie was taking care of the minx, was she not? Of course, the girl was all right! If Mary couldn't rely on Dulcie, who *was* there, really? Mary's sisters were both in new governess positions she'd helped them procure—and already complaining. Mary wished she had money enough to set them up with a new school, but there was none to spare at the moment. She accepted a second glass of claret when Paine lifted the bottle to pour. For what she had to do, she told herself, she would need the wine.

CHAPTER XII.

Broken Glass and a Missing Girl

༄

ROGER PEALE awakened, confused. Then remembered he'd been removed to a damp cellar room—barely eight feet square, with stone-and-mortar walls. It was his punishment for breaking a hole in the wall, Mrs Bludgeon had said. He'd admitted to breaking it—he hadn't wanted to get the woman on the other side in trouble.

At first he thought he had lost a leg, then realized he had no chains. It was as though without the chains, part of his leg was missing. When he moved the leg, it was stiff and painful. He knelt on the straw mattress to see through the mullioned window above the cot. Two wooden bars had been nailed across the inside, but he could see out between them to a thicket of trees. It was not the same wood, for this window faced east, but it contained a whole grove of chestnut trees. He could see the sun inching slowly up over the leafy tops.

The place was quiet as a copse on a winter day. He watched a spider crawl toward the window, then disappear into a crack. While he remained captive. "It's cold in here. I need a fire!" he called out. But no one answered. A sparrow flew past the window, and off into the woods. He called out again—silence.

Anger took his breath at the thought of this dank prison—no better than Newgate; he reached between the bars and hammered his fists; one of the panes cracked—but not big enough to push an arm through. His knuckles bled but he felt no pain, only the familiar despair of the trapped—as if he were beast, not human. Was that what he was—a mere animal? He howled and heard the howl beat itself against the walls. Outdoors, he thought he heard something screech back, a kindred spirit.

But unlike himself, free.

FOOLISH, no doubt, Joseph thought: this wild chase to Grosvenor Square to look for an object some trickster had alluded to in an anonymous note. Had it been anyone other than Mary, he would not have taken part. But he had no children of his own—Mary was his family now, and impetuous and unpredictable as she was, he adored her.

When Mary had come knocking on his door, fresh off the boat from Ireland, he had taken her in. She was a feral cat, starved for the flesh of intelligent discourse; a woman with seemingly few prospects, and no sign of surrender to man or God. No great writer either, he had thought at the time: her *Education of Daughters* an innovative but flawed work—the unsold copies gathering dust in his warehouse. Yet when she entered his shop like a onrushing wave, he gave up his shore. And she soon showed him what she could do. Her *Vindication* was now in several languages.

And here she was herself, bursting out of the carriage, banging on the dead woman's door, shoving through it, in spite of the housekeeper's daughter, who was understandably upset at this passionate entry. "We have come to search the cellar," Mary announced, and marched past the bewildered girl. "I was Mrs Frothingham's friend. We're looking for—oh, what does it matter? I needn't explain."

Nor could she explain, Joseph might have told the frowning girl, but he held his tongue. He knew what they both wanted to find, but why the deuce would the stolen painting be here, of all places? Nevertheless, he nodded at the maid and followed Mary as she snatched up two candlesticks—one for each—and headed for the stair to the cellar. Down they went: past the kitchen, down into the bowels of a mansion that was far more elegant than his own home. Somewhere the bluestocking had acquired the means.

They must search in two directions, she decided when they entered the dank, cobwebbed cellar. And here *he* was: an asthmatic man who hoped to show his protégée how absurd it was to bungle about in the dark with little more to go on than an anonymous note, an obscene sketch. Her impetuousness would come to no good end, he'd warned—neglecting, of course, to remind her of the outcome of her foray into the Fuseli household. She had undoubtedly felt enough remorse in the aftermath of that pitiable affair.

She would not break down and cry over it, though, not in front of him—nor anyone, he supposed. She wanted no pity, she would inevitably say, though he could see the heart fracturing under the façade of confidence.

"Have you found anything?" she called from somewhere in the cellar.

"How can I find something," he called back, "when I don't know what I'm looking for? I see only an ocean of wine. Mrs Frothingham might well have drunk herself to death. I suspect she was already dead when the fellow found her and trussed her up."

"Not her," Mary said. "She had a life force. She was going back to adopt her Annie, did you know that?"

He did not. "Who told you that?"

"Why, Annie herself. And, the governor, yes, mentioned something of the sort."

Dreaming again, he thought. Imagining things: like a positive reception from Sophia Fuseli. As if any self-respecting English wife would accept a second into her household. "Writers are a mad species," he said aloud, thinking not only of Mary, but of William Blake with his angels; young Sam Coleridge, with his opium dreams. Even Erasmus Darwin, writing a long love poem to his plants (though Joseph had published *The Botanic Garden* the year before—and with profit, for once.)

Publishers and editors had to be wholly rational. Without them, writers would ride off into the sunset without a map. But try to tell them that.

"Mr Johnson! Come look at this." Her voice sounded far away, as if issuing forth from an empty wine bottle. He heard a clonking sound, like bottles banging against one another, then clunking to the hard dirt floor.

He stumbled his way toward her, his breath coming raw from the damp. What legal right had they to be here? If the housekeeper were to summon a constable—and himself already in trouble publishing pamphlets that outraged church and state...

He straightened his shoulders and pulled up a shuddery breath. He must make Mary come to her senses and leave this place at once. But he started coughing before he could get a word out. "P-please," he choked as he made his way toward the spectral voice.

He halted. Three bottles lay on the floor, oozing wine. Such a waste, he thought, and set the broken ones upright. Then, looking up, he saw a rack of remaining bottles moving aside; she'd found a hidden catch to press and lo, the rack had swung out of the way. Behind, to Joseph's surprise, was a hiding place, a kind of safe. She cried out.

"What?"

"Look! Open your eyes."

"If you move aside, I will. I can scarcely breathe. I have to get out of here."

"As soon as you help me remove this painting."

"Painting?"

"*The Nightmare!* Can't you see? It was here all this time, rolled up. This is where she hid it. Or someone hid it."

He looked, and it was so. She was slowly unrolling the canvas. And there was the sleeping woman, the incubus, the leering horse. My God, he thought. My God. But who? And why? She was on her knees, staring at it, with lidded eyes. As though praying. Praying for what?

"We must inform Henry," he said, his blood heating with the excitement of the discovery.

Now she was up, facing him, those witch-hazel orbs penetrating his. "We will do no such thing, Mr Johnson."

"You don't mean to appropriate it y-yourself!" Upset, he tended to stutter. "You can't do such a thing. You w-wouldn't!"

"Not for me. Not to keep. Why would I want such a monster? No. We must leave it hidden, don't you think? Until we find out who put it here?"

"Why, it had to be Mrs Frothingham," he allowed. "This is her wine cellar. She hired someone to steal the painting and bring it here. S-sounds just like her. She was a collector. You've seen her drawing room. Though surely she'd have admitted—"

"Possibly, yes. But we must prove beyond a doubt that it was not Mr Peale. We can't let Fuseli have his way over the poor fellow. No, we must find out who left that note about the hiding place. It was someone who knew me, I wager, who came into my home."

"But my d-dear girl—be reasonable."

"Pray, help me roll this monster back up, if you will, and put back these bottles. We must make the place appear untouched."

"Impossible, my dear. Wine seeping into the dirt floor? Broken glass? Any fool would know someone was here." Oh, why was he doing this? If it were anyone but Mary he would leave at once. But for Mary... and for Henry, too, his old friend. Both of them irrational at times, but highly original, and he valued that above all attributes. "Mary, dear, let's take the painting and leave. Or you'll be carrying a dead man up the steps. Is that what you want? Who will publish your next book?"

"You're trying to blackmail me," said Mary, but he saw the sly smile. "Go on up, dear man. But call the housekeeper to bring a broom. Tell her the wine bottle we were looking for has shattered. I'll close up the false panel."

"I will clean it up," said a shrill voice, and Joseph turned to see a sharp-faced woman descend the stairs with a broom and cleaning rags. Resigned, he sank down on a bottom step of the staircase, to wait.

Mary was a cat caught in the cream. But nevertheless, quick on her feet. "You do remember me from Mrs Frothingham's soirées?" she soothed, addressing the woman. "She and I were well acquainted."

"And let me help you with that panel," said the woman—the housekeeper, most likely.

"You knew what was in there," said Mary.

"Didn't I help put it there?" said the woman, looking indignant.

"Then how—that is, who was responsible for its concealment? Surely you know what it *is*!" Mary looked at the housekeeper, and then at the publisher.

He kept his silence. He knew better than to come betwixt two strong-minded women.

"I only helped Mrs Frothingham," the woman said, sounding defensive—though no one had accused her. "But good riddance, said I, when the painting was concealed. A disgusting thing, I have to say! And I was sorry for that young man in gaol. 'A sacrifice,' the mistress called it." She set about cleaning up wine and bits of glass. Her bottom loomed like a round hillock.

"Did Mrs Frothingham herself take the painting?" Mary said, standing over her. "Surely she had help to remove the frame. Though undoubtedly it was someone else's idea, not hers. What, I ask, have you overheard? Pray, tell me."

"Madam, I do not eavesdrop," the housekeeper said.

"Come now," said Mary, "you heard my question perfectly well. Speak up. It could mean the life of a young artist—falsely accused!"

The housekeeper gave a resigned sigh and a series of snorts. Finally she stood upright. "Mrs Frothingham spoke only of *he*. *He* took the painting, and *he* wanted it stored here 'till *he* could retrieve it. And then *he* would give Mrs Frothingham a share of what he earned from disposing of it—in America, I believe he said. My employer—well, I know for a fact—needed the money. You've no idea how she overspent! With never a thought to the future." She groaned to think of the extravagance.

"You never saw this man? You never saw a man in close conversation with her?"

"My employer entertained many gentlemen, madam. And all in close conversation with her. As I said, I do not eavesdrop. The affair was none of my business." The woman had done with her harangue. She went back to her task of cleaning the floor. (*Who was paying her, with the bluestocking dead?* Joseph wondered—and felt he should help out.) Mary was staring at the bent back as though her eyes might somehow glean the information. Joseph would never understand the minds of women. His own mother had been an enigma to him, never expressing her thoughts or feelings. Always wanting to control *him*. And he'd had his frustrating confrontations with the bluestocking, though he pitied the manner of her demise. She was a clever woman; her novel sold well in spite of Mary's less-than-enthusiastic review.

The housekeeper kept her peace. She marched back up the stairs with her rags and broom. When Mary helped Joseph off the step and sent him up the crumbling stairway in front of her—she would catch him should he fall, she said—he went. He did not want to be drawn into this nightmare. He had problems enough of his own. And here was the authoress on a foolhardy quest for a thief and killer—when she should be writing the second part of *Vindication*, earning them both a bit of money. He might just as well send her to Paris, as she'd hinted, to write about the ongoing Revolution. It would serve, too, to stifle gossip of the Fuseli disaster.

"For now, get back to work," he said, stopping on the stairs to cough and draw breath. "Go home and write."

Did he hear the impudent creature laugh?

DULCIE had had enough of that girl. She had tramped up and down London Bridge searching for her, a frightening experience, what with the strong current below that spun small boats into a whirlpool and sucked down the sailors, folk said. She didn't dare look into the choppy waters for fear she'd see the desperate fingers of the victims sticking up.

A red-haired girl at the far end of the bridge was walking hand in hand with a tall boy; Dulcie elbowed her way through the crowd. But it was just a pasty-faced milkmaid, and Dulcie shrugged. She could only hope the girl had reconsidered and gone home. Anything could happen to a female alone in this dangerous city. Hadn't Dulcie herself, at one time or another, been solicited by bawds? And what of Miss Mary?

A figure bumped into her and she felt a tug at her pocket. She wheeled about to see a young footpad flee down the street—then trip on a protruding tree root. She raced to catch up with him and retrieve her favorite handkerchief—it ripped in the struggle. "Thief!" she screeched. But no one turned a head. No one cared about a servant girl.

Her bladder was full, so she ducked into an alley, pulled up her skirts, and let go. Hurried out just as two smirking youths swaggered past.

She practically raced home through the streets and burst in, calling the girl's name: "Annie? Answer me, girl. Where've you been, Annie?"

She tramped through the rooms, calling.

But no Annie.

Now *she* was in trouble. She had promised Miss Mary to keep the girl inside and the wench had gone out and got herself lost. All of it Dulcie's fault, the mistress would say, and point, as warning, to the door. And if Dulcie were to leave here, where would she go? The publisher would not keep paying her wages.

When it was Annie's fault, not hers!

Though the girl wasn't really bad: she was just headstrong. It wasn't so long ago Dulcie had been thirteen, in that charity school. And oft-times whipped till her skin was red and raw. She had to remember that. Sorry for herself, she dropped onto the sofa beside the cat; the creature opened a slitted eye, and closed it again. And now her nose was running. She groped along a side table for something to wipe her face with—and came up with a stocking she'd been meaning to darn. When she could half see again, she recalled leaving Isobel's will on that table. She groped for it. But it wasn't there. She searched under the sofa and all around the room. And no will.

Oh, Lord in heaven! Now she had plenty to cry about. She let go, loud and clear; she watered the cat. The lazy black thing jumped off the sofa and scampered from the room. It didn't care. Nobody did. And all because of that child. That miserable Annie!

LATE in the day Roger heard children's voices outside the window. He recalled hearing a child call out a few weeks ago when he was in the upstairs room. A neighbour's child most likely. He couldn't imagine a child living in this place of misery. The children's voices sounded melodious, like a running stream. Whenever he painted children, he heard them in his inner ear. He thought of his neighbour's little girl, her tinkling laughter. But she and her mother had gone to America to join the woman's husband in Ohio.

The voices danced through the wood. At least it seemed to him that they danced. Happy people danced—not Roger. He could scarcely lift one foot in front of the other. He pulled himself to his knees to see through the window. "Ho," he called out. "Ho!"

The voices ceased. The dancing stopped and the wood was quiet again. He cursed himself for calling out. He needed those voices in his head. He lay back on his cot, depressed, ready to die. Perhaps he would, and soon. It were best that he die, for if he came out into the light he'd be punished for the escape from Newgate, for a theft and murder he was innocent of.

Now the voices sounded again, and he pulled himself back up to the window and rapped on it. Two brown heads looked up, both boys. He tried to smile but he couldn't: the muscles in his cheeks were slack. He lifted a hand and gave a weak wave. One of the boys threw a chestnut at the glass, and laughed. Roger wiggled his hands and put his fingers in his cheeks the way he did with Lillian's child—that always made the lad giggle. The boy grinned and threw another chestnut. Roger clapped his hands; he put a thumb to his nose and waggled it. Another chestnut—the smaller boy joining in. Children loved a game. Then a pebble striking the window directly, between the inside bars—the first boy was a good shot.

More faces, more pebbles. And then a rock. A rock that cracked the glass in the place Roger had earlier struck it. He wiggled his nose and blinked and banged on the window to encourage the throwing. For the children might make a hole in the window. A hole that he might crawl through in the night. And they wouldn't tell. Children who broke windows did not tell, for glass cost money and windows were taxed.

It had begun to rain, and the boys were running away now, giggling. The smaller one turned back and put a finger to his lips. "Don't worry, I won't tell," Roger mouthed, but of course they couldn't hear him.

The rain darkened the room, but he could smell lilacs in the air that blew through the hole. It must indeed be April by now. He didn't know where he was—what part of England, though the carriage had headed south when he and St Pierre left Newgate. But he would find his way home. Animals did, and so could he.

A key turned in the lock and the apple-faced woman came in with a tray. He lay back again on the cot so the old woman would look at him and not at the cracked window—though the room was darkening with dusk, he needn't worry. She plunked down the tray on a wooden chair, nodded, and without a word, as though she had been instructed to abstain from talk, turned and went out.

Tonight he would enlarge the crack with the aid of the chair, and then with all the strength he had left—and more—he would try to wrench apart the wooden bars. He was weak, yes, but he had read about men accomplishing miraculous feats in their desperation. He thought of the castaway surgeon Henry Pitman, who had escaped from a penal colony, then shipwrecked on a desert island—and survived; he thought of Scottish Alexander Selkirk, four years alone on a Pacific Island—both of them, no doubt, models for Defoe's Robinson Crusoe. Yes, the children's voices had revived Roger's hopes. He was not mad. He would find his way back to his Lillian; they would take ship to America. Lilly would bear his children; he would farm, and paint. They would live out their lives in peace.

He wanted, too, to paint those children who had saved him. He would paint them dancing, tossing up leaves, chestnuts, and pebbles. He would paint himself into the background, a man frail but not broken, watching in the shadows.

Waiting to dance.

MARY carried her morning coffee to the sitting room and dropped onto the sofa—the cushions, she saw, already required patching from the kneading cat. She had just sent ten pounds from her royalties to a needy Everina and she could not afford new cushions. She was at the end of her patience. Everything she had touched of late had turned to straw. She had tried to find true companionship, and was cruelly rebuffed. She had braved a madhouse, only to discover the victim was gone. She had crawled about Isobel Frothingham's wine cellar and found that the bluestocking herself was involved in the theft of the painting. Another blow for literary women, who were already called unnatural females. Now Annie had willfully disobeyed and stayed out all night. Was this to flout Mary—or was the girl in some kind of trouble? Edgar Ashcroft had seen her with a man, he had told Dulcie, and Mary was worried. Young girls were at risk in this feral town.

She will come home. She will come home today, Mary told herself, and felt better for having said it.

But here was Dulcie stomping into the room, moaning about a missing will. "What will?" Mary said. "I have no will. No will to go on at all."

"Not that kind of will," Dulcie said. "A death will, you know—what you leave folk when you're underground."

Mary sighed at the thought of a death will. She had her whole life ahead of her, did she not? And what had she to leave anyone? "Have you, Dulcie, made a will at the tender age of nineteen? And what valuable jewels," she teased, "are you planning to bequeath?"

Mary was worn down by the wine cellar adventure. Her nerves were jumping like fleas. If she couldn't have peace at home, she might as well fling herself into the river. Had she done it the day Henry rejected her, she would not have had to endure the averted glances of her peers.

"Mrs Frothingham's will!" Dulcie cried. "Not a sealed and signed one, but a will, all right. It said so at the top. Last will and testament, and so forth. I was going to show it to you, but it disappeared. It was with those papers I took from her drawer."

"What? You took papers from her drawer? Without her knowing it?"

"How could she know it? She was dead. I was just trying to help *you*, ma'am."

"By stealing what might be evidence? And you never told me?" When Dulcie hung her head, Mary sat up straight, and gulped the last of the coffee. "Then sit down and tell me about those papers. You took them from her drawer, you say? Well, it's true, she'll never know, poor thing. And where, pray, are the rest of those papers? Go find them at once." Mary waved an arm to send the grinning girl thumping up to her room.

But the bluestocking had died intestate—or so they said. Mary's solicitor was investigating, but he had not found a will. The fat, feathered cousin who had laid claim to the estate was still trying to make it hers, and might succeed, while Mary was hoping to have the estate fall to Annie. At least she had sent a petition to the lawyer to that effect.

Minutes later Dulcie was back and Mary had a lapful of papers. They spilled over onto the floor; the cat was making a nest in them. "I assume you've been through these." She was secretly pleased that Dulcie had found them, but had to remain stern: else the officious girl would be shuffling through Mary's own papers. And that would never do. The girl would find out she had been writing nothing—nothing of value at all—as she sat at her writing desk.

"Some, madam, not all."

"Then show me what you find of most interest." Mary was too weary to paw through everything; she needed a shortcut. "And refill my coffee, would you. I require something to stimulate my brain."

Dulcie pulled out a handful of sketches and pointed. "Who is that boy? The one standing all alone like he smelled bad?"

Mary had to smile. Dulcie had a way of cutting to the core of things. "Unattractive, yes. But what about the coffee? And bring one for yourself if you like. Oh, and you'll never guess what I found in Mrs Frothingham's wine cellar." She had to tell someone—it might as well be Dulcie. The girl might be giddy, but she had a brain—she wouldn't always be a servant. Not that she considered herself one, anyway.

Dulcie was obviously torn between the coffee and the discovery in the wine cellar. She stood on one foot, and then the other.

"The coffee first and then I'll tell about the wine cellar. And bring me a slice of bread with butter and raspberry jam, please. I'm starved. I ate almost nothing yesterday."

Dulcie sighed loudly and pounded down the steps to the kitchen. Her wooden pattens made her sound like an elephant—too often she forgot to take them off in the house. Mary rubbed her temples, and squinted at the papers Dulcie had handed her. One was a rough drawing, done, it appeared, by an adolescent. The mother's eyes were dull and averted, the father's stern. The girl had to be Isobel herself: the arched eyebrows, sly smile. And then the boy, standing apart, legs spread, staring insolently ahead. A bastard son perhaps? In a second drawing the sketcher, perhaps young Isobel, had drawn tiny horns on the boy; in a third, she had drawn a tail. A naughty child. A wicked child. Or so the unknown sketcher perceived him to be.

Turning the drawing over she saw a black thumb print, and in the next drawing the thumb print blocked out the boy's face as though pushing him out of the picture. In the next, the thumb print covered young Isobel's face. Some careless person had been looking at these pictures.

The coffee arrived—too hot, and Mary let it sit there while she thumbed through more papers. She found nothing to indicate a father for Annie. She scanned a sheaf of poetry: childhood verses, begging for love; adolescent verses, longing for love; adult poems steeped in love that wasn't love—but lust, envy, ambition. Ambition for what? Like Mary perhaps, wanting to be taken seriously as a writer? A new genus of woman and writer, Mary had told her sisters (but sometimes, with the disapproval of some, feeling an imposter).

For a moment she wondered, like Joseph, if the bluestocking had swallowed a vial of pills, then had a trusted friend or servant arrange her to look like the painting. As if the death scene were a final poem, one that had succeeded this time. It was entirely possible: the woman could have done it.

But no, she thought, sipping the coffee: Isobel had been full of life when they last met. She had talked of poems that would soon be published. She would not have wanted to die before her time.

"So what did you find in the wine cellar? What? Tell!" Dulcie's enthusiasm hurt the listener's ears.

Mary licked the last bit of raspberry jam off her lips while Dulcie waited. Then she described in considerable detail what she had found.

Dulcie was smiling. "She said it might be a woman who took the painting."

"What? Who said?"

"Mrs Frothingham. At her party when I served the iced plum cake. The thief might be a woman, she said. And the French lady clapped her hands."

"Something else you never told me?" Mary frowned. "Well, too late. *Now* we must discover who sent that note. I had almost forgot with all this talk about a missing will, and Mrs Frothingham's papers. You were here, were you not? Who brought that packet?"

"It was Mr Ashcroft. He said he'd found it on the doorstep. He said he'd something important to say to you, and he'd be back later for your reply."

"My answer is *no*. You could have told him that, Dulcie. I do not wish to see Mr Ashcroft or hear his solicitations. I gave him my answer before, and it was final." Mary slapped the sofa pillow for emphasis and papers sprang up amidst the dust.

"I did remind him of that, madam. At least I tried."

"Ah, you're a good girl. Sometimes. But how do we know he was telling the truth about *finding* the packet? It might have been himself who wrote the note and merely *said* he found it? He lies about everything else in his foolish newspaper."

Mary swallowed the acrid dregs of the coffee. She supposed she would have to speak to the arrogant fellow. She fancied she could tell if a person were lying. Had there not been a half dozen suitors in her life who had thrown down their affections like flowering weeds at her feet, and then deserted her? No, she had given up all hope of finding an honest man of sensibility.

"Send for Mr Ashcroft," she told Dulcie.

"Send for him? I don't know where he lives."

"His place of work is in Fleet Street. They tell me he has rooms above. Find a porter. Here, take this." She scribbled out a message on the back of an envelope.

Then as Dulcie stood, she tore it up. "I must be mad. Send for him? Why, he'll think I want him to come! When it's the last—"

"Madam, he said he would come here."

"Ah, then, we will have to grit our teeth and wait. And where could young Annie have gone? I told you to keep her in, didn't I?"

"So you did, ma'am. But she's willful, that one. Disobedient. Of course I said no. And when my back was turned—"

A knock on the door and Dulcie went to answer. Mary sucked

in her breath. It couldn't be Annie: the child wouldn't knock; she would simply barge in with a made-up excuse. She steeled herself for who it probably was.

It was. "Mr Edgar Ashcroft," Dulcie announced, with a smirk.

The man charged in and flung himself down to kneel at Mary's feet. Oh, dear. Close up, she saw the furrows in his forehead, the parentheses around his mouth, the saggy belly. The bobwig came off with his hat and he clapped it back on. But not before she noted the bare circle in the centre of his greying head.

"Madam. I have to confess. Madam, you must hear me out. About that painting? I know you were at Grosvenor Square—I saw you leave with Mr Johnson. Nay, not a word!" he shouted, though she hadn't uttered one. "Just hear me out."

"For heaven's sake, stand up, will you?" said Mary. "My shoe is covered with spit." She seated herself in a parlour chair while he blathered on. "Now, pray, get to the point."

She had small patience with those who could not state their purpose in a few well-chosen words. The man was dancing all about the subject, tossing out compliments like peppermint drops; she had a headache. She'd had a headache upon coming home yesterday, finding Annie gone. Today, with Edgar Ashcroft at her feet, she ached from head to toe. For he had not risen at all when summoned, but crawled over to a stool, pushed aside the sleeping cat, and dragged the stool to her feet. She put a hand to her temples and sighed.

He took this for a sign of acquiescence. "Miss Wollstonecraft. Madam?"

"*Mrs* Wollstonecraft, if you please," said Mary. She had just this minute decided to take on the mature *Mrs*. Why not? Other women did. It was a mark of distinction.

Though at heart she felt herself to be the same Mary. Her old failures would not disappear with a new title. Or a new book. It wasn't easy to become a *Mrs*.

"You need protection, miss—missus. You are in danger. Protection I can give you. I have many assets. I own two warehouses—well, one now. I own a newspaper."

"So you said. Many times."

"Though admittedly, I lost money through unwise investments. But I've—"

"Pray, enough. Now who wrote that note about a wine cellar? It was you, was it not? Confess now: you wrote it. You brought it here, hoping I might go to Grosvenor Square and look for *The Nightmare*. So I went, yes, and I found it. And now I must ask you: how did *you* know it was there? Had you something to do with the theft?" She leaned forward to look him squarely in the eye. He looked ridiculous with his satin buttocks squashed over that small, round stool. He had a hole in one of his white stockings.

He gazed back, blinking. His mouth quivered. For a moment she thought he might cry, and she couldn't bear that. "Speak," she ordered, and handed him a handkerchief.

He held it to his lips as though he would kiss it; then wiped his eyes and pocketed it. She did not ask for it back. "I was at Mrs Frothingham's," he began.

"Asking her to marry you."

"Oh no, madam, it has always been you I wanted. I was merely, well, taking solace."

"In her bed. If she would let you."

"No, no," he protested. "It was always—"

"So you said. Now go on. You were at Mrs Frothingham's, and you or she or some mysterious *he* spoke about the painting."

"Yes! It was *he* who brought it to her. Not for *her*, mind you, but because he needed the money for—well, I am not at liberty to say precisely what for. But rest assured, to this man at least, the money was paramount."

"Mmm. And what part had you in the theft of this painting?"

"None at all, I promise you. Absolutely none! Oh no, no. Why would I take a painting of the most prurient nature? Risk all my—"

"Yes, yes, go on."

"I had to close my eyes just to look at it. Unseemly, aye. An insult to the feminine gaze. I hope you don't think—"

"But you helped to hide it."

"No, not that either, though Mrs Frothingham begged. And then made me swear to keep silence. *He* was with her when I arrived. The painting was there in the drawing room. I couldn't help but see it. She wanted it taken to the cellar at once, before the other servants arrived. Only the housekeeper was there."

"So I discovered."

"The painting was huge," he said, describing it with his hands:

"They had to pry it off the frame and roll it. It barely fit through the door."

Mary glanced at the fleshy bum that overlapped the width of the stool; it might have been Edgar Ashcroft, not the painting, that barely fit through the door—she couldn't imagine he had sat there and done nothing. She heard Dulcie giggle in the hall and almost broke down herself.

"*He* might have had help for that—someone waiting, I don't know. She had a false panel where she kept her best wine," he went on. "It was exactly wide enough, Mrs Frothingham said, for—"

"I saw it, I told you," Mary interrupted. "I was there."

"Ah. So I hoped you would be. I want the painting returned to its creator. You see, I've been torn with guilt. That young artist falsely accused. And you in need of help and support—I had to tell you. I happen to know how cruelly Mr Fuseli treated you when you, um—"

Mary was on fire; her voice rose. "So you thought to gain my favour by telling me all this. Making me a partial conspirator, because now the painting remains in the wine cellar. Don't you think I'll tell Mr Fuseli? It's not as though we don't speak at all."

Though it was. They had not spoken a word since his betrayal; he had completely cut her off. What *had* she intended to do with the painting? Joseph didn't want to be further involved. They had left the thing there like a snake one doesn't want to handle, and walked away.

But there was one thing she had to know. "The housekeeper, too, mentioned this mysterious *he*. Name him! I must know."

He gave a sly smile and rubbed his satin belly. "Pray, madam, is it not enough to know the painting is safe? That it was not Peale, and the bluestocking is dead so she will not suffer when the painting comes to light. The housekeeper discovers it, but no one knows how it got there, you understand?" He was off the stool, down on his knees again, hands clasped, imploring. "If you will come to see me in my quarters on Fleet Street, I might be persuaded to tell you the name."

"I will not come. Now will you please stand up?"

"Madam, I can give you acres of land. I have a country house up in Stratford-upon-Avon. Shakespeare country, madam. I know how you revere the Bard."

Mary held up a warning hand. "Mr Ashcroft. If you are so torn with guilt, then you will tell me. A young artist, abducted. A bright, young (*well, not so young*) woman murdered. Myself threatened—of course you know that? The killer left a warning."

There was a knock at the door. Edgar Ashcroft wobbled on his knees but didn't move.

The knock came again, and at Mary's nod, Dulcie went to open up—reluctantly. She would want to hear what the man had to say. But his lips were now sealed.

"Mary! He's back!" And here was Lillian Guilfoy bursting in. She paused, astonished to see Edgar Ashcroft on his knees. But in a moment the man was up and moving.

"I will come again," he told Mary as if he were tossing a pound note at her. "We will speak further. I cannot betray a promise. But I will help you to return that—object to its owner."

"Nay," Mary said to both. But he was already hustling out the door. Then back in again to retrieve his hat. And mercifully out for the last time. *Bang!* A welcome sound. She turned toward a smiling Lillian.

"It's Roger!" Lillian cried, running to take Mary's hands. "He'll need a physician, but he's alive!" She dissolved into happy tears on Mary's shoulder, snuffling into the neckerchief Eliza had embroidered for Mary's last birthday. "He's home. He's sleeping. He's safe! No, not safe, but home. My darling love, home!"

"Really? Astounding!" said Mary, though she was still feeling unstrung from the encounter with Ashcroft. "Do sit down. Tell me how—"

"I don't believe a word that man said," Dulcie scuttled past to hiss in Mary's ear. "Did you see his nose twitch when he spoke? He has Miss Isobel's will all right. He's the one would've picked it up. We must get it back."

"Quite true," Mary said, sotto voce. "But I've a guest, Dulcie. We'll speak of that later."

"Mary, will you come? To hear Roger's story? I don't know what to do. I don't know how to keep him safe." Lillian peered into Mary's face, her eyes shiny and wet, a gloved hand outstretched.

"Of course I will! You can count on me." Mary squeezed the hand.

"I daren't leave him alone for long," Lillian said breathlessly, jumping up. "I must go. I'll expect you at four, shall I? We must find him a place to hide. I only wanted to give you the good news."

Mary was glad for Lillian, but after the young woman ran out, she felt as if she had been put on a rack and stretched. How was she going to keep Roger Peale safe? It was clear that he hadn't taken the painting, but he was still a suspect, and he *had* escaped from Newgate. And Ashcroft had given her a confidence she didn't want to harbour. All she really wanted now was to sit down and write— write out her feelings, her frustrations. It was not Part Two of *Vindication* that she wanted to write: it was fiction. Or fact disguised as fiction. She longed for happy endings, to bring order into the chaos of her world. And though Peale was out of his madhouse—in part a happy ending—was he really free? He must go into hiding—but where?

And furthermore, she thought, looking at the mantel clock that was marching on towards one o'clock, where was Annie? Why had she not come home? Why did she have to keep her mistress in a constant state of worry?

Mary would go to see Roger Peale; she would find a place to hide him. But on the way she would report a missing girl.

CHAPTER XIII.

A Sinful Fragrance

∾

ROGER LOOKED up to see two women. His beloved Lilly on one side, reaching now for his hand—he knew her by the scent of lavender. A woman on the other, in a green dress...his sight was blurred: he could not identity her. He had arrived shortly before noon, slumped into his lover's arms, endured a bath, then fallen onto the sofa for a deep, exhausted sleep.

"Where were you, Mr Peale? How did you get here?" The Green Dress was leaning over him now, worrying him with questions. Why was she here?

"It's Miss Wollstonecraft," Lillian said. "You remember. The authoress? She has been trying to help us."

"We had already met at my publisher's, Mr Peale. I know you're weak—and I'm more than happy to see you out of that terrible place—but you're still in danger. You're not safe here. Though we can prove your innocence—in regard to the painting, that is—I'll explain later. But you did, well, you did escape Newgate. They don't like that, the authorities."

He almost smiled. No, the authorities would not like that. He widened his eyes to see the woman and tightened his grip on Lillian's hand. She squeezed back and gave him strength. What could he tell this demanding female? He had no idea how long his journey had been. He had escaped through the broken window a little after midnight, taken a horse from the madhouse stable, ridden hard, then left the creature at an inn some forty miles beyond Slinfold. It was broad daylight by then; he was disoriented—that vast, blinding space of the out-of-doors! For a time his legs seemed frozen to the ground. Until desperate, hungry, he stumbled to a farmhouse where he found a man milking his cows—Roger called himself an itinerant artist.

"Which I was, was I not?" he asked the two women. "I did a quick sketch of the farmer's daughter, promising to finish it later in my London studio, then send it back, in return for a ride to London. It was a fair likeness, though my hands were weak." He held them up and they saw the raw and bruised fingers.

"Poor lamb. Poor darling," Lillian soothed. "Try not to speak now."

But he needed to finish his story. "I claimed I had met with an accident, been the victim of an assault. The farmer's boy brought me to the southern edge of London in his waggon. From there I walked north to George Street. No one took notice; I was one of a hundred beggars. I never realized—how many beggars in this world. I can see why the French peasants, the *sans-culottes*—"

His voice gave out. He lay back, spent from the long speech. Lillian caressed his hand and he gazed up at her gratefully. So many nights in prison, in a madhouse, he had dreamed of this homecoming.

But the woman in green would not leave him alone. Who put him in that place, her insistent voice asked. Who took him there? She knew he was exhausted, she said, but the perpetrator must be brought to justice. Yet at this point he remembered only the blessed children. He had their faces, their free-wheeling bodies still in his mind's eye. He could only gaze at the woman mutely and shake his head. Squeeze his Lilly's hand again and again to prove he was alive and here with her, the nightmare over.

He sat up, but was once more struck down by a torrent of words. This time something about a wine cellar, the *Nightmare* painting, a *he* who had taken it. So it was found? Ah. But no, he didn't know who that *he* was! He had been at Mrs Frothingham's twice only—the second time with St Pierre and Lillian: to appeal his innocence and ask for help. Talleyrand, he recalled, was there at the time, talking about the Girondin cause in France. The bluestocking had been more interested in French politics than with a poor artist.

It struck him that perhaps Miss Wollstonecraft thought he himself was that *he*. "No! I did not take the painting! No!"

"Of course not, Mr Peale," the authoress said, rubbing his shoulder. "We've been trying to prove otherwise, have we not?"

He squeezed his eyes shut and rolled toward Lillian. The effort cost him his equilibrium; he had a sharp pain in his ribs. He had no

idea how he had ridden that horse. He wondered if he still had legs.
He tried to move them but they were chunks of wood. He was—
"paralysed!" he cried out in despair.

"No, no, you're not paralysed, my dearest. You're just fatigued,
weakened. Try to sleep. Miss Wollstonecraft: he must sleep. We
must let him. No more questions, please."

"We must move him," Miss Wollstonecraft said. "I'm so sorry,
yes, but you must see, for both your sakes, that he can*not* stay here.
This is the first place they'll think to look when they find him gone.
That matron will send out alarms. She'll discover he escaped from
Newgate, as well as her madhouse. The authorities may already be
on their way."

"Monstrous!" Lillian cried. "Where, then?"

Miss Wollstonecraft was thinking hard. She was pressing her
lips together and sighing. All at once she brightened and said, "Mr
Johnson, my publisher, yes! We'll go there at once. Mrs Guilfoy,
pray, send your nursemaid for a carriage."

No, Roger thought. No, no. They are not sending me away. He
pushed his abused body deeper into the mattress. The pain sub-
sided. He wouldn't go. He had only just arrived. No.

"For your safety, love." Lillian's cheek wet his face.

"He must go *now*," Miss Wollstonecraft said. "There is no time
to waste." The bright eyes blazed into his as though she would set
his face on fire, like her own.

She was not to be argued with, the eyes said. "Mr Johnson's,"
she repeated. "We must go to him. Now."

"Now," he echoed, giving in, and struggled to rise.

JOSEPH Johnson took a long, slow swallow of claret and blew
his nose into a white linen handkerchief. He had been sitting in
his rocking chair with a manuscript to edit, his feet in the daily
basin of hot water. His toes tingled, his sinuses filled, as though
nose and toes were conspiring to do him in. A kettle of hot water
was steaming on the hearth: he breathed in the vapours. Outside
the chamber window he heard the snorting of horses, the creak of
wheels stopping at his door. Mary Wollstonecraft's voice sounded
below, then a second woman's high, sweet treble—familiar, though
he couldn't place it. Then a man's hoarse voice. What hungry devil
was she bringing now with a story to peddle?

He heard Mrs Murphy downstairs, ushering them in. Chatter, chatter, chatter. Mary's voice rising above the rest. A moment later she was thrusting through his bedchamber door. Had a man no privacy?

And here she was, her cheeks pink and quivering with what she was about to ask him. He did not want to hear it. But what recourse had he? He was defenseless with his feet in a basin of water.

"Sir, I have brought Roger Peale. He is escaped from his madhouse and downstairs with Mrs Guilfoy. There is no one to harbour him. You see, his pursuers would go at once to her house. Or to my house. Nay—don't say a word," she ordered when he held up a hand and tried to catch a breath. Excitement, or anxiety (the two went hand in hand) worsened his asthma. Mary, though he loved her, brought anxiety into his life. Anxieties surrounded her person like a swarm of buzzing bees.

"Of course they will come to *my* house, Joseph—they will search roof to cellar. They would undo my writing, undermine my schedule."

What writing? he wanted to ask. What schedule? She was doing too much chasing after an art thief—or an artist—to have a schedule. Well then, she should know that her old Joseph had still not ruled out Roger Peale as thief. The man was jealous; his work had been maligned. He could perfectly well have taken that painting. Had Fuseli maligned *him*, he, too, might have fought back. But Fuseli knew where his bread was buttered. Years ago Joseph had published Fuseli's books and taken him into his own house to live. And what happened after that? The house burned down, devouring books, paintings, everything they owned. He squeezed his eyes shut to think of it.

Mary was still talking—about some missing person; he didn't catch the name. He clapped his hands to his ears. She wasn't looking at him; she was pacing the room, skirts swishing, quick excited breaths. He tossed a slipper at her; it struck her on the backside.

"Sir!"

"I said, that is—what I want to say, is—" he gasped "—I cannot have him here. Only think, my dear, Fuseli comes often, and you know he has the run of the house. All it would take is a cough from the garret, Fuseli wandering about looking for a book or a chamberpot, and *voilà*! His art thief!"

Now she'd got him coughing. He waved at her for water and she handed him his glass. Then stared down at him, her cheeks flaming. She had not thought it out clearly; she was far too impetuous. She would have an early death—it had come to him in a dream. No, in a nightmare. He couldn't bear to lose her....

But she had to understand. "My shop is under surveillance by His Majesty's men." He enunciated each word in his hoarse voice. "My person is under surveillance. We're all being watched. Not only you, dear lady." He drank down the whole glass and shut his eyes.

The silence was a moment's reprieve. He breathed it in with the steam from the kettle. "So you see, my dear, we cannot have him here. 'Tis impossible."

"Where then? We can't throw him to the lions." She flung herself at his wet feet and gazed up at him imploringly. Wrung her hands. It was a gesture that always moved him: his mother would do it when the money jar was empty.

He dropped his head in his hands and considered. How many times had Mary come to him for a solution and he always found one? But this time...

"You must know of someone, Joseph. Someone we can trust. It won't be for long. Just till we can find out who did take that painting. And oh, I have a thread of hope! An indication. A certain person who knows the identity of Mrs Frothingham's *he* the housekeeper spoke of. If I can find a way—"

He looked her in the eye and she gazed back. Her pupils were huge and dark. Perhaps she did have an "indication"—he did not want to ask of whom. He had his own life to lead; he was in enough trouble as it was. Some of his writers were in trouble, too. Tom Paine, he told her, had fled to France. The howling crowd at Tom's departure in Dover threatened to tar and feather "the great Satan," as they'd labelled him. His own government, finding Tom guilty of seditious libel, had exiled him.

"Never to see his native country again. Any day they will break down *my* door, shut down my shop. End my life's work. Think on that, madam. You will lose your publisher."

"I couldn't bear it, sir, you know that! But it hasn't happened yet. And now, this very moment, I need your help. There must be someone, dear man," she implored, "some friend or relative of yours with conservative sentiments whom the authorities would not suspect, but whom we can trust. Someone who owes you something. Come now, sir. Mr Peale is downstairs—did you know that? (*Good God, no, he didn't.*) Even now they could break in here, looking for him. We've little time. Who, sir, who?"

She was lifting his feet out of the hot water, rubbing them with a towel, too hard. "Stop!" he cried. "*Oww*, my ankles! Let me have that towel."

She handed it over with a smile. But she wouldn't relent, not that one. He had to come up with a solution, a place for an escapee to hide. In his head he ran though the possibilities. Dulcie, already with Mary in Store Street—nay, that would not work. His Aunt Hannah—no. His something-something cousin, Grace, a fussy housekeeper, a gossip, who would give the lad away the first hour she kept him. No. His old friend Randolph, a violinist who a decade earlier had brought the young composer Mozart to play in London—poor Mozart, dead a year ago of exhaustion. No, Randolph was as much a Dissenter as he. The king's men were watching *his* house. But maybe…

Mary was watching him think. It was unnerving. He could feel her breath on his cheek. "Go down and see that they have a bite to eat," he said, struggling up out of his chair. "Then send Mrs Murphy up here. We'll need a porter. I have an idea."

"I knew you would. Oh, you darling man, you never fail me!" She gave him a fierce embrace, a sloppy kiss. Now she'd got him laughing! He wheezed when he laughed. She rushed out of the room and his mother's portrait nearly fell off the wall.

Cyrus Hunt, yes, he told himself. A distant relative of his father's sister-in-law—he never quite knew the connection, if indeed there was one, although Hunt had used it to gain work. The printer did his job well, even when he disagreed with one's orders. But he kept his peace. He was conservative, aye, a Trinitarian, but content enough to let people have their opinions without challenging them. And he needed the work the publisher sent him. He needed the rooms Joseph had arranged for him on Whitefriars Street. He needed Hetty Croup, the wife of a distant relation whom Joseph had sent as servant; Hetty was the only one forgiving enough to work with a dozen birds flying about the apartment.

Joseph would call the new lodger Ransome, a creative fellow

who needed a period of quiet for his nerves. Ransome Brown, who'd been attacked by a highwayman and was injured but was now recovering.

What he would not be able to tell Hunt was how long Ransome would be in his care. His mad Mary was the key to that.

"Send a boy for Cyrus Hunt," he told Mrs Murphy when she entered his chamber, looking put upon, her grey head in its white cap quivering with indignation. Before she could complain, Joseph said, "No, the fellow is not staying here. Have the boy give Hunt this note, if you will. He'll find him on Fleet Street, at Jones and Hollister, Printers."

"Cyrus Hunt?" said Mrs Murphy, who seldom spared him her opinion. "That old fuss-patch? He'll not like it one bit to have an escaped prisoner thrust upon him."

Joseph lifted a hand for peace. "He won't know who the man is. Just give the boy this note, I said. Then bring me a draught of porter. It cuts through the mucus." When Mrs Murphy left he wheezed and coughed and his elbow struck the wall; his mother's portrait lost its mooring; the glass shattered. It was all Mary's fault. "You'll be the death of me yet, madam!" he shouted down the stairwell.

MARY was pleased as she walked up the steps to her house. The young artist would be safe with Cyrus Hunt; Joseph had assured her of that. Herself, she had never cared for the churlish fellow: he always looked at her as though being female meant she was somehow soiled. But he was loyal to Joseph. She had seen the way Hunt looked adoringly at the publisher. Roger Peale would be safe. She only worried now that Lillian Guilfoy might try to visit there. She had warned the young woman that she might be followed—not to tell anyone where her fiancé was, not even St Pierre. But lovers could be impulsive. She knew that from her own impulses that didn't always turn out...well, as she'd hoped. Though at Joseph's urging she had sent Sophia Fuseli an apology, had she not? With no response, of course.

Dulcie greeted her at the door, not with tea but with a letter from Annie. A wave of relief swept over her. The letter had been shoved under the door, Dulcie said; she had found it when she went to polish the handle.

I am well, the letter read in Annie's childish handwriting, smudged with ink and poorly spelled and punctuated—something Mary must correct.

I am at the home of a frend from the hospittal, I plan to stay with her a week or more. I need frends of my own age do I not? Do not come looking for me, my frend's mother be ill. I will see you by and by. Ann.

Ann, not Annie. Back to formality, Mary thought, are we?

"So you see how the girl repays your hospitality," said Dulcie, hands on her aproned hips, her mouth a stiff pink bow. "After all you done for her."

"*Did,* Dulcie, not done. Did." But it was one more blow. And just when she had reported the girl missing, and was feeling pleased about helping Roger Peale to find sanctuary. Just when she was nearing a solution (she hoped, for Bow Street had none) to Isobel Frothingham's murder: she would soon be on her way to see Mr Ashcroft and make him name the painting's thief. She crumpled the note in her hand. Relief led to pique. It was exasperating to have the girl stay with a friend and not first come to ask permission.

Yet Mary was fond of the girl, for all her faults. She wanted her home, safe. In spite of the letter, a lump lodged itself in her throat. She tried to swallow it down, but it kept coming up. Her intuition again, her proclivity to worry.

She swept a pile of papers off the sofa, and sat. She must steel herself to disappointment in love and war. To disappointment in family matters as well, for on the side table was a peevish letter from her father, asking for money. It lay beside an earlier letter from Everina, enclosing a note from Eliza, in which the latter called Mary "already dead to us." A metaphoric death, Mary thought—her sisters envious, perhaps (like Fuseli?) since the publication of the new book. When she had sent them half of her proceeds. Celebrity, it seemed (or was it notoriety?) came with a price. She loved her sisters, she didn't want the new book to come between them!

Now a rolled-up painting worth thousands of pounds lay in a dank wine cellar. What was she to do with that? A throbbing pain was creeping up her neck and into her temples. Dulcie held out a glass of burgundy and she took it; drank it down.

Ah. The wine flooded her with purpose. First things first. She would seek out Edgar Ashcroft and demand that he reveal the iden-

tity of the mysterious *he*. She would see that the painting was returned to Henry—see that he knew it was she, the spurned Mary,
who had recovered it. But not before he absolved Roger Peale of
all culpability.

"More wine, Dulcie." She held out her glass. "And sit down
and have one with me."

Which Dulcie did, of course. The girl never needed a second
invitation. Between them they emptied the bottle. After all, it took
fortification, a virtual suit of armour to seek out Edgar Ashcroft.
She would go the next morning. Her wit would be her weapon.
She would not come home without an answer.

MARY went to the Fleet Street rooms of Edgar Ashcroft by way of
Grosvenor Square. She wanted to speak privately to Isobel's housekeeper. Joseph had been with her when they found the painting;
the housekeeper might have kept something back.

She found the woman with a wineglass in her hand; the broad
cheeks coloured when her daughter announced the newcomer. It
was just as well, Mary thought: she would speak more freely. Smiling, she waved the woman back down into the settee and took a
chair opposite. "I just happened by. I had been thinking about the
painting. It is still in the wine cellar, of course, amongst all those
barrels and bottles? You've been down there to see?" They both
looked at the glass in the housekeeper's hand.

Though what if the painting were not there? What if *he* had
returned to find that someone had meddled, had not put back the
false panel correctly? Had teased out a confession that Mary had
found the painting? She hadn't thought of this before. She should
have informed Fuseli at once. She should have sent Joseph to his
house. It was true: she didn't always think things through.

"No one has been here, madam. I am sleeping here now. When
the mistress was alive, she preferred to be—alone. Most of the servants have been dismissed; it's just myself and my daughter. We
would know if someone came in."

"Of course you would. And I'm grateful. You've more than fulfilled your duty to Mrs Frothingham and to—" Mary coughed.
"To God," she had thought to say, but what did God have to do
with a false panel in a wine cellar?

The housekeeper shifted her position and planted her legs firmly
on the floor. "What is it you wish, madam? I have work to do. I was

only, well, only—" She clutched the empty wineglass in both hands as though she would make it disappear.

"Taking a moment for relaxation," Mary said. "A well-earned moment, I'm sure." She cleared her throat and leaned forward. "I've come about that gentleman you mentioned when we found the painting." She held up a hand when the woman started to protest. "I know you couldn't identify him—you made that eminently clear. But in the interest of discovering who killed your mistress—that is, the theft and the killing might be related in some way. One never knows, does one? In that interest—I would like you to scour your memory. Tell all you know about this man you saw in close conversation with Mrs Frothingham. It was just before the painting arrived, you said?"

The housekeeper had not said. Mary was setting a trap; she was pleased with her sleuthing. She felt a rush of blood to her cheeks.

The housekeeper bent her head. Her legs splayed wide under the blue woolen skirt. She was still clutching the wineglass. Mary waited. Finally the woman said, "I did not see him. I only heard him. It was before the painting arrived."

"Ah," said Mary. "You didn't tell us this before. And what did he say?"

"I told you, madam, I do not eavesdrop." The lips glued together; the eyes gazed piously at the ceiling.

"You do not eavesdrop, but you might overhear. And what did you overhear?"

"Only—only a word here and there. He and the mistress were speaking of the painting. What hour of night he would bring it. Madam, I heard very little. I'm telling the truth now. I heard little—although there was that smell—"

"Ah. And what smell was that? Was it *he*?" Mary was delighted.

"Of liquorice root and saffron, madam. 'Tis an expectorant. The odour isn't strong, but I'd know it anywhere. I remember it from my cousin Esther who has weak lungs and is in fear of becoming consumptive."

"And what, pray, does it smell like, this combination of liquorice root and saffron?"

"Like—like—oh I can't describe it!" Her hands patted the air and then dropped in her lap. "The saffron dominates, yes. You will have to smell for yourself."

So now Mary would have to go about looking—nay, sniffing—

for a man who smelled of liquorice root and saffron. How close would one have to be to such a man? It was not a pretty thought. She liked liquorice, but she was unfamiliar with saffron—she only knew it was a costly spice, coloured an orange-yellow. And it was the predominant odour, the woman said.

"As I said, most folk would hardly notice, madam. It's just that my cousin Esther—"

"Poor woman, yes, and did you notice anything else about the smell or sound of the man?"

"He had a rather soft voice, as I recall. That was why I couldn't always hear."

Mary smiled. "How frustrating for you. But the voice—was there an accent? French, perhaps?"

The housekeeper shook her head. "There were dogs barking. Cook was singing in the kitchen. I could hear only the pitch of his voice. But the smell... My cousin Esther—"

"Yes, and thank you again." Mary took her leave. She would go now to Edgar Ashcroft. She would make him divulge the name of this mysterious man who smelled of saffron. She prayed it would not be Mr Ashcroft himself. She couldn't bear to lean close enough to smell him.

MARY found Ashcroft at his desk, scribbling notes for an editorial: skewering the Dissenters, no doubt, in scarlet ink, upholding the status quo. He was looking particularly garish today in a purple cravat and canary yellow coat that could not quite contain his belly. She coughed, and the editor jumped up. "I knew you would come," he said.

Mary was not pleased with that greeting. She liked to be considered unpredictable; surely her life to date confirmed that attribute. Still, she forced a smile. She had facts to extract from the man.

She pulled herself upright; felt her bones resist, but she did need height. Mr Ashcroft had money and influence—within the king's party, that is; she wanted equal opportunity to be heard. He was trying to draw her hand up to his puckered lips. He obviously saw her as someone to be overcome with money and perseverance. But, she determined, he had met his match.

"Sir," she said, pulling back her hand—she smelled a malodorous perfume on the man; was it saffron? "This is not a social call. I have come on business."

"I can offer you publication," he said. "Not for woman's rights, no—not my dish of tea, you understand, but something light. A bit of fiction perhaps, a romance?"

She let out a sibilant breath and waved away the offers. What a fool he was to think she would write something so frivolous as a romance. Though, in truth, she did have in mind a sort of love story, followed by—yes, a betrayal.

"Pray sit down, Mr Ashcroft." She would not have him standing while she sat. He carefully lifted the tails of his satin coat, and sat down; he made a steeple of his fingers and smiled provocatively. "You know, sir, why I've come," she said. "And not because you invited me. I want you to tell me the name of the man who took the painting. The man who brought it to Mrs Frothingham's house to be concealed there. I must know."

His smile widened at the corners. It was a lopsided smile: one side curled higher than the other. He resembled a monkey she had seen in a cartoon. "If I tell you, what can you do for me?" He leaned over the broad desk.

She gripped her hands together in her lap. So. He would exact a prize for his gift of the name. It was not a prize she intended to give. "We'll play a game," she said. "I'll give you three names, and if I come close to the name of the man who stole the painting, you must ask to kiss my hand, and I'll reward you."

She sat back, satisfied with her plan. A kiss—on the hand—repulsive as it would be, was as far as she would go for her answer. And as close as she could to smell him.

"Name them," he said, getting up, pouring claret for them both (though she refused it) from a decanter on his desk. He scraped his chair close to hers.

She thought hard. She came to the names of three Frenchmen. All three had admired the painting. All were in need of money—for themselves, or for France. Any one of them would have had access to Henry's studio. She named them, one at a time:

"Alfred de Charpentier."

He smiled. "Close," he said.

"Jacques St Pierre."

He smiled again. "Closer still." He moved his chair nearer; his foot encountered hers and she moved her own.

"Bishop Talleyrand."

"Ah! *Touché!* Closer still." Grinning, he leaned over the side of his chair; she let his lips brush her hand. But then he pulled her close and pressed his mouth hard on hers.

She wrenched away. She straightened her neckerchief and glared at him. "It was Talleyrand who stole the painting, wanting funds for the Girondin cause? To overturn the radical Jacobins? Offering you money, no doubt, to keep quiet? And of course you would tell me all this, since you do not support the Revolution in any manner. A bit of revenge, sir, as it were?"

"I said, *close.*" He giggled. "Close for all three Frenchmen. They might all have had a part in it. I did not say any of the three *stole* the painting. For, madam, the fact is, I simply do not know."

Mary swallowed her frustration and lifted her chin. "I am not asking if they *might have*, sir. I am asking for the *one* man who helped to conceal it in the wine cellar."

"Ah, but you did not say that. You said 'come close' to the man who *stole* the painting. And I do not, I said, know who originally stole it. Shall we resume the game? For higher stakes this time?"

He was playing with her. He had no intention of divulging the name. She had no intention of playing with *him*. She arose, and arranged her cloak about her shoulders. "Goodbye, sir. I shall not trouble you again."

"You'll be back, Miss Wollstonecraft," he called out as she reached the door. "You'll be back because you will want to know who the man was. But you will have to pay for it. Aye, you will pay for it, Miss Rights of Woman." He giggled that asinine giggle.

"*Mrs*," she said, and swept out the door.

MARY was in her kitchen the next day, sniffing saffron mixed with a little liquorice root, which she had purchased at a spice shop. The mingling of scents made her quite dizzy. But she was at last certain that she could identify one or the other should she come upon it. For now though, she needed to leave the kitchen with its competing smells of sour milk and rotting fish that Dulcie had not yet removed. Upstairs the maid was sweeping the hearth and singing at the top of her lungs—not at all a dulcet sound. She thought of Annie's soprano hum while she read her book. Mary always knew when the pace quickened in the book, for the hum would grow louder and become a vibrato. The girl had been gone three days now, without another word since that letter, and Mary was starting to panic. The letter had seemed authentic enough: it was signed in

Annie's careless handwriting—but one could be forced to write a letter.

Oh God. She had denied facts far too long. Someone had kidnapped Roger Peale for self-gain of some kind—it could happen to Annie.

But why? A poor orphan girl?

The thought nagged at her. Her nose was still full of saffron; she sneezed—once, twice, and blew her nose. She put on her light cloak—for the sun was shining—and went out. She breathed in the spring air; felt the wind fan her face. Her April birthday had come and gone, with only a note from Everina and a cake from dear Joseph. The soot polluting the air was not as thick here as in other parts of town; she could almost imagine she was back on the farm in Barking, where she had spent her early childhood beside a river. She had been happy there, making up songs, and like her friend William Blake, conversing with angels. She had been happy, that is, before her hapless father moved the family again, looking for the greener fields he never found.

She walked briskly down Store Street, through Russell Square, and over to Coram's Fields where the Foundling Hospital rose up, shouting with children. She went at once to the governor's office to inquire about Annie's friends. It was a new governor: he had not heard of Annie. Without waiting for him to shuffle through his files, Mary moved on to the kitchen where four women were chopping and slicing under a matron's supervision. Mary thought she smelled saffron, and had to ask for a glass of water to quiet her nerves.

"Aye, I knowed the girl, but she had no friends." The matron was a middle-aged woman with large, agile hands, and a belly the size of a balloon.

"But she said in a letter she had gone to visit a friend—and it would have been from here."

The woman was obstinate. "She was a loner, that one. Had to be dragged away from a book to do her work. Ask Bessie, she'll tell you." She stuck out a thumb in the direction of the yard where a dozen girls were racing after a large hide-covered ball. Mary was struck twice in the stomach as she struggled to catch Bessie.

"Not my friend, that one," the girl said, shaking her head emphatically. "Not nobody's friend, uh-uh."

Mary felt a renewed surge of warmth for Annie. She herself had few female friends as a child. It wasn't until Jane Arden, and her beloved Fanny, and then her pupil Margaret, that Mary had female friends she was truly close to. But Jane was occupied with her school and a new beau, Fanny died, and now Margaret was married.

"If you want my opinion, she run away," Bessie said. "Lor', I 'member two, three times she said she'd run off if she'd 'alf a chance and a farthing in her pocket. Aye, she run off, you can bet. You want her back, you go find her. She won't find you."

"Thank you for your opinion," said Mary, sighing, and set out for Bow Street, where she had earlier reported the missing girl. The magistrate had promised to send out a set of Bow Street Runners in pursuit. But where would they look? What could they promise?

"We got hundreds o' younguns missing," said a bewigged fellow with a scar curving below his mouth like a second set of lips. He cleared his throat of phlegm, settled his gaze on Mary's bosom, and wrote down, for a second time, Annie's name and description.

Mary drew her cloak across her chest and rose. She had little hope from that quarter.

Law and order in this country, she told herself grimly, were laid largely on the individual. If justice were to be done—a young girl found, a friend's murderer brought to heel—it was up to Mary herself. A heavy task indeed. Perhaps a hopeless one.

She thanked him and left.

There were children everywhere running about the streets, but none was Annie. Once she chased a group of young girls around a corner, but they turned out to be dirty-faced urchins—one in a red wig. The smallest of them stuck out a tongue, and Mary wept from frustration—she couldn't help it. The tears rolled boldly, shamelessly, down her cheeks and into her neckerchief. She tried to contain them with a sleeve, but still they flowed.

She hurried back through the teeming streets and towards her home. Turning into Store Street, she heard hooves beating up behind her, but was still too overcome with emotion to even look. In seconds the horses were upon her. Shrieking, she flung herself behind a tree. The carriage hurled up mud and pebbles, but kept moving at a smart pace.

When Dulcie found her she was still clinging to the tree: a sorry, soggy muddle. "Laws," Dulcie cried, "you been fighting, have you?"

Mary nodded; she supposed she had. She let Dulcie lead her up the steps and into the house where even a warm fire, hot tea, and a purring cat couldn't stem the tide of woe.

CYRUS Hunt was not happy. No sir, he was not. It was not fair to burden him with an invalid, no. He felt cornered, run over, like one of the freshly dead birds he'd pick up from the street to sketch. It was as if he'd sold his soul to the publisher in return for work and three small, chilly rooms. And one of the three occupied now by an unhealthy stranger. A suspicious stranger. A brother, Mr Johnson claimed, to that painted female who was with the man now. Hmph.

Cyrus detested painted women. It was just such a painted woman who had lured his father into her bed, given birth to himself, then deserted them both. A Frenchwoman, aye. It was for good reason Cyrus hated the French. He made the sign of the cross: he had recently converted to Catholicism. It was something solid in his life: a religion that stood for something, that told him how to live—unlike Johnson's Unitarians who had no creed.

He touched the painting on the wall of the sitting room; caressed the pale cheek, the blue curve of robe, the sacred foot in its white sandal. He dreamt sometimes that the Madonna was his mother: chaste, and loving. Not painted pink and red and smelling of scent like that woman now with her invalid brother. Or was it her brother? He had seen the way they greeted one another—lust in her eye. Cyrus knew lust, yes, but he was able to overcome it. He was content, a bachelor. One of the yellow cockatiels landed on his shoulder and he stroked it. The female squawked in the cage, too shy to fly about the room. He would replace her with a male.

He would go to Johnson. He would explain that he could not sanction this visitation. He would remain loyal—loyalty was in his nature. But there were limits beyond which a man could not go.

Besides, he needed the rooms for his work. For the wood engravings he made of the living and dead birds, and then coloured by hand. He used a graver to leave a line that didn't print—a white line rather than a black line; the finished engraving was far superior to a woodcut. Even superior, he felt, to some of William Blake's copperplate engravings. When they saw what he, Cyrus, could do with copperplate and lead and the technique of aquatint, they would see himself as the truer artist. He had developed a bluish-purple colour, for instance, that more closely matched the grackle or the blue grosbeak than any he'd seen on prints of birds in the British Isles or North America.

The wood-gravings would take the better part of a year to complete. Then he would print two hundred copies, with one hundred varieties of birds. He would need capital to complete the project, but he had a plan already in progress. And now Johnson was presuming upon the very space he needed for his work. Already one whole table was filled with the publisher's seditious pamphlets. Pamphlets that Cyrus had set in type without reading, for to read them, he thought, would fill his mind with anguish.

He wanted to live free of the publisher's charity. He wanted to be able to rent his own rooms—nay, buy a house, a whole house to roam in, to set up his printing business. He no longer wanted to work for someone else. For this had been Cyrus's life. To obey, to suffer in silence. To endure.

But no more. He clenched his fists. He would endure no more!

He moved to the door of the chamber where the woman's brother (so-called) lay on the bed, and squinted through the keyhole. Saw. Drew back. He sucked in a breath that sent waves of pain through his body—let it out slowly, and felt a vertigo.

If this was the woman's brother, it was incest. Unspeakable sin! If not her brother, why, then a lover. But who? And what had the man to hide? The face was familiar—a face Cyrus might have seen before, though with the ragged growth of beard he could not be certain. But he would find out. He must know who he was housing.

When the woman laughed, it was more than he could bear. He filled with rage. He wheeled about and banged on the chamber door. "Get out," he cried. "I said no visitors. I cannot have it. Cannot! I've work to prepare. Leave my rooms at once!"

The chamber was suddenly quiet. He staggered back into the sitting room and collapsed onto the sofa with a manuscript. Buried his head in it, though he couldn't read the scrawl of words. He smelled the woman as she passed, the sinful fragrance. She paused near the door as though she would speak; he held his breath, and she moved on.

The outer door shut behind her and he let out the breath. Mrs Croup came up out of the kitchen with a tray and he said, "Not now. Later. I'm feeling poorly. Take it back."

"It's for him," she said, pointing a stubby finger at the stranger's bedchamber. "Ye want him to starve, do ye?"

He hated the way the servant talked back to him. Women took advantage, they always had. He would not dignify her with a reply. He heard her enter the chamber, and then the stranger's soft "thank you." Too much! He would go to Joseph Johnson and demand that the stranger leave.... And if the man didn't leave—what would he be forced to do then?

CHAPTER XIV.

No Way Out

∼

THEY WERE not going to keep Annie in this ugly little room with only a journal to read: *The Ladies Pocketbook for the Year 1776*—almost twenty years out of date! And who wanted to read pages and pages about hats and dresses or a letter from Her Majesty to the King of Prussia, or the rates of coachmen and chairmen. And all "compiled at the request of several ladies of quality." Quality, pooh! They all had to sit on the pot, like herself.

Still, she read it over and over till the pages shredded.

She flung the journal down on the floor and went to the third-storey window, to the one tiny unbricked pane that gave her a view of the river. If she refused to eat she might lose weight enough to squeeze through that space and then throw herself into the waters. She could paddle back to shore, couldn't she? But if she grew thin enough to wriggle through the single pane, why she would be too weak to swim, or run through the streets when she reached land again. She might even be dead when she struck bottom.

There was no way out, it seemed. The door was locked and bolted on the outside, and the woman was strong—Annie saw the muscles bulge when she raised her arms to knock down a bat that had come in. And who was that other man? When Jib forced her into the house, she'd seen him with his back to her, drinking wine. Jib shouted, "Got her," and the man grunted but didn't turn round. Then the woman came to drag her upstairs and lock her in the room.

The knob was turning now in the door and Annie braced herself. Neither Jib nor the second man had come in to see her, yet she always expected one of them. Had she a stool in the room, or even a book, she could whack him with it—or the woman, too. But what hurt could *The Ladies Pocketbook* do? If only she had her mother's quill pen Miss Mary had found: she could poke the woman in the eye, and then run out the door.

But they even took away her shoes. And she owned only the one pair. What would Miss Mary say?

It was the woman, Peg, with a tray of bread and soup and the emptied chamber pot. "Chicken soup, dearie, special for you," the woman said in her Scots brogue. "Wi' potatoes, a treat from America. The Indians grow 'em, ye know. They be taking ye there, they say. Ain't you the lucky one? Me cousin Agnes went over with her man, and started a grand farm with a byre and a wee cow. Sent back a few pounds, they did, to me gran."

"I don't want to go to America," said Annie, contemplating the soup and bread. Should she drink it—or pour it into the chamber pot when the woman wasn't looking? Why, anyway, were they keeping her here? They didn't ask for money in the letter they made her write. Were they planning to take her to America and turn her into a woman of pleasure? She'd heard about such things—she'd barely escaped right here in London!

"Why, it might not be America. It might be Australia they'll be takin' ye—I canna be sure. Australia's a grand big land full o' sheep, they say. A lass like you could make a brand new start there. And a warmer climate, too, than the north of America—'tis all snow and ice there, I hear tell."

Annie did not want to go to Australia *or* America. She wanted only to stay in London and live with Miss Mary. Something throbbed behind her eyes. But she would *not* cry in front of this woman.

She decided to eat their gruel and grow strong. She would lift the chamber pot up and over her head a dozen times to strengthen her muscles. Then one day she would hit the woman with it, and escape. When the woman went to pick up the chamber pot after she got up, she said, "Leave it be. I think there's more coming."

The woman looked hesitant, and then shrugged. "Weel, ye'll find out where the ship's bound in five days' time, lass. The South Seas maybe, for aught I been told. And won't you have a grand time then?"

She flashed a "too bad" smile at Annie and marched to the door. Annie hurled a soup spoon that hit her in the small of her back; bits of potato sprayed the apron strings. The woman spun about with a hissing sound. She tucked the spoon into her belt. It made a high-pitched ring against her iron keys. "I wouldna do that again if I was ye, lass. Ye might not get anything atall to eat and then ye'll be going nowhere, but into the ground, eh? Now lap up yer soup like the helpless bairn ye be."

Annie kept a stoic face until the woman left. When the lock turned in the door, she let the angry tears water down her soup.

But she had to drink it. She picked up the bowl and gulped it down: tears, potatoes, and two small chunks of chicken that stuck in her throat and came up again. She spat them out, then picked up the chamber pot and heaved it up and down, up and down, until her thin aching arms hung useless at her sides.

"'TWON'T bring Annie home, you know, miss, starving yourself like this. The girl's run away, like that orphan said. And that's that."

Mary stared up at her maidservant, who was standing over the bed with a tray of porridge and milk, glaring down at her with two heads. She was feeling poorly: her muscles still ached from the latest accident. She blinked and her vision cleared.

"You're not helping nobody," Dulcie went on, "just lying in bed like an old woman." Dulcie held a spoon to her mistress's lips and, abstracted, Mary sipped from it.

Old woman? Oh, dear. "How long have I been here like this?" She was suddenly ravishingly hungry. She snatched up the bowl in two hands, and gulped down the liquid.

"Two and a half days. And there's a message from Mrs Guilfoy, wants you to go see her. And two bouquets of flowers from Mr Ashcroft."

"I don't want them. You know that."

"I know, ma'am. I already give one bouquet to the almshouse in Chenies Mews. Put the other on the table downstairs. Seemed too bad to throw out pretty spring flowers."

"Just keep them out of my sight. And next time shut the door in that man's face."

"It wasn't him as brought 'em, 'twas an errand boy. I'm not going round shutting doors in innocent faces."

"All right then. Bring me a dish of tea, would you? I'll drink it while I dress."

"You're not going out, Miss Mary! That horse and carriage—I seen the hoofprints. They swerved up onto the grass. Accident, you said?"

"The tea, Dulcie. And I will not be a prisoner in my own house. Mrs Guilfoy wants to see me, does she?" Mary would walk to George Street, she decided. She felt safer on her feet than in a carriage she couldn't control.

"Yes, ma'am. But that galloping horse. You might've been kilt."

"Accidents happen every day in London. Now the tea, Dulcie. With a heaping spoonful of melted sugar. And stop assaulting me with dire warnings."

"Yes, ma'am."

"No, never mind. I'll take my tea at Mrs Guilfoy's. Now, off with you, while I pull myself together."

IT was not tea but a glass of porter that Lillian Guilfoy thrust into her hand, and then sat beside her, hip to hip, to pour a flood of complaints into her ear. Cyrus Hunt had forbidden access to her beloved. "For three days now. He said he wouldn't tolerate such 'excesses of passion.' As though I were some—some woman of the street! And worse, he wants my fiancé removed from his house. Oh, Mary, but I must—*must*—see Mr Peale. He needs proper care; he needs a physician. He's still weak, poor lamb."

Lillian was burrowing her head into Mary's shoulder, inching her into a corner of the sofa as she waxed on. Mary put a hand on her arm: "Pray, calm yourself, dear girl. One concern at a time. Let's begin with the phrase 'excesses of passion.' Would Mr Hunt have grounds to say such a thing?"

Colouring, Lillian rose to her own defense. "But we hadn't seen each other for weeks, you know that! We were in the bedchamber, I had shut the door—the other rooms are filled with birds, gabbling in their cages. Sometimes he lets them loose and they fly about the room, dropping you-know-what on the furniture. I worry about disease. But the printer came in and the chamber door cracked open—it doesn't have a proper latch."

"He saw you embracing, did he?"

"Well, perhaps, I can't say. Embracing, nothing more! Whatever he saw, he misconstrued. He said it was the second time we had—whatever he thought we'd done."

"I believe Mr Johnson told him you were brother and sister."

Lillian gasped. "I hadn't thought of that. Oh! How could he think such a thing of Mr Peale and me!"

"Men have minds like that. As for the nursing care, Mr Johnson is sending his own physician. And we don't want Mr Hunt suspecting who your fiancé is, do we? I'm sorry, dear lady, but it would really be best you do not go back. I'll speak to Mr Johnson, and warn him about the printer's concerns. We must keep your fiancé there." Mary patted the young woman's elbow. "It's only for a short time. Until we can find things out. You see, we're moving closer to an answer. Did you hear that we found the painting?" Mary smiled, and Lillian nodded. "Yes?" Mary put a finger to her lips. "Mr Fuseli doesn't know yet. It will soon be back in his hands, but I want him to stew about it a bit longer. He won't thank us anyway, the ingrate. He'll just go into a tirade against the one who put it there. Against poor Mrs Frothingham, who is already dead."

"What? Mrs Frothingham took it?"

"Oh, she doubtless just stored it for someone else. Who knows what they bribed her with? We don't really know yet, do we?"

"Then why, if you have the painting, should Mr Peale stay at that bird-man's house? Why can't he come home to me?" Her hands were clutching at Mary's arm, the arm Mary had bruised, escaping the horse. There was no reasoning with a woman in love. Mary knew. She herself was no longer in love—she had shut off that part of her. But her body ached to remember.

She carefully extracted the pinching hands. "Think, dear girl. Mr Peale broke away from Newgate. He must yet face a charge that he hired a fellow to run down that poor footman. No, your fiancé is still in danger. He can't stay here with you." He might have to take ship to Australia, Mary thought, but she wouldn't suggest such a fate today.

Lillian blew noisily into a lacy handkerchief. Somewhere in the house young Tommy was having a tantrum; the nursemaid was trying to quiet him. Henry's son, yes. Mary thought: we have both been betrayed by Henry. We are sisters in betrayal. She leaned into Lillian and let the latter's head sink onto her shoulder. The wailing quieted in the far corner of the house. The white cat purred where it lay sprawled on the wide window seat.

There was a rap on the door. Two raps, and Mary lifted her head. A voice called, "*Ma chère Madame Guilfoy. C'est moi.*"

"Ah, it's Monsieur St Pierre," said Lillian, and went to greet him.

St Pierre, yes, in a somewhat shabby royal blue coat and waistcoat and white worsted stockings. He flung a bouquet of violets on the table, embraced Lillian, held her away from him a moment, and then drew her close. He did not seem aware of her abstraction. Did he know that his rival was back in London? Mary had warned the young woman not to tell anyone. For a moment she was sorry for the man. But when he bowed stiffly to acknowledge Mary's presence, she nodded back, and sighed. Of course, she thought, he wants to see Lillian alone. I am the unwanted chaperone.

Mary was unprepared for what happened next. Lillian had scarcely extricated herself from the Frenchman's arms when she hurled herself back into them. "I have to tell you," she cried. "Mr Peale is safe! You must know that. You must be glad for me."

Oh, my God, Mary thought.

The Frenchman's face was a whirlpool of emotions from the frowning brow to the trembling mouth. His mouth said, "*Eh bien, excellent.*" But his eyes said he was not happy that Roger was back, and safe; his fists pressed into the young woman's back.

Lillian broke free and flung her arms high. She whirled about, her skirts swishing with her. Then seeing his struggling face, she embraced him again. "Oh, *mon cher* Jacques. I shall always be grateful for your help. But I love my fiancé. I can't help it. He is my—my soul mate. You must understand that, and be my friend. Will you be my friend? For ever and always?"

Slowly he recovered himself. The trembling stopped, the hot eyes cooled. He let his "friend" go, and sat on the edge of a wing-back chair. He adjusted a dented buckle on his shoe that had come undone. Mary felt she was at Covent Garden, watching a drama play itself out. He began to ask questions. How had Monsieur Peale escaped the madhouse? Where had he been in the interim? "Where is he now?" he asked, trying to smile.

Mary saw the gleam of the man's white teeth, and her imagination soared. She thought of the children's tale of Red Riding Hood and the Big Bad Wolf and wondered how she could get closer to him so that she might smell him. Oh, dear. Would she spend the rest of her days smelling men, trying to determine their guilt or innocence?

She tried to catch her hostess's eye, but the latter was already bubbling out answers to his questions. "We have Miss Wollstonecraft here to thank," she said. "She and the bookseller have found him a refuge on Whitefriars Street, with Cyrus Hunt." The foolish woman blew a kiss at Mary, and seeing Mary's distress, said: "We can trust Monsieur, Mary, he's my dear friend. He helped my Roger to escape, did he not?"

"You can, you can, my dear—*mais oui, absolument*," the Frenchman said warmly, and this time his teeth seemed smaller, less shiny.

Lillian rang for the nursemaid, and when she appeared, Tommy clinging to her skirt, she said gaily: "Tea for us all. And cake."

"Cake!" the boy shouted, and climbed onto his mother's lap. The nursemaid scooped him up, laughing, and whisked him back to the stairs.

"Cake, cake," she sang, "we ache for cake," and the boy giggled loudly.

Let them eat cake, Mary thought absurdly—a phrase Marie Antoinette was rumoured to have said in reference to her starving people—but probably hadn't. Who could be so cruel?

"Forgive me, but I must forgo the cake," said the Frenchman. "I stopped in only to see if you were well and to bring the flowers. I have an appointment. My mind has been so scattered lately, with all that has been happening in my beloved Paris. This guillotine they are building: it is more than we expected—it has already taken the head of a highwayman. A quick and benevolent death, they say. They would have *my* head if they could. I have friends I worry about now. They waited too long to leave. And one is already in La Force Prison—the most cruel!"

He coughed after the torrent of words, and then rose and bowed over Lillian, taking her hand to kiss. He bowed towards Mary, and she held out a hand. He looked surprised, but took it, his lips just missing the fingers. *His* fingers, she saw, were tinged with yellow as if he had jaundice. But it was not jaundice. She breathed him in. She knew the aroma: that sweet, thick, musky aroma. She had studied well.

"Nor can I stay," Mary told a disappointed Lillian once her visitor took his leave. "We are looking for Annie, you see; she has been gone several days. We had a letter—she might be with a friend. Though I worry. I go twice a day to Bow Street Court to ask if there have been any sightings. I've asked everyone I know to keep an outlook for her. I should have asked St Pierre. Do you know where he lives?"

"Why, in Green Street. He has rooms there over a spice shop. I've only been there once, but it smells to high heaven." She laughed.

"They sell saffron there, do they?"

"Oh yes, yes. Jacques brings me the powder. My maid bakes it into buns and cookies and churns it into butter. It turns butter into a brilliant yellow. Will you try some on white bread?"

"No, no. But thank you, I must be away. I, I—" Mary couldn't speak coherently; she was consumed with what she had to do. Go first to Hunt's, and if St Pierre was not there… But why would he be there?

The Frenchman is Roger Peale's rival for Lillian Guilfoy, she thought as she pulled on her cloak. To what lengths would he go? If he were not at the printer's, and she hoped he would not be, then she would go to his rooms in Green Street. One way or another she would confront him and make him confess that he had stolen the painting. Or had been put up to it by Talleyrand.

The bishop, yes. Hadn't he enlisted St Pierre to help him raise money for revolutionary France? They had sat in her own parlour speaking of it. Talleyrand had a reputation for taking what he wanted—with impunity.

She embraced her hostess and pocketed a piece of cake (she had not fully breakfasted); outside she hailed a hackney coach. The Frenchman was nowhere in sight—there was no time to walk. When she arrived at her destination, she would send the coachman after a constable.

Talleyrand, she realized, was too big a prey for her. She would have to bring him to heel by attacking the underling—pulling the carpet out, so to speak, from under his big warped foot. Though it was a temptation to let the bishop have the painting and sell it for the cause of the moderate Girondins who would allow women to hold public office and who wanted Louis XVI exiled, but not killed. And thereby to defeat Henry Fuseli. She would think on that.

But if she thus defeated Henry, young Peale would be hanged

and the lovesick Lillian remain an old maid, her son a natural child, unadopted. That could not be, no.

She felt suddenly weak as she climbed into the coach, and overwhelmed with responsibility. She must prove St Pierre a thief and Peale an innocent. She must return the painting to Henry Fuseli. He must see that he was *wrong*. That had become her whole mission in life.

"Whitefriars Street," she told the coachman. "And hurry!" She held out a shilling. It was her last shilling; she should share it with her sisters. But for now, they would have to sacrifice to *her* cause.

THE physician sent by Joseph Johnson pronounced Roger to be in moderately good health, and left "Mr Brown" a bottle of Collett's Elixir: a mixture of French brandy, Madeira wine, and the salt of millipedes. It would make him drowsy, if nothing else. "You're a lucky young man," the smiling doctor told Roger. "I've seen men go into madhouses whole in mind and come out—if indeed they come out at all—a wreck, an animal. Have you been to Bedlam?"

"Not Bedlam in particular," said Roger, "but I feel I know it well." He had seen more than he wanted of madhouses. He thanked the doctor and locked the door behind him as Hunt had instructed. The latter had been home less and less often the past few days—most likely to avoid his unwanted guest. Roger didn't like the enforced union any more than the printer did. For one thing, Lillian had been told not to visit. And Hunt had given Roger a lecture on morality he most decidedly did not need.

God, but he was lonely here—almost as lonely as in the madhouse. Of course he could leave: he could just walk out and go. He could deliver himself up to the authorities. And perhaps he should. Hiding out, he feared, would only worsen his punishment.

There was a knock at the door and he gave a start. His muscles were not his own: they jerked and creaked. Mrs Croup was out; he was alone with the birds. A cockatiel flew out of a cage Hunt had left open and landed on his shoulder; the talons dug into his flesh. He didn't like the feeling, but he couldn't bear to return the creature to its cage.

Again, a knocking. Then a voice, calling, "Monsieur Peale! *C'est moi, moi,* Jacques St Pierre! Open up if you are there."

He pushed the bird back in its cage and unlocked the door. It was indeed Jacques. His friend grasped him by the shoulders and bussed him on both cheeks. "Where have you been? How did you get here? Your *belle fiancée* has sent me. She says she cannot come, so here I am, to welcome you back."

"Enough," Roger cried, pushing him off. "I'm still bruised— you can't imagine what I've had to endure."

"Oh, *mon pauvre ami. Eh bien,* it is only my great joy to see you again. We have all been looking, you see. Madame Guilfoy heard about your escape from that terrible madhouse, but then lost track again. What happened? Where were you?"

"South of London—I can't tell you exactly where," Roger said. "I escaped in the dark. Mrs Guilfoy can tell you more precisely. She went there to search for me—did you know that?" Poor darling, he thought. And he was there the whole time, locked in that damp cellar.

St Pierre was pacing about the room, picking up prints, slapping them down again, his fingers already purply-blue. "Ah—this fellow is an artist, like you, *monsieur*?"

"A printer by trade. But an artist of sorts, yes. His sketches are quite good, the colours he mixes. At least for the birds. Not for the human beings."

Seeking paper for his own sketches, Roger had found lewd drawings of women—including women copulating with birds. Instinctively he had disliked Hunt, and now he was certain. Besides, the printer was too religious for a Dissenter like Roger, too cold, too hypocritical. The way the fellow had been shocked coming upon himself and Lillian embracing, as if he were some popish priest— and yet those salacious drawings... Dear God, Roger wanted out of here. Out!

"Find me another place to stay," he told St Pierre. "Have you rooms?"

"Ah, *oui, mon ami,* but they would go there at once, the authorities. We must look elsewhere, eh? I have a plan. I have come to tell you about it."

"Sit down then," Roger said, dropping onto the couch. The fellow was making him nervous, the way he paced about. Or the man himself was nervous. But St Pierre had helped him escape the prison, had borrowed money, he said, to do it. Roger owed him some courtesy. "I regret I can't offer you food or drink: the housekeeper is out. At any rate she doesn't care to serve my guests. She barely tolerates *me*." The woman looked a martyr each time she brought him his meagre serving of food. He would gain no flesh in this place. Although the elixir might bring him an ounce or two. Already he could feel his muscles slackening since the physician's visit.

St Pierre sat for a moment, fidgeting on the stained blue seat cushion, further upsetting Roger's fragile nerves. "I cannot stay. I just want to take you from here to a safer place. My kinsman in the country—the one awaiting us before the highwayman came? He would be happy to accommodate you. You said you are ready, eh? Well then. Come. Come!"

He leapt up and extended his hands. "I have a carriage outside. You are not safe in London, you should know that. We will go at once. Get dressed. Gather your things."

Roger hesitated. The thought was compelling, but for some reason he had doubts. He didn't know what they were—he hadn't had time to think them through. But they were there, under his skin.

"Madame Guilfoy will be able to visit you there, *monsieur*. Till we find who really took that painting. So come, come. Where are your clothes? Is that your bedchamber?"

When Roger nodded, St Pierre put an arm about his shoulders and led him into the room. "Here, I'll help. Is this your coat? It looks like a farmer's barn coat. Someone gave it to you, I suppose? Your breeches?" He laughed. "All ripped at the knees and hems. We will buy you new ones. My cousin is your height. A bit more in girth, but you will grow into one of his. Oh, we must talk! I want to hear about every moment of your sad adventure. From the time we were stopped by those miserable highwaymen."

He helped Roger step into the breeches. The proximity to the man gave Roger a sense of déjà vu. Something, he couldn't think what…

"I want to go. But tonight I'm too weak. Tomorrow perhaps. Next week. I'll take my chances here."

St Pierre chuckled. "Come, come. You will be happy there. Just for a short time. Button up now, we don't want your breeches falling down before we reach the carriage, do we? *Non, non*, that would never do."

Still chuckling, he pushed Roger out of the bedchamber, back into the sitting room. "The key, the key, *s'il vous plaît, mon ami.* Ah! It is still in the lock."

Before St Pierre could reach the handle, the door opened, and there stood that woman, that authoress. Roger could tell she was angry by her quick breath, the lips pursed, the cheeks a blotchy red. She went straight for St Pierre and grabbed his arm.

"It was you who stole Henry's painting," she accused. "Oh yes, Edgar Ashcroft saw you. He was at Mrs Frothingham's when you entered with it. He helped you hide it in her wine cellar, did he?"

"I beg your pardon, madame? We were just taking our leave. Now kindly let us pass."

"And why does Roger Peale have his cloak on? He's not well. He is not ready to go out of doors." The woman's face was a pink sunset; she still had the Frenchman's arm. St Pierre was laughing and shaking his head. Roger was confused—what was the woman saying about a painting?

Still holding on to St Pierre, she locked the door behind her and pocketed the key. She looked hard at Roger. "You don't know what he's done? He has stolen *The Nightmare* and let you be accused of taking it. If you were in a madhouse, whoever put you there— whatever hireling—it was St Pierre at fault. Yes, I see that now. He let you, Mr Peale, take the blame."

The Collett's Elixir was taking over Roger's brain. St Pierre had stolen the painting? Fuseli's painting? What would he want it for? Roger could not think what, or why…

"The saffron. I could smell it." She had St Pierre by the collar; she was shaking him. "Mrs Frothingham's housekeeper smelled it, too. You were indeed there, sir. Edgar Ashcroft and the house-keeper can testify in any court of law. Outside—I've a constable."

A window of light was forming in Roger's head. The smell. He knew the smell—not what it was precisely: it was simply Jacques St Pierre to him. "It was you," he said, pointing a shaky finger. "It was you, St Pierre!"

St Pierre had turned on the authoress. Holding her wrist with one hand, he fished in her pocket with the other—for the door key, no doubt. She was fighting him back with her free hand, crying out at the top of her lungs, a veritable Amazon. Roger tried to pull him off the woman but he was too weak. Spinning about, the Frenchman knocked him on his back; then snatched a bottle of printer's ink and flung it. The bottle struck the woman's arm; purple ink sprayed back on the thrower: "*Merde!*" A second cockatiel's cage sprang open in the mêlée; the bird flew at St Pierre and clung to his scalp. The Frenchman howled.

The Amazon was at the window, calling down; a male voice replied. "Get back," she told Roger, "back in the bedchamber." But Roger was weary of hiding. They had the painting—he understood that much. It was St Pierre who had stolen it. St Pierre, who had masqueraded as a friend and broken him out of Newgate—then put him in that madhouse. For God's sake, why?

He saw the woman open the door for the constable and then lock it again. The key fell on the floor when she tried to return it to her pocket, but she didn't seem to notice. "That the rogue?" the constable cried.

St Pierre was at the second-storey window, pushing it wide, propelling his body through, reaching for a branch of an oak tree— Roger saw a blue carriage waiting below. He lunged, and this time grabbed him by the seat of his breeches. Someone grabbed *him*— and shoved him aside. His hand groped for a chair-back to keep himself upright. The constable was clubbing the Frenchman on the back and shoulders, tying a cord around his wrists, propelling him toward the door.

"Take him to Bow Street Court," the woman cried. "Inform Mr Fuseli that his thief is found. The painting is safe. This man can tell him where it is."

Roger backed against the wall and hung frozen there, the bird clinging to his shoulder. The authoress was triumphant. Her dress was askew, her hair like a nest of swallows. A shoe had come off in the turmoil. But she was smiling from ear to ear. Roger had heard she wanted to go to Paris "to see what's going on." He could imagine her running down the Champs Élysées, shrieking *Liberté, Égalité—Féminité!*

"You call yourself a revolutionary?" St Pierre cried out while the constable fumbled with the door handle. The door was still locked and the woman searching now for the key. "You do not know," he bawled, "what revolution is. *Mon Dieu*, they will have half of Paris beheaded before it is over. Blood flowing in the streets— you would soak your feet in it. That painting would have brought

money to keep the atrocities under control—to buy help for those
with some measure of reason. Fuseli can paint another. There must
be sacrifices!"

Roger spotted the key on the floor beside the empty ink bottle.
He picked it up and she snatched it from him. The ink had painted
a dark blue bruise on her cheek.

"For the Girondin cause, yes. But not the sacrifice of Mr Peale!"
she shouted at St Pierre. "It was because of your love for Mrs Guilfoy, was it not? When she does *not* love you, you know that."

"What do you know, officious *femme?*" he cried. "She loved me
once. What do you know?"

She unlocked the door for the constable. She was going with
him, she said, to be sure the Frenchman did not break free. "You
may have more than a thief and abductor," she told the constable.
"You may have a murderer."

Mercifully the door shut behind the trio. Roger returned the
cockatiels to their cages and collapsed onto the couch. He didn't
know if it was St Pierre or this madwoman—why did her name always elude him?—who tired him the most. She had saved his neck,
yes. But she had taken the door key. Cyrus Hunt would stage a
scene over that.

At least the constable had paid no attention to *him*. Though
someone would come back, he was certain of that. There was no
way out of the black hole that St Pierre and his plan had put him in.

When the authorities came, he would be here, waiting. He
could no longer hide.

CHAPTER XV.

Wild Horses Wouldn't Stop Her!

⌒

THE STORY St Pierre told the Bow Street magistrate was astonishing, and Mary believed it—despicable though it was. There had been a "terrible conflict" in his mind: a conflict of passion. He had taken the painting, he insisted, to sell abroad and help fund the moderate Girondins. To create a measure of sanity—and with it, a hope of regaining his estate. The magistrate nodded at the word "sanity." The Frenchman went on to say that when Fuseli accused Roger of the theft, he, Jacques St Pierre, used the accusation as a means of exculpating himself.

"But I was not in my right mind, you see. There was Madame Guilfoy. I was in love with her—am in love. *Sans espoir,*" he cried, breaking down, while the bewigged justice sat squinty-eyed and solemn. The sour-faced court clerk scribbled down the Frenchman's words with equanimity.

When St Pierre recovered his breath he admitted to arranging Roger Peale's escape from Newgate. He could not bear—ah!—to think of Peale free to return to Madame Guilfoy. He had hired the highwaymen to halt the carriage and take the artist to a madhouse.

"I never wanted him hurt, or dead, *mais non, non!*" he cried, pounding his fist on the bench. "I had nothing against him except—except—" They all knew what the "except" was. They waited while he wiped his eyes with a sleeve. "You see, I hoped that with his absence Madame Guilfoy would give up hope for him and come to me—and later I would find a way to help Peale—I truly thought that." He gazed at the courtroom through a glaze of tears.

"I did it out of love." He turned his head and stared at Mary.

"Love for the great cause as well. *Vive la Révolution! Vivent les Girondins!*" He collapsed onto the bench; his tears leaked into the cracks of the ancient oak. Mary thought she could smell saffron, even at a distance.

The magistrate looked on, steely-eyed. He had no love for a revolution. He had no pity for a lover. He would send St Pierre to Newgate to await trial—a final irony. There the Frenchman would be interrogated as well about the murder of Mrs Frothingham. In the interim, a Bow Street Runner was to meet Mary at the Grosvenor Square house to retrieve the painting, to see that it was returned to Henry Fuseli. Would she like to accompany the fellow to the Fuseli home?

Mary hesitated. She would like to see Henry's face when he realized it was not Peale but St Pierre who had stolen the painting. And that, in addition to the bluestocking, he had an accomplice in the theft he yet refused to name: most likely Talleyrand. Ashcroft, too, Mary thought—but then decided that the man was merely a dupe, a tool. He was probably telling the truth; he wouldn't dare to steal a painting. And he deplored revolutions.

Ah well: the law and Henry Fuseli would have to find out for themselves when the case came to trial in the Old Bailey.

As for Mrs Frothingham, she would have felt she was helping the great cause: *La Révolution.* Poor idealistic lady: everyone's pawn. In bed for this cause, for that one. Mary was a staunch revolutionist, yes, but she was principled; she would not stoop to steal a painting (or live with someone she didn't love, for that matter). She wanted Henry to know that she'd had a part in apprehending the criminal, in returning *The Nightmare* to him. But she could not set foot again in that house of humiliation.

"I will meet your man in Grosvenor Square," she said. "But he will take the painting himself to Mr Fuseli."

MARY arrived at Grosvenor Square a quarter of an hour before the constable, who had to stop en route, he had earlier said, to bring an elixir to his ailing wife. The housekeeper's daughter opened the door: a giddy, black-eyed girl whom Mary surprised in the company of a young male. The girl had taken a long time answering the knock; her hair and clothing were in disarray.

"I shan't bother you," said Mary. "I have come to pick up a

painting that did *not* belong to your mistress. A constable will join me shortly." When the beau looked panicked, she said, "He will not detain *you*. But I suggest you leave at once."

The fellow shot out the door. Mary took a candelabrum and a small kitchen knife—it would be unpleasant, alone, in that dark cellar—and trudged down the narrow steps.

At the bottom, she stood, dismayed. There were three aisles of bottles, all looking and smelling alike. She marched up and down, running her hand over the sticky shelves.

Nothing. Good Lord, had someone removed the panel? Should she not have trusted the housekeeper? Had that rascal who just left stolen the painting? What a fool she was not to take the painting at once when she'd discovered it!

She must collect herself; steady her nerves. It was here. It had to be.... She passed once more through the aisles, pushing and pressing the walls.... In the last aisle, on the righthand side, she felt something give. She gave a shout and pushed harder; the panel gave way....

And there it was behind the bottles, rolled up in its sheath of paper and linen. But was it the stolen painting? She had to be sure. Someone had certainly moved it—the housekeeper perhaps. She pulled aside the wrapping, and with effort, unrolled the canvas. Held her breath.

Ah-h. It was. *The Nightmare*. The candelabrum with its three slim tapers lit up the eyes of the little incubus; he seemed to be staring directly at Mary, eyes narrowed and gleaming as if he would take her next. For a moment in the dark cellar Mary *was* that sleeping woman, that erotic dream. That nightmare. The horse's head ogled and waggled toward her; the magnetic eyes of the incubus drew her into the painting. She cried out—then held a hand over her mouth to stifle the sound.

She hated the painting, hated it! The trouble it had caused, the heartbreak! She wanted to destroy it. She pulled the knife from her pocket. Her hand trembled; the colours vibrated in her vision. Reds, golds, palest blues, one colour running into the next. Amazing colours. *Incroyable*: she recalled the French word. She saw the delicate curve of the sleeping woman in the way the arm fell, twisting slightly at the wrist, fingertips touching the carpet, the texture of skin taking on the salmon red of the drapery. The folds and creases in the bed linen—wondrously depicted. Henry's art. Henry's genius. The genius that had first drawn her to him.

One had to separate a painting from the painter: she saw that now. Art was neither good nor evil: it merely depicted human nature—her friend William Blake had said that.

She put the knife back into the sheath of her pocket, then gripped her hand to keep it still.

Now, as she continued to gaze at the painting, she saw Henry himself atop the sleeping woman. Why, it was Henry, the incubus! It was his own human nature he was painting, was it not? Not the painting that was diabolical, no—but the painter. Did not Blake say his art came from above? That he was merely the vehicle through which inspiration passed? And was it too much of a leap to imagine that after Henry had had his fill of that designing woman, he had killed her? Perhaps it was not St Pierre but Henry himself, full of wine, or something stronger, who had joined the bluestocking in bed—and then strangled her? Arranged her to resemble his painting? And then made light of it to allay suspicion...

"Miss Wollstonecraft?" Upstairs she heard the voices of the constables. It would take two men to return such a valuable painting.

"Down here," she called. She quickly rolled up the canvas in the linen cloth. It was just an object now, an artifact. She didn't know where the frame was—St Pierre would have to lead them to that. The Bow Street Runners were on the stairs; she heard the crunch of gravel from their shoes. She did not want them viewing the painting. "It's the right one," she said, "I assure you. But be careful, please. We don't want a single scratch. It is a very, very valuable painting. A work of genius. Mr Fuseli will be much obliged to you for returning it in perfect condition. Surely there will be a substantial reward?" Not for her, of course, although she could use the money, but would never in this world accept it! "The reward is yours."

The men smiled. They were good men, bluff and hearty—one could see mutton and gravy in their eyes; pubs and mugs of foaming ale. One of them picked up the rolled canvas—it seemed of little worth in his beefy arms. Still, she felt the man's awe. He looked as if he were carrying a large baby, holding it up in front of his face. The second man, equally sombre, guided him through the wine cellar and up the steps.

"Are you sure, madam, you won't come with us?" the first man asked when they reached the street door. She saw they had a hackney coach waiting; they would not want to hand-carry a valuable painting through the hazardous streets of London.

"Nay," Mary said. "Tell Mr Fuseli that Jacques St Pierre has confessed. That it was not Roger Peale who stole the painting. Tell him he was wrong about that."

The men started down the steps with the painting and she ran after them. "Tell him that Mary Wollstonecraft said that. That he was wrong. Wrong!"

THIS time the Wollstonecraft woman barged right into the flat, and Roger was relieved to see her. It was the next morning, she told him before he could utter a word about the door key, that she realized she still had it in her pocket. Had he lost the key, he would have had the printer's wrath down upon his head—but luckily the printer had not come home last night. As it was, Roger had not the energy to clean up the debris from the tug-of-war with St Pierre. He waved a weak arm at the spill of paper, paints, ink, and feathers. "I can't let the housekeeper see this," he said. He was as worried about the tyrannical Mrs Croup's reaction as he was about Cyrus Hunt's.

Miss Wollstonecraft stood before him now, all business. She was handsome, yes, one might say voluptuous, but today he found her quite formidable with her wind-blown hair and that fierceness of hers—he might call it *passion*.

"It will require water and soap," she said as she dove into the heart of the chaos. "Mrs Croup will have to help. But I can at least try to clear up the clutter. We'll have to explain what happened to Cyrus Hunt." While she cleaned, she related the story of St Pierre and the Bow Street Court.

"The villain!" he cried, his heart reeling to hear precisely how St Pierre had sacrificed his friend to steal his fiancée. "Let them put *him* in a madhouse! See how he fares there."

"He *is* in a madhouse, she said, dropping to her knees to pick up a sheaf of papers. "He is in Newgate, awaiting trial. Just as you once were."

"Ah," he said. The woman appeared decidedly less formidable now; he smiled down at her, and she smiled back.

"The decision on whether he obtains a reprieve," she said, looking up from her kneeling position, "or whether others are arraigned in connection with the theft, must rest in the hands of the justices—and Henry Fuseli. Mr Fuseli has a large ego. Huge. Stealing that celebrated painting was like stealing his very self. I'd say that was why he was so monomaniacal about pursuing you." She smiled. "Though, thank God he never caught you. Oh!"

The cockatiel landed on her head, its talons in her hair. She returned it gingerly to its cage and latched the door. "But Fuseli may argue that Monsieur should be hanged. I wouldn't be surprised. He can be vindictive."

Did Roger want that? A man's death? He didn't think so. Prison, yes, until the fellow repented what he had done. But not hanged. Roger pitied the bird, crying now, in its cage.

"Hanged, yes, if they find that he killed Isobel Frothingham." She brought up an armful of papers and dropped them on the desk.

"But why would he kill Mrs Frothingham? For what end?"

"For the painting, perhaps. She'd have wanted her share of the money for selling it, and he wanted it all for the Girondin cause. Or so he implied. No doubt he'd have taken some of it for himself. Had you noticed his shoes? How scuffed they are? The tarnished buckles? When he fled France he took little with him."

"But why kill her in that horrible way? By simulating the painting?" Lillian had described the murder scene to him, as she'd heard it. It was beyond comprehension. St Pierre was selfish, even cruel, but he and Lillian had once been close. Nay, he couldn't imagine Jacques killing a human being. Not with his own hands, at least.

The authoress gave no answer. She was at Hunt's desk, sorting out documents and drawings, her jaw lowered as though she would devour them. "My God," she was muttering, "my God." Her mouth was open; she was running her hands through her hair—it stood practically on end. He would so like to paint her! In bare feet and breastplate, flinging one leg up onto a white horse, a helmet on her Medusa-like hair.

He picked up a piece of drawing paper from the floor and glanced about for a pen and ink to begin sketching. He sneezed, and the paper flew from his shaky fingers and under the couch where he was seated. It was not drawing paper, nor even a single sheet of paper he discovered when he retrieved it, but two pieces clipped together with handwriting on the other side—a slight rip on the lefthand corner of the top paper.

"Curious," he said, and read aloud: "*I, Isobel Jane Amelia Froth-*

ingham, of the city of London..." Why, it appeared to be a handwritten testament. Nothing legal of course—he flipped over to the second page—there was no signature but her own. "Perhaps the draft of a will," he told the Amazon, who was staring at him. "Something she might have taken to a solicitor, or planned to take."

In a flash she was back across the room, snatching the papers from his fingers. She held them close to her flushed face. "My God," she said again, "how did this get here?"

He couldn't tell her. He knew only that he wanted—needed to sketch her. He pushed himself off the couch and picked up a blank piece of paper from the printer's desk. When he turned, the woman had his seat. Shrugging, he took her former seat at the desk, shoved the other papers aside, and began to sketch her.

The room was quiet for a time. He had almost forgotten she was there in the flesh when she suddenly shrieked: "Annie! Everything goes to her! House, furnishings, paintings—well, almost everything. Two hundred pounds, of course, to the Foundling Hospital."

He turned his chair about so he could see her more clearly. Now she was a mother whose runaway child had to be snatched back from an onrushing horse. He couldn't describe the expression, but he could paint it. That mix of anger, ferocity, determination: to bring a child safely home to hearth. He sketched with excitement, with abandon. They had found the art thief—he himself was going to live! They would realize he could not have killed that footman. And surely not that bluestocking. He was going to paint again.

"When does he come home? Tell me, when?" The woman was up on her feet, wobbling in her worn black boots, waving the papers in the stale air.

"Who?" He was already back to his work. By the time she had finished talking, he couldn't recall what she had said.

"Cyrus Hunt, I said. When will he return? Is he at his work place now? Is he in Fleet Street?" Good Lord, she was standing over him, a hand clutching his shoulder. He looked up and tried to concentrate on her questions. He didn't know where Hunt worked. He only knew that the fellow came home sometimes to change clothing before he went out again. Sometimes not until late in the evening, around midnight.

He told her what he could. She said, "Fleet Street. I must go at once to find him."

He went back to his sketching. He heard the door shut. He hoped she had remembered this time to leave the key. The printer would be angry to find it missing. Mrs Croup would be furious to find the carpet stained with paint and ink. She would not want to hear about any fight, any coming-to-justice of a thief. She would want to know why the sitting room was not as she had left it.

It didn't matter, not really. He was drawing again. For the first time in weeks he was drawing; he was creating—even on the backs of papers with lewd drawings and notes that said BEWARE... He could still see the helmeted authoress riding into battle, her eyes fierce and shining, her body bent over the horse, over the stallion—she would be riding a stallion, yes. No docile mare for this woman. Mary Wollstonecraft: the eighteenth-century Amazon, riding a stallion!

Roger was laughing. For the first time, perhaps, since he'd been imprisoned, he was wholly letting go. Laughing, while the tears poured down into his rumpled collar.

THE cat had spit up on the rug. Mary stepped carefully around the stain. "Dulcie?"

It was not for the cat mess she wanted Dulcie, although that, too. She wanted the girl to look at the papers she had brought, to compare them to those in her hatbox. She wanted her to see if the will from Hunt's place was the one Dulcie had taken from the bluestocking's house.

The girl appeared, trailing soapy puddles. She had been washing her hair, she said; the next-door maid had deliberately emptied a chamber pot out the second-storey window.

"For heaven's sake," Mary said, "go bind it up with a towel and come back down here with those papers. And be quick about it. There's a killer at large."

"Is that news?" Dulcie said, wringing out her hair over the worn rug.

"Don't argue, Dulcie. Just bring them. And a rag. I'll clean up the cat mess. That is, eventually. He didn't ask to go out?"

"No ma'am, not that I heard. Not in English." Dulcie grinned and ran lightly upstairs.

Mary sat down and smoothed out the will she had taken from the printer's house—the will that made Annie her mother's heir. It was only a handwritten draft, but she would have her solicitor look into this. "Hurry, will you?" she called up.

"Aye, that's the one I found," Dulcie said, back with a hatbox and her hair tied up in a neckerchief. "I know it from that little rip in the corner. It said, 'I, Isobel Jane Amelia Frothingham—'"

"Yes. Now get out those early sketches. The ones with the sour-faced boy. Are there any drawings of birds?"

Dulcie shuffled through, then held one up: a sketch of a starling, its blue-black wings extended, ready to fly. "Ah!" Mary pulled out a similar drawing she'd taken from Cyrus Hunt's. A drawing of a birdcage, with a colourful bird on each perch: a redbird, a bluebird, a yellow bird, a green parrot in the bottom left-hand corner. All exquisitely painted—she had seen such a cage of stuffed birds in the bluestocking's bedchamber. There was a purple-blue smudge on the top of the drawing as though the artist had not cleaned his hands before painting the last bird.

A smudge. Where had she seen that? "Dulcie."

"Ma'am?"

"This smudge. On the back of the will. Was it there when you found the paper in Mrs Frothingham's drawer?"

Dulcie held it up to the window glass. "I don't think so, ma'am. I can't be too sure, but—no, I would've noticed. I only remembered the rip."

"Then it *was* Cyrus Hunt who took the will! When he left that dull book to review, I suppose." Mary laughed out loud: "*Hunt* was the sullen boy in those childish sketches, I've no doubt of it, ha! He was Isobel's bastard brother—do you think?" She sprang up; the papers flew off her lap and landed on the cat. "Now, Dulcie, I want you to take this draft of a will to my solicitor, William Boskin—at Gray's Inn in Chancery Lane. Tell him it was Mrs Frothingham's intent to make Annie her heir. And remind him to look into Cyrus Hunt's birth records—to see if he *is* the bastard son—I've already sent a message to that effect. Hunt was surely no brother that Isobel acknowledged. If, indeed, she knew. Here, I'll write it out for you."

"I can't go out with a wet head."

"It's warm outside, Dulcie. Wear your cap. That's all you'll need. And take a chair. I don't want you running through the streets with precious papers." She should do this herself—not leave it up to a maid, but she had another mission—she couldn't be in two places at once.

"I'll need a shilling." Dulcie extended a palm.

Mary didn't have a shilling, did she? Unless hidden somewhere... She got up to rummage through her purse and then her greatcoat pocket—and *voilà*! Wrapped in a hanky, a shilling and a bronze halfpenny. She placed the shilling on Dulcie's palm. "Go then, at once. Directly there. Don't dally—I'm putting my trust in you." Dulcie gave a bobbing curtsy. "And meet me afterward—at Jones and Hollister, Printers—Fleet Street. I'll be there with Cyrus Hunt. That is, I hope to be. And bring a constable."

"What? Where do I find one of those?"

"Number Four Bow Street, Dulcie, you know that. It's not far from Fleet. Tell them I sent you. Ask for that nice Mr Lawson, who helped arrest St Pierre. Tell him I think I know who might have taken our Annie—might even have killed her birth mother. It was not St Pierre. Though he did sufficient mischief as it was." Mary had seen a blue carriage outside the printer's house after St Pierre had arrived, and it was a blue carriage that had run down the footman. She tossed out the halfpenny she'd found. "Now run!"

The door banged behind the girl. Mary's nerves were playing a lively tune under her skin. What had she just said? What plans had she made for herself? Ah, yes. Go to Hunt, accuse him of strangling the bluestocking. Though why he'd have trussed her up to look like the painting she couldn't fathom.

And what if it wasn't Cyrus Hunt who had killed her? What if it was Henry Fuseli? Rejected by the bluestocking—a blow to his hubris? Suspicious of her role in the theft of his painting? Or had Hunt been hired by Henry Fuseli? For truly, she couldn't imagine Henry soiling his hands with someone's blood, no (unless, perhaps, to render a painting more realistic).

What of those others? Alfred de Charpentier, the spurned lover? Edgar Ashcroft? The editor's activities were still suspect. Was he lying when he said he just happened to discover St Pierre and the painting in Mrs Frothingham's drawing room? Who could prove that he was or was not? Edgar Ashcroft, whom Isobel had rebuffed and humiliated in front of her guests (not to mention her own rejection of his distasteful proposal).

Or was it St Pierre after all? Wanting the stolen painting all to himself—and not for Bishop Talleyrand. In Talleyrand's service, but feeling betrayed by the Revolution, what it was becoming—like

the émigré, Alfred de Charpentier, who had lost his title. *Arrgh!*
She didn't know. She was on a giant wave, rushing out to sea—and
full of doubts as to how she would get home to shore.

Always, always, those doubts in her mind: about herself, her
writing—was it good, or was it worthless, as some contended? She
ran her fingers through her hair, a rat's nest, indeed. She should not
think of the murder or the controversial book now, but of Isobel's
young daughter, Annie: with a good life ahead of her in the house
on Grosvenor Square—good, yes, if not wholly prosperous—for
didn't the housekeeper say her mistress was overly extravagant?
Who knew what was left of the Frothingham estate? Perhaps nothing at all.

Mary had no plan, but she had her suspicions. She had a bit of
evidence—however it would hold up in a court. She had kept back
the sketch with the birds to show Cyrus Hunt what she knew. She
would drive him into a corner. If only she had a sword and a horse!
Foolish thought, but she would like to ride through the print shop
door and skewer him to the wall. Make him confess then and there;
tell where Annie was.

Oh, Annie, child!

She thrust the papers into her pocket and ran bare-headed out
into the sunny afternoon. Fleet Street was eleven or twelve streets
away, but she would run the distance. No one would dare knock
her down today, no. Wild horses wouldn't stop her now!

DULCIE could do but one, possibly two things at a time. Not
three. Three was too many. She left the papers with Mr Boskin,
who said he had already done a little research, and would soon
look up the birth of Cyrus Hunt. "Though I cannot do it today,
this hour," he said, his fingers beating a tattoo on his scarred desk.
"Your mistress is always wanting things done yesterday. She's
a delightful woman. A clever mind. But she must realize—" He
smoothed his fuzzy chin feathers.

"But this is about a murder." Dulcie manufactured a tear. She
rather enjoyed pitting her wits against a solicitor. His uplifted eyebrow said, *I have important things to do. Run along, little maidservant, and let me work.*

"This is about someone who might kill Miss Mary," Dulcie persisted, reminding him of the note: BLUESTOCKINGS BEWARE.

"Ah. That."

"Even now, sir, she's in danger. At the printer Hunt's shop—lecturing him—you know how she can be." Giving a quick curtsy, she ran out on the lawyer's "Gad."

She had frightened herself with her words about danger for the mistress. Bow Street was out of the way, so she would bypass the constable. She raced up Oxford Street and down Chancery Lane to Fleet; stopped breathless at the sign of Jones and Hollister. She knew she was at the right place when she heard the shouting inside; she opened the door.

Miss Mary had cornered the printer and was waving a paper in his face. Such a spate of words! Dulcie caught a few here and there: "Isobel... birdcage... killer!" He was denying everything Miss Mary accused him of. For a moment Dulcie wanted to take his side. Had she been cornered by the mistress she'd have wanted to get away, too, and quick.

The printer was resisting his accuser: now he had her hands locked in his hairy ones. He had strong hands from setting type. He gave a giant shove; she fell against a freshly inked printing press, then slipped down onto her backside. Dulcie ran to help her and the mistress shouted, "Where's the constable?"

"Constable!" Dulcie shouted to placate the mistress, though there was none outside.

The printer fled at the word "constable." His coat-tails flapped as he ran towards a rear door. Miss Mary was a heap of skirts on the dusty, inky floor. "Send the man after Hunt!" she cried. "And help me up, will you?"

But Dulcie was already out the door. She would hope to find a constable on the way. "Help! Thief! Murderer!" she shouted. A dozen bystanders took up the cry and raced after the printer. He dodged in and out of carriages, hawkers, carts, dogs, beggars, shoppers, and finally darted into Chancery Lane.

"Stop him!" Dulcie cried again—then stopped herself, clutching her chest, breathing hard. The devil take the wicked fellow. She had lost sight of him.

"AT least you're alive," said William Boskin, extricating Mary from the black type that had printed *Revolutionary* on her right wrist. "When your maid said you were coming here, I worried."

"He's gone, fled. Guilty," said Mary, looking up at the wispy chin hairs, the black cravat, undone in the solicitor's haste. "My maid brought a constable—he's in pursuit." She stood upright and caught her breath. "Have you looked up Cyrus Hunt's birth? Is he related to Mrs Frothingham? Can you help me find my Annie?" Oh dear, she would have to soak her dress in lye—it was covered with inkprint.

Mr Boskin shook his head. He had not had time to look up Hunt's birth. "But I did a bit of sleuthing on my own after I got yesterday's message. I had him followed—I never did like the little toady… He has a mistress, a coal heaver's widow; she lives in Dark House Lane, off Lower Thames Street. He could be on his way there now."

"Good fellow! Then Hunt could have brought my Annie there."

"And what, may I ask, has your Annie to do with Cyrus Hunt?"

"Good heavens, can't you see? You're a man of law. If Hunt is the girl's uncle, though both are illegitimate, he might—"

"We don't know that," said the stubborn solicitor. "I have not had time, I told you."

"Then find out. Find out, Mr Boskin. I'll go see the mistress. Tell me where she lives on Dark House Lane. In which dark house, if it's a street for coal heavers?"

He was stroking his chin hairs, giving her that familiar women-are-impossible look. This time she didn't care. "Just discover his background, sir. The relationship to Isobel Frothingham. I must know."

Now he was shaking his head. The chin hairs made him look like a sea lion; she had to smile. He would stop at Bow Street, he said, on his way back. "I'll have them send a Runner to the house. You mustn't go there alone."

"The directions," she pleaded. "The number of the house."

"End of the street, that's all I know. It ends by an inlet of the river."

Boskin was a friend, who had published a book of rather incomprehensible essays with her publisher. But he was too literal, too precise, too full of quibbles when immediate action was required. "Now find me a hackney coach, Mr Boskin," she said. "I must be there before he is."

CHAPTER XVI.

A Lucky Catch

∽

D ULCIE HAD last seen the printer running up Chancery Lane, the way she'd come. He could easily double back and go to Whitefriars Street where, Dulcie knew from Miss Mary, the man had his rooms. If the printer was going to escape London, he'd want his things, would he not?

The problem was, when she got to Whitefriars Street, she didn't know the number of the house. There were three houses, all alike. Would she have to rap on the door of each one? If so, it might give warning to Mr Hunt if he were inside.

A child was playing with a small dog in front of the first house. She called out and the girl said, "There's no Mister Hunt here. This be my house on the first floor and me sister's on the second. Her man left her and she looking for a boarder. You need a place?" She threw a stick and the dog brought it back. The beast sat on its haunches, wagging its scrawny rope of a tail.

"Thank you, not at present," Dulcie said, though she might one day have need of it. Miss Mary could be put in Newgate, or killed, if she didn't stop poking her nose in other folk's business—or try to move in with folk who didn't want her—and then Dulcie would be alone. She had come to think of the Store Street house as her home. She blew her nose thinking of it. She was starting up the street when the girl called back to her.

"You want Mister Hunt, he lives two houses down, on the first floor. It's me mum's friend Hetty Croup's the housekeeper. She don't much like him—he keeps dead birds in his scullery and now she got some sick man puking up the place. But she needs the money."

Dulcie hurried on up the street. She heard the girl's pattens tapping along behind her.

A flight of rickety outside stairs led to the first floor. She stood on the landing to gather her thoughts. What would she do if she found the printer at home? But he knew who she was; he might think she'd come with a constable. The thought of the imaginary constable gave her courage. She took a breath to steel herself, and knocked.

"He's not there," the child called up. "I seen him go out just afore you come. He got in a hackney. He told the man to hurry up. Hurr' up, hurr' up," she crooned, and rode an imaginary stick horse back along the muddy street.

Dulcie was turning to go down the steps when the door opened and a hatchet-faced woman confronted her. She had a shopping bag in either hand. "He's gone out," said the woman. "And we don't need no more help in this establishment. So run along."

"I was just leaving," said Dulcie. "And I'm not looking for work. I work for Miss—Mrs Mary Wollstonecraft. You might know her book."

"Nay," the woman said, like Dulcie hadn't spoken a word, and hustled past, nearly knocking Dulcie off the landing.

The door opened again behind her and a man beckoned her in. "Come in, miss. If you work for the authoress, then I've something to show her."

Dulcie hesitated. It could be that Mr Peale, lately of a mad-house. The man might still be mad. In her view, madness was a contagion. And Mr Peale was an escaped convict. No matter what they said about his innocence, it was a fact. He was a convict. Though with his comely face and longish dark hair, he looked more like a wronged lover than a convict. There was a wronged lover in the romance young Annie had been reading aloud.

"It's important," the man said, holding out a drawing. "Your mistress should know about this. I didn't discover it till after Hunt left or I'd have found a way to detain him. He was just here. But he'll be back."

"I don't think so," Dulcie said. "I think he's flown the cage." She pictured Cyrus Hunt flapping his wings as he sailed over a high fence.

When she entered the room, a bird landed on her head and she shrieked, thinking it the reincarnated printer. But it was only a yellow cockatiel. The wronged lover shooed it off.

"Take this to her," said the lover, "and don't lose it. It's evidence. The man is mad, you see. You must warn your mistress. Here, I'll tie a cord around it." He coughed, and Dulcie put a handkerchief over her mouth.

While he rummaged in a drawer for a piece of cord, she peeked at the drawing. It pictured a naked woman in bed, a devil on her chest, a horse. Gad, it was *The Nightmare* again. That ugly little imp of Mr Fuseli's. Why would Mr Peale want to give Miss Mary a sketch of that? The mistress already had her fill of nightmares. Dulcie had heard her cry out a dozen times in her sleep.

Though when Dulcie looked closer at the drawing, she saw that the horse was not a real horse, but a hobby horse (Dulcie recalled it with horror). The devil not a devil but a monkey. In the background a great black bird flapped its wings over monkey and woman. And the woman's face was Mrs Frothingham's! "Guard it well," the man warned.

Dulcie tucked the roll of paper under her cloak and ran down the outside steps, but not towards home. She'd had another thought— from those birds in the printer's front room. Mr Hunt worshipped his birds, Miss Mary said. He wouldn't want to leave London without the biggest prize of all, would he?

Dulcie knew where that prize was. It was in Grosvenor Square. In the bluestocking's bedchamber. She would go there first, but with a constable this time. Definitely with a constable—that Mr Lawson if she could find him. Dulcie was no fool. She was not going to put her own sweet neck in a noose. Miss Mary had taught her that—though the mistress was always putting *her* neck into one, was she not?

LOWER Thames Street led into Tower Hill and then the Tower of London, where thousands had lost their heads. It gave Mary a chill to see the eleventh-century stone prison loom up at the far end of the street. She fancied she could hear the menagerie of lions once kept there, roaring out their anger. She thought of the little princes incarcerated in one of its turrets in the time of Richard III. That led to anguished thoughts of Annie, and she hastened her step. She knew what had become of the queens and princesses who were locked in those towers—just because they couldn't produce a male heir, or were in the way of a male heir, or had lost their youth. She was angry all over again at the damage done to women through the ages....

She wound her way down the street through fishmongers, fish-wives, drunken sailors; turned down Dark House Lane and halted in front of the last house. It was a well-kept building of sandstone with a small garden in front and a path that led down to an inlet of the Thames; a battered blue skiff floated back and forth. Beyond, she could see merchant ships and fishing vessels; she smelled the stench of fish and sea coal. Not far to the east, one could take ship to France, or north to Scotland and thence to the former Colonies, as her brother Charles would soon do.

She stood a long moment in front of the house, wringing her hands. She was only a woman, yes—one must face reality. Men, especially desperate men, were bigger and stronger than she. How else had they managed to subjugate women all these centuries? Surely not by their wit! Though Dulcie and the constable might already be here. Had Hunt eluded them? Or were they on his heels, perhaps en route to the wilds of Scotland? They might never find him if he hid out among those savage clans.

A woman with a yellow dog and a bundle of wash in her arms crossed her path. The dog sniffed Mary's gown. She nudged him off with a foot, squared her shoulders, and marched up to the black-painted door. She knocked. And knocked again. Presently the washerwoman trotted up behind: "Ye can knock till the cows come 'ome but they won't let ye in. They's funny people what lives 'ere. Not neighbourly, no. Won't give ye no work neither, if that's what ye're after."

Looking down at her smudged gown, Mary said, "Yes, I *am* needing work. I came to see the woman of the house. Is she in, do you know?"

"I think not, madam, I seen 'er go out, 'alf an hour back. But would she give me a nod? Oh no, she wouldn't think on't! She were all dressed up, too, waiting for 'er fancy man."

"A fancy man? Oh, you mean her lover?" Mary asked, smiling at the woman who might be a source of information.

"Sure and 'e's got her set up nice in this 'ouse. Though 'e's a queer one, too, never speaks to a body, 'e don't. Queer 'ouse 'tis, funny noises coming out all hours of day and night. She sings, says she, that's what the noise is. But sometimes it sounds like someone calling for 'elp. But I know who that is."

"And who would that be?" Mary's heart pounded to think of Annie calling out.

"Why, the ghost. The ghost o' Agnes Brown what used to live 'ere when I were a girl. She were strangled in that 'ouse, aye, she were. They found 'er in a tub o' lye, a stocking round 'er neck, 'er skin 'alf et by the lye."

Mary planted her feet firmly on the path for support. "And did this woman's, um, fancy man know Agnes Brown? Would he have—killed her?"

"No, no, ma'am, for that were afore 'e come. Least I don't think e'd of knowed her. Maybe 'e did though. Could be. I seen 'im come and go from 'ere—never once smiled or took notice o' me, like I were a ghost meself."

"Thank you," Mary said, needing to move her inert legs and get into the house. She knocked again, and again the woman told her it was of no use to knock. Mary kept her back turned, and the woman drifted back up the street with her wash and her yellow dog.

When no one answered, Mary walked around behind the house. A clothesline was stretched between two trees with linen and a white flapping nightshirt pegged to it. On a second line: ah! Annie's petticoat and shift! A closer look discovered the words PROPERTY OF FOUNDLING HOSPITAL scrawled in faded blue ink on both. Mary snatched them off the line—they were damp from river spray; the girl would need them.

"Annie!" she shouted, looking up at a window, bricked-up but for one pane. "It's Miss Mary, Annie. I'm here to bring you home!"

A flock of crows cackled past and landed on the branch of an oak tree; they stared down at her with beady eyes. A pair of gulls dropped at her feet to scoop up something black, swooped up again, and out over the water.

"Annie," she called again, and a rear door thrust open. "She not here," said a short, pasty-faced girl. "She gone to Australia."

"No!" Mary rushed toward the door. "Not my Annie."

The girl stood calm. "I don't know who's your Annie. But my mistress's Annie who I make porridge for every morning, went this afternoon just. Off with the mistress to take ship for Australia."

"The Annie who wore this," Mary pleaded, holding up the white shift. "A girl of thirteen, red hair and sea-green eyes? A girl who was forcibly abducted by your mistress's man friend and brought here?"

The maid went to shut the door against the intruder, but Mary pushed her way in. "Take me to her room. I must see it. And don't lie to me, miss." She put her hands on the girl's shoulders, and stared her in the eye.

"Leave me be! They'll whip me, they know I let you in."

Mary let the girl go and held up her purse (though it was devoid of coins—she'd have to recompense the girl later). "Her chamber."

"Up there then," the girl said, looking at the purse. She pointed to a narrow staircase. "Chamber's empty. I tole you they took 'er this afternoon. An hour ago. Less."

Mary ran upstairs, feeling dizzy, desperate, into the room at the top. Annie had been here, she saw that at once. There was the green cloak, the secondhand one Mary had given her after she brought her home from the orphanage. She was taking ship without her cloak—what did that mean? Australia, the girl had said? What was the weather like in Australia? She ran back down the stairs, the cloak in her arms.

"What ship, where?" she said. "I've a constable outside, you know. What time do they set sail?"

"'Ow should I know?" the girl said, in tears now. "I didn't want 'er locked up in there. Neither the mistress did. But it's 'er bread and butter, she say. Without Mister 'Unt, she can't pay to live here."

"Hunt? And where is Mr Hunt?" She opened her purse invitingly. It was Cyrus Hunt then, putting her on that ship. Or sailing with her—a sudden decision perhaps, God forbid.

"I don't know. I don't know nothing. They went that way. St Katherine's Dock." The girl stuck out a thumb to the east. "He told 'er, be there. They took a boat, I tole you, me mistress, Jib, and the girl."

"Don't just say 'girl.' She has a Christian name. Annie." She grabbed the maid's wrist.

"Ow-w! Don't I know it? Leggo. I'm not stopping you. Go on down that dock. Maybe you'll find them. Maybe they're not there yet. I don' know, don' know, I tole you." The girl's face exploded with hot tears.

"All right, all right." Mary let go the wrist. "But if Mr Hunt returns, don't you say I was here. You'll have your reward. Not this moment, but you will indeed, I promise. I do!"

Hearing her name called, Mary ran out and around to the front of the house where a phaeton had come to a halt: it was indeed the constable the solicitor had sent. "Down back," she called out. "It's quicker by boat. St. Katherine's Dock. You'll see Annie there. They're taking her to Australia!"

If we see them, she thought, and she stumbled down the embankment to the weathered blue skiff she had seen earlier. The constable was a big-boned fellow with arms like rakes. He held the boat for her to get in, then got in himself as if to take the oars. But she already had them—she heard the man sigh. She offered a quick smile and rowed the boat east.

AT Grosvenor Square the housekeeper's daughter, Dulcie saw, was drunk. She lay snoring on the drawing room carpet, a bottle on the floor beside her, leaking wine. But someone was upstairs—she heard thumps. She tiptoed up to the hall outside the bedchamber. And there was Mr Hunt on his knees, gazing at the birdcage with its stuffed aviary of red, blue, green, and yellow birds. He had the glass cover off; he was stroking the feathers of a bluebird. He coveted them, she could tell—all those dead stuffed birds.

That's why he killed the bluestocking, she thought: he wanted to put her on a golden perch in a cage—that's what Miss Mary would say. Miss Isobel was just another dead bird to him. The printer's mouth hung open. Bubbles of saliva formed at the corners; his lips held a smirk. He hung the glass top back on the golden base and then, oh so carefully, placed it in a large cloth bag.

Where was the constable she'd sent an errand boy for? She turned back to wake the servant to summon help. The pug trotted up behind, and began to growl. The printer saw her; he was wedged in the doorway with his bag. She held onto the banister, trying to calm her hands that were fluttering like swallows.

"It's not yours to take," she said. Her voice was brave, but she was a mouse in the face of this scowling man. A man in the very room where he'd strangled a clever woman. She wished now she had not come alone. But she had to act bold. She hadn't read eight pages of the mistress's *Rights of Woman* for nothing.

"It belongs to Mrs Frothingham," she said.

"Mrs Frothingham is dead." His steely eyes fastened on hers.

"Then it belongs to her kin."

"Then it belongs to me," he said. He put a hand to his cheek, and for a moment she recognized the boy in the sketches, the one thumbing his nose at a young Isobel.

"Annie," she cried righteously. "Mrs Frothingham's daughter. It's her that owns it now. You want it so badly, you go ask her. Maybe she—she'll let you have it."

Dulcie ran down the stairs. She'd been daft not to fetch the constable herself. She dashed into the drawing room and shook the sleeping maid. "Wake up. There's a thief in the house. Run! Fetch a constable!"

"Thief!" the girl cried. "Sweet Jesus, what'll I do? How'd he get in? Mo-ther!" Stumbling up, she banged into a chair, knocking it over.

Dulcie heard the man on the stairs. When she turned back, he was heading for the door with his prize.

"Help, thief!" Dulcie cried, running after him into the street. She shrugged off one of her pattens and hurled it at his back. He yelped, and stumbled on a loose stone. She snatched the bag and ran back to the house—she would lock him out. He tackled her as she went and the rolled-up sketch of the bluestocking's *Nightmare* flew out of her pocket; the bag dropped on the stone step. The cage glass shattered. The printer roared with anguish. A rock struck her on the back of the neck; the day brightened a moment as she pitched forward, and then slowly darkened....

ANNIE was in a fog. It was something, maybe, they'd put in her porridge. She'd gulped it down to make herself strong, but instead she fell asleep. She was still groggy when they got her up: the woman of the house and the brother, Jib. They'd dragged her out of the chamber and down the stairs into a small green boat. "Pick up yer feet, damn ye," the man kept saying, while she wanted only to lie down and sleep.

She opened her eyes wide, and willed herself to wake up. She heard the lap of water, ships' horns, faraway voices, laughter. Finally they pulled up to a pier, and dropped her on a landing bench. "Leave her sleep here, she won't run," she heard the woman tell the man, and then the man: "Her's a tricky one. Take no chances till the ship sails." Then his voice went away. Annie tried to get up but something kept pulling her back down. She was a boat sinking into the sea, and she could only go down with it.

Moments—hours later (how long had she slept?) she woke in a ship's tender crammed with young people, her hands tied before her. They were on the river; people on the pier growing smaller as she watched. "Young thieves," she heard one sailor tell another. "They'll know what to do with 'em when they get there."

"I'm not a thief!" she cried, and the girl beside her laughed and said, "Tell 'at to the navy. All I done was take a mutton chop for me mum, and 'ere I am. Though Australia may be better'n eight o' us in two rooms. I ain't had a whole night's sleep since I were born, I 'aven't."

"Nor me," said a boy. "Six in a bed, and every 'alf hour a new shift coming in. But any place's better 'n Cheapside. Me old lady were glad to see me off, I could tell."

"Well, I won't go!" Annie said. "I'll drown myself first." She tried to lunge over the side but a big-fisted boy caught her about the neck with his two roped hands.

"Don't be stupid," he said. "You'll make out, you will. Just go along with 'em. They'll make a stop in France, I heard say. We'll try then, I'll help you."

Annie did not want to go to France. They didn't speak English there; they ate snails and cut off people's heads. She wanted to go home. She bit hard into the rope that held her wrists together. It was an old rope: she'd break it even if she pulled out her front teeth. Freedom was more important than teeth—Miss Mary said so. Liberty, equality, fraternity: she chanted the words over and over under her breath while she stared down into the choppy waters. Liberty, equality... Except for that pond she'd long ago floated in, she'd not been in water deeper than a wooden tub full, and she'd hated that. Even so, she let her wrists dangle in the river, thinking to soften the rope. The tender was rocking with the swift current; the motion made her want to puke over the side, then slip off. But the rope, though fraying, still clung to her hands.

Back by the shore folk were shouting; a dozen small boats were converging. She couldn't hear what the shouting was about—a flock of gulls was squabbling over a crust of bread someone had dropped overboard. One gull picked it up and the others followed into the sky, protesting. They were victims, like Annie.

She pulled her numb hands out of the cold water, and asked the boy to tug on the slack rope. He did, though he warned her: "They find out, you be punished. Maybe hung."

"Pull hard," she ordered, and he pulled, and nearly wrenched her wrists in two but the rope slipped off. "Turn your head," she ordered. He didn't, but never mind. She tugged off her filthy gown. "You'll drown!" he hissed, and for a moment she hesitated. Then she held her nose the way she did off that creaking board at the pond, and went head-first into the grimy waters.

And sank. Good night, good night...

CYRUS Hunt jumped out of the carriage with his cloth bag. The nosy servant girl wouldn't follow him this time. He had the birds, the golden perches, and the base—he'd have a glass top blown later. He'd made arrangements for Isobel's girl to be on that ship with the other thieves; she'd stolen one of his handprinted books, he told the magistrate; he'd hired a "witness." Peg was on the pier with her brother—Jib was a rogue; he wanted his share of the estate. Cyrus was prepared for that: three pounds in the fellow's pocket, promises of more. "Estates aren't settled in a day," he reminded Jib. But the fellow just stood there like a raven, waiting to lick the bones clean. "Off with you," he told Jib. "Ready?" he asked Peg. She waved her arm at a line of carriages.

"Aye, ready and packed." She blew her nose, then blinked up at him. He nodded, and squeezed her arm. Peg was good for what he required. Though he would have to drop her—he didn't need a live-in mistress; he couldn't bear one in the house all day. He'd take Peg with him to the Scottish border, then disappear.

He had a ticket for America—a single ticket. He would leave from the port of Leith. There were birds in America he'd never seen—birds as yet uncatalogued, unsketched. He would change his name; he would make something of himself under a new name. He would give up the printing for his art. America was so vast, so lawless, he'd heard, you could hide a hundred wanted men in a square mile of its forests. In a year or two when it all blew over, the girl out of the way in Australia, he'd come back and claim his property. He had every right. He and Isobel Frothingham had the same father, didn't they? That made them half siblings.

The Wollstonecraft woman was all smoke and no flame. He had heard about her foray into the Fuseli house. Ignorant. Scandalous. Never mind her disagreeable book that he'd put into print. He'd wanted to drown it in ink.

He touched Peg on the arm. "The girl's on the ship?"

"No, Mr Hunt, no. Now prepare yourself. Annie's dead. Drown-ded," she whimpered. "She pitched overboard—never come up. I seen it meself. It was her. I'd recognize that red hair o' hers fifty yards off, 'deed I would. She's gone, Mr Hunt. Drownded." Peg puled into a handkerchief.

He stood a moment in shock; felt the sweat on his brow, a needle of pain. Then slowly a wave of relief flooded his body. He hadn't intended to kill the girl. Just have her gone before she knew enough to make a claim on the estate. The girl out of the way, he might not have to go to America, after all. He had proof that that other fellow killed Isobel; he had the shoe the man lost, climbing into her bedchamber, strangling her. It was that fellow, no doubt about it. He had the letter the angry man would've flung at the bluestocking, saying "Be mine or die!" But he couldn't tell anyone, that was the bloody thing of it. They would ask how he came by the shoe and the letter. They would think he did it. When he was not a killer, no. Not that.

Though Isobel's girl—well, that was an accident, her own foolishness. Not his fault.

It was that other one killed Isobel, aye. All Cyrus had to do, when he saw, was arrange her. He couldn't help himself. The hobby horse in her chamber, the one they used to ride on, him and her. The stuffed monkey—it was his, and she took it! She was always cruel to him: a tease, a little snob. Playing tricks, at his expense. In later years—she never *acknowledged* him, even in the print shop. He didn't want to think of the hundred little humiliations.

But then he had heard footsteps, and Cyrus had to make a quick exit—without the birdcage he'd come for. But he had the shoe the murderer left. He'd found it under the bed, the pug gnawing on it. He'd taken it on a whim. A kind of self-defense.

"The bags are in the coach?" Peg nodded. "Then we'll be on our way." He nudged her elbow. "Hurry, will you?"

Still she balked, staring out at the river where a small blue skiff was moving up towards the dock, and farther off, a fishing boat with two men aboard. "I said now, woman. Pull yourself together. Move, will you, woman!"

ANNIE was paddling with cupped hands, the way she'd seen a dog swim a pond—and scissoring her legs. Though this was no pond—she had to heave her body against the current that might rush her out to sea. She spit out a mouthful of brackish water and kept her feet and hands churning. For now she was able to stay afloat, even advance slowly towards shore. She dropped her face into the waves and saw she could go faster that way, though she must keep coming up for air. She lifted her right arm and scooped the water. It propelled her farther still from the tender that wasn't turning about, though a far-off, wind-blown voice was shrieking, "Girl overboard... Pick 'er up... She'll drown..."

The voice inside her said she was not going to drown: she must get to shore. And then what? Would they send her in a second boat to the ship? It seemed pointless, and she let herself sink again.

She was exhausted now, her arms and legs like logs. The water was spurting into her mouth, though she tried to keep it shut. She couldn't go on, couldn't... couldn't...

When someone close by cried, "Ahoy! Girl there in the water. Drop a rope," she could only hold up a weak hand and try to clasp it.

A strong arm hauled her up and into a boat. "Lucky catch. Biggest o' the day," a man said, and the other one laughed.

In moments she was face down and spewing bilge water into a net full of squirming fish.

IT was the printer, there on the dock. Mary rowed harder, her arms nearly pulling out of their sockets. "It's him," she said to the constable. Already Hunt was turning, hurrying back to a row of waiting conveyances.

"Let me." The constable's blue coat was drenched, like her gown; she squatted in the bottom of the boat and let him take the oars—the boat nearly overturned with the awkward change of places.

A fishing boat passed to starboard and blocked her view of the shore. She urged him on: "Hurry!" The printer might have Annie with him—tied and gagged, and lying in a carriage. Or was she already on that ship out there, which was preparing to weigh anchor? "Pull!" she yelled. "Pull, pull, pull!"

The fishing boat landed at the far end of the pier, and then they, too, were skimming up on shore. Folk milled about, waving, shouting, laughing. But no Hunt in sight. She and the constable raced to the row of sedan chairs and carriages, peering inside, one by one. But no young girl. No Cyrus Hunt.

Then she saw him at the far end of the line: heaving a fallen case onto the top rack of a coach—shouting at the driver to get moving; shoving a woman into the interior.

"Halt, you're under arrest. Halt, I said!" The constable raced forward. He brought the man down with his truncheon; the printer's head knocked against the rear wheel of the coach. The woman jumped down and tried to run off. Mary caught her sleeve and yanked her about.

"Where is she? Where is Annie? Where is my ward? Is she on that ship? I know who you are. You brought Annie here to take ship." She had the woman by the throat. The woman was gagging, begging, flailing her arms. Mary loosened her grip.

"I never wanted…" the woman pleaded. "I only did it for *him*." She turned towards the printer, who was being thrust headlong into the coach, his wrists tied. "He said she was an orphan. I been good to her, fed her nice. We had us some grand talks."

"Is she on that ship?"

The woman shook her head, then threw up her arms; tears creased her cheeks. "Gone. Drown-ded. I seen the red hair. Och, I seen her jump out and go down, G'bless her soul."

Mary was in shock. She couldn't speak. The constable was calling to her: "Taking the rogue to Bow Street. I should take that one as well?" He pointed to Hunt's mistress.

The woman was clutching Mary's legs, howling her innocence. Mary waved the driver on and yanked the woman up off her knees. "It was someone else drowned—it had to be! It was some other poor girl. What proof have you? Because if Annie's on that ship we need to halt it." Far out on the river she heard sailors shouting commands.

"I seen 'er jump," the woman persisted. "Seen that hair. Didn't come up. 'Twas her."

"But she might be swimming to shore." Could Annie swim? Mary herself could barely swim, though she knew how to stay afloat, tread water as she had on hot days in the childhood river at Barking. She'd done it instinctively, as Annie would have. Annie was wily, a survivor. Annie was not a drowning kind of girl. Mary would find someone to row her out to that ship.

She ran back to the dock. A dozen or so people were gathered about a fishing boat that had just pulled in, its nets crammed with fish. And more than fish. A half-drowned rat—a red-haired rat, dripping and wailing—she hadn't wanted to be brought to this shore. "Not a thief," she cried, "I don't belong on that ship.

Find Miss Wollstonecraft. I belong to her—she'll tell you. Find her!"

Mary couldn't call out; she was overcome. She staggered over to embrace the girl, to hold her tight. It seemed to be young Fanny, up from her bloody childbed, up from the grave—no, a live Annie, up from the depths of the sea, clad only in her shift. She wrapped the child in the green cloak she still carried, though it was soaked from spray. Then, finding her tongue, in spite of herself, she scolded. "Why did you run off like that? If you hadn't gone, you wouldn't—I wouldn't—" The words clung to her tongue.

"I didn' run off," Annie said, water spilling out of her nose and mouth—Mary mopped it up with her damp skirts. "I had to get out of the house. It was that Dulcie. She was horrid to me. She said I got into the sugar when I did *not*. Least not so much as she said. I had to get out, and I saw that man who—" She coughed and spat up more water, and Mary rubbed her back. "And—and I followed him—just trying to help. 'Twas awful. That man wanting to send me to Australia! Where is he? Put him in gaol!"

"And so we shall," Mary said. The printer's mistress had disappeared, but it was all right now, she had Annie.

"And what would I do in Austra-li-a?" Annie was sobbing—a bystander put a hand on the girl's head; another made the sign of the cross. Mary gathered the girl into her arms and hustled her off to a sedan chair. She had no money but the chairmen wouldn't know that until they arrived at the house. Sometimes coins dropped between the sofa cushions—she'd look there.

When an official came to interrogate her about Annie's identity: "Who is she? Should she be with the others on that ship?" she shrugged him off. "I'll have the law on you for attempted abduction," she scolded the astonished man. "For calling my ward a thief. Now let us pass. This girl needs a hot bath. She must be kept warm—she almost died in that frigid water. Did you not, child?"

"I did. I almost died." Annie broke down into sobs that wouldn't subside until Mary held and rocked, and rocked her, all the way home to Store Street.

CHAPTER XVII.

The Father Exposed—and Neck or Nothing!

⤸

B UT WHY would that Frenchman kill Mrs Frothingham?" Joseph Johnson asked two days later. He and Mary were in his
library: she in an ancient rocking chair; he by the hearth, his swollen feet up on a stool. Galleys and manuscripts were scattered about
on the floor, awaiting his attention.

Mary sighed. She had tried to explain to so many people. To the
Bow Street magistrate, to her solicitor, to a footsore Dulcie—the
latter had staggered into the house shortly after Mary bathed and
fed a bedraggled Annie. On that evening of her rescue, they were a
household of invalids.

"You don't kill someone simply because she rejects your advances," Joseph said. Mrs Murphy lowered his feet to place a kettle of
steaming water on the stool, and he leaned forward to breathe it in
sonorously. It transformed his hair into grizzled ringlets.

"You do if you're desperate to *have* someone," said Mary. When
Henry betrayed her on that terrible afternoon, she had wanted to
race up the stairs and strangle him, there and then. She knew the
impulse.

But unlike her, Alfred de Charpentier would act on his desperation. He might well have ravished her, would he not, in that carriage? Though it was not herself he was enamoured with. If that
is, he truly loved any woman. He couldn't bear rejection, that was
all. He had endured exile from his homeland, loss of property and
title—and the final blow: humiliation at the hands of a clever, rich,
desirable woman. It was all too much for his male *amour propre.*

Joseph's expression was sceptical inside his wreath of steam. He
was a wholly rational fellow; he couldn't seem to comprehend so
much passion in others. Though before Fuseli's marriage, the artist
had shared Joseph's house for several years, and the two were still

close. Was it true affection? Or merely need—someone else to mirror one's self-image...

"The Frenchman is an anti-revolutionary," Mary said. "He didn't care for Isobel's politics. I once saw him snatch away her red cockade—a joke but maybe not. And she'd just laugh and refuse him. In those last moments that anger would have exploded into violence. Love—or whatever you might call it—turned to hate. Besides, he despised bluestockings. He thought they were all affectation and pedantry."

"Wait now," said Joseph, looking up, wet-faced. "It was Hunt, not Charpentier, who wrote that note, *Bluestockings Beware*. You told me that, my dear—your Dulcie found a copy in his room. Hunt—my best printer, Mary, lost to me now (*he frowned*)—wrote it after he set up her body to parody *The Nightmare*, yes? It was not the French count but *Hunt* who despised bluestockings. By extension, that means you, too, are a bluestocking, my dear—more or less. Others are discussing your *Vindication* in their salons, did you know that?"

"Really? Ah."

"And what of that poor footman, Mary? Was he not murdered as well? Was it Cyrus Hunt again?"

"Not he. I don't think so—not for the footman. Cyrus would have no interest in him. More likely it was St Pierre who ran him down, wanting to halt the search for the painting thief. Remember: the footman had seen the thief, very possibly St Pierre. I told you I'd seen a blue carriage outside the printer's lodging. And it was a blue carriage, according to Fuseli, that ran down the poor fellow."

"St Pierre doesn't have a carriage," Joseph said. "Not in England at least. He comes and goes on foot, or in a hackney."

"Hired, then, most likely. By Talleyrand, perhaps. Though Talleyrand would let St Pierre do the nasty business for him—give the footman a fright, not meaning to kill him. With the king's refusal, they were desperate for the money the painting would bring. They didn't want the footman telling whom he'd seen taking the painting. Why, I do believe all three absconded with it: St Pierre, Talleyrand, and Isobel Frothingham—what a conspiracy!"

"Or it was simply an accident," said the perverse Joseph. "Carriages run into one another all the time, do they not? But less often into people on foot, like yourself, my dear. Who could *that* have been?"

She sighed. She wearied of this guessing game. She wanted to put it all to rest. But the publisher was waiting for her to speak, his brows, damp from the steam, like question marks. He would have her answer.

"Well, sir, if you must: it was the count, I think now, trying to avenge my leap from his carriage, another hired or borrowed one— I'll tell you about that later. Or, more likely, to discourage me from seeking Mrs Frothingham's killer. Or was it Cyrus Hunt's man Jib, who abducted Annie? Jib will talk when we find him. Or Ashcroft again, a form of intimidation. Men do that to women, you know."

"Some men, some, my dear. I would never—"

"Of course *you* would not! On the other hand, we might never know. I'm sure it was in *all* their minds to keep me from interfering. Mary Wollstonecraft, the 'hyena in petticoats.'" She smiled. She could smile now about that infamous label of Horace Walpole's; at the time, the blood was pumping furiously in her head. "But you're a Dissenter, Joseph, a Unitarian. You know we don't have the answers to all of the questions."

"As far as your accidents, Mary, I put my money on Hunt, with his head full of copper and lead," Joseph said. "He was the one who arranged the bluestocking—including the stocking itself, no doubt, after Charpentier strangled her. He was a misogynist; I've heard him curse women's manuscripts he was setting in print. In particular, your *Vindication*, Mary."

"Oh, the villain!" Mary was definitely *not* a bluestocking, no. She was not so much a woman wrapped in a Grecian gown, quoting from literature, as a rational woman *writing* it (when, that is, she had the time and quiet to write). There was a difference, yes. Besides, she did not have a salon, or the funds to maintain one. Had she one, she would no doubt speak her mind to her guests, and then no one would return.

"Hunt came to her chamber after a birdcage, a foolish birdcage, did he?" Joseph croaked. The steam was beginning to loosen his congestion.

"Yes. Dulcie discovered him. The back of her neck is all black and blue from that rock, poor girl. Mrs Frothingham's poem, 'My Bedchamber's Birdcage,' was in the chapbook Hunt was to set in type. Doubtless he read the poem and determined to go after the cage. Or perhaps it was an heirloom he'd seen as a child."

"And he found her there on the bed. But he didn't see Charpentier."

"I told you, dear man. He found the man's shoe! It was one of those fancy red-heeled leather shoes made in Paris, with his initials inside. Surely you noticed them at the bluestocking's routs. What could be more damning? But it was the letter that made the count confess."

"Letter?"

"Really, sir, you don't listen to me! I told you yesterday: Cyrus found a letter that the count had earlier left on her dressing table. It was his ultimatum to her: *Be mine or die!* She would not, and crazed, he killed her. What a brave soul she was to reject him!"

Already a fictional plot was brewing in Mary's head: she must write it down or it would fade. She picked up a pen and a bit of foolscap from his table and began to write on the back.

"Stop! That's Barlow's work!" Joseph's feet slapped the floor. The kettle tipped and a rivulet ran down and under a cabinet full of books.

Oh dear. It was a revolutionary pamphlet: Joel Barlow urging the French Convention to establish a democratic republic "on humane principles: no death penalty, no standing army, no colonies," she read aloud. She righted the kettle, and blew a kiss.

He waved her away, and smiled. Then his face changed. They were rounding up priests and nuns in Paris, he told her— "Threatening to kill them. The news just came in. Now some of our Dissenters are condemning the revolutionaries. Blake has put off his red cap of liberty. Doesn't that tell you something?"

He was having doubts himself, he said; he was horrified at the thought of *La Guillotine*; he made a zzzz-ing sound, and slashed at his throat. "They'll have King Louis's head, you watch. And Antoinette's. You, Madame Sleuth, have been running about chasing fools and knaves while blood is spilling in Paris. Come back to the world, Mary. The real world. The cruel world." He coughed from the effort of his impassioned speech.

She sat for a moment, thinking of that *cruel* world—she had seen it these past months in London, had she not? Then she rose, and kissed him on his grizzled head.

"By the way," she said as she took her leave, looking at a portrait of Joseph's mother on the wall. "You told me once, I believe, that your mother had red hair? Would it have been the shade of my Annie's?"

Joseph looked up: drops of moisture stood out on his forehead. "Why, what are you trying to say, my dear? There are redheads all over London. Yes, indeed. Wild Scots and Irish. You see and hear one on every corner, oh my, yes."

Mary smiled down at him; she rubbed his neck. "And how did *you* know that birdcage was in the bluestocking's bedchamber? *I* never told you that detail."

"What? Why—I just assumed, I mean, you said—you, you d-didn't? Well..."

"Isobel Frothingham was always daring men. Trying to seduce them. She once told me so. Men who were considered inaccessible, who would never approach her on their own. Perhaps Annie's father was one of those."

"Oh! You think so?" His face was scarlet.

"Thirteen years, Joseph, almost fourteen years ago? Look in your diary. She seduced you, plied you with claret—you love claret. She took you up to show off her precious birds, and for once, a little tipsy, in spite of yourself, you—"

She paused. Now his face was a sunrise.

"Goodbye then, dearest man—my publisher, my surrogate father," she said, leaning down to kiss his cheek. "I am off to the real world, as you told me I should be." She felt his breath on her own cheek. "To Paris. To see for myself what is going on there."

"Oh, but Mary—*La Guillotine.* So much has happened in France since we first spoke of going."

"No worse than what I've been through these past weeks in London." She thought a moment. She would need funds. For the boat, the coaches, her lodging—though a friend of Everina's had rooms there, did she not? She could prevail on the woman's hospitality. Still... "I've a new book in mind. A sort of historical and moral look at the Revolution in Paris. It cries to be written, does it not? From an Englishwoman's point of view? You underestimate women, sir. We *want* to know what is going on in our world. We want to play a part in it."

"Yes, of course, dear lady, have I ever denied that? But that other book, Part Two of your *Vindication?*"

"And Annie," she said, ignoring Part Two. "You will keep her here with you while I'm gone? She loves books; she would be a great help to you. You could call her 'Mary's ward.' Just a short visit, yes? To get to know her?" She did not wait for his assent, though she saw the gleam in his eyes, the wonder. The apprehension.

Downstairs, she warned a startled Mrs Murphy about a new

young house guest, and strode out the publisher's door. She walked
with her arms swinging all the way to Store Street where she had
left Dulcie and Annie arguing over who was going to clean up after
the cat that had disgorged again; and went up to her chamber to
sort out clothing for the trip to Paris.

She must see *La Guillotine* for herself. She could not let the
world spin by and herself not there, for the ride. And she *would*
write that book on the Revolution (she would ask Joseph for an
advance of funds). She would leave Dulcie in charge of the house—
have her look in on Annie now and then at St Paul's Churchyard.
In truth, the thirteen-year-old might benefit from Mrs Babbit's
School for Young Ladies on the corner of Store and Gower, as
she would suggest to Joseph; Babbit's had a solid curriculum. She
would not be long away—six weeks, six months at the most? Who
knew?

"I shall soon set out for Paris. Alone," she told Dulcie when
she came downstairs with an armful of linen that needed washing.
"Neck or nothing is the word!"

Dulcie drew a stubby finger across her neck, and let her tongue
loll; Mary laughed. "But don't go," Dulcie pleaded. "Please, miss,
don't go, I beg you. 'Tis madness to go to that bloody place."

Mary smiled. What had she to lose? Henry Fuseli was gone from
her world. Annie would be with her father. Her brother Charles
would soon (she hoped) make his fortune in America and offer her
sisters a home—though for the time being at least they were em-
ployed. She would one day bring Eliza to meet Annie, and perhaps
adopt her: a girl to make up for the loss of her own child. She would
send her father a few guineas each week through Joseph. Her mind
was free, uncluttered, ready for adventure. For revolution.

"I'm a spinster on the wing," she cried. Dropping the laundry, she snatched up a sofa pillow and moved about with it. "Who
knows?" she said, gliding close to Dulcie, stage-whispering in her
ear. "In Paris I might even take a husband. For the time being, that
is."

"Poor fellow," said Dulcie. And neatly dodged the pillow that
Mary flung at her.

Afterword

AFTER BEING dismissed as governess in 1787 by the haughty Kingsboroughs in Ireland, Mary Wollstonecraft returned to London with the manuscript of *Mary, a Fiction* in hand, and was fed, housed, and published by bookseller Joseph Johnson, who became her patron and surrogate father. (The titles bookseller and publisher seem to have been virtually interchangeable in that era, since booksellers were often publishers.) She became both famous and infamous when in late January, 1792, he published her signature work, *A Vindication of the Rights of Woman*, and critic Horace Walpole labelled her a "hyena in petticoats." In February, she told her sister Everina that the book had instigated a marriage proposal, but "a handsome house and a proper man did not tempt me."

She was living on Store Street in London during that winter and spring of '92, seemingly unable to write. Whether this writer's block came from some psychological fear of success, or from her obsession with the artist Henry Fuseli, I doubt even she knew. But the fact remains that she was not working on the projected Part Two of *Vindication*, in which she would expose and offer solutions to the biased laws governing women. It was only after her unsuccessful and humiliating attempt to join the Fuseli household in a platonic *ménage à trois*, that she went to Paris in the autumn of 1792 to see the Revolution for herself, and at her publisher's urging (and with a monetary advance), to write a series of "Letters from the Revolution." As the world knows, she did write the work, but lost her head (metaphorically speaking) to an American adventurer, and her reputation in the process.

What else was she doing during that winter and spring of seeming desuetude? Little that I've been able to ascertain, other than reading "to improve" herself, conversing with like-minded Dis-

senters at Johnson's literary suppers, and handing out money to
her needy father and siblings. So my mystery would seem to suit
her restless and curious mind, along with her outrage at injustice
of any kind.

Apart from her fellow Dissenters and other acquaintances whose
short biographies are listed below, I have added a number of fictional characters: the maid Dulcie; the printer Cyrus Hunt; French
émigrés Jacques St Pierre and Alfred de Charpentier; editor Edgar
Ashcroft; Lillian Guilfoy and her fiancé Roger Peale; the bluestocking Isobel Frothingham and her natural daughter Annie. (Mary did
for a time take in a motherless young girl named Ann who had
"animal spirits and quick feelings," but who stole sugar and lied
about it.) And Mary never did call herself a bluestocking, although
literary women read and discussed her *Vindication of the Rights of
Woman* in their salons.

Biographical Notes on
Real Characters in the Novel

Anna Laetitia Barbauld (1743–1825) was a English essayist, poet, and educator. Her revolutionary politics brought threatening letters when she refused to sign loyalty oaths to the government; her 1792 poem written to Joseph Priestley after the king's mob burned his home and laboratory laments his fate as "the bandied theme of hooting crowds." Her happy marriage to a fellow Dissenter turned tragic when he became mentally ill and abused her. A frequenter of Johnson's literary circle, she enjoyed lively conversation with its like-minded participants, including Mary Wollstonecraft.

Joel Barlow (1754–1812) was an American poet and journalist. After the failure of his scheme to sell Ohio land to French immigrants who found only disputed acreage and angry natives, he published political pamphlets with Joseph Johnson, and then went to Paris to join Gilbert Imlay in an illegal shipping business. Wollstonecraft, who disliked "commerce," was used as an innocent go-between. Barlow's mysterious involvement with a ship full of silver confiscated from the estates of French émigrés seems to have brought him great wealth.

William Blake (1757–1827) was an English painter, poet, and printmaker. The Bible inspired many of his imaginative works, along with "archangels" he said, who helped him to create. He frequented Joseph Johnson's literary soirées, and like its other habitués, upheld racial and sexual equality; his devoted wife, Catherine, worked beside him as engraver. He wore the red Phrygian liberty cap of the French revolutionaries until he lost faith during the Reign of Terror. He illustrated Wollstonecraft's *Original Stories from Real Life*, and published, among other works, *The Marriage of Heaven and Hell*.

Thomas Christie (1761–1796) was a Scottish historian and political writer. With Joseph Johnson he founded the *Analytical Review*, for which he and Wollstonecraft both wrote. Like others in the publisher's circle, he supported the French Revolution: in 1792 he entered into politics and commerce in

Paris, trading in flour. He and his wife, Rebecca, were arrested during the Terror, and then released; Rebecca later nursed Wollstonecraft after a suicide attempt in London.

Samuel Coleridge (1772–1834) was an English Lake poet and critic who, with fellow Dissenter William Wordsworth, founded the Romantic Movement in England through their joint work of poetry, *Lyrical Ballads.* One of the younger members of the publisher's circle in Wollstonecraft's era, he is best known for his poems *The Rime of the Ancient Mariner* and *Kubla Khan.* The latter allegedly was written under the influence of opium—the antidote, perhaps, for his lifelong bouts of anxiety and depression.

Henry Fuseli (1741–1825) was an ordained Swiss clergyman turned artist, who learned to paint by copying Michelangelo's frescoes. He moved to London when his romance with the niece of his friend, Johann Lavater, failed; Fuseli's erotic painting, *The Nightmare,* is allegedly based on that unfulfilled passion. A seeming misogynist, he painted Sophia, his wife and model, as a Medusa who turned men to stone. His surreal paintings reputedly inspired some of Poe's mysterious works. While living with publisher Johnson, he lost many paintings when the latter's house and shop burned. He was attracted to Wollstonecraft and enjoyed her company, but turned his back on her after she tried to establish a platonic *ménage à trois.*

Stéphanie Félicité de Genlis (1746–1830) was a French harpist, writer, and educator, whose innovative methods, such as teaching history through magic-lantern slides, were popular in England. Wollstonecraft especially admired her *Adèle et Théodore: Lettres sur L'éducation.* She kept a glittering salon in Paris until the moderate Girondins, including her estranged husband, were guillotined, and she was forced to flee to London. Though she called herself a revolutionary, some claimed she never really betrayed her class.

William Godwin (1756–1836) was a novelist, religious dissenter, and philosopher. His work, *Enquiry Concerning Political Justice,* was a virtual text for the radical thinkers of his day. His first meeting with Wollstonecraft at a 1791 dinner given by publisher Joseph Johnson for him and Thomas Paine, was a failure: "for I heard *her,* very frequently, when I wished to hear Paine." The pair remet after her disastrous affair with Gilbert Imlay, fell in love, and married when she became pregnant; she died eleven days after giving birth. The griefstricken Godwin wrote a candid memoir of her life, which shocked its readers. Their child was Mary Wollstonecraft Godwin, who grew up with Mary's natural child by Imlay, married Percy Bysshe Shelley, and later wrote *Frankenstein* and other novels.

Mary Hays (1760–1843) was an English poet, novelist, and liberal thinker. At the age of nineteen she fell in love with a young man of whom her parents disapproved; he died on the eve of their wedding. She later had an unre-

quited love affair with a Cambridge mathematician, which she drew upon
for her novel, *Memoirs of Emma Courtney*. After reading *A Vindication of
the Rights of Woman*, she became friends with Mary Wollstonecraft, and
remained loyal when the latter was ostracized by others because of her illegitimate child. Surprisingly, Hays did not include Wollstonecraft in her six-
volume *Female Biographies* published in 1803—perhaps because any praise
of the controversial authoress might have hurt sales of the book.

Joseph Johnson (1738–1809) was the most innovative English bookseller
and publisher of his time, known for his promotion of young writers, whom
he served as editor, banker, and father-confessor. The most famous authors
and poets of his day became part of his legendary circle. When in 1787 a
destitute Wollstonecraft came to him, manuscript in hand, he housed and
published her, and opened the way to women becoming professional writers. He published inexpensive, accessible books upholding the rights of per-
secuted groups, yet he also printed works of opposing views. When he was
arrested for disseminating "seditious libel," his followers attended his soirées
in prison. When he died, possibly as a result of his chronic asthma, he left
two hundred pounds to Wollstonecraft's natural daughter, Fanny Imlay.

Theophilus Lindsey (1723–1808) was the minister and co-founder of the
Essex Street Unitarian chapel—so-called because at that time non-Anglic-
an denominations such as Puritans, Quakers, Catholics, Baptists, and Jews
could refer to their meeting houses only as "chapels." Dissenters were not
allowed to hold office, serve in the armed forces, or attend the great univer-
sities—although Lindsey received degrees from Cambridge before he became a minister. Among those in his first congregation were Wollstonecraft's
mentor Richard Price, Benjamin Franklin, Joseph Priestley, and publisher
Johnson. Like most Unitarians, he advocated social reform, equal rights for
all, and the abolition of slavery.

Thomas Paine (1737–1809) was an English intellectual and revolutionary
pamphleteer. To avoid debtor's prison for a failing business, he emigrated to
the Colonies, where he wrote his bestselling *Common Sense*. He participated
in the American Revolution and became a Founding Father. Later in London he was a part of Johnson's circle; his radical *Rights of Man* influenced
the French Revolution but got him expelled from England in 1792 for seditious libel. In Paris he wrote *The Age of Reason*, but his arguments against
institutionalized religion alienated readers. After arguing against the execu-
tion of Louis XVI, he was put in Luxembourg Prison, where Wollstonecraft
frequently visited him.

Joseph Priestley (1733–1804) was an English Unitarian minister and chemist, with a doctorate of laws from the University of Edinburgh; his experi-
ments in electricity helped to gain the friendship of Benjamin Franklin. He
was a friend and mentor to Wollstonecraft and part of publisher Johnson's

circle. His arguments against the virgin birth led the Birmingham church and king's mob to burn his home, books, and laboratory. Forced to flee England, he ultimately moved his family to America, where he founded the first Unitarian church in Philadelphia. His sermons were attended by John Adams and Thomas Jefferson; the latter called him "one of the few lives precious to mankind."

Charles Maurice de Talleyrand-Périgord (1754–1838) served as diplomat for Louis XVI, and later for Napoleon. A limp kept the young Frenchman out of the army, so he entered the church, and despite his agnosticism, became Bishop of Autun. He supported the Revolution, but spoke out against the guillotine; he later recalled "the sweetness of living" under Louis's reign. In 1792 he was sent to Britain to avert war; Wollstonecraft dedicated her *Vindication of the Rights of Woman* to him. A complicated man whose principles conflicted with his love of money, he was a hedonist and a womaniser, whom Napoleon called "a shit in a silk stocking."

Edward John Wollstonecraft (?1737–1803) was the father of Mary and her six siblings who squandered an inheritance from his master weaver father and failed in his various occupations as weaver, farmer, and businessman. He was often drunk and abusive to his first wife, Elizabeth, and after her death, quickly married his housekeeper, Lydia.

Elizabeth Dickson Wollstonecraft (?1740–1782), born in Ballyshannon in County Donegal, Ireland, was the mother of Mary and her six siblings. Ignored and mistreated by her husband, she died in Enfield, England, after a long illness.

Edward (Ned) Bland Wollstonecraft (?1758–1807) was Mary's elder brother who, through primogeniture, was his grandfather's heir; he was apparently unwilling to share any of it with his siblings. If, as a solicitor, he tried to obtain the requested legal separation for Eliza from Bishop, he failed; and divorce was virtually impossible in that era.

Henry Woodstock Wollstonecraft (1761–?) was apprenticed at age fourteen to an apothecary-surgeon and former mayor of Beverley, England, and then disappeared from record. The family was uniformly silent, as if he had committed a crime or gone mad.

Elizabeth (Eliza) Wollstonecraft Bishop (1763–18—?) was Mary's pretty, spirited, younger sister. She had an unhappy marriage to Meredith Bishop at the age of nineteen, and when Mary arranged an escape, lost all rights to her infant; in Bishop's custody, the baby girl died within a year. Unable to divorce, Eliza became an unhappy governess in Wales and Ireland.

Everina Wollstonecraft (1765–1843) was Mary's youngest sister, who studied French in Paris, and like the impecunious Eliza, accepted Mary's financial support and was a frustrated governess in Ireland and England. After Mary's death, both sisters allegedly offered to bring up Mary's natural daughter, Fanny, but the griefstricken William Godwin would not part with her. At age twenty, an unhappy Fanny died of an overdose of laudanum.

James Wollstonecraft (1768–1806), Mary's middle brother, went to sea at the age of fourteen. With Mary's help he studied mathematics at a military academy, and later sank into debt. At his request she sent him to Paris, but he was arrested as a spy and deported. He finally joined the Royal Navy, became a lieutenant, and died of yellow fever.

Charles Wollstonecraft (1770–1817) was Mary's youngest and favorite brother, whom she helped send to America in 1792. There, he failed in business, joined the American army, and became brevet major; he never made enough money to bring his sisters to America as he'd promised. He divorced his first wife for adultery, and remarried; his widow, also called Mary Wollstonecraft, was a New England botanist and educator.

Llyn Rice

About the Author

Nancy Means Wright is a longtime teacher and author of fifteen books, including nine mystery novels. Her short stories and poems have appeared in dozens of magazines and anthologies, including a collection of poems written in the voice of Mary Wollstonecraft. A former Bread Loaf Scholar for a first novel and Agatha Award winner and nominee for two children's mysteries, Wright lives and writes in the environs of Middlebury, Vermont. She welcomes visitors at www.nancymeanswright. com and her Facebook page, "Becoming Mary Wollstonecraft."

MORE MYSTERIES
FROM PERSEVERANCE PRESS
🕱 *For the New Golden Age* 🕱

JON L. BREEN
Eye of God
ISBN 978-1-880284-89-6

TAFFY CANNON
ROXANNE PRESCOTT SERIES
Guns and Roses
Agatha and Macavity awards nominee, Best Novel
ISBN 978-1-880284-34-6

Blood Matters
ISBN 978-1-880284-86-5

Open Season on Lawyers
ISBN 978-1-880284-51-3

Paradise Lost
ISBN 978-1-880284-80-3

LAURA CRUM
GAIL MCCARTHY SERIES
Moonblind
ISBN 978-1-880284-90-2

Chasing Cans
ISBN 978-1-880284-94-0

Going, Gone
ISBN 978-1-880284-98-8

Barnstorming *(forthcoming)*
ISBN 978-1-56474-508-8

JEANNE M. DAMS
HILDA JOHANSSON SERIES
Crimson Snow
ISBN 978-1-880284-79-7

Indigo Christmas
ISBN 978-1-880284-95-7

Murder in Burnt Orange
ISBN 978-1-56474-503-3

JANET DAWSON
JERI HOWARD SERIES
Bit Player
ISBN 978-1-56474-494-4

KATHY LYNN EMERSON
LADY APPLETON SERIES
Face Down Below the Banqueting House
ISBN 978-1-880284-71-1

Face Down Beside St. Anne's Well
ISBN 978-1-880284-82-7

Face Down O'er the Border
ISBN 978-1-880284-91-9

ELAINE FLINN
MOLLY DOYLE SERIES
Deadly Vintage
ISBN 978-1-880284-87-2

HAL GLATZER
KATY GREEN SERIES
Too Dead To Swing
ISBN 978-1-880284-53-7

A Fugue in Hell's Kitchen
ISBN 978-1-880284-70-4

The Last Full Measure
ISBN 978-1-880284-84-1

MARGARET GRACE
MINIATURE SERIES
Mix-up in Miniature
(forthcoming)
ISBN 978-1-56474-510-1

WENDY HORNSBY
MAGGIE MACGOWEN SERIES
In the Guise of Mercy
ISBN 978-1-56474-482-1

The Paramour's Daughter
ISBN 978-1-56474-496-8

DIANA KILLIAN
POETIC DEATH SERIES
Docketful of Poesy
ISBN 978-1-880284-97-1

JANET LAPIERRE
PORT SILVA SERIES
Baby Mine
ISBN 978-1-880284-32-2

Keepers
Shamus Award nominee, Best Paperback Original
ISBN 978-1-880284-44-5

Death Duties
ISBN 978-1-880284-74-2

Family Business
ISBN 978-1-880284-85-8

Run a Crooked Mile
ISBN 978-1-880284-88-9

HAILEY LIND
ART LOVER'S SERIES
Arsenic and Old Paint
ISBN 978-1-56474-490-6

LEV RAPHAEL
Nick Hoffman Series
Tropic of Murder
ISBN 978-1-880284-68-1

Hot Rocks
ISBN 978-1-880284-83-4

LORA ROBERTS
Bridget Montrose Series
Another Fine Mess
ISBN 978-1-880284-54-4

Sherlock Holmes Series
**The Affair of the
Incognito Tenant**
ISBN 978-1-880284-67-4

REBECCA ROTHENBERG
Botanical Series
The Tumbleweed Murders
(completed by Taffy Cannon)
ISBN 978-1-880284-43-8

SHEILA SIMONSON
Latouche County Series
Buffalo Bill's Defunct
*WILLA Award, Best Original
Softcover Fiction*
ISBN 978-1-880284-96-4

An Old Chaos
ISBN 978-1-880284-99-5

SHELLEY SINGER
Jake Samson &
Rosie Vicente Series
Royal Flush
ISBN 978-1-880284-33-9

LEA WAIT
Shadows Antiques Series
**Shadows of a Down East
Summer**
ISBN 978-1-56474-497-5

PENNY WARNER
Connor Westphal Series
Blind Side
ISBN 978-1-880284-42-1

Silence Is Golden
ISBN 978-1-880284-66-7

ERIC WRIGHT
Joe Barley Series
The Kidnapping of Rosie Dawn
*Barry Award, Best Paperback
Original. Edgar, Ellis, and Anthony
awards nominee*
ISBN 978-1-880284-40-7

NANCY MEANS WRIGHT
Mary Wollstonecraft Series
Midnight Fires
ISBN 978-1-56474-488-3

The Nightmare
ISBN 978-1-56474-509-5

*REFERENCE/
MYSTERY WRITING*

KATHY LYNN EMERSON
**How To Write Killer
Historical Mysteries:
The Art and Adventure of
Sleuthing Through the Past**
*Agatha Award, Best Nonfiction.
Anthony and Macavity awards
nominee.*
ISBN 978-1-880284-92-6

CAROLYN WHEAT
**How To Write Killer Fiction:
The Funhouse of Mystery & the
Roller Coaster of Suspense**
ISBN 978-1-880284-62-9

**Available from your local bookstore or from
Perseverance Press/John Daniel & Co. at (800) 662-8351
or www.danielpublishing.com/perseverance.**